USA TODAY BESTSELLING AUTHOR
DALE MAYER

Lovely Lethal Gardens
01-02

Arsenic in the Azaleas
Bones in the Begonias

LOVELY LETHAL GARDENS, BOOKS 1–2
Beverly Dale Mayer
Valley Publishing Ltd.

ISBN-13: 978-1-773364-01-8
Print Edition

Books in This Series

About This Boxed Set

Arsenic in the Azaleas

A new cozy mystery series from USA Today best-selling author Dale Mayer. Follow gardener and amateur sleuth Doreen Montgomery—and her amusing and mostly lovable cat, dog, and parrot—as they catch murderers and solve crimes in lovely Kelowna, British Columbia.

Riches to rags. … Controlling to chaos. … But murder … seriously?

After her ex-husband leaves her high and dry, former socialite Doreen Montgomery's chance at a new life comes in the form of her grandmother, Nan's, dilapidated old house in picturesque Kelowna … and the added job of caring for the animals Nan couldn't take into assisted living with her: Thaddeus, the loquacious African gray parrot with a ripe vocabulary, and his buddy, Goliath, a monster-size cat with an equally monstrous attitude.

It's the new start Doreen and her beloved basset hound, Mugs, desperately need. But, just as things start to look up for Doreen, Goliath the cat and Mugs the dog find a human finger in Nan's overrun garden.

And not just a finger. Once the police start digging, the rest of the body turns up and turns out to be connected to an old unsolved crime.

With her grandmother as the prime suspect, Doreen soon finds herself stumbling over clues and getting on

Corporal Mack Moreau's last nerve, as she does her best to prove her beloved Nan innocent of murder.

Bones in the Begonias

Riches to rags. ... Chaos continues. ... Murders abound. ... Honestly?

Doreen Montgomery's new life in Kelowna was supposed to be a fresh start after a nasty split from her husband of fourteen years, plus a chance to get her bearings and her life back on track. Instead her first week in her new hometown was spent digging up dead bodies, chasing clues, and getting in Corporal Mack Moreau's way.

But now that the old cold case has been solved, and the murderer brought to justice, Doreen believes things might go her way this week. When Mack hires her to whip his mother's garden into shape, it seems like a second chance, both for Doreen's new beginning in Kelowna and for her budding relationship with Mack.

But, instead of digging up Mrs. Moreau's struggling begonias and planting them in a better location, Doreen discovers another set of bones ... and another mystery to solve. As the clues pile up, Mack makes it abundantly clear that he doesn't want or need her help, but Doreen can't resist the lure of another whodunit. As she and Mack butt heads and chase red herrings, Doreen's grandmother, Nan, sets odds and places bets on who solves the crime first.

All while a murderer is watching ...

USA TODAY BESTSELLING AUTHOR
DALE MAYER

Arsenic in the Azaleas

Deadly Gardens SERIES #1

Chapter 1

Day 1, Wednesday: The First Day of the Rest of Her Life...

THIS IS WHAT she'd come to? A thirty-five-year-old soon-to-be divorcée, penniless, living in her grandmother's dilapidated home? Doreen Merriweather—back to Doreen Montgomery now—parked her aging Honda Civic in the driveway of what was her new residence in the Lower Mission area of Kelowna, British Columbia. And stared.

Goodness. This was not how she remembered the house. It was just another lump to take in a long line of lumps she'd already taken.

She blew the errant curls of blond hair off her face. The warm spring sunshine highlighted the two-story house's ancient clapboard siding, windows in desperate need of cleaning. Shutters in need of paint or repair, and a roof more covered in moss than shingles. It had a lost-in-time and forgotten-by-the-world air to it.

She could relate.

For just a moment she allowed herself to wallow in self-pity. Her previous home had been an eight-thousand-square-foot mansion in West Vancouver with an in-ground pool and four staff to look after it and her soon-to-be ex-husband—and now Doreen's younger replacement. A smart Barbie doll of twenty-eight. A *very* smart Barbie doll, as Doreen had found out belatedly.

"Just be grateful you have a home at all," she reminded herself. "Without Nan giving this place to me, we'd be on the street at this point." Feeling better, she turned to her pedigreed basset hound, Mugford Horace III, but *Mugs* to her, and said, "Right, boy?"

He gave her a droopy-eyed look.

"I know. You're not impressed either. Still, it's what we have, and we're thankful for Nan's generosity." Just because Doreen's life had changed, didn't mean she wasn't up for the challenge. She knew there would be days when it would all seem to be too much. But she should be used to that as it described most of the last six years of her marriage anyway.

Doreen had signed the separation forms some two weeks after her husband had asked her to leave their house and their marriage. Right before Thanksgiving, in fact. On her lawyer's advice, Doreen signed the divorce settlement papers as well—to have it all over with, even though the divorce couldn't be filed until after she and her husband had been separated for a year. *This way offers minimal emotional pain for you, Doreen. You can move on without having to revisit the painful time in your life.*

Only, shortly after signing all those papers, Doreen had found out that her divorce lawyer was her husband's lover… Yeah, life's a bitch.

And so was her divorce lawyer.

She hadn't figured out what to do about it yet—if anything. Part of her wanted to walk away and leave him to his money—and new girlfriend. Another part of her wanted to fight him tooth and nail and take the house right out from under him.

But how?

She had no money. Or connections. And although her lawyer was as crooked as they came, how did she trust another one to help her right the wrongs done?

Money bought people. And apparently their loyalty too. She couldn't afford to lose any more of either.

Mugs nuzzled her hand. She shook her head, bringing herself back to the present, sitting in her car still parked outside her grandmother's house. Doreen's new reality. She pulled the keys from the ignition and exited her car.

She walked up to the front door. Her grandmother—*Nan* as she preferred to be called to avoid the old-age stigma surrounding "grandma" and all such other labels—had said the keys were atop the doorframe. Doreen reached up and found the key ring, and, with relief, she unlocked the door, pushing it wide open.

For better or for worse, this was the first day of the rest of her life.

Pulling her phone out of her suit pocket, she dialed Nan's number. "Nan, we're here. Just wanted to let you know."

"Thank you for calling, dear."

Doreen heard a rustle on the phone, like Nan covering up the speaker, then she called out as if to someone else in the room, "She's just arrived. A few minutes before noon. Write that down."

And that made no sense. While Doreen was still trying to figure out what her grandmother meant, Nan was talking to her again. "Glad you made it safely, dear. Now make a cup of tea and settle in. We'll talk tomorrow when you're rested." Just as Doreen went to hang up, Nan said, "It's lovely to have you close. I'll get Marge to stop by in a few days. She's gone on a holiday so perfect timing, dear."

Click.

Doreen hung up, shaking her head. Nan was still as quirky as ever. Who was Marge? She wracked her brain looking for a mention of that name and drew a blank. She'd find out later. She had more pressing problems right now. She headed back to the car, to her faithful pet. "Come on, Mugs." She opened the passenger door and waited for him to jump down. He raced across the lawn, his nose down, big floppy ears bouncing with every step.

"Mugs, over here."

He woofed and raced behind her toward the front door.

With him at her side, she stepped across the doorway. She was immediately hit with that *lovely* aged smell that came with the ancient house.

Knowing her circumstances, Nan had convinced Doreen to move into her house with her until a spot opened up at Rosemoor then she could have the house all to herself. Unexpectedly, a spot opened up and Nan had moved in before Doreen had time to adjust her plans. Doreen had been living with friends—or their empty apartments—since leaving her old home. The last place had belonged to a woman she'd been close to. Unfortunately she hadn't realized that without the husband, the prestige, the money... the woman no longer considered Doreen a friend. And her hope that this woman's brother, a lawyer, could help her fix her divorce mistake went out the window.

She'd overstayed her welcome waiting for him to get back into town. Only to realize he'd been in town the whole time and was waiting for her to leave... she'd left the next day.

As part of Nan's decision to live at Rosemoor, she had also decided to give the house to Doreen, Nan's only living relative, so she'd always have a home to live in.

And Doreen was incredibly grateful to have it. She walked to the nearest window in the living room and pushed it wide open, letting in some springtime air, then went to the next room, the formal dining room. It had been a long time since she'd been in the house, and her present reality warred with her past memories.

There was just something about the house of an older person who had lived in it for the last forty-odd years. The living room and dining room overflowed with furniture, all covered in brightly colored afghans. The walls were full of mementos, the shelves full of knickknacks. Decades of items that added joy to Nan's life.

Her gaze roamed the small space, made even smaller by the clutter. In the ensuing weeks Nan had been gone a fine layer of dust had settled over every surface... It would take hours to clean all this...

It would take more time to declutter this place, and Doreen would feel terribly guilty if she disposed of anything without Nan's permission.

Nan might love all these mementos, but Doreen felt claustrophobic with all the large dark furniture crammed into the front two rooms. She walked through to the kitchen and stopped. It was cute, quaint and old. Still, if it functioned, it was more than she had otherwise. She opened the back door and stepped out onto the porch that ran along the back of the house. Outside she found the rear garden, rioting in color and completely overwhelmed with knee-high weeds and out-of-control bushes.

As her gaze wandered the length of the gardens she gasped in delight. "Oh, boy, Mugs," she said. "We have our work cut out for us here."

Yet the gardens thrilled her. Gardening was her thing. During her former life she directed gardeners to do the work. Anytime she'd managed to get her hands dirty, she'd been reprimanded because the cuts from the thorns would mar her skin and digging in the soil would break her nails.

She glanced down at her self-manicure. In no way did they resemble the perfect nails she used to show off. "Well, they've already taken a beating, so what's another one."

Mugs stood in the rear doorway and sniffed the air. When a growl came from deep inside his chest, Doreen hurriedly stepped back and peered around the doorframe. While the house fronted a cul-de-sac and sat in the middle of the circle with neighbors on both sides, the backyard went on seemingly forever. Even at the half-collapsed fencing at the back of Nan's property, more land flowed beyond, unmarred by buildings.

"What's the matter, Mugs?" Doreen glanced around nervously. He obviously took well to his new role as protector.

Before this, she'd never paid attention to his heavily wrinkled eyebrows that shifted and moved when he was upset. He really was a watchdog. And something out there bothered him. Feeling a little spooked, she caught him by the collar and dragged him inside and closed the door.

"First thing we need to do is unload the car. Then I want a cup of tea. Afterward we can explore."

She returned to her car. Emptying the contents from the back seat and the trunk of her Honda to the concrete driveway, she stood amid her measly pile of belongings and shook her head. After fourteen years of marriage, she was reduced to five suitcases and two carry-on bags. What a change. Resolutely she grabbed several of her suitcases and took them up the front porch steps and into the house.

She dropped them at the bottom of the staircase. She didn't even remember how many rooms were upstairs from her last visit, years ago, to see Nan. Wouldn't matter now. Nan could have knocked down walls and made two bedrooms into one for all Doreen knew. She wondered if a usable bed was to be found in any of them.

She collected the rest of her luggage from the driveway and added them to the growing pile inside. Afterward she retrieved Mugs's food and water dishes from the front passenger side of the car. On her last trip, she collected his bag of assorted dog food and treats, then made a clean sweep of the Honda's interior to make sure she hadn't left anything behind. She locked the car, walked inside, and shut the front door.

She leaned against it and studied her new home.

Nan had said something about looking after her Maine coon cat that generally lived outside. So far there had been no sign of it.

"Oh." Doreen brightened. "Mugs, is that what you smelled out back? Was it the cat?" She walked to the back door again and opened it. "Hey, kitty, kitty. This is your home, kitty, but Mugs lives here now too."

Mugs growled. Then came a howl and a hiss, before a screaming cat ripped inside the house between Doreen and Mugs. Instantly the dog barked and gave chase. Standing with her back to the rear doorway, in her three-thousand-dollar Chanel suit she had traveled in, Doreen watched as her professionally pedicured dog happily chased the crap out of the ragtag cat that looked to be almost bobcat size.

What the heck had Doreen gotten herself into?

Chapter 2

PROMISING HERSELF A cup of hot tea in the near future, Doreen took her glass of water and left the back door open—so Mugs could join her if he wanted, especially to avoid that cat. "*Goliath*," she murmured, finally remembering Nan's cat's name. Doreen wandered outside to the veranda, which drifted down the full width of the house, noting a matching set of steps that led to the deck, one from each end of the veranda.

She wasn't hungry, even though it had to be noon or later. After all, she had spent all morning driving here.

With peace established inside—Nan's cat taking refuge under one of the many pieces of furniture cluttering the living room and Mugs no longer barking but feeling proud of himself—Doreen collapsed into the nearest of the two wooden chairs on the veranda and stared at the backyard. A nice deck connected the back of the house to the grassy area of the yard.

It was such a gorgeous afternoon. The sun cast beautiful beams of light across the property, and the waist-high overgrown garden added some shadows too.

Nan's property.

Now Doreen's property.

Legally. Or soon to be. Nan had already started the transfer documents.

Odd to consider this was the first home Doreen had owned herself. Never in a million years would she have expected to end up here in this stage of her life. It was both daunting and exhilarating. Her marriage had been on the rocks for years, and she'd been desperate for a change... but wow. Watch what you ask for.

Looking back, she felt a little guilty and wondered what Nan's life had been like during Doreen's marriage, when Doreen had been led around the world on her husband's arm for years. When Doreen had been a child, she had been best friends with Nan, until Doreen's mother had married up in life, and Doreen had been shipped off to boarding school.

Her mother's death years later had brought Doreen and Nan closer together again, until Doreen had married her own wealthy nightmare. Then Doreen's relationship with Nan had been shunted back to phone calls and the odd solo visit. Mostly when she could get her husband to allow her the time away. Now Doreen and Nan only had each other. And that made it lovely to move closer so they could spend the most of what time they had left together.

Doreen's previous life seemed so far removed from where she'd landed now. Although this house was paid for, she still needed to find a way to make a living to pay her monthly bills and to put food on her table as well as to pay for the dog's food. According to Nan, the water bill here was horrific, and the power companies were thieves. Doreen had not worked the whole time she had been married. Her controlling husband had deemed it "demeaning." So Doreen had job searches and job applications and job interviews to look forward to as well.

But what did she *really* want to do with the rest of her life?

She sighed, shook her head. Those were tomorrow's messes to deal with. Today was about getting moved in and settled for the night.

Mugs walked over and sat down beside her.

He had something in his mouth, but she had no idea what. When he crunched it with a bone-breaking noise, she bounded to her feet and stared at him, aghast. "Where did you get that?"

A bit of grass stuck out one corner of his mouth.

Whatever it was had come from outside the house. But, since Mugs hadn't been in the garden in the front yard or in the backyard yet, chances were that the cat had brought it inside. And that could mean all kinds of horrible things. Doreen had no experience with cats, but she'd heard the horror stories... "Mugs, that's disgusting. Drop it."

When he didn't, Doreen's face twisting in distaste, she leaned over for a closer look. Was it a bone? But what kind of a bone? "Mugs, give it to me. Let me look at that."

He gave her a grunt and backed away.

Crap.

She got on her hands and knees to peer closer. A bone wouldn't be so bad, but something appeared to be sticking out the end of it. She tried to grab it from him, only Mugs backed up again.

Slowly she followed him on all fours. "Come on, boy. You don't want that nasty bone. Give it to me, and I'll get you some proper dinner." Inspired by the idea, she hopped to her feet and ran inside to his stash of goodies, found his treats, shaking the bag as she ran out the back door.

Immediately Mugs dropped the bone and raised his nose to sniff the air. When Doreen held out a chicken twist for him, he smelled it, then decided he preferred the bone at his feet.

"No! Wait, Mugs. No." She shoved the treat into his face a second time.

He gave her an offended look but slowly took the treat, dropping the bone once more.

Instantly she snatched it out of his reach. She turned it over and screamed, tossing the small fleshy thing to the wooden floor of the veranda. Mugs raced for it, but she shooed him away. Using a piece of old cardboard found on the side of the veranda, she scooped up the bone and placed it on the little outside table. Gasping, her heart pounding, she peered closer.

The bone had skin on it—and a fingernail at the end. A nicely manicured man's nail.

Mugs had been chomping on a human finger.

Chapter 3

A N HOUR LATER Doreen faced yet another *first*.

Police. They were as foreign to her as the world they worked in. She'd never met anyone who worked for the police. And hadn't ever needed their assistance. Was there a specific etiquette she should follow? Typical of her husband's overall mind-set in ruling her world and her actions, Doreen shouldn't be so surprised that she would even consider such an issue.

She really couldn't expect to undo all her bad habits formed in her fourteen-year marriage in only six months' time. Yet, she was working on that.

While waiting for the police to arrive, Doreen had transferred the finger from the small table on the rear veranda to the little matching table on the front porch. And she had made sure Mugs remained inside the house, separated from the finger, although she had lost track of Goliath.

As the RCMP car pulled into her driveway behind her Honda, she headed outside and stood on her front porch, wondering at the strange turn her "new" life had taken. The driver got out, and she plastered a bright smile on her face and then immediately wiped it off. This was hardly a social occasion. She could shake their hands. That was businesslike, right?

When the first officer arrived at her front porch steps, she was lost as to what expression was appropriate for the occasion. So she just blurted out, "I think there is a body on the property."

The older man remained silent, surprise lighting his taciturn face.

She stared, fascinated, as his bushy eyebrows rose into his forehead. How did that work? They were like Groucho Marx's in size, only longer. She gave an inward shudder. She wanted to run inside and grab scissors and clip them into shape. If she did that, he'd lock her up as being a lunatic. Half hysterical, she wondered if she could make a business of eyebrow trimming. There was obviously a need for her services in this town, but would they pay her or would she have to pay them to give her the opportunity?

"I'm sorry, ma'am. What did you say?"

She took a deep breath, clenched her fists against her belly, stiffened her spine and said, "Maybe you should come on the front porch, and I could show you instead."

He seemed to be waiting for his partner, who was bent over the cop car, talking on a handset pulled through the open window, standing just outside the car door. The first man was as old and grizzled as the second man was young and dynamite—a tall blond Adonis.

Her breath escaped slowly as she tried to calculate his age.

Early thirties she figured.

Immediately her mind calculated their age difference. There were all kinds of rules to such a relationship. She wanted to race back inside and check. She had them written down somewhere. She should know them by heart. But after Sally Browning had had a relationship with somebody thirteen years her junior and had been ostracized from all the tea parties, Doreen wasn't sure she had the appropriate rules to go by in this instance. After all, Doreen was only a couple years older than Adonis, right?

Right?

Regardless, she thought Sally should've been totally fine dating a younger guy. It wasn't that she and her much-younger boyfriend were doing anything other than having an affair. Everyone knew that, when having an affair, age didn't count. It was only when that affair turned to something long-term that age differences caused eyebrows to raise.

Unless of course money was involved—then all rules were off. Because everyone knew that money made age go away.

And made wives—future and former—come and go too.

"Ma'am, what is it you wanted to show me?" the older officer asked.

She dragged her gaze from the younger officer until he tossed the handset on the passenger seat and stood fully upright. Crap. He was as cute standing as he had been slumped over. Only taller than she expected. Much taller.

Finally pulling her attention back to the officer in front of her, she pointed at the small table off to the side of her front porch where she'd carefully placed the offending bone. "It's that."

He glanced at the table, back at her and asked, "What is?"

She half turned and pointed at the table again. "I put it on the table."

The second officer joined them. She beamed at Adonis.

Both policemen stared at her. "What about the table?" the older man asked.

She exhaled heavily. "Not the table but what's on the table."

Both men stared at the table from where they stood on the ground next to the porch steps. "Just a piece of old cardboard is on the table." The second man's voice was lighthearted and cheerful.

Too cheerful. As if he were humoring her. Instantly his cuteness rating dropped several notches. She glared at the table and froze. *No. No, it can't be.* "Oh, my God, it's gone."

"What's gone?"

She spun around and stared at the younger officer. "I told the dispatcher that I think a body is here."

"And what... made you think... that?" the older officer asked in a slow and patient voice.

She glared at him. "Because of the finger."

At the word *finger*, both men straightened to attention.

She nodded with satisfaction. "I should think so. That dratted cat brought it inside. I swear it was him. Mugs would never have touched it first. But then Mugs took it away from him," she admitted. "I brought it out here and put it on the front porch table, waiting for you guys to show up." She glared at the table. "I bet it was Goliath's doing. He never forgave Mugs for stealing it away from him."

"Mugs? Goliath?" the older officer repeated.

She raised both hands, palms up. "Aren't you listening? The cat brought it in."

The younger man smiled. "Is the cat *Goliath* by any chance?"

"I just said so, didn't I?" She turned her back to the men, now so flustered that she didn't know what to do. If she couldn't produce the finger, no one would believe her. Therefore, no one would check out the backyard because she certainly wasn't going to until she got an all clear from someone. Neither would she let that cat back into the house to bring home more body parts. Turning, she announced firmly, "We have to find the finger. The cat probably stole the darn thing back again."

"When did you last see him?"

She stared at the young man she had thought was cute. His brand of *cute* was only on the outside. He had to have a fully functioning brain going on inside to rightly earn the term. "I saw him just a while ago, of course. He couldn't have gone far." She shook her head. "Never mind. The finger must be around here somewhere." She searched the furniture on the front porch. "Check the floorboards. Maybe the cat dropped it. Or maybe he took it inside." She opened the front door and then stopped. "No, it can't be inside. It was here when I heard you drive up." She shut the door and frowned, facing the officers again.

"I haven't seen the cat since we arrived, ma'am," said the younger officer.

The older man walked up and down the length of the porch, supposedly looking for a finger, but he didn't appear to be putting too much effort into it.

She sighed. Loudly. She so didn't need this.

"But Nan did have a big Maine coon cat. She used to take it with her everywhere," the younger man added. "It was a character. Then Nan is too."

"She's my grandmother. So is she yours too?" She studied the man closer. "Are we related?"

The younger officer laughed. "No, the community knows her as Nan also."

"*Great.* That'll make for a confusing few weeks." But it pleased her that Nan was so well-known and apparently well-loved.

Not to mention that she and Adonis were not related.

"She had a cat *and* a parrot," the older man murmured, his gaze still on the flooring of the porch.

"Well, if a parrot is here, I haven't met it yet," Doreen said. "I just arrived. I'm still finding my way through the house. It's a maze of clutter." She frowned. "But I believe Nan did tell me a bird was here. I assumed it was outside."

"Thaddeus tends to wander where he wants. He flies but not terribly well. When you see him, you'll never forget him." The officers looked at each other and grinned.

From the far side of the front porch, she heard a wild squawk. She pivoted and saw a beautiful blue-gray bird standing on the railing, facing her. He was at least a foot tall with long red tail feathers. "Oh, my goodness! Is that him?"

The cops laughed. The younger man said, "Yes, that's Thaddeus."

"Thaddeus is here," the bird said with great stage presence, strutting along the top of the railing. "Thaddeus is here."

"Oh, great. He talks," Doreen muttered, staring at the bird. That was the last thing she needed when Goliath had been dragging human body parts inside the house.

As if understanding her thoughts, the huge orange feline erupted from under the front porch. It raced up a few of the porch steps, then stopped and looked at the humans disdainfully. He took two more steps, dropped his butt, shot his hind leg into the air and proceeded to lick his behind.

In front of one and all.

The only thing that Doreen could think of was how horrified her husband would be with this scene right now. She had to chuckle at that image.

On cue, Thaddeus squawked before speaking. "Thaddeus is here. Thaddeus is here."

Doreen groaned with a shake of her head. "That'll get old very quickly."

"He doesn't say very much, but he is a character." The younger officer walked over and brushed the feathers along Thaddeus's cheek and neck. "He's very personable. Most of the townsfolk know him. Nan, of course, took him with her everywhere too."

"Wonderful," Doreen said half under her breath. "I sure hope no more pets are around here. Mugs is having enough trouble adapting to the cat. I can't imagine him with a parrot, particularly one that talks."

"Mugs?" asked the older man. "Who's that?"

"My dog."

He gave a half snort. "Fun times ahead."

She shrugged. "Not so fun if I can't find the dratted finger again. You two will never believe me without proof." She glanced at the floorboards and found a small hole. She dove to the porch floor and studied the shadows below. "Something's down there. It's just out of reach, and even two of my fingers can't fit at the same time inside this hole. Plus it's hard to see for sure." She thought it was the finger. She darn well hoped it was. She'd already made a fool of herself. She sure didn't want them to think she was a liar too. "I accidentally bumped the table when I came outside. It must have rolled off then."

"Let me see." The older officer got down on his hands and knees. "Well, something's there all right." He twisted his head sideways. "I can't rightly say it's a bone though."

"I've got a pair of tweezers in my purse. Let me go grab them." She dashed inside the house, leaving the door open for just a moment. She found the tweezers and returned to the front porch to find that Mugs was now outside, his tail wagging, as he slobbered his joy all over the officers.

"Darn it... I walked inside for two seconds. What kind of watchdog are you anyway, Mugs?"

"So he only barks when he feels like it?" the older officer joked.

"So far, just when the darn cat ran through the house with the finger. Probably jealous because I think he wanted a fresh bone too."

The two men looked at one another in fascination.

"Sorry." She winced. "I guess you both think I'm a little odd."

The two officers shook their heads very slowly. "No, ma'am. We know Nan well. You are very similar." The older man grinned and stuck out his hand. "The name's Arnold, Constable Arnold Depruis. Welcome to town."

She flushed and shook his hand, still flustered. She brushed her hair back and smiled at the younger man. "And you are?"

"Constable Chester Pearson. But you can call us Arnold and Chester. Nice to meet you."

Tossing a bright smile his way, she dropped back to her knees on the floorboards, positioned over the hole again. The finger had fallen into the hole and rested on a crossbeam underneath. If it had dropped any farther, she'd likely have lost it forever.

She focused and very carefully pulled the offending item out between the boards. "Well, Arnold and Chester, do you think I'm telling the truth now?" She held it up triumphantly and said, "See? I wasn't lying."

Both men leaned in to take a closer look and immediately turned more businesslike. Arnold shifted his hat back and said, "Well, look at that. It's a finger all right."

Mugs barked at her feet and tried to jump for her hand, and somewhere close by a cat howled. Likely Goliath was pissed that he had lost his treat.

Doreen smirked as she laid the nasty thing back onto the cardboard triumphantly. "See? The rest of him has to be around here somewhere too."

But Thaddeus put the icing on the cake. He squawked loud and long, then cried out, "Body in the garden. Body in the garden."

Chapter 4

WHILE THE POLICE searched the property, Doreen searched the kitchen in vain for a teakettle. The police had been here for what seemed like hours, and she needed the comfort of a hot cup of tea. After hunting through the cupboards, she had only found a well-stocked pantry, confirming Nan had lived off canned goods. There were canned beans, canned soup and canned fish. Doreen saw what appeared to be canned potatoes. She stared at it, shuddered and closed the cupboard quickly. Did Nan have any teeth left? Maybe that was the problem.

Doreen knew Nan was a big tea drinker, but Doreen couldn't find any kettle to plug into an outlet. When she opened another cupboard, she found an old-fashioned stovetop kettle. The trouble was, Doreen and stoves didn't get along. Then, of course, she hadn't had much of a relationship with one either. She never had to cook during her entire marriage, and she'd never cooked growing up either. Now that she was single and on her own, she had yet to fathom the depths of how that whole producing-wonderful-food thing worked.

But, if there was ever a time to force herself to try, it was now. Because, above all else, she desperately wanted a cup of tea. That was, if a double-shot no-fat latte or a latte with sprinkled cinnamon on top wasn't available. And, considering her current lack of finances, those fancy coffees would likely never be available to her again.

She pulled out the funky-looking kettle, clicked the button at the top to open the lid and filled it with water from the sink. She walked over to the ancient stove and put the kettle atop one of the rings. She studied the stove for a long moment, but, for the life of her, she didn't know which knob would turn on the right-hand burner in the front. Age had taken its toll on the stove, wearing off all helpful markings—the same as the rest of the house had aged.

She would just have to experiment. She turned on both knobs on the right side where she'd put the kettle. Surely this was intuitive. Unfortunately the smell of gas immediately hit her nose. She shut off both knobs and turned on the other two on the far left side. When she smelled gas again, she quickly turned off those.

Back to one of the cupboards again, she pulled out a couple teacups to peer farther inside, then grinned. She reached far back into the cupboard and pulled out a bright and shiny electric kettle. Nan might not have liked it or used it, but Doreen was thrilled. She filled it with water and plugged it in. "Now we're in business."

For Nan and Doreen, teatime was a beloved hobby. Yet no teapots were visible. At least none that she'd found. But there were teacups. She took out a large one, then found a drawerful of different tea bags and tins full of loose tea leaves.

Studying the varieties, she was astonished at their names, like chamomile tea and dandelion leaf tea. Why would anybody want to put hot water on top of dandelion leaves? Dandelions were considered weeds, the bane of her husband's gardeners. She just didn't get it. But she spied a box of black tea bags, and she figured that was her best option. She dropped one into the teacup and waited for the water to boil.

Leaning against the sink, her back to the window, she deliberately didn't want to look out the window because police officers crawled all over the property. That lovely bone came from somewhere.

As she'd found out on her drive into town earlier this morning, Kelowna was smallish, and the Mission area was tiny. Thus the Kelowna RCMP detachment had only ten full-time staff, as Chester had shared. She swore they were all here in her backyard. Surely they'd be done soon. The property wasn't that large. But she was afraid that, if she went outside, with her luck, she'd be the one to find the body.

Raising even more suspicions from Arnold and Chester.

Beside her, the teakettle whistled. She frowned as the little silver lid snapped up and down. She took that to mean the water was boiling. She poured hot water into the teacup. She sniffed the air experimentally above it, and it did smell like tea, regular old-fashioned black tea. Embolden with that simple success, she opened the back door and stepped onto the veranda.

None of the officers were close to her now. She figured it was safe to sit down and watch their shenanigans. Who knew she had such a gruesome curiosity? Plus her feet ached, and she needed to get off them. She was used to wearing high heels all day long but couldn't for some reason here in Nan's house. Maybe it was the uneven floor. She didn't know.

Her entire wardrobe was completely unsuited for her new lifestyle. Along with that fact came another—she had no money to change it. And she wouldn't have a clue where to buy everyday jeans. The only jeans she owned had designer labels on them, were skintight and didn't wear worth a darn. Whereas everybody she'd seen so far in this town wore blue jeans or leggings that looked durable.

That was what she needed. Something she could afford and which would last. She might have to follow Nan's advice and go to the church bazaar and find something secondhand. Just the thought made her shudder.

She wasn't snooty or too proud. She just wasn't at that point yet of trying to navigate the process. Wearing other people's hand-me-down clothes made her wonder about the original owner. Who they were? Why they'd discarded the clothes? Had they gained weight? Lost weight? Changed jobs? Speaking of jobs, how much could she expect to earn from a job here in the Mission? Heck, she had no idea what kind of a job she would be suited for. Would anyone want to hire her? Her, a discarded rich man's trophy wife?

As she looked down at her Chanel suit, she figured it would probably take a year's wages at whatever new career she found in this small town just to pay for another one of these. On the other hand, she didn't need any more Chanel suits. She had those already, should they ever be needed on occasion in Lower Mission. Still, it would probably take a year's worth of time for her to no longer worry about whether she was perfectly coiffed, all to avoid getting snarky, nasty remarks from her husband.

Only after she fully got away from her marriage did she realize the stress and pain involved in maintaining appearances for his sake. And how his constant criticisms—when she didn't achieve the required level of perfection—were more about him and not so much about her.

How her nails had always been the wrong color, her lipstick had always been too bright. Her eye shadow had never been stylish enough. He said her hair, the last time she had it done, made her look like an old woman.

Of course it hadn't made her look old, but, in his eyes, he was ready for a younger trophy wife. Well, he had found her in Doreen's divorce lawyer.

How was that for irony?

One thing Doreen had learned from that mess was to laugh at herself. She knew she was an anomaly. Nobody would feel sorry for her after her years of the rich and lavish lifestyle. But rarely did people see the other side of that lifestyle. How Doreen needed to be perfectly fit, a perfect decoration always. To smile, even though she hated the people her husband brought through the house. And, when his hand cupped her butt blatantly in front of others, how hard it was to not turn around and smack him for his lack of respect.

She took it because, most of the time, he was fine. He was worse in front of his peers. When she had first met him, she'd been totally in love with him. That had faded quickly. But, by then, she had already been groomed for her role as his wife. Another pretty bauble for him to show off. Never mind that she had a brain.

But what about her growth as a person? Nobody ever really cared about that. A decade into her marriage, well, that was a whole different story. She finally woke up to seeing how much she was missing in life. Things she'd never have a chance to experience. She didn't know who she was, what she was, or who she wanted to be. All she knew was what *her husband* had expected her to be while married to him. But what did *she* expect to be, to do, to become?

"Find time to figure that out, idiot," she said out loud but with affection. "And you promised to never put yourself down again."

She had taken enough of that from her husband. Almost worst was his sister. That woman had hated Doreen. The feeling had been mutual. Doreen had never been allowed to say anything catty or mean to her back then. Of course not. Her dratted husband wouldn't have allowed that. And he'd ruled the roost.

"Ma'am?"

Startled, she stood, her tea sloshing, almost spilling on her suit. She walked to the railing to see the younger officer, Chester, standing at the foot of the nearest veranda steps, which led to the uncovered deck in the backyard. "Yes?"

"Have you been in the backyard at all?"

She shook her head. "I told you that I just arrived today, around noon, moving into the house."

She really wondered why the people in this town didn't understand what she was saying. She was a British Canadian living in a British Canadian town. It wasn't like she was French Canadian with an accent. Before she'd lived only a five-hour drive away in the British Properties area of West Vancouver. Yet it seemed she had to keep repeating everything she said three or four times since arriving here. "I can prove that I drove all the way from Vancouver this morning," she said, "if you don't believe me."

He gave her a surprised look and shook his head. "It's not that I don't believe you. But we found a lot of footprints back here."

"What?" She leaned forward but couldn't see anything

where he pointed. She set her teacup on the little table and walked down the veranda steps using the wobbly railing for support. The old place was falling apart. As soon as she stepped on one of the wooden planks of the deck, it squeaked and groaned under her weight. And she knew for sure that, at five feet seven and 125 pounds, she was not overweight. No matter what her husband said.

Shrugging off her husband's insults, she walked toward the officer, now at the far edge of the deck, and noted as he pointed out several footprints in the yard. The area had been roped off to avoid any further contamination of the scene.

"But those could've been here a long time. Maybe they are Nan's."

He looked down at her, his head cocked. "You don't have anything to compare them to right now. But they're large, like a man's size eleven."

Her eyebrows rose. "No, not Nan's. Those are big feet."

He pointed at his. "Mine are a ten. Those footprints are bigger than mine."

"Maybe they belonged to the dead man?" she asked, her voice rising in horror.

He stopped and stared at her. "Do you know who the dead man is?"

She frowned. "No." *Be patient, Doreen.* "Remember? I just got here." Man, she wanted to put that sentence into audio format and just hit the Rewind and Play buttons. It would save her a lot of time and effort.

But Chester still stared at her as if he couldn't figure out what made her tick.

Good luck with that. How could he know when she didn't?

Finally he shook his head and said, "No sign of a body

yet."

"Well, unless somebody is walking around town with an amputated finger and just accidentally left the appendage here on my property, I suggest you keep looking." She glanced at her heels and said, "I could change my shoes and come out to look too."

"No, just stay where you are. The less people out here, the better."

She chuckled and looked at the dozen people already on her property. "What possible difference could one more person make?"

"We're all professionals, ma'am. We know what we're doing."

"It doesn't look like you do, when you haven't found the body yet," she said in exasperation. She held up her hand to stop him from speaking. "Okay, fine. I'll go sit on the veranda." She delicately made her way to the steps. Before she reached them, she turned to Chester and asked, "Did you check under the deck?"

He instantly spun to address her. "Why would I check *under* the deck?"

She stared at him wordlessly for a full moment, getting a grip on her frustration. "Because it's a possible hiding place to put a body?" From the doubtful look on his face, she didn't think she would get any kind of a meeting of the minds here.

"Of course it's a great hiding place. I just thought maybe you knew that's where the body was."

"Let me tell you *one more time*. I haven't been in this house in years until I arrived about noon today from Vancouver. I don't know who the man is who belongs to that finger. In the three hours or so that I've spent here today—the last two hours of which I have had policemen crawling all over my property—I never saw anybody else in this place, and I did not put a dead body under the deck." On that note she turned away, gingerly went up the steps, retrieved her tea and stalked into the house. Her last act of revenge was to slam the door. Hard.

Chapter 5

BACK INSIDE SHE decided to take Mugs for a walk. She changed her heels for Nan's bright pink garden shoes on the back veranda, put Mugs on a leash, grabbed her purse and walked out the front door. If the police wanted to talk to her, they could call her. Because she'd had enough of them. She sauntered down the street, waving at a couple neighbors who called out to her. She pretended not to hear them when they asked questions, and she just kept on strolling by.

What was she supposed to say? *Oh, the police? No problem. I just have a body in the garden.* Or how about, *Oh, it's nothing. I'm sure that finger I found wasn't connected to anything to be concerned about.*

She refused to contemplate what happened to the poor man normally attached to that finger. Best scenario was a neighbor lost the finger in an accident using power tools. Her husband always said they were dangerous things.

As a vehicle slowed while passing her, the driver's gaze curious, she stared resolutely ahead. Not the preferred first day to her new beginning that she'd hoped for. These people barely knew her, and Nan was already eccentric enough. Apparently everyone was checking out Doreen sideways to see if she would be a chip off the old block. According to Chester and Arnold, she probably was.

Just as she got to the end of the block, she heard a single *flap* sound behind her. She turned to see Thaddeus flying— no, make that coasting—toward her. He landed on top of Mugs, who immediately twisted in a circle, trying to get at the bird riding him like a horse.

Goliath streaked past too, the huge cat brushing up against Doreen's calf in the process.

"Oh, for God's sake." She brushed the bird off Mugs's back. The bird immediately hopped to her arm and did a weird slide step up to Doreen's shoulder.

"Thaddeus is here. Thaddeus is here," he squawked in her ear.

"Really? Like I didn't know that already?" she cried out, trying to stare at him. He cocked his head at her. "You can't just sit there." She'd come to a complete stop on the sidewalk. How was she supposed to walk with him on her shoulder? But Thaddeus had no problem with it. His claws dug into her shoulder but never hard enough to really hurt. Nan had obviously trained him well. Besides, he was beautiful.

He looked down at her... as if waiting for her to sort herself out.

"Okay, fine. But you behave yourself."

"Thaddeus is here. Thaddeus is here." Instead of shouting it, he crooned it softly, rubbing his head along hers.

She nuzzled back, grinning in spite of herself, and then proceeded to walk toward town.

Instead of being upset by the crap going on in her backyard, she had a spring in her step. Maybe this would work out after all. She didn't have any chosen direction to walk or any definitive purpose for going to town. She just needed to take Mugs for a walk and, well, to get away from the madness at her house.

She turned right, taking a path along the creek.

She crossed one of the small footbridges and stopped, looking at the water below. It really was beautiful here. She could see how Nan would've enjoyed her years spent in this town. Doreen brightened. Maybe that's what she should do—visit Nan. The retirement home wasn't very far away. Nan had one of the outer studio apartments on a corner with lots of light where she had French doors leading to a patio and a small garden. She could have her meals at the main center, or she could do her own cooking. But Doreen knew Nan. She didn't do much in the way of cooking. And only cooked what came from a can, apparently.

Doreen grabbed her phone and called Nan. "Are you up for a little bit of company?"

"Oh, my goodness. I would be delighted," Nan said. "When?"

Doreen laughed. "I'm walking toward you right now. Thaddeus is on my shoulder, and I've got Mugs beside me. And the cat is sauntering close by too."

"Oh, my dear, that would be absolutely wonderful. I'll put on the kettle."

When her grandmother hung up the phone, Doreen had to laugh. Nan wasn't one to hold the phone to her ear while preparing tea. But then Nan had been late getting into the Technology Era. She still felt the phone—a plugged-in landline no less—belonged in the hallway near the front door and nowhere else.

Doreen changed direction and kept walking until she could see Rosemoor, the retirement home, up ahead. It had both full-care and partial-care facilities. She really didn't know anything else about it. She had never known anybody who lived in one, until Nan. And this one appeared to be unique in a town that didn't have a large population, so they had gathered together a lot of people with various needs into a single building. One end was a full nursing home for people mostly bedridden. On the opposite side were small independent living apartments. That was where Nan currently lived. Doreen assumed, when people's conditions worsened, they were moved to the north end of the complex.

That kind of sucked. But, on the other hand, Nan was still in her right mind, so maybe it was all good.

As Doreen walked up to Nan's apartment, Nan stepped onto her patio and waved. Thaddeus immediately left Doreen's shoulder and flew across the beautiful lawn toward Nan and landed on her shoulder. Even from this distance, Doreen could see the affection between the two. Her heart warmed. Maybe having Thaddeus around wouldn't be so bad after all.

Doreen was supposed to go inside the main lobby entrance and around to the front door of Nan's apartment, but, with Mugs and the bird and the cat, she knew she wouldn't be allowed inside. So, ignoring the Do Not Walk on the Grass sign, she cut across the lawn and quickly stepped onto the stonework patio.

Hearing the horrified gasp at the edge of Nan's patio, Doreen turned her head and stared at an older man. She hadn't seen him working in the gardens from the sidewalk. He glared at her and pointed at the sign.

She winced, gave him an apologetic smile and quickly turned away. *Shoot.* She didn't want to make a bad impression in her new life, but, so far, she'd done nothing but.

"Don't worry. That's Grumpy George," Nan said with a chuckle. "He's a stickler for rules and keeps track of the blades of grass here, like a farmer does his sheep."

Chuckling at the nickname, Doreen bent to give Nan a hug, amazed at how strong her grandmother's hug was. Nan, while aging gracefully even with her somewhat gnarled fingers, was petite with her tiny wrists. And the smile on her face was, as always, full of pure love. It brought tears to Doreen's eyes. She'd missed this woman a lot.

"Take a seat, dear."

Doreen pulled out the other little wrought-iron chair and sat down at the small bistro table. The patio wasn't much bigger than a ten-by-ten-foot square, so there wasn't a whole lot of room for furniture. It was cozy and suited this downsized version of Nan. As Doreen looked at the teapot, she frowned. It appeared to be a flower upside down with its stalk as the spout. "That's quite a teapot, Nan."

She laughed, her voice rippling around the garden, seemingly making even the sunshine brighter. "Isn't it? I picked it up at a secondhand store. You have to go over there, my dear. They have treasures unlikely to be found anywhere else in this world." She shook her head and smiled, patting the little teapot. "I know it's an oddity, but, at my age, I should be allowed a few of those."

"We should be allowed those at whatever our age," Doreen said with a big smile.

"And yet, you don't." Some of Nan's bright laughter fell away, and Nan's voice sharpened. "You were barely even living before, my dear. But look at you now. You're not coated in makeup, and your nails look like you have lived a normal person's life instead of a model's. That smile of yours—it's the best part—because that's the first real emotion I've seen on your face in a long time."

"That's not true," Doreen protested. Inside, she hoped it wasn't true.

"No, maybe not," Nan admitted. "Your only other emotions lately have been the pain and loss of your husband to your divorce attorney and the loss of your marriage—or more the loss of a way of life and your complete lack of comprehension of what that meant for you." Nan shook her head. "I never said anything all those years you were married. But you never looked happy. It's like you were shaped into a Barbie doll, and that was the role you played. And you played it well. Until your husband was no longer happy with Barbie and changed it for a china doll." She waved her hand up and down at Doreen. "Look at you. Your super expensive suit, and yet, those must be my gardening shoes." Nan bent forward under the table to stare at them. "Oh, my goodness, where did you find them?"

Doreen kicked out her legs. "They were on the back veranda."

Nan laughed. "See? That's what I mean. A year ago you never would've been caught dead in them."

"But they're comfortable," Doreen said. "Besides, I had to run out of the house and get away from the cops."

Silence fell at those words. Nan stared at Doreen, and her jaw slowly dropped open. She leaned forward. "What have you done that the cops are in the house?"

Nan didn't know anything about it. "Oh, my goodness, I didn't do anything. I blame your cat for this." She quickly explained what the cat had brought home and how Mugs had stolen the finger from the feline.

When Doreen got to the part about the dratted thing dropping the bone onto the front porch and then disappearing in the cracks of the floorboards, Nan shook her head and giggled. "You are a disaster." Then her giggles turned into full-blown laughter. "I love it."

"You love that a body's on your property?" Doreen stared at Nan for a long moment, wondering where her grandmother's humorous reaction came from. As far as Doreen knew, her grandmother was one of the sweetest old ladies ever. On the other hand, sweet old everyday ladies could have a dark side. Doreen leaned forward and asked, "Nan, did you kill somebody and bury him in the back-yard?"

That sent Nan into absolute hilarity. By the time she finally calmed down, Doreen wondered if she should call somebody. Tears poured down the old woman's face, and she held her sides to the point that she looked to be having a heart attack.

Just as Doreen rose to race inside to get medical atten-tion, Nan said, "Oh, my goodness, I needed that. You have no idea how boring my life has gotten lately. I'm so glad you decided to move to town, my dear."

Doreen settled back in her chair and stared at her grandmother. "So does that mean you did or did not murder somebody and bury him in the backyard?" She narrowed her eyes suspiciously at her grandmother.

Several more chuckles slipped out as Nan regained con-trol. She wiped her eyes with a napkin from the table. "No worries. I never murdered anybody." She pointed a finger at Doreen. "Now I might have wanted plenty to be murdered. But it's just so messy."

Doreen stiffened at those last words. She knew her grandmother would never have been involved in a murder. But, when she said how it was *too messy*, Doreen fixed her gaze on her last living relative and asked, "How would you know it's messy?"

That sent Nan off again.

Grumbling about being the center of so much laughter, Doreen reached for the teapot and poured the two of them some tea. Maybe that would help Nan calm down. Or maybe not. She appeared to be enjoying herself way too much.

Chapter 6

THE WALK HOME was bright and sunny. After an enjoyable hour with Nan, where it appeared she hadn't had anything to laugh about in months, the two women had settled down to a nice chat. Nan tried to explain how the stove worked, but it was a bit too confusing for Doreen. Especially in the abstract, what with the ancient stove not on hand for an actual demonstration. The discussion on how the washing machine worked also went over her head. But she promised Nan that—somehow—she would figure it out.

It seemed like Thaddeus had the best visit, as he'd spent much of his time on Nan's shoulder, crooning and rubbing his beak along the older woman's cheek.

With tears in her eyes, Nan lightly stroked the beautiful bird. "The worst part was leaving the animals behind. I do so thank you for bringing them for a visit." She stroked the sprawled-out cat, acting sedated around Nan—not like the hellion at the house earlier.

"And I'll bring them again. Besides, you can visit any-time you want," Doreen said as she gave the woman a goodbye hug, dropping a kiss on her cheek. "Do take care."

"*You* take care, my dear. You're the one who has a dead

body in your garden." And she snickered.

"Murder is not exactly a joke, Nan," Doreen admonished. "Let's hope there's no body at all." She walked across the lawn, and Thaddeus flew to join her, perching on her shoulder. With Mugs happy to be once again on the march, and the cat lollygagging behind, the four of them slowly walked toward her house.

She stopped on the little footbridge and stared at the happy creek bubbling under her. It really was a beautiful place here. She still hadn't spent the night at the house or bought any food, so her dinner would be whatever traveling snacks she had left from her car trip.

Doreen had lived in a world where food arrived on platters, beautifully presented. And now she lived in Nan's world, where food was prepped overnight, and then something magical was done to it the next day. *Or cans were opened up*, she thought with a shudder.

Since her separation, take-out and sandwiches were more the norm until even takeout cost too much.

And all that kitchen magic from her mansion-living days was black magic to her now because Doreen had yet to make anything work in her grandmother's kitchen, other than an electric teakettle. She sighed. Her new life was a challenge. But she had often thought she was bored before, so maybe this was a *good* challenge for her.

As her little house came into sight, her good mood fell away. Some people were hanging about the yards nearby, watching her place. And the police were still there. Really? How long would it take them? How was she supposed to adapt and spend her first night in the house in this her latest version of "alone" when she wasn't even alone?

With a heavy sigh, she walked up the front porch steps

and into the house. She unclipped the leash from Mugs, who ran to the back door and barked. Thaddeus jumped off her shoulder and flew to a tall perch in the living room. *So that's what that was for.* She likely would've tossed it out otherwise. But Thaddeus stood tall and proud, surveying the world below him. Goliath slunk into the kitchen, probably to scare the bejesus out of Mugs. They were darn near the same size. She closed the front door, crossed into the kitchen to put her purse in a cabinet and stared out at the rear garden.

She pushed the back door open and stepped onto the veranda, leading out to the adjoining deck in the yard. A half-dozen men were working underneath the wooden slats.

"Did you find anything?" she asked.

Chester, the younger police officer, popped his head out from under the deck and smiled at her. "There you are. Yes, it looks like we found something."

"Under the deck?"

He nodded. "Appears somebody was buried underneath. It was a garden at one time. And this deck was built over the top."

She stepped back and looked at the deck, only six feet wide maybe. New planking was on the far side, above the spot where they searched. And, of course, a body was darn near the same size as this newer deck addition.

Also a large cutout on the deck accommodated a huge azalea bush. *How odd.*

She hadn't really noticed the azalea growing *through* the decking or the new extension before now. But both made sense under the circumstances. And the police would surely destroy the newer deck area to get to whatever lay underneath.

As she watched, one of the officers tested the supports

and found several beams perpendicular to the ground with the newest deck section atop them. With four big strong men strategically positioned, they literally picked up this extension and moved it off to the side. Everyone stared down at the space below. Several flowering bulbs had sprouted through the ground but were suffering without sunlight.

"Oh, my goodness. Those are begonias."

An officer pulled out the green-brownish shoots and stared at her in surprise. Then at the handful of gnarly bulbs he held. "What are they?"

"Begonias," she said in delight. "I didn't realize they grew here. I figured the winters would be too hard."

"Lady, I don't have a clue what you're talking about." And he proceeded to dump his handful of bulbs onto the ground, off to the side.

"Oh, be careful," she cried out. "Those are beautiful plants. We need to give them a chance to grow."

All the men stopped to peer up at her, then looked at the backyard's massive garden, completely overwhelmed with weeds and unruly overgrown bushes, and finally at each other.

She frowned. "I just got here. Like five, six hours ago. You have to give me an opportunity to fix the garden before you judge me for it."

A similar piece of cardboard to the one the finger had been resting on had been discarded halfway under the railing. She snagged it up and then headed down the deck steps until she was at ground level. She picked up all the discarded begonias and placed them on the cardboard. "When you pull out more," she instructed the policeman, "put them all here."

"Lady, this is a murder investigation," the officer said.

"We are not concerned about where we put the garbage."

"They are not garbage," she snapped in outrage. "And, if you are pulling out any true garbage from this spot and are planning to throw it all over my property, then you're wrong to do so in the first place. You can darn well get a garbage can or a garbage bag and put the trash in it." She glared at him. "Do you understand me?"

The cop who'd spoken turned to look at the others. Then he shrugged. He pulled up a few more of the bulbs and said, "Whatever." But he did add those to the indicated cardboard.

"That's much better. Thank you."

The other officers rolled their eyes at her.

"It's not that hard to save a life." Nobody had any appreciation for plants. She'd found that out a long time ago. It had been one of the hardest things to accept with her gardening staff. So often they were there for the job and didn't give a darn about the plants. She'd had enough of that attitude.

That wasn't her. And, if she could get along with these policemen, then they would have to get along with her too.

Suddenly one of the men gave a startled exclamation.

The others rushed to his side. She looked where he pointed. All the men gathered around, squatting around something. She walked closer and peered over their shoulders.

And, sure enough, a hand missing a finger poked through the dirt. "Oh, finally you found it. That's excellent." She beamed. "Now kindly remove it please."

Arnold, the older grizzled cop who she'd met first, stood and said, "All in good time. It won't happen that fast. You need to be prepared for that. The coroner will be here shortly. Properly digging out a body takes a lot of time, and we need to gather forensic evidence as we do." He spoke in such a ponderous tone, as if this was super important.

She sniffed. "It wouldn't take ten minutes to dig up that body, if you really cared to."

"It's because we care that we aren't doing it that fast." He glared at her. "If any forensic evidence is in this dirt, we need to find it. We need to know who put this body here and what killed him."

She stared at Arnold for a long moment, her jaw opening as realization dawned. "You're talking *days*, aren't you?"

He shrugged. "Potentially. But likely tonight and tomorrow. So why don't you go on back inside and let us do our job."

She fisted her hands on her hips and stared at the group of men, all shaking their heads at her. She tapped her foot and said, "Okay, but if you find any more begonias, you put them all in one pile. I'll collect them later and give them some water. Don't kill them. I've got to have one place where I can put them and keep them alive without the police destroying them."

She turned and headed inside. What she really needed was food and a cup coffee. Her blood sugar was dropping. That was the only explanation for her being more concerned about the begonias than the dead body. But really, begonias were so much easier to think about than a body in her backyard, you know?

Not exactly a warm welcome to her new home. And a rather ominous start to her new life.

Still, she was here, and she had to make the best of it. And while the men worked outside, she searched the tea drawer for coffee beans. Thankfully she also located a simple-enough coffeemaker. Now if only she could find the blasted coffee, figure out the portions, and find something to grind the beans in. Meanwhile, the hostess in her wondered if she was expected to share her coffee with the uniformed officers outside. Because that would put a major drain on her resources and her patience. *Was she supposed to feed them too?* She wasn't sure there was food enough for her own dinner.

She forgot about making coffee as she heard several more vehicles pull up her driveway. A look outside from her living room window confirmed more people had gathered out front. And two more police cars parked behind her Honda, confirming in no way would she get a meal prepared if she couldn't drive her car to buy some groceries. Damn. She did have some nuts, cheese and crackers, leftovers from her travel snacks. That would be a pitiful dinner, but it looked like that was all she had. At least until the men were done. Or maybe she could order some dinner in. A walk back to town would not happen. She was already tired, and her feet still hurt.

Nan was her best source of information for takeout.

With that bright idea, she picked up the phone and called her. "Nan, I can't get out because of all the police cars here. Is there any place I can get food delivered?"

"There's a lovely little Chinese restaurant around the corner," Nan said. "I used to always get their wonton soup. Win and Len Yee run it. Lovely couple."

Nan rattled off the phone number while Doreen quickly wrote it down. "Thanks, Nan." She hung up, wondered if it would be too expensive for her present situation. But she had to eat. And, so far, today was a complete wash. She had a sinking feeling that tonight would be just as bad. She had to wonder if she would get any sleep as she watched the new arrivals bring out what appeared to be large floodlights and tarps.

By now a bigger bunch of onlookers stood on the street, watching all the activity too. This *so* wasn't the impression she'd wanted to give on her first day in town. She sighed and muttered out loud, "The Mission will never recover from my arrival."

Chapter 7

AFTER TOO MUCH of her lifetime spent worrying about appearances, this didn't exactly bode well. She peeked out the living room window to see dozens of strangers standing outside watching the goings-on at her house. She wanted to creep out the back, run around, and join them, blending in so they wouldn't know who she was.

She walked back into the kitchen, Mugs very close to her heels. *The poor guy is hungry after walking into town and back again.* She should have fed him before they left, but she had been too angry to think straight. Yet, his food was easy to take care of. She had both wet and dry food for Mugs.

She lifted the appropriate bag onto the table, and gathered his food and water dishes. With his bowls now filled, she looked around the kitchen for an out-of-the-way spot where he could eat in peace. There really wasn't any area that worked with the natural traffic patterns in this room.

She could put Mugs's food and water bowls on the deck, but not right now as dozens of people were working around the house. And probably not a good idea anyway given she didn't know what other animals were out there. She went into the entrance hallway where a bench had been situated so people could sit to put on their shoes, and that vacant space underneath the bench would work, but it would only be a temporary fix—not exactly where she wanted to keep the dog's food and water bowls when company arrived. She returned to the kitchen and studied the lower cabinets.

One of the lower cupboard doors hung at a slight angle. She opened it up to find the shelf on the inside was askew too. This house was falling apart. How had Nan stayed here for so long without repairing stuff? Doreen tried to straighten the shelf so it would be usable again, only it broke into two pieces while in her hands. "Great."

She tugged the pieces of wood free. It came loose suddenly, sending her flying to her butt. Doreen sat there, glaring at the now-empty space. It was a rather large cupboard, accessible. "Mugs," she called out.

Mugs sniffed around, already at her side, his big jowls waggling back and forth in joy. She glanced at her messy suit, Nan's old gardening shoes on her feet, while considering the fact she sat on the dirty kitchen floor, holding a busted shelf. Tears came to her eyes as she dropped the shelf pieces beside her. She threw her arms around her beloved dog and held him close. But he could only stand that for a few minutes before he wiggled free. She moved her legs out of the way, and instantly Mugs walked into the cupboard.

The cupboard was at least three feet across. It didn't make any sense to have it here. The door didn't fit properly. She assumed a different door had been here at one point in time. Neither did the flooring go all the way to the end of the cupboard. How wrong was that? On the other hand, it was a potential place to put Mugs's food and water bowls.

At least with them in there, the bird wasn't likely to eat it all either. She hoped. She kicked off Nan's old shoes, got to her feet to retrieve the dog's food and water bowls, and put them inside the cupboard. Mugs didn't seem to mind his accommodations at all. He dug right in.

"Dinnertime. Dinnertime."

She spun to see Thaddeus strutting back and forth on the kitchen table. He stopped beside the open can of wet dog food and pecked away at the little bits of food still stuck to the bottom of the can. As if getting the scent of the dry dog food, his head flew up. He cocked it sideways to look at her first and then at the bag where the dry dog food came from and carefully walked forward, his neck fully extended. When he got to the bag, he stuck his head inside, pulled back, and stuck it in again. This time he came out with a dry kernel. He put it on the table and pecked at it, then said, "Dinnertime. Dinnertime for Thaddeus."

She wasn't sure she would survive all this domesticity, taking care of not only herself and Mugs but now a bird and a cat. *Probably like taking care of children.* Something else she had no firsthand experience with. Not even secondhand experience. Too bad she and Nan couldn't share this old house now that Doreen had arrived and also share the pet-related responsibilities. But hopefully she would be working a day job, away from home, so she knew it was better that Nan have twenty-four-hour assistance available at Rosemoor.

Groaning, her legs not working quite the same as they had before her walk, Doreen trudged over, while Thaddeus pulled out one more kernel from the dog food bag and put it on the table. She said in a firm voice, "That's Mugs's dinner."

She closed the bag, cleaned up the kitchen, and then studied the room. Surprisingly Thaddeus had been quiet all this time. She needed to get Thaddeus some food, or they would have an all-out war over the dog food soon. But where was the bird food, and what did a parrot like this eat? She'd forgotten to ask Nan about that. Darn. Mugs had already adjusted to a much cheaper dog food than he was accustomed to, but she didn't need Thaddeus eating it any faster.

Who had Nan left in charge of him and Goliath for these three weeks before Doreen arrived? Or had Nan walked back and forth each day to feed her animals? Or was that the Marge Nan had mentioned when Doreen first arrived? Nan cared for her animals meticulously and obviously wouldn't have let them suffer. Thaddeus was an African Grey, Nan had said. It would outlive both Nan and Doreen.

That didn't bear thinking about.

She searched the kitchen cupboards, looking for bird food but finding none. She turned in frustration, the bird staring at her, his head cocked to one side.

He spoke again. "Thaddeus is hungry. Thaddeus is hungry."

She glared at him. "Do you have to say everything twice?"

"Yes. Yes."

She groaned. "Enough."

"Thaddeus is hungry. Thaddeus is hungry."

In defeat she pulled out her phone and called Nan. "Have you got food here for Thaddeus?"

"It's in the front closet on the top shelf," Nan said with a giggle. "Is he eating the dog food yet?"

"Well, he is trying to. I presume he also eats Goliath's food too?"

"Who's Goliath?"

Silence overtook her. Doreen frowned into the phone. "Your cat?"

"Oh, well, Goliath is a better name than I gave him." Nan giggled. "Cat food and bird food are all in the closet. Don't leave the door open, or Thaddeus will get in all the food."

With Nan still on the phone, Doreen headed to the closet and tried to open it. "Why would you lock this closet? The bird can't turn a doorknob."

"It isn't locked. It's just got a strong spring, so it shuts firmly. Turn the handle and tug real hard."

"Really?" She squeezed the phone between her ear and shoulder, and, with both hands, she turned the doorknob and gave it a sharp tug. It opened easily enough, considering, sending her backward. "Well, you're right about it sticking." She looked up at the corners, realizing the door had swelled, and that was why it had been stuck. "This door should be taken off its hinges and sanded down," she said to Nan. "There are some things I know need to be done as I oversaw the work at the estate, I've just never done it myself."

Nan laughed. "That's a minor thing. Wait 'til you see the rest of the things falling apart in the house."

"Oh, great." But bags of pet food were up on the shelf. She pulled out the cat food and some of the bird food. She found another set of food and water bowls that she could use to feed the cat, since Doreen hadn't seen any others out in the house already. Did Thaddeus eat and drink from a bowl? So far she'd seen him eat off the floor and the table. The rest of her conversation with Nan was about how much Doreen was supposed to feed Thaddeus and Goliath and where to feed them.

"He has two bowls. One for water, but he prefers my tea," she chuckled. "And loves the blue bowl with chips out of the side. He's partial to that one but will eat out of anything. It's important that you put Thaddeus on his roost after eating. He's very good at keeping the house area clean in general, but you have to change the newspapers around the base of his stand."

While Thaddeus ate on the kitchen table—a habit she really didn't want him to continue—Doreen walked to the bird's perch and stood, staring at the soiled newspapers positioned around the base of the stand, and saw what Nan had been talking about. Doreen's long-sounding sigh had Nan giggling on the other end.

"Did you really think he didn't have to go to the bathroom when inside the house?"

"How many times a day does he go?" Doreen asked suspiciously.

In a way-too-innocent-sounding voice, Nan said, "Not too often. Just change the newspapers whenever you can. Every day would be good." And then she hung up.

"Darn." After the day Doreen had had, what was a little poop? She rolled up her sleeves, gathered the dirty newspapers together and laid out fresh newspaper from a nearby stack—now understanding why they were in this corner. Along with a collection of plastic grocery bags. She grabbed one of those too and filled it with the newspapers to discard.

She certainly didn't want this mess inside the kitchen. She looked outside at the people standing around where her garbage can was. What a long walk it would be to get the bird-poop papers down there with everybody's gaze on her. And how hard it would be to get past those people watching her without them noticing her.

Then she got mad. So what if they were watching? She'd been through a heck of a lot worse since the holidays last year. So many people had looked on, snickered and outright laughed at her circumstances.

She'd be darned if she'd let these gawkers make her sleep in the same house as the rather overwhelming collection of bird poop. She walked back into the kitchen, slipped her feet into Nan's shoes, picked up the bag of poop-coated newspapers and opened the front door. Instantly a murmur arose from the crowd at the base of the driveway. She closed the door behind her and strode, staring straight ahead, to the garbage can. There she lifted the lid, put the garbage inside and slammed the lid down a little harder than necessary.

Instantly silence surrounded her.

And still the *clang* of the metal-on-metal rang clear. She winced, turned and walked back toward the house. Not a soul said a word. As she entered her front door, neither had she.

She stopped in the threshold, wondering how to turn this around. Normally she'd say she was a wonderful hostess, knowing how to smooth over any awkward moment. She'd prided herself on that to make her husband's social evenings work. Yet, here she was, in the middle of two worlds, a bridge that she had crossed. But she had yet to figure out a way to bring her previous experiences with her.

She pivoted for one last look at the crowd. And tried to smile.

All eyes stared back at her. Nobody moved.

She took a deep breath, twisted fully to face them and said, "Hello. My name is Doreen. Nan is *my* grandmother."

Not a word was spoken in response. She shrugged. Well, she had tried. She turned again.

And just as she was about to shut the door, somebody from the middle of the crowd called out, "Did you kill him? Did you kill the man in the garden?"

"Of course not," she yelled. "I just arrived today."

"And yet, there is a dead man in your garden."

"No," she hollered at the top of her voice. "There is a dead man in Nan's garden."

And with that the crowd gasped in shock.

"Nan wouldn't kill anyone," someone yelled.

"And neither would I," Doreen yelled back. She glared at them, spun on her heels, then slammed the door shut. If only she could shut out the world that simply. She leaned against the door, tamping down the scream in the back of her throat.

Just then Mugs raced through the hallway, Thaddeus riding his back and screaming at the top of his lungs, "Thaddeus is here. Thaddeus is here."

Doreen grabbed her hair, pulled and joined in, screaming at the top of her lungs.

Chapter 8

FROM THE DIN inside, it was almost impossible to hear the knock on the door. Wiping the frustrated tears from her eyes, Doreen scrambled to peer around the corner of the living room window. A massive crowd remained outside. If anything, it appeared to be larger.

She glared at them from her hidden position. But someone at the door pounded again. The whole darn frame seemed to shake at that movement. She peered around the corner, but all she could see was someone big, and she chewed on her bottom lip, wondering if she should answer. By this point Mugs thought he should add to the noise again. He barked and barked and barked.

What now? I'll never get to eat at this rate.

If for no other reason than to shut him up, she walked to the front door. With her chin held high, she flung it open. And her jaw dropped. A man—huge, broad, sexy as hell, and a bit older than she was—filled the doorway.

He looked at her and smiled and asked, "Doreen Montgomery, I presume?"

She stared at him suspiciously. "How do you know my name?"

"I work with law enforcement. So I already know who you are. Besides you're in Nan Montgomery's house."

"But my married name was Merriweather."

"Have you reverted back to your maiden name?"

"Paperwork is in progress," she admitted. "But Montgomery's the only name I'll answer to now."

He motioned to the living room behind her. "May I come in?"

She crossed her arms over her chest and glared at him. "Why?"

He laughed.

That made her even more suspicious. "Are you just one of the many who wants to come here and gawk?"

"Hell, no, I don't. I'm the investigating officer for the Serious Crime Unit here in town."

She bolted backward. "Does that mean I'm a suspect?" She outstretched her arms as if to ward off an attack. "I didn't do anything, honest." Then she stopped and stared at him suspiciously. "Do I need a lawyer to talk to you?"

"Whoa, take it easy. No. You are not a suspect but more of a witness after-the-fact. My brother is a lawyer, if you *want* to talk to one. I almost went to law school with him." He smiled reassuringly at her. "We both work on the side of the good guys."

"There is no such thing when it comes to a lawyer," she snapped. She narrowed her gaze at him and asked, "ID?"

He raised an eyebrow, pulled out his wallet from his back pocket and extracted a card from inside. With two fingers, he held it out to her.

She read it. *Mack Moreau.* He looked like a man called *Mack* should look, as he was the size of a freaking Mack truck.

And the card presented him as Corporal Moreau of the Kelowna RCMP Serious Crime Unit. So at least he was who he said he was. If that made any difference. "Why are you here, and do I need to get a lawyer of my own choosing?" Yet, she had absolutely zero trust in them at this point in her life.

He shook his head. "No, you don't. Things are done very casually here. I came to welcome you to our town and to see what the hell was going on in your backyard. More cops will be here anytime now."

"*More* cops?" She waved at her backyard. "How can there possibly be more cops working for this small town? They're all in my backyard already."

"A lot of times we deputize civilians if we need them."

She stared at him as the information computed in her brain. "So you can deputize me to work in my own garden?"

At that he gave a boisterous laugh. "Well, if it wasn't your garden, and there wasn't a body found on your property, without that conflict of interest, if you are in fit physical form to assist us as needed for the case, then it's possible."

She stared at him, disgruntled. "I'm fit."

His gaze went from the top of her no-longer-coiffed hair all the way down her very bedraggled suit to Nan's pink garden shoes on her feet. In a very gentle voice he said, "It looks like you've had a very difficult day." He motioned to the kitchen. "Why don't we put on a cup of tea?"

She couldn't decide if he was being patronizing or compassionate. She decided she'd had enough of the bad guys, and she'd take his compassion if it were there. "Fine. But watch out for Mugs and Goliath." She turned to find the giant of a man busy rubbing Mugs's belly as he lay on his back, his stubby legs in the air, a serious groan coming from his mouth. "I don't think I've ever heard him make that sound before." She stared at the man and shook her head. "I suppose you think you can charm anyone?"

"Nope. But dogs are easy."

"How do you feel about cats?"

Goliath snuck around the corner of the hallway toward Mack. He gave the cat a great big scratch on its back and under its chin. And, just like that, he'd won over Goliath too as the traitor dropped to the floor and purred like a lion. Doreen stared at Mack. He had an affinity for animals she'd never really had a chance to explore. Before today.

"How's Thaddeus?" Mack straightened and walked toward Doreen, glancing over at Thaddeus on the tree post. "I'm used to seeing him on that roost all the time."

"He seems to like that place." She put on the teakettle, grateful she knew how to do that much. Too bad she hadn't made any coffee. She'd have it to offer him now. But what would she serve him with the tea? "I haven't had a chance to go shopping yet," she said. "I wasn't sure the crowd outside would let me."

"If they're bothering you, I can have them dispersed."

She faced him. "Can you?"

"Sure. They're just curious. Those are all your neighbors, plus a few from surrounding neighborhoods it seems. They want to know what's going on. They're harmless enough."

"How can you tell? One of them might be the murderer. Isn't it true that murderers often stick around when the police arrive at the scenes of their crimes?"

"Usually with a fresh one. Not so much when it's been buried for a while. Although this one is a relatively recent murder, as I understand flesh is still on the bones." He tilted his head toward her. "But you are correct in that criminals do return to their crime scenes. And they do seem to enjoy watching everybody scurry around to solve the mystery."

"I thought so." She opened the tea drawer. "I don't know what tea to serve you."

"How about coffee instead?"

She eyed him suspiciously. She had heard the hopeful tone in his voice. "The coffeemaker is right there. Feel free."

He walked over, swung out a basket from the top of the coffeemaker she hadn't known existed and dumped out its contents in the trash can under the sink. He opened the drawer below the coffeemaker, pulled out a coffee filter, stuck one in and then reached for a bag of coffee.

And she didn't even know it had been coffee. She walked over and studied the bag. "Nothing on it says *coffee*." She felt his stare of surprise.

He quietly said in a calm voice, "It says *espresso*."

She nodded. "I read that. I didn't realize that was the same kind of coffee one could use to make coffee in a coffeemaker."

"Absolutely. Espresso makes some of the best coffee."

"Good, because I really could use a cup." She walked over to the table and sagged into a chair. At that moment, Thaddeus decided to walk across the kitchen floor, strutting his stuff but coming from the other side of the kitchen. "Where the heck were you?" she asked in an accusing tone.

"Thaddeus is here. Thaddeus is here." He ruffled his feathers and jumped onto the table.

And then she got it. She leaned forward and studied the dog food. "You were in the cupboard, eating all the dog food, weren't you?"

"Thaddeus is here. Thaddeus is here."

"You might not be for long though," she threatened.

"Thaddeus is a long-term character around this place." Mack walked over and brushed the side of the African Grey's cheek. "Hello, Thaddeus. How are you doing?"

Thaddeus lifted a foot to the man's finger, bobbed his head, proceeded to hop on, and then walked all the way up to Mack's shoulder, where he sat quite comfortably. "Thaddeus is fine. Thaddeus is fine."

"Glad to hear that, big guy. I'm sure it's been a pretty tough adjustment for you not having Nan around."

"Nan is gone. Nan is gone."

But Thaddeus's tone of voice had changed to a soulful mourn, so much so that Doreen could feel his grief.

"Nan is not gone," she reassured Thaddeus. "Remember? I took you to see Nan today."

"Did you? How is she?"

Doreen looked over at Mack and said, "Honestly, she seems quite happy there. I was expecting her to be in worse shape."

Mack pulled out a chair beside Doreen. As he sat down, Thaddeus maintained his position perfectly on his shoulder.

The smell of coffee filled the air. She turned and looked at Mack. "I should've asked earlier. How much coffee did you put in?"

"Two scoops," he said without missing a beat. "And the scoop's inside the bag."

She stored that information away for later. She so wanted to learn to make a decent cup of coffee. Even if it took her ten pots to get there. She was a little desperate for her caffeine.

"And your relationship with Nan?"

Her gaze focused on him, her mood mellower now that she knew coffee was coming. "My grandmother. She's the only family I have left. I didn't get to see her very much when I was married. We did phone a lot though." She smiled. "Nan used to tell me how her life was busy and not to worry if I didn't have more time for her."

"Did you believe her?"

"No, I think she often said that to make me feel better." Doreen looked at him. "My marriage wasn't exactly the easiest. Nan seemed to call at my low points. She always cheered me up. Just hearing her voice made me happy. She was also the one who constantly told me how I had choices in life."

"Did you agree with her?"

There was no probing. His questions just seemed like simple curiosity. So she answered him the same way. "At the time, no. When you're in the middle of a situation, it's very hard to see options. But now I can laugh and realize—looking back over the years—how upsetting the situation was, and yet, how many options I did have at the time. I wish I'd listened to her earlier."

At the last gurgle of the coffeepot, Mack nudged his shoulder, and Thaddeus walked to the table. Mack rose and filled two mugs with coffee, bringing them back to the kitchen table. "I think everyone feels that way at some time or another about their lives."

"And, if they're smart, they'll listen to the advice given to them by those who are older and wiser." Her gaze fell on Thaddeus, busy preening himself. After all, he had just finished eating the dog food. Time to clean himself afterward, right? "I'm surprised Nan didn't find a home for her pets though."

"Except for one thing," Mack said quietly. "She *did* find a home for them."

She raised her gaze, startled at his words. "Me?" When he nodded, she laughed. "I meant a *good* home."

He tilted his head to the side and studied her carefully. "And why is it you can't provide them a good home?"

"I have no idea how. I haven't had to provide for myself until now, and, at this point in time, with three animals…"

"But you're resourceful. You're a survivor. You can do this."

She openly stared at him. And she had to wonder. Was he right?

One thing she did know. He was too handsome, too suave to believe most of the time. But maybe those most recent words from him were just what she needed to hear.

Chapter 9

"WHAT QUESTIONS DID you want to ask me, Corporal Moreau?" Doreen studied Mack, wondering at his earlier insight. Mugs walked over and sniffed his shoes.

"Just call me Mack. I'd like you to tell me what you saw outside and what you found." He gave her a gentle smile. "Just start from when you first arrived."

She rolled her eyes. "That'll take a while. I've been here a whole six or so hours, and unlikely events have taken over my life." But she launched into her story. Doing the best she could to leave nothing out, she brought Mack up to date on everything that had happened so far.

"Do you have any idea why there would be a body in the garden?"

She looked at him and said, "No."

"Any idea why Nan would have somebody buried in the garden?"

She narrowed her gaze at him. "No."

He nodded. "Do you have problems with anybody from this area?"

"Maybe the entire neighborhood for all I know," she

snapped. "Remember that part about how I just got here? Today? At noon?"

"What about Nan? Did she have any enemies?"

Instantly her ire subsided. "Hell no. Nan is one of the nicest people I've ever known." She waved her hand around at the small house. "Maybe you should talk to the neighbors about that. Because I really don't know. If they do have something to say, maybe you'll fill me in. As far as I know, Nan didn't have any arguments with anybody. However, Nan is alive and well in the retirement home, so maybe you should talk directly to her."

"And I will," he said, tucking away his notepad.

He'd been writing something on those pages. She watched him pocket his pen. "Can you tell all those policemen to get out of my backyard now?"

"Not until they are done."

"And the mess they're making?"

He glanced out the window at the completely overgrown garden and said, "How can you even tell?"

She stared at the garden area. "Nan couldn't do very much gardening for the last few years."

He waved at the grass. It was well over knee-high, so were the weeds all throughout the yard. "At least that long."

A few trees in the back badly needed pruning. When she had the time and energy and money, she would get those done. Nan must've needed help with everything. All of it piling on top of her and just not enough energy to even care anymore. Between the garden, the house and the animals, it had all gotten to be too much for her aging grandmother.

Guilt shot through Doreen. Poor Nan. She'd really hoped to stay here in her own home until she died. Maybe Doreen should ask Nan once more if she wanted to come live here with her.

"Any idea what brought about her decision to move?"

Doreen slowly faced him, her eyebrows raised. "You know? I never asked her. Maybe I should."

His voice dropping yet again, he said, "Maybe you should."

As he walked away, she studied his back suspiciously. "What do you mean by that, Mack?"

He turned and smiled. "It might just have something to do with your circumstances."

She stared at him blankly for a moment, and then it hit her. She gasped in horror. "You're not saying Nan moved into a retirement home so I could have her house? That would be horrible."

"Why would it be horrible?" He leaned against the doorjamb, crossing his arms as he studied her. "Sometimes it takes other people's circumstances to make us realize it's time for a change."

She huffed.

He grinned. "Then, because of your circumstances, it might've been the final straw that led Nan to making that decision."

Somehow that sounded better, but, at the same time, it wasn't what she wanted to hear. She planned to ask Nan... she just needed the right time... She didn't want to make it sound like she was ungrateful for all Nan had done. Neither did she want Nan to feel obligated to help her out. Doreen could stand on her own two feet. She had no experience doing so, but she was gutsy and getting more so every day.

There was something incredibly freeing about her new life.

Just then a knock came at the back door, and she opened

it, amid Mugs's crazy barking, to let in the same grizzled cop she had met at the very beginning of this strange day—Arnold. She couldn't begin to remember his last name. Carmichael maybe? No, that wasn't it. No matter. Chester said to just call them by their first names.

He nodded, took note of Mack and said, "Good evening, sir. I didn't realize you were here."

Mack nodded back at him. "Any forensic finds?"

"Not that we noticed yet. The coroner is ready to take away the body. Did you want to see the backyard?"

Mack said, "Yes, actually I would like to."

"I would too," Doreen growled. She headed out to the back veranda behind them. When she saw how much of the garden they had dug up getting to the body, she winced. "You know? The least you guys could do is dig up the entire thing." Several blank faces raised in her direction. She sighed. "Never mind."

Mack laughed. "They will get the joke later."

She followed Mack from the kitchen back door to the far set of veranda steps down to the decking nearest the grave. She stayed on the veranda steps while Mack walked around one six-foot-long pit, a couple feet wide, barely big enough for a body, and only a couple feet deep. "I thought you're supposed to bury bodies at least six feet deep so that animals can't smell them?"

One of the officers turned to look at her. "That would be in ideal circumstances."

She nodded. "So somebody didn't intend for this body to be here for very long?"

Arnold faced her. "Maybe *somebody* buried it just recently."

A sour note had entered his voice. As if Doreen were

somehow responsible. She glared at him. "It wasn't me. Remember that part about me not being here until six hours ago?"

"But you could have been here a couple days ago, coming in secretly, burying a man in the backyard and then coming back again when you moved in. All looking innocent like that." He brushed most of the dirt off his hands and clothes.

She glared at him. "Why would I bury a body in my own place?"

"I haven't figured that out yet. But I will." Arnold gave her a surly look and walked around the house.

Several of the other men were busy walking the rest of her property.

She waved a hand toward them. "What are they looking for?"

"Anything and everything," said the younger cop, Chester. "We must search to find any forensic evidence that would explain how and why this happened. And, most important, by whom."

"I understand that, but do you have to check in the garden like fifty yards away?"

"If you were to stand on that deck," Mack began, "and were to toss a murder weapon into that mess, how far do you think you could throw it?"

She turned to Mack and answered his question. "I don't know. Maybe thirty to forty feet?"

"If you were a fit teenaged male, how far do you think you could throw it?"

She studied the back of the garden and said, "Fine. I guess somebody good at pitching a softball could throw all the way to the back of the property. But it's getting too dark to see anything."

The young cop said, "That's why we will be back first thing in the morning."

She stared at him in surprise. "You guys will be here again tomorrow?"

Mack cleared his throat beside her. "We'll be here every day until we have searched the whole place."

She stared at him. "Why?"

"Because a dead body was found on your property."

She closed her eyes, hating the idea of starting a brand-new life immediately ravaged by something as nasty as a murder. Then she nodded. "That's fine, but I want to know exactly what you take out of here."

"We can do that. We'll give you a list of items before we leave with them."

She asked Mack, "If you guys are leaving now and coming back in the morning, how the devil will you know if the killer comes back and takes whatever it is he might've thrown out there?"

He looked at her and just smiled.

She shook her head at his failure to answer her and was about to go back inside, but Mugs sniffed around the bottom step. "Did you happen to check under these veranda steps?"

Everyone still in the vicinity stopped and looked at Mugs. He sniffed from one side of the step to the other. Then he jumped down into the grave. "No, Mugs, no."

But Mugs ignored her command. With his short stubby legs, he dug deeper in the spot where the policemen had dug. Instantly several of the cops came back over with flashlights to look closer underneath that final step nearby the grave. And she had the sinking feeling they'd found something.

Mack, disregarding his suit, jumped into the grave, picked up Mugs and put him at the top of the veranda steps beside her. "Can you keep him here until we find out what it is he smelled?"

She nodded and grabbed Mugs by the collar. Goliath wandered out, completely oblivious to the fact that a dozen men surrounded the veranda. "What is it, Goliath?" She didn't expect the cat to answer, but he walked back and forth over the top of the same step Mugs had sniffed and swished his tale. She wasn't sure what that meant in cat language, but she presumed it was significant. Between the findings of the two of them, something had to be under there.

When somebody tore off the bottom veranda step from its supports, set it to one side, and dug underneath, she winced and said, "Please tell me a second body isn't down there."

"I don't think so." The cop pulled out what look like a briefcase. "A man's laptop bag or something similar." In the dark, it was hard to see, but the item was black and about the right size for a briefcase.

The men kept digging a little more and came up with a dead squirrel.

"Oh, that must be what the dog was after."

The cops shrugged. The squirrel was tossed into the nearest garbage bag beside them. One of the men asked the cop holding the briefcase, "Now this briefcase, that's a different story. The animals weren't necessarily interested in it. But is it the dead man's briefcase?"

"It's a reasonable assumption," said the cop holding the new evidence.

With a flashlight turned on the briefcase, the cops opened it up to find papers. Lots and lots of papers.

Doreen leaned in to make sure nothing pertained to Nan. A couple of the cops looked at her funny, but none told her to go away. They'd better not. Without her and Mugs, they wouldn't have known the briefcase was even here.

Mack pulled out several documents. "These look like investments, stock portfolios."

"And is Nan's name on there or not?" Doreen asked.

Mack looked at her and understood. He walked up the steps and turned on the outside light for more light on the veranda and the deck then he went through several of the papers. "I'm not seeing Nan's name on any of these forms."

Doreen's shoulders sagged with relief. "Thank you. I just want to make sure this guy hadn't ripped her off or something. Nan must have had a really bad time financially these last few years, and I'd hate to think somebody took advantage of her."

"Forensics will get these original documents first. I'll get copies and go over them in detail," Mack said. "If there's any mention of Nan on these, I'll let you know."

He collected the pages, put them back in the case, gave it a good bang to ensure some of the dirt came off and then joined the other policemen on the yard.

Chapter 10

DOREEN LOCKED THE front door once Mack and some of the other officers had gone, then, needing a better outlet for her growing frustration, ended up kicking it too.

"Ouch." *Okay, that was stupid.* Hobbling gently, she walked to the kitchen window where she watched from behind the curtains as the policemen slowly collected their tools and belongings and then left her garden. When the backyard was clear, she walked into the living room, just in time to see several cop cars pull away.

A few stragglers remained from the crowd that had been outside, standing around, staring and talking. Several even had what appeared to be mugs of tea or coffee. She supposed this was their local entertainment. With a sad shake of her head, she turned toward the coffeepot.

At least she'd learned how to make coffee. If she were lucky, there'd be a cup left.

She perked up at the idea and walked to the pot. No such luck. It was a small pot, and between her and Mack, the coffee had been finished off. She pulled out the coffee from the drawer where she'd seen Mack grab it, and, true enough, the scoop was inside. So now she could make coffee herself.

But, just in case, she jotted down his instructions on a notepad so she wouldn't forget.

She was hungry too and still had her lack-of-food issue to deal with. The Chinese food delivery would have to wait for another day. She was just so tired, but she forced herself to sit down and eat the rest of her traveling snacks. After the first few bites she felt better. By the time she'd polished off her meager meal, she was more than ready to go to bed.

She grabbed several of her suitcases and marched upstairs. She hadn't unpacked her bags yet, not with so much happening on her first day here.

With all the animals following behind her, she opened the first room to see a small bedroom with ancient wallpaper and dingy curtains on the windows. In spite of the looks she smiled. This had been the room she'd stayed in as a child. There had been a bathroom across the hallway. Crossing the hallway she found the bathroom as she remembered, which at least looked serviceable. The master bedroom was at the end of the hallway. This was Nan's room. She gasped in delight as she walked in. It was huge. This would work.

Of course it was also jam-packed with all kinds of shelves and old furniture. She had no idea what Nan needed with all this stuff. But amid all this clutter was a very large bed in the center. She walked over and sat down experimentally. Loud squeaks and groans of metal springs erupted from underneath. She closed her eyes in defeat. "Really, Nan?" Was this the same old bed she'd always had? Hadn't she upgraded anything? Doreen stared at it in disbelief. "This thing will break my back. I just know it."

Immediately she chastised herself for the uncharitable thought. It was probably all Nan could afford.

Doreen pulled back the bedding to see that, indeed,

clean sheets were underneath. Nan had probably left it ready for Doreen's arrival. Which Doreen appreciated, but, at the same time, she wondered at the sense of just taking the mattress off the noisy steel springs and putting it on the floor. She wasn't sure she'd be able to sleep on the bed as is. She was starting to feel like the princess with the pea—only right now she was more pauper than princess.

Two very large double closet doors were on the opposite wall, and that was a plus. But as she opened the doors, the closet overflowed with everything else stored away in this house. It would take days, if not weeks or months, to sort through and toss all this clutter. Why hadn't Nan done this first? She'd known she was leaving this house.

When Doreen had a chance, she'd ask Nan. Doreen's little Honda was too small to haul everything out of here, and she had no money to pay for somebody else to get rid of it all. The living room and dining room downstairs were full as well. But she hadn't really expected this bedroom to be also. She turned to see Thaddeus, sitting on the foot railing to the bed. "Oh, I don't think so. This is where I sleep, not you."

But as she studied him and the newspaper on the floor under him, she wondered if that really was his sleeping spot. "Oh, my God! Please don't tell me that you poop in here too?"

As if knowing exactly what she said, Thaddeus gave a tiny squirt, and a white splotch appeared on the floor.

It was just too much. It was *all* just too much. She could feel hot tears burning in the corner of her eyes. She brushed them away impatiently. By the time she cleared her eyes, she could hear a weird groan. She glanced over at the bed again to see Goliath dead center, curled up in a ball. Nan probably had lived with her pets as if they were family.

The trouble was, they were *Nan's* family. Doreen wasn't at all sure they could become hers. Did she have any choice?

Mugs stood up on his back legs, his front paws on the bed, took one look at the cat asleep there and barked.

Doreen rushed over. "Oh, no you don't. You're not jumping on that bed." But before she reached him, he lunged and ended up on the bed too. The bed squeaked and bounced with his movements. The cat didn't even open an eyeball. Mugs sniffed at him hard and then circled around and dropped at the foot of the bed, stretched out, taking up over half of it.

If she'd ever wondered how much her life would change now, here was her answer. The proof was right here in front of her. She would never be the same again.

She turned her back on them and surveyed the rest of the room. She couldn't deal with the animals right now. *Later.* Spotting a door on the far side, she walked over and pushed it open. And cried out in joy. Of all the things she hadn't expected, it was this huge en suite bathroom with a large soaking tub, a separate shower and double sinks. When had Nan redone this room? Whenever it was Doreen would be forever grateful. And right now a hot shower would do a lot to ease her mood.

She walked to the window to check if anybody could see her. The master bathroom looked over the backyard. Outside of the neighboring yards, only trees and grass stared back at her. She stood here, slowly unbuttoning her suit jacket as she stared out at the massive garden. Tracks and shovel marks and trampled grass reached all the way back to the dilapidated fence. Such an invasion of privacy. She knew she shouldn't feel violated, as it didn't feel like home yet, but she was more outraged for Nan's sake.

Yet, she knew Nan didn't give a crap. In Nan's mind, this was done and gone, and she wasn't coming home again. And that was just that.

As Doreen glanced back out into the evening light, something twinkled. It winked and flashed as if something metallic or mirrored had moved. She frowned and stepped behind the curtains. Was somebody out there?

Of course people were out there. She had had curiosity seekers watching the events here all evening. Just because the cops had left, did that mean the gawkers had too?

No other houses were behind hers. She should have complete privacy here. Except for whatever was twinkling in the night.

As she glanced up, she could see the moon rising off to the left, sending a sharp ray of moonlight down on the back garden. Well, that explained the twinkling and flashing going on, but what was the moonlight hitting? She contemplated heading out there to look but knew that she couldn't see anything in the dark. Did Nan have a flashlight among all the stuff stored in this house?

Sleep would elude Doreen while that shining thing was out there. She didn't know if it was important or just a piece of garbage. But what if it had something to do with the murder?

This was Nan's house—regardless of what Nan thought or said or did—and Doreen had to do what she could to protect it. With a groan, she buttoned up her suit jacket once more and headed back downstairs, shoving her feet into Nan's shoes. Doreen searched the kitchen drawers until she found a flashlight and then headed outside.

With both Goliath and Mugs moving excitedly at her

side, she propped the back door open so the animals could come and go as they pleased and then headed outside. She went down the veranda steps, carefully making her way around the huge hole that the police had left, striding toward the area where she'd seen the twinkling light. Thaddeus flew up, joining the trio, and landed on her shoulder. She stroked him, her heart more affected than she thought.

He crooned against her cheek, "Thaddeus is here. Thaddeus is here."

And she was so grateful that she would not be totally alone in Nan's house.

With the animals at her side, the flashlight giving her limited visibility, she slowly made her way through the backyard. Going by the landmarks she'd memorized while looking out her upstairs window, she focused on the big window in the master bathroom, gauging where she'd find the shiny thing. She shone the flashlight around but saw nothing. She walked the area for a good ten minutes but couldn't locate it.

"Well, Goliath, you're the one who brought the finger bone inside. Can you find this other thing? How about you, Thaddeus? Can you find the reflective thing?"

Maybe his species was attracted to shiny stuff. Or was it magpies that stole the shiny things? Crows? She shook her head, not having any answers to her own questions. "What about you, Mugs? How about you root around and dig up stuff? Isn't this what you wanted a garden of your own for?" She knew she was talking out loud just to keep herself focused on why she was here. In the dark. By an empty grave.

Mugs had been denied access to the garden in the big house where they used to live. He had his own little dog run where people came and cleaned up behind him every day.

But now he had a real garden, where he was allowed to roll around in the dirt. She knew he'd be much happier here. Just like she would be.

She stopped, took another assessment from the angle upstairs where she'd been and walked about eight feet forward. As she moved ahead, Mugs dove into the grass in front of her. It was tall enough and deep enough that it darn near split and flattened in half with his weight. She shone the light to see what he'd found. And, sure enough, something was in his mouth. She grabbed his collar so he wouldn't run away with it. She'd had more than enough of that earlier with the finger bone. She shone the flashlight at what was in his mouth, and it was indeed metal. It was a small flat piece. But Mugs wouldn't drop it easily.

She found a stick and made a trade.

Grudgingly he accepted the stick. She stared at the metal and wondered what the heck it was. Probably nothing but garbage. She checked out the spot where it had been. With the dog now happily chewing on the stick beside her, the cat roaming the garden and Thaddeus staring over her shoulder, she found the rest of it.

It was a small metal box half buried in the garden. She didn't know if it had been uprooted by the police or whether one of the volunteers had found it or if it had lain here for decades. She dug around it and lifted it from its surprisingly deep home, realizing it had been in the same position for a long time. Nothing was inside the metal box, but, as she removed it, she found something below it. Gradually she moved away more dirt and grass and then reached inside the hole. And what she brought back up made her blood run cold.

Thaddeus squawked in her ear. "Murder in the garden. Murder in the garden."

Chapter II

"MACK? CORPORAL MACK Moreau?" she said into the phone. She rubbed her hand across her forehead and stared at the item she'd brought into the house.

"Yes, this is Mack. Who's this?"

She rolled her eyes. "It's Doreen."

"Doreen?" he asked cautiously.

"Remember the crazy lady with the bird, the dog, the cat and the dead body in the garden?"

There was an abrupt silence before he said, in a much warmer tone, "Yes. What can I do for you?"

"I found something in the garden. Honestly I wasn't looking. I wasn't trying to interfere. But I was getting ready for bed, and I could see something shining in the back corner of the garden. I guess the moonlight hit the metal. Anyway the four of us went outside, and I found a metal box. It looked like it'd been disturbed while everybody was searching, but nobody probably really did see it because it was covered in dirt."

"And what was in the box?"

She said, "Nothing. But a bottle of arsenic was buried below it."

"What?" His voice turned businesslike. "Please tell me you left it in the garden."

"Oops," she said into the ever-widening gap of silence.

"Of course you didn't. Did you bring it all inside?"

"No, just the bottle of arsenic. It appears to be empty though," she hurriedly added. "Honestly I didn't want to leave it out there. What if some animal got a hold of it?"

She could almost see him ready to pull his hair from his head. It was very nice hair. She really didn't want him to pull it out. But she understood how his lack of control over her could be a little on the frustrating side. "You have to understand. This is my property, and it reflects on Nan's reputation, and I am feeling a little responsible for what's going on here."

"Where is the arsenic now, Doreen?"

"In front of me," she said. "On the kitchen counter."

"I'll be right there."

"No, you don't have to—" But it was too late. The phone was dead in her hand. "Wonderful." She glanced down at her clothing. "And my shower will have to wait. Again."

No getting away from this visit. She'd called him, and she would have to see this through to the end. She walked to the front door, opened it to let in the evening air and stepped on the front porch, waiting for Mack to show up.

She was grateful that, at this time of night, her house had long lost interest for all the neighbors. For the first time, she could see the beauty of the small cul-de-sac with its collection of little houses. Everyone took care of their yards. They were large properties. Nobody could see into the other houses' windows. There was a lot to be said for this place. She would enjoy seeing more of this area as she walked into town to visit Nan every day or so. She just wasn't so sure about that whole gossipy thing going on right now.

Or the dead body.

Of course, if she hadn't been at the murder scene, maybe it would've been just fine. She sat with Goliath in her arms, Thaddeus walking back and forth on the porch railing and Mugs sleeping at her feet until she saw headlights coming. A car drove up her driveway and stopped.

Mack got out and walked over to her. "You okay?"

She shrugged. "I'm exhausted. I'd really like to get this over with." She stood slowly, handing him Goliath. "The arsenic is in here." She proceeded to lead the way.

Goliath didn't seem to care that he'd been passed over to the big man. And neither did the man. She watched Mack as he shifted the large cat in his arms and followed her.

Now that was a decent guy. Her husband would've stepped back before the cat made contact with his suit. He'd have shot Doreen a horrified look, as if she'd tried to kill him. But then he hated cats. Apparently Mack didn't. And she trusted Goliath to know a good man when he saw one. Although she had no idea where she'd heard that old wives' tale about cats being able to discern that. So far Goliath hadn't been around many people. But what did Doreen know? She'd been a cat owner for less than half a day. And so much had happened in that time to distract her from watching Goliath's reaction to various people.

In the kitchen, she pointed out the bottle. Mack glanced at her. "I don't suppose you wore gloves when you picked it up."

She winced and shook her head. "No, I never thought of it."

He directed her to the sink. "Wash thoroughly."

Immediately she turned on the water, soaping up, chastising herself for not thinking of that first. She could have poisoned her pets. She glanced at Goliath. "I was petting him too."

"When you're done, grab the brush and give him a good brushing. Chances are, he'll be fine, but you don't want to take a chance. Then I want you to show me where in the garden you found it."

She grabbed the towel, quickly dried her hands, walked over to the pet closet where she'd seen a brush along with the cat food and pulled it out. Between the two of them taking turns, Mack and Doreen made Goliath think he was royalty. They managed to get a solid layer of fur off him.

When that was done, she picked him up in her arms, and tossed him over her shoulder to carry him like a baby. Armed with her flashlight again, she led the way to the far back corner of the yard. It took a moment for her to find the exact spot. She had to look back at the master bathroom window several times. But finally she pointed. "There."

She shone the light on the metal lid she and Mugs had discovered. Of course Goliath sat right beside the place she'd been looking for. Was it on purpose? Or a coincidence. She shot him a suspicious look but he just stared back at her.

Mack walked over, pulled some gloves from his back pocket, put them on and squatted beside the lid. Mugs snuffled the ground at his side. Mack gently scratched his neck as he studied the box. "Did you move anything?"

"Just the box and the bottle," she said. "The metal box was on top of the bottle," she said. "I think the lid caught the moonlight and was twinkling, which drew my attention. When I realized it was a box, I lifted off the lid. But the box was empty. So I unburied it, and then I found the arsenic." She shone the light around the area and cried out softly, "Oh, my goodness! These are azaleas."

He turned to face her. "I gather you're a gardener."

"I'd love to be a gardener. Up until now I've only directed gardeners."

He shot her a look of wonder.

She shrugged. "What can I say? My soon-to-be-ex was extremely wealthy. I wasn't allowed to touch anything, including cutting flowers from the garden for vases inside the house."

He shook his head. "A different world."

"A very different world."

He lifted the lid, checked it, found nothing. He lifted the metal box. Examined it and again didn't see anything. He shined his flashlight all around and took a closer look at where the box was. "I'll take the box and the lid with me. I doubt any fingerprints are left on it—other than yours." He shot her a look.

She gave him a half smile of apology. "I'm really not up to all this stuff. Not exactly sure what I'm supposed to do when I find things like poison in my garden."

He nodded. He collected the box and the lid and straightened. "In the morning I'll come back and take another look." He motioned to her. "Lead the way back to your house."

Scooping up Goliath again, who seemed to be completely content to be carried, she led Mugs and Mack back to the house. Thaddeus half-flew, half-walked beside them.

When they got to where the big empty grave was, Thaddeus perked up. "Murder in the garden. Murder in the garden."

Mack laughed. "Did you teach him that?"

She shot Mack a look. "You really think I want him to repeat that?" She shook her head. "He said that when we first found the arsenic."

Mack studied Thaddeus. "Interesting. I wish I knew where he learned that from."

"I don't know much about him," she admitted, then considered Mack's words. "You don't really think someone taught him that, do you?"

"I doubt it. Why would anybody? It's hardly something you want your bird to tell people. They would start to wonder if it was telling the truth. *Body's in the garden. Body's in the garden.*" He mocked the bird with his last words.

She stopped, looked at Mack. "Actually that's what he said when we found the finger. *Body in the garden.* Now he says, *Murder in the garden.*"

"Smart bird."

"Why?"

"Because the progression of events is exactly as he said. First, it was a body in the garden. But now it's proof of a murder in the garden."

"You're saying that man was murdered...? Of course he was!" She felt a little ill at the thought. She hadn't really considered it an actual murder. A real murder. "I know I've called it a murder and even asked about murderers watching in the crowds, but the reality of that event just now sunk in." She had assumed from her nice, easy, safe existence that he had died of natural causes and that someone may have buried him. No, that really didn't make any sense. She was such a fool. Why hadn't she jumped to this conclusion immediately?

Frowning, she walked back into the kitchen. "Sorry," she muttered. "It never occurred to me. I guess maybe I am still in shock over this whole mess."

"Don't worry about it. We don't have any details on it yet. But I highly doubt he met his death in any natural way."

"Well, he might have. What if he just keeled over and had a heart attack?"

"Then why bury him? Why not call an ambulance to haul away the body?"

She stared and shook her head. "I don't know. I can't come up with any scenario that makes sense."

"Exactly, which usually means murder."

"But neither can I come up with a reason why anyone would bury the body so shallow and so close to the house with the animals all around."

"Usually it's a case of expediency. Accidents happen, or an argument gets out of control. Somebody kills somebody and must get rid of the body real fast. Or maybe they couldn't move the body very far. If you think about it, the grave was right near the bottom of the steps."

"Which is a stupid place to put a body."

"Let's say a garden was already there."

She frowned at him. "Well, the cops did pull out begonia bulbs. Normally they come up in spring. It's an unseasonably warm April, but it's still too soon for begonias to show much more than shoots. And, depending on the climate, they could be left in the garden. Although they have to be insulated in cold climates or better yet they get pulled and replanted after the ground warms."

"So, the garden is likely freshly turned, with bulbs breaking up the dirt underneath, so that makes it easy digging." He cleared his throat. "And of course there's the new deck over top..."

She stared at him suspiciously. If anybody said anything

against Nan, Doreen wasn't having any of that. "I don't like what you're implying, that this could be Nan's work."

His eyebrows shot up. "Why is it I would be implying it's Nan?"

"It's her house. It's her garden. She's a small and aging woman who couldn't pull the body very far."

He nodded soberly. "And, in that case, you'd be quite right. However, it also fits other people."

"Like who?"

He gave her a grim smile and said, "There is somebody else. She's standing right in front of me. She could've come several days ago and done this. She's not very strong, but she's certainly determined."

Chapter 12

Day 2, Thursday

DOREEN WOKE UP the next morning to a sore back and the not-so-musical sound of the bed springs. Mugs had taken up residence at the base of the bed near her feet. Goliath had taken up the other half of the bed. And, yes, Thaddeus appeared to be snoozing on that old metal railing at her feet. And every time she rolled, the bed springs squeaked and groaned.

"Not sure how long I can live with this noisy tortuous bed. It's not conducive for actual sleeping. But getting a new bed is out of the question for a while."

She stared up at the old ceiling and thought—although it would take a lot of time, effort and money to fix the house—it was a gift in her time of need. It was a far cry from where she'd been, but it was hers alone. There was a certain sense of peace and security with that.

With a hard realization, she looked back over the years where she'd spent money indiscriminately because it was always available. It was... there. She'd bought jewelry, clothes and knickknacks for the house, and she'd never thought to put away any cash. When she'd married, she had believed in forever. And, sure, she'd wanted out of her marriage a lot of times. But it had never occurred to her she would be replaced. How was that even fair? Or legal?

She'd been married for fourteen years. He had built up his business during that time, with her help as his hostess for all his social events. She had no intention of ripping off her husband, but she'd wanted some compensation for all those years she had invested her time and effort into his businesses. But, according to her lawyer, Doreen wasn't entitled to anything of his, including the house, his cars and their bank accounts. The only reason she had the Honda was that it had been her personal car before they married, and she had convinced her husband to keep it, if only for having on standby so the maid could run to the grocery store.

So Doreen was lying here, not even able to afford a new bed, and he had the contents of the whole house to himself. Well, he and his new arm candy, Doreen's divorce lawyer.

Doreen did have one thing from her marriage. Her survivor's spirit.

Of course, she'd been the fool for signing the divorce agreement—only she hadn't realized it until afterward, when it was too late. Or was it? She'd revisit that thought later.

One crisis at a time, please.

She threw back the covers, hopped out of bed and walked over to the bathroom. Once again she stopped in the doorway and smiled. Not only did she have her spirit, she had this bathroom. And this was one room in the house that mattered. She danced inside and turned on the shower, delighted to feel lovely hot water almost instantly with copious pressure.

After a vigorous scrub and several shampoos of her hair, she almost felt clean again. Between the dead body and rummaging through the weeds, she was dang sure she'd brought in more than her fair share of the dirt. She'd like to blame the animals. But she'd been in and out constantly herself.

Back in her room she opened her biggest suitcase, looking for a pair of pants she could wear around the house. She had no idea what she was supposed to do with all her expensive clothes. Her designer shoes. The thought of ever wearing them here was highly unlikely. Could she sell them? She knew it was probably a foolish idea. But she'd do almost anything to get a new bed.

Once again the animals waited for her as she made her way, now dressed, to the kitchen for her next attempt at making a pot of coffee. While it dripped, she fed the animals. At least their food would last them for a while. Then she turned her attention to herself, because, after all, dinner had been almost nothing, and this morning's offerings weren't looking much better.

With a fresh cup of coffee, she opened the fridge, another archaic-looking thing she couldn't believe still worked. She'd seen them in old movies but never imagined they'd be in household use today. It was empty except for a box of baking soda on the shelf. She didn't understand why that was there. The half-freezer above was also empty.

So Nan had used up or given away or tossed all the perishable food before she left, and that was probably a darn good thing. But it also meant Doreen couldn't put off grocery shopping for much longer. She gathered all that was left of her traveling food on the table—some dried fruit and nuts. Obviously that was her breakfast.

As soon as she ate, she grabbed her purse, poured the last of the coffee in her travel mug and headed for her car.

As she opened the front door, she gasped to see an older woman, her hand in the air, ready to knock.

The two women stared at each other in surprise before Doreen pulled herself together. "Hi. How can I help you?"

The older woman smiled. "I'm Ella, your neighbor." She turned to point at the house on the far right of the cul-de-sac. "I just wanted to say hello and to welcome you to the neighborhood. It's been a bit rough for you, so I wanted to let you know we're not all nosy busybodies."

How lovely. Doreen beamed at the first true welcome she'd had. "Thank you so much. You're right. Yesterday was a bit rough, but today is a new day."

Ella laughed. "I see you're heading out." She motioned at the travel mug in Doreen's hands while backing down the front porch steps. "So feel free to stop by and say hi sometime. We'll have a cup of tea together."

She skipped down the last few steps, waved and strode home, leaving Doreen to stare after her neighbor, wondering if she should have changed her plans and visited with the woman. Still, the moment had passed. Shrugging, Doreen got into the car. Nan had said a grocery store was just down the road. If nothing else, Doreen could live on bread and peanut butter for a while. The peanut butter was a memory from her childhood. She'd never been allowed to have it while married. Like so many other things.

She hated to leave all the animals inside the house. Plus, she expected the cops back again, but she had to leave before they blocked her in once more.

She drove down Lakeshore Road, ignoring the many people out walking their animals and staring at her. Several blocks later she came to a grocery store. She pulled into a parking spot, got out, grabbed a cart and went in. Now she had to enter that food nightmare. If she could cook, it would be a different story, but chances were she'd burn everything. Although the coffee this morning had tasted like coffee, which was a huge improvement.

She still didn't understand the mystery of grocery stores. She understood fresh food was supposed to be on the outside perimeter, and the food she was to avoid was on the inside of the store. Why would they sell food that you're supposed to avoid? And why put it in the middle of the store, exactly where everyone was going? Her husband had been a fresh-food freak, and that was great as she'd obviously remembered some of his rantings. She wandered down the store aisles, figuring out just what she could buy in this small town with an even smaller budget.

She quickly collected fresh greens, spinach and kale. Maybe she could get her smoothies back into her routine again. She didn't know if Nan had a blender. Checking the secondhand store for one was a place to start. Maybe she could find a teapot too. She kept on going through the fresh veggies, picked up some fruit and wandered into the meat section. This was where that whole cooking mystery began. Nothing made sense to her. But she needed to eat protein too.

By the time she finished her shopping, she was confused, tired and frustrated. But she pushed her small cart to the cashier. The clerk, Cherry, according to her name tag, gave her a wide-eyed look, then pinched her mouth shut and rang up the groceries. Doreen assumed Cherry must have heard about the body.

Figures. Doreen pushed her prepaid card into the card reader and punched in her security code so she could access her remaining funds, heaving a breath of relief when the transaction was approved. She had saved most of her "allowance," then had bought a prepaid card before she made the five-hour drive here. She didn't want to carry any cash on her while traveling alone, and she felt the prepaid card was safer, plus it was insured for theft.

But she did need to check its balance. She was afraid to look and confirm how little was left, but, at the same time, she needed to know the exact figure. She sighed, deciding to check the balance once she got home.

Just as silently, she grabbed her bags, put them in the cart. She thanked the clerk with a polite smile before wheeling the cart to her car. It was such a relief to be back out in the fresh air and sunshine again and to not have to worry about anybody saying anything. As she thought about it though, nobody spoke to her at all—as if a town conspiracy of silence was the best way forward.

When she drove into her driveway and parked, two unmarked vehicles were already parked at the curb. She figured they were cops, working in the back garden. She opened her trunk, pulled out her bags and walked up to the front of the house. Instantly Mugs barked.

"Mugs, it's okay. It's just me."

Mugs barked again, not having any of it. Since strangers were in the street and the backyard, she couldn't blame him. She unlocked the front door, let the dog race outside to confirm nothing was there and carried the bags to the kitchen. Setting everything on the table, she walked back to close the front door. She shrugged out of her sweater, laid it over the back of the couch, dropped her purse on the kitchen table beside the groceries and opened the rear kitchen door so she could step out and see what was going on. Mugs barreled ahead of her.

Sure enough, four men were in the garden where she had found the arsenic last night. She recognized Mack, who raised a hand in greeting. Beside him, she acknowledged Chester and Arnold with a wave and returned to the house. She stood just inside the door and wondered aloud, "Should I put on coffee? Or tea? I'd offer cookies if I was at home." She frowned, walking over and staring out the kitchen window.

She'd been forced to learn a lot of etiquette rules when she'd been married, as they were different from the ones for unmarried women, according to both her uppity mother and her controlling husband. It had taken forever before any of it came naturally to Doreen, but eventually it had. With her separation, that had been one of the first things she'd stopped worrying about.

Until moving here for some reason.

She decided it was probably prudent to be ready with coffee if Mack did come in. At least she'd have a cup for him. So she put on a second pot. It was a small pot after all, and she'd drink it all herself if she had to. She quickly set the coffee to dripping, put her perishable foods in the fridge and then figured out where to put a few canned goods of her choosing when the cupboards were already full.

A knock came at the back door. Mack filled the open doorway.

She smiled brightly at him. "Good morning."

"Good morning. You weren't here when we arrived, so we went straight into the backyard."

She nodded. "I needed to get a few groceries." Her tone was formal. Even though she was trying to be friendly, it was still odd to see somebody like him doing what he was doing.

He nodded formally as well. "How was your night?"

"Outside of the fact that you were here late last night, and the bed I slept in must be from the early 1900s, and every time I rolled over, the bed squeaked and bounced and pinched my spine..." She gave him a wan smile. "I'll probably be heading for a nap at noon because it was so bad."

"Sorry about that." He winced. "It's really important to have a good bed."

"Well, I won't be getting one anytime soon, since I have no money for anything like that."

He shrugged. "At least you have a home."

She gave him a flat stare. "There is that."

"You know..." Mack began.

Her eyebrows raised, she waited for him to continue.

"I don't mean to meddle," he said.

"Go on. I can at least listen to what you have to say, then I'll decide. Right?"

"You could have an estate sale."

"But, but... isn't that when someone has died?"

"Call it a garage-and-house sale if it makes you feel better. Get rid of what Nan doesn't want and buy a new bed."

"*Hmm.*" She wasn't sure what that type of sale entailed but it was an idea. She just wasn't sure it was a good one. And would it actually bring in enough money to buy a bed?

"You could make it one day, or a weekend or even a one-week-long neighborhood event, where you could get the neighbors to join in. It would give the community a new way to view you after all this murder business."

Her eyebrows shot up at that. "I don't know," she said slowly. "I will consider it, but it's going to take time to sort through this stuff. I have to ask Nan about most pieces."

"There's no rush though, is there?" He smiled at her.

"Except you could use a new bed sooner than later."

With a nod of her head, she said, "Thank you, Mack."

Thaddeus walked in and straight up to Mack. "Thaddeus is here. Thaddeus is here."

She smiled down at the bird. "Good morning, Thaddeus."

He tilted his head sideways and rolled one eye up at her. He hopped onto the kitchen counter and walked back and forth. "Coffee. Coffee. Thaddeus smells coffee. Thaddeus smells coffee."

"I've never heard that word out of him before," she exclaimed. She brushed a finger down the bird's neck. "I really have no idea what I'm doing with him."

"Looks like you're doing just fine."

"Just goes to show you that appearances can be deceiving." She straightened and gave Mack a pleasant smile. "Did you need something?"

He nodded. "That's why I came in before we left."

"Left?" She glanced out at the garden and saw it was, indeed, empty. "Oh, good."

"You don't have to sound quite so happy."

"Given what I've been through these last twenty-four hours, I so do. I want this over with." She motioned at the coffee. "Would you like a cup? It's fresh."

His face lit up. "I'd love a cup, thank you." He pulled out a kitchen chair and sat down at the table. "Besides I have some questions for you."

Crap. She knew she shouldn't have been so friendly. "Questions about what?" she asked as she poured two cups full of coffee.

"Questions about the murdered man."

Chapter 13

DOREEN STARED AT Mack in shock. She sat down hard at the table and said, "I don't know who the murdered man is."

"His name is James Farley. He was an insurance salesman."

"Well, Mack, I'm not at all surprised an insurance salesman was murdered," she murmured. "According to my almost ex, they are all scammers."

"Well, you're *almost* not married anymore," he said shortly. "Make your own decisions."

She narrowed her gaze at him. "Somebody murdered him. Why do you think I would know anything about him?"

"That's why I'm here." He proceeded to ask her questions, like; did she recognize the man's name? Did she know the family? Had she any insurance? Could she have bought some from this Farley person? What about Nan? Did she have any insurance?

The answers were easy, as she didn't know anything about the dead man or insurance. Neither did she know anything about Nan's knowledge of the dead man's family or if Nan had purchased insurance from him. "You'll have to ask Nan." When he was done, she crossed her arms and slumped in the chair. "You've told me who he is. I still don't *know* him."

"Have you seen any correspondence from Nan around the house with that man's name on it?"

She shook her head. "I've been a little busy over the last twenty hours or so since I arrived here, so you need to direct those questions to Nan."

He nodded and stood. "That's where I'm heading next."

He walked to the front door, she trailed behind. "Don't upset Nan when you go there," she said. "The last thing I want is for her to have a heart attack over this."

"I won't do anything to upset her if I don't have to. However, we do have to find out who killed this man."

And then he was gone.

There was no friendly belly rub for Mugs or a stroke behind the ears for Goliath. Not even an acknowledgment of Thaddeus. Businesslike and simple. A few questions and he was gone. But it left a chill.

She locked the front door behind him. She knew how this looked. Yet, that didn't change the fact that neither she nor Nan had killed this man. Perhaps somebody had known the house was empty and thought nobody would notice, so they had deliberately placed the body here to implicate Nan or Doreen. Or as a temporary measure until they could move it again but... *ewww*. Not to mention that decking over the body looked pretty permanent.

Either way it sucked. Nan was a wonderful person, and she didn't need this. And that meant somebody had to find the right answers. Not just the answers that would fit and make a case for the police. Because, if that case closed around Nan, then the conclusion was wrong. Somebody would have to set them straight. That somebody would have to be Doreen.

Nan had done a lot for Doreen over these last few rough months, and that was without taking into account all the times she'd been there for Doreen over the years. The least she could do was return the favor. She'd find out who killed that man. She rolled up her imaginary sleeves and stormed into the kitchen.

She snagged a cup of coffee and stepped onto the back veranda, considering what to do to clear Nan's name. Her gaze studied the proximity of her house and yard to the neighbors' yards, wondering if she should talk to the neighbors. Maybe they had seen something between the time Nan moved to Rosemoor and when Doreen arrived yesterday.

But the state of the backyard distracted the gardener in her. Nan's back garden was fully fenced although those fences were badly in need of TLC, like the gardens themselves. Doreen had lots of TLC to give, but she wasn't so sure about the fence repairs. Still, if a hammer and nail would do the job, she could work with that. Besides the physical work would help rid her of some of the building stress.

But solving the dead man's mystery came before gardening. Her laptop was still packed away upstairs. She went inside, retrieved it, set it up on the kitchen table and searched for James Farley. Thank heavens the house had internet. Thanks Nan.

He'd lived and worked in Kelowna, in British Columbia, Canada. But he wasn't from the Mission area of British Columbia. Not that that made him an outsider. Mission was just one of many communities that had pulled together and suddenly became a town as it grew. No way to keep the growing parts and pieces separate anymore, so they'd been incorporated into the city of Kelowna.

Farley was employed by an insurance company downtown. Maybe it was time to take Mugs for a walk along the boardwalk and check out where this guy had worked.

Had the insurance company called him in as a missing person? Or had he been one of those employees who traveled most of the time and only checked in occasionally, and the company didn't know when he was coming back? Didn't they realize he was missing?

Unable to leave it alone, she quickly toasted herself a piece of bread to-go, then loaded Mugs into the car. She locked Thaddeus and Goliath in the house. With both cat and bird staring out the living room window at them, she got in the car and drove downtown.

A lot of the downtown parking you had to pay for, unless it was on a weekend. Today was Thursday. So she parked for free down by the beach, hooked Mugs on his leash and proceeded to walk toward the business district. Several blocks later and around a corner, she found the small insurance company. She glanced up at the second floor to see the company name written on the window. Lifelong Insurance, Inc.

"Yeah, it didn't do him so well, did it?" she asked Mugs. "His lifelong ended up being a pretty darn life*short*."

As the words fell off her lips, the door opened and out stepped a balding redheaded mailman with more freckles than she'd ever seen. A big bag over his shoulder, mail in his hand, he smiled at her and moved out of her way. "Sorry," he said cheerfully and, with a jaunty step, headed down the sidewalk.

She pulled open the door, and with Mugs at her heels, they climbed the stairs to the small office. Lifelong Insurance was on the right at the top of the stairs. No lights appeared to be on inside. She turned the handle and pushed, but the door was locked. No Closed sign was on the door though. She knocked several times, but there was no answer. Did James Farley own Lifelong Insurance? Was he the only employee?

With those thoughts running through her mind, she slowly made her way back downstairs, stopping at the first landing. And came face-to-face with Mack, who was on his way up.

She smiled. "Great minds think alike," she said gaily.

"What are you doing here?" His tone was much less than happy.

She stuck out her chin. "I wanted to see if I could find some answers myself. I don't want you thinking that Nan had anything to do with James's murder. And I know I didn't do it, so, therefore, somebody else did."

"Oh, no you don't. I don't want you nosing around, asking any questions," Mack stated in an unequivocal term. "You leave that to the police."

She'd perfected a flat stare a long time ago. But it seemed to have no effect on him. She gave up and smiled sweetly instead. Nan had always said honey worked better than vinegar. "Obviously I don't want to step on any of your toes. I just wanted to know where Farley worked." She glanced over at the door above and behind her. "It's his own business, is it not?"

Mack nodded. "Yes, he's the owner and operator of Lifelong Insurance."

"Right." She was pleased to find that out on her own.

She tossed him a bright smile. "Have fun."

He probably had the right to go inside the office, even if locked and vacant. She watched as he carried on up the stairs, unlocked the door and entered Farley's office. Unable to help herself, she tiptoed back upstairs and stood in the open doorway. And cried out.

Mack stood in the middle of the destroyed office and glared at her. "Don't come in here."

Immediately she shook her head. "I won't. I promise I won't. But look what they did."

"They?" he asked, suspicion coloring in his tone.

She glared at him. "What? I didn't do it."

"Didn't you? Funny how I just came in as you're leaving."

She pointed at the doorknob. "It was locked, remember?"

This time his smile was less than pleasant. "Easy to lock it if you had already unlocked it to get in."

She glared at him. "I had nothing to do with this."

"Good. Keep it that way." He made a motion with his hand to shoo her out of the doorway. "I've a forensic team coming in here. Don't touch anything, and stay out of the way."

She backed away but went to touch the door.

"What did I just say?"

She pulled her hand against her chest. "I tried to open it earlier. So my prints will be on the doorknob. And I knocked, so my knuckle prints are on the glass," she added in a rush.

He shook his head and glared. "Great. Now you mucked it up with your prints too."

She winced. "I'm sorry. It just never occurred to me that

trying to talk to someone at an insurance company would cause trouble."

"That's because you didn't think. Everything regarding James Farley is now a police issue. Please go home. Let the police handle it before your prints are everywhere and cannot be ignored."

She sniffed, turned on her heels and slowly walked back down the stairs. Trouble was, Mugs didn't want to go. He stared at the top of the stairs, and short of dragging him all the way down, he wasn't interested in leaving the office. Groaning, she stepped up a couple risers and said, "Mugs, what's wrong with you?"

"What's going on?" Mack asked from the doorway.

"I don't know. I just asked him that," she said in frustration, glaring at Mack. "He doesn't want to leave."

Mack walked over, and in a mood completely opposite to the cold, irate cop from seconds earlier, he bent and scratched Mugs behind the ear. Mugs wagged his tail, sniffing all over Mack's shoes. While Mack was busy scratching the dog, she hadn't been paying attention, so when Mugs tugged on his leash, it fell from her fingers and he darted right between Mack's legs. Right inside the insurance office.

"Oh, no," she cried out. "We have to get him." She darted around Mack, dashing into the office.

Mack was on her heels.

Inside the office, she stopped and stared. There was no sign of the dog. She spun on her heels and cried out, "Where is he?" Turning back to the trashed floor, she called out, "Mugs! Mugs, come on, boy. Where are you?"

No answer came.

Mack searched the other rooms. She followed. There was a single small office, a bigger office and a private one that looked like another small office in the back. By the time they made their way to the bathroom and the storeroom, she found the office was larger than she'd initially thought, deeming it just one of those tiny seedy-looking single rooms with a bathroom. But it was set up to hold five to six staff offices.

Only there was still no sign of Mugs. "Where could he be?"

Behind her was a muffled bark. She spun around to see Mugs underneath a large boardroom table, but with all the chairs pulled up around it, she couldn't see him there. She pulled out a couple chairs to find Mugs lying on his belly, panting. A mess of papers was on the floor in front of him. She grabbed his leash and tugged, but he wouldn't move. He stretched his neck forward and barked at the papers.

"No, Mugs, you can't have those papers. I know you love to rip apart paper, but you can't have these papers."

Instead of listening to her, he lunged for a big stack, growled and backed up under the table. Mack grabbed the leash and brought Mugs out from underneath. By then Mugs had a mouthful of paperwork.

She gently opened his jaw, telling him, "Who's a good boy, Mugs? I promise I'll find you a newspaper at home. You can rip that up."

He gave her one of those hangdog looks, as if to say, "Sure you will."

"Wait." Mack dropped to his knees beside the dog. Using a pressure point in the back of the dog's jaw, Mack forced Mugs's mouth open. The stack of papers dropped. Mack snatched them up but not before she saw the top page.

"That's got Nan's name on it."

"Yes, it does." He patted Mugs. "Thanks, Mugs. This is a great lead."

Chapter 14

DOREEN MOVED CLOSER to read more, but Mack removed the papers from her sight.

He glared at her. "Official police business, remember?"

She shoved her chin out front and forward. "Official family business, remember?"

He chuckled. "You've got a point." He laid the papers on the table, and together they searched through them for Nan's name.

Doreen tapped three different sheets. "These relate to Nan."

Mack pushed the first one off to the side. "This is her personal history, medical, etc. You always get that done when you make an insurance claim or when buying insurance coverage. This one appears to be his notes about Nan's family history. Your name is on it too." He tapped the center of the page.

She peered closer, and there was her name. She tapped the mention with her fingernail.

He set those two sheets beside each other, then pulled out the third one and studied it. "And this is a copy of a life insurance policy on Nan... until she reaches age 95."

Doreen focused on it and snatched it from his fingers. "Why would she do that?" She studied the document. "This is for half a million dollars!"

"Yes, but this was taken out a long time ago. And it's not from Lifelong Insurance. So he found an insurance company that had a policy for Nan. And it lists you as the sole beneficiary."

She stared at him. "Does this mean it's still in effect?"

He turned his gaze from the paper to her. "It appears to be. You didn't know anything about it?" he asked curiously.

She shook her head. "No. I had no idea." She stared at the paper in wonder. "She had no money. This must be important to her."

"Do you know for sure she had no money?" Mack asked delicately. "Because, many times, older people just can't spend their money or don't feel like they should spend it or aren't interested in spending money. They like the comfort of all the old things they have around them."

She pulled out a chair and sat down hard. "I honestly don't know. And I feel very invasive having that conversation with her. She used to travel a lot when she was younger. Then she stopped. I figured it was because the money ran out. Plus, look at her run-down house and gardens. If she had money, wouldn't she have renovated her house and the yards?" Doreen shook her head. "I've never asked Nan for any money or for anything else for that matter. I thought she was broke. Why buy a life insurance policy?" she muttered under her breath. "I always thought they were just scams."

"Lots of people believe the whole life policies are, and yet, lots of other people believe the term life policies are a good investment. Plus these term policies are the cheapest, so it may not be the hardship on Nan that you think. Then there are equity insurances and too many other combinations to list."

"How can it be a good investment if it only pays off after you die?"

"So true." He laughed. "But it also goes to show you that Nan loves you."

What a lovely thought. She stared at the sheet of paper and thought about how much her husband didn't love her and then thought about how Nan was in the background doing something like this for Doreen. And never telling her. "I'd never have known about this if I hadn't come here."

"Maybe it's not a good thing for you to know." He shuffled the rest of the papers. "If she runs out of money and can't maintain this, then you might have the expectation of money when she dies, but it won't be there."

"If she needs the money, I'd be happy for her to cancel it. She doesn't get any money back, does she?"

"Not on a strictly term policy. Not any way of knowing that without reading the policy. Some of them are structured differently."

"My soon-to-be-ex-husband is paying for one on me. I didn't know about it until he flung that information at me during a fight in our last year. It still makes me cringe, even after the first few months of our separation. Just the thought that maybe he'd knock me off somewhere. But, since I wasn't the one paying the premiums, I didn't have a copy. So I have no idea what the details are."

He shook his head. "You have every right to go to the insurance company and say you fear for your life, and you want the policy canceled. I don't know what they'd say, but, if you are seriously worried, then you should do something about it."

"And that'll likely involve a lawyer or cops. And lawyers are not people I trust." She forgot who she was talking to.

He straightened and focused on her again. "Lawyers get a bum rap. But they are not all bad."

Her gaze went flat, and she stared at him. "My lawyer completely screwed me over on the separation and upcoming divorce and is now my husband's current fiancée. According to her, I wasn't entitled to anything. And I, fool that I am, believed her."

He stared at her. "Oh, shit."

"Oh, shit, indeed." She turned her focus to the papers atop the table. "Are you taking these? What about the stuff on the floor?"

"I need to spend a few hours going over some of these papers. It's hard to know exactly what's been going on here, but with the vandalism, I have to consider somebody was looking for something."

"How can you tell if they found it?"

He shook his head. "With a mess like this? The only person who knew for sure is dead. So likely we'll never know."

For her that wasn't good enough. She needed answers, not more questions. "It doesn't make any sense that he'd have copies of Nan's old insurance papers. If he was trying to sell her insurance, he would know she wouldn't need another policy."

"Perhaps he was hoping to get her to transfer it or to create a new policy or to sell her something else."

"That's possible. I don't know what Nan is like with business. She always kept that to herself. In fact, I can't ever remember her talking about money."

"Is that why you believe she doesn't have any?"

"Yes, plus everything in the house is in disrepair and seriously in need of updating. Lots of canned food but no fresh food or new furniture and the bed..." She closed her eyes, a shudder rippling down her spine at the reminder of the night. "That bed is something else."

"Maybe she has many happy memories of all that furniture. The house is worth a fair bit. It's in a nice little area. The whole of the Mission has skyrocketed in real estate prices. She could've sold her home at any point in time if she needed to. Instead, she gave it to you. That, in itself, means she obviously felt she had enough for her own needs without selling it."

She stared out the window. The Okanagan area—including a lake, a valley and a river—was well known for its resort-like location and balmy weather almost every day of the year. And, true to form, a blue sky and sunshine were out there today.

The talk of her grandmother made her homesick to see her again. She'd stop off on her way home for a visit. Maybe she'd bring up this insurance policy.

"Was it that tough?" Mack asked, pulling her back to the conversation.

"Between my husband and my lawyer, I get nothing." She said it in a brisk tone, hating to let him know just where she was at financially. But there was no point in putting on airs that she was anything but completely destitute. "My lawyer explained how I had signed all my rights away."

"How long were you married?"

She looked at him. "Fourteen years. I helped him build his business, clear off his debts, yet somehow ended up with nothing."

"How long have you been separated? Have you actually

divorced yet?"

She frowned. "Separated for months, almost six now. He told me right before the holidays. And, no, we can't file the divorce papers until one continuous year of separation later, but I've already signed everything. I just didn't realize I had other options when I was signing. *Obviously*. I let my lawyer handle it. But, of course, I didn't know my lawyer was on my husband's payroll and had screwed me over." Her laugh was bitter. "And apparently screwing him at the same time." She shook her head. "I didn't even think things like that could happen." She turned and strode from the room. "Believe me. Some lessons you just can't walk away from."

"But there might be something you can do about it."

She froze, turned and looked at him. "And just what would that be?"

"You could see another lawyer. Yours obviously did not have her client's best interests in mind."

"She only had her own interests in mind. And a lawyer means more money. Remember that part about being cleaned out and not having anything?"

"Another reason to have the garage sale."

Doreen shook her head. "I'm buying a bed first. Everything else will have to wait." She picked up Mugs's leash. "Come on, Mugs. We've had enough of a bad trip down memory lane for today. Let's stop at Nan's and see if we can find a little sunshine in her life today."

"And consider letting me and my brother take a look into that separation agreement before the divorce goes through," he said. "My brother is a practicing lawyer, and he's a good, fair man."

She looked over her shoulder at him. "I don't have any money, so your offer, although generous, still requires some form of payment. I don't have anything to give. Maybe later." She nodded at the forms on the table. "I'll ask Nan about James and the insurance policy. Maybe she can shed some light on this." She headed down the stairs.

When she got to the front door, Mack called out to her. "You didn't even ask how much he'd charge."

She looked up the stairs to where he stood. "Doesn't matter. My last one got every drop of money out of me. So it doesn't matter how much he charges. Even your idea of a garage sale, if I pull that off, is only a one-time thing. I need money coming in monthly. If I don't find a job soon, I'll be heading to the food bank." She turned and walked out.

As the door slammed behind her, she smiled. There was something freeing about stating the truth about her current situation.

Instead of depressing her, the action made her feel better. If there was one sentiment Nan had impressed on Doreen repeatedly throughout the years it was, *When you're down, look up. That's the only place left to go.*

She glanced up at the bright blue sky and the sunshine beaming across the small town. "You know? I'll be totally happy to go up for a change. Being down really sucks."

She walked to her car, loaded Mugs into the back seat and went around to the driver's side. She closed the door and buckled up her seat belt to find Mack standing at the front of the car. She rolled down the window and called out, "Now what? Did you find something?"

"You mean, besides a very frustrating, irritating woman?" he asked. "No."

She glared at him. "Then what do you want?"

"To offer you a part-time job," he said in exasperation. "But why I want the added frustration, I have no idea."

She froze. Then stared up at him in delight. "What kind of a job? And, yes, please."

He shook his head, stared up at the sky for a long moment, then raised both hands in the air and said, "Whatever." He walked around to the driver's side, leaning in the window. "You might not like it."

"It doesn't matter if I like it or not," she admitted quietly. "I need it." She waited for him to say more.

"Do you like gardening?"

She nodded. "I love gardening."

"My mother's house is only a couple blocks away from you, and she can't get out into the garden anymore. I told her that I'd come and look after it, but it's more than I have the time for. I wouldn't be able to pay you a whole lot... but maybe an hourly wage that we could agree on would make us both happy."

She grinned. "Absolutely. Give me the address, and I'll look at it on my way home."

He gave her the address, watching as she wrote it down. "Don't talk to my mom yet though."

She merely shook her head. "Okay, I won't. I just want to see what kind of work I'm looking at."

"Good idea. And, after you do, give me a shout. We'll discuss price." He pulled out another card, this one with his home number on it and handed it to her. "In the meantime, stay the hell out of my case." He glared down at her as if for good measure, then abruptly walked back into the Lifelong Insurance building.

She turned on the engine, and in a much happier mood, she said to Mugs, "See? Like Nan said, there's only one place to go, and that's up."

Chapter 15

DOREEN DECIDED TO visit Nan tomorrow and to check out Mack's mother's garden today. When she finally located the address, it was within walking distance from Nan's house. Just a couple blocks down, like Mack had said. In that sense, it would be perfect. She wouldn't have to use the car to get to work, so the cost of gas wasn't an issue.

She drove past the house slowly, looking at the front yard. It had a lovely front garden with a bed full of perennial bushes with a few annuals dotted around. A nice combination of colors. And it was in decent shape. The grass needed to be mowed, and that could present a problem as she didn't have her own lawn mower.

Neither did she have the money to buy one. As for the weeds, well, some had definitely taken advantage and needed to be pulled. Many of the bushes were overgrown and needed to be trimmed too. She wanted to get out and wander around to the backyard, but she didn't want to disturb his mother. Looking at the yard, she thought she saw an alleyway behind the house.

She drove around to the back of the house, parked and got out, then looked over the short fence at the backyard.

She couldn't remember if he had said both gardens or just the front. But the back garden was in worse shape. His mother probably tried to do what she could out in the front to keep up appearances. But the backyard required more than she had to give. Like so many people who owned homes, the work got ahead of them, and catching up was brutal.

Considering how much work Doreen had to do on Nan's garden, she understood. In Doreen's case, fences needed mending, the patio was overgrown with weeds, and likely the concrete blocks making up the patio weren't worth keeping either. Not to mention the beds had to be redefined. She'd need a full-time paycheck just to get it back into shape.

But some of it had to be done, even without money, applying a lot of physical labor.

It would take a day or two to fix up the front yard of Mack's mom's house, but the back property would need a full week, and she could use some added muscle. Several shrubs needed heavy pruning. And some fallen garden logs needed to be replaced. Still, it was all doable.

A dog barked at her side. She spun in surprise to see an older gentleman staring at her, his nose in the air, a disapproving look on his face.

She glanced from him to the fence she'd been peering over and flushed. "I was just looking at her garden," she rushed to say.

His gaze narrowed.

Flustered, she returned to the driver's side of her car and quickly backed out the alleyway. As she came to the end of it, she realized she could have just driven forward past the older man.

"Crap," she muttered, still flustered. But at least she

hadn't backed into anyone's fences on her way.

Smack.

She froze, then closed her eyes and dropped her forehead on her steering wheel. Finally she raised her head and looked behind her. And grinned. She'd hit a harmless street sign delineating the road and alleyway. She hopped out and walked around the car to see the damage but could only find a scrape on her bumper. And it was hard to see because the bumper had been well decorated in the same manner long before she'd bought it.

Happier, she got back in her car and drove home. She pulled into the driveway, parked and let Mugs out. He barked immediately. She looked around but didn't see anything. "Mugs, what's the matter?"

He kept barking, then ran around to the rear of the house. She followed at a slower pace. In the back, she couldn't see anything wrong, but she could hear Goliath inside the house, howling. Obviously he wanted out too. She made her way up the back steps to the kitchen door and opened it. Instantly Goliath shot out, screaming across the backyard property. Now the two of them were out there. She propped the kitchen door wide open to let some fresh air in, and, sure enough, Thaddeus flew out the door to land on the railing.

"Thaddeus is here. Thaddeus is here."

"Of course you're here. I can see you," she said in exasperation.

The bird cocked his head at her, and the big guy blinked. She tilted her head to the side and patted her shoulder. Instantly he hopped up. She threw her purse and keys down on the outside table and marched to the rear of the property.

For whatever reason, both the dog and cat were howling at something in the back corner. As she made her way to them, she assessed the manpower needed to restore the back garden to its former glory. And groaned. It would take a lot of work. A lawn mower would help a lot, but again she didn't have one.

The fence wasn't as bad as she had thought, if she looked past the multiple types of fencing that dotted the yard. The support posts were solid. A hammer and nails would put the sagging boards back in place. A can of paint would give it a face-lift. Part of the fence was an open-picket style, with just crossrails instead of solid wood. Several of which had fallen off. Still, she could see the neighbor's house on the one side and out the back alley.

Alley? That was the first time she realized an alleyway was behind the house. In that case, it would've been easy for somebody else to access that side of Nan's backyard to bury the body.

Nan's property backed onto Crown land. One of the advantages was owning a home where you could open a gate and walk the dog for miles out on public property. Or a disadvantage if Mugs ran off.

"Mugs! Mugs!" she called out. As she reached the back fence, she found the gate was open. "Oh, dammit, Mugs. Come on, Mugs."

She pushed the gate wider and stepped out. Instead of grassy fields, she found a good-size creek ran along here. She looked back at Nan's house and the fence. "Why would you fence off the river? This is too pretty to hide."

What she'd thought had been an alleyway was a bit of a walking path alongside the back of all the fences, which buffered the creek edge to the fence line. Plus a little

ARSENIC IN THE AZALEAS

footbridge was built over the water. "Oh my, this is beautiful."

"Beautiful. Beautiful," Thaddeus crooned in her ear.

It would be even nicer to get rid of the broken-down
fence to open up the view of the creek to Nan's house. It
would also allow her to see the wildlife, as plenty of small
critters of all kinds would gather at the water. That would be
something she'd love to watch.

Feeling so much happier at the sight of the creek, she
studied Nan's house from here. A lot of bushes and trees
blocked the view. But, with a good heavy pruning, she could
turn this backyard into something spectacular.

She hopped up onto the little bridge and called out,
"Mugs! Mugs?"

On her shoulder, Thaddeus opened his mouth and
cried, "Thaddeus is here. Thaddeus is here."

"I know you're here, silly," she said. "But where's
Mugs?"

Suddenly Thaddeus made a great big screech and flew
off her shoulder, down to the far side of the bank.

She ran after him. "Wait, Thaddeus. What did you find?
Mugs? Where are you?" She ran over the little bridge. As she
put her foot on the last board, it gave way beneath her. And
down she went.

She cried out as one of her feet hit the water, her other
knee buckled and her butt hit the little bridge. Taking a deep
breath, she tried to assess what just happened. One foot was
caught in the framework of the little bridge. She was forced
to twist around, using her hands to clamber back up, afraid
to put any weight on her ankle or the bridge.

She glanced down at her designer jeans and sandals and
cried out, "And these are ruined now too?" She shook her

head but was much less concerned over her outfit than her missing dog. "Mugs, where are you?" She whistled for him.

Still there was no answer from Mugs. Clumsily she stood on her feet and tried to shake the water off her sandal. But it and her jeans were drenched to her knee and covered with mud. Hesitantly she placed her weight on her sore ankle, grateful it could at least sustain her weight. Her leg was scraped by the broken slats, but her ankle didn't appear to be sprained.

Now that she was on the other side of the creek, she could see a small pathway, overgrown by brush. She managed to get up onto the path and followed it after Thaddeus. "Come on, you guys. Where are you? Don't make me search for you."

Bedraggled and limping as she was, she hoped to heck she didn't meet anybody. It was bad enough being Nan's crazy granddaughter in the eyes of a few. But, if anybody saw her now, they'd have no doubt she was nuts.

In the distance, she heard a bark. "Mugs?" She ran, although lopsided. But at least she was moving. She got a few steps down the path when she heard Mugs's barking go up a notch. She picked up her speed, broke through a pile of brush and came to a sudden stop, staring at her crazy trio. Mugs was still barking like crazy. Goliath sat on a tree stump staring up a tree, his tail making short hard twitches. Thaddeus wandered back and forth like a bloody little soldier. Marching ten steps, turning, and marching back again saying, "Thaddeus is here. Thaddeus is here."

She shook her head. "What is wrong with you guys? Why did you take off?"

Only Mugs wasn't listening. He insisted on barking as he looked up a tree. She groaned and walked closer. She grabbed for his leash. As she looked up, eyes looked down at her.

She shrieked and stepped back. That set Mugs off again. She hesitantly took another step forward and peered up into the foliage. "Hello?"

"Hello" came the boy's small voice.

"Are you okay?" she asked. "Mugs won't hurt you."

"He's barking."

"Yes, he does that a lot all of a sudden." She sighed. "I can't seem to find a way to stop him." She peered through the foliage to see a young child sitting on a branch way too high up for her to even reach. "How did you get up there?"

"I climbed."

"You climbed?" She shook her head. "Do you need help getting down?"

The child looked down at her and said, "You're the crazy lady, aren't you?"

"I'm not the crazy lady," she protested with a winning smile. At least she hoped it was. "I'm Doreen. I'm just a normal person."

The child giggled. And pointed at her leg. "But you're wet and covered in mud."

"Yes, but that doesn't make me a crazy lady," she protested. "I fell through the slats on the little bridge back there when I was chasing after my animals. Now that I've got my dog and Goliath, not to mention Thaddeus..."

At that moment Thaddeus flew up and landed on her shoulder again. He stared up into the tree. "Thaddeus is here. Thaddeus is here."

"I know you're here. Stop talking, for crying out loud." She groaned. "Okay, maybe I look a little crazy. But I'm not, honest." Then she shrugged. Why was she explaining herself to a child?

"Why do you call him that?"

"It's his name. What's yours?" she asked, wondering if he could get down on his own.

The child swept to the bottom branch and scampered down the trunk like a monkey. He stopped and looked up at her. "I'm Travis. And you look crazy to me." And then, without another word, he ran full steam in the opposite direction.

Leaving her standing with her mouth open.

Chapter 16

S HE HEADED FOR the kitchen, determined to face this room of such mystery. She had deliberately picked up simple foods at the grocery store this morning. Everybody can make a jam and peanut butter sandwich. Trouble was, she wasn't interested in having one now. She'd bought sliced ham for sandwiches, and also she could fix cucumber sandwiches with mayonnaise too. Or a ham-and-cucumber combo sandwich. Each, she knew, she could manage.

Just to find some success in her day had her keeping her lunch to a simple sandwich. She pulled out two slices of bread and started building. It was fun. She could see that maybe this cooking thing wouldn't be too bad after all.

With a sense of pride, she cut her sandwich into four triangles, placed it on a plate, put on the teakettle to make a cup of tea and sat down at the table to enjoy what she had made. She took the first bite when Thaddeus landed on the table beside her.

He cocked his head and said, "Thaddeus is here."

"Thaddeus is here," she joined him. "I wish you would stop saying that all the time. Please."

He opened his beak and to shut him up she reached for

a piece of cucumber still on the cutting board and held it up to him. He looked at it, snagged it in his beak and laid it down on the table where he broke it off into little pieces and pecked away at the center, then lifted the food with his foot, and ate it.

But at least he ate it. So that was good. Or maybe it was not good. Were birds supposed to eat cucumbers? She had no idea. She grabbed her laptop and pulled it toward her and quickly checked. *Yes, cucumbers are allowed. Good.*

She glanced around to see Goliath, sitting on the chair beside her, studying the ham left on the cutting board.

"Oh, no you don't. That is for me, for another sandwich. And I might just need a second one." She was starving.

She hadn't had very much to eat since she'd arrived in town. And she really wanted a full meal. The thought of making it herself was daunting. Most of her earlier attempts while at the apartment had ended up in the garbage. And she couldn't afford to waste food then or now. When she counted that cost of ruined food against what the restaurants charged, she'd chosen the restaurant more times than not over the last six months.

But she didn't know very many restaurants here in Mission. And, if she could just learn to cook for herself, it'd be that much cheaper. She picked up the second quarter of her sandwich and studied it with a smile. "This was easy. So surely I can find something else just as easy to fix too."

She set up a search on her tablet for easy meals for new cooks. And she munched away on her sandwich and studied the recipes.

"They don't look that hard." She chose one with a chicken breast and vegetables. When she finished her sandwich, she rose, walked to the fridge and studied the package of chicken. It was too much for one meal, so she opened it, put one piece on a plate, added the spices the recipe called for, putting it in a quart-size zip-bag, placed it back in the fridge, and froze the rest. She'd done her first step to getting dinner ready. Good. Next step was to clean up her lunchtime mess. Something else she never had to do while married.

She turned to see Goliath running off, a big piece of ham hanging out his mouth. And Mugs in chase.

"Mugs! Come back."

But the dog not only had a chance to chase the cat but ham was his prize. No way would she be able to call him back from that. She took advantage of both of them being gone to quickly pack up the rest of the ham and put it back in the fridge. As she turned around, she caught Thaddeus working away on a large bit of cheese. She lifted the package, dumped the little bits and pieces on the table for him and wrapped up the rest.

"I can see that keeping food away from you guys will be as much of a challenge as not burning it," she scolded. "You might be cute and fluffy, but you can sure destroy a block of cheese fast."

As she turned around after closing the fridge, Goliath sat there, staring at her with a grin lighting his eyes.

"Oh, no you don't. You had your share, and that's all you're getting."

But the cat didn't move.

And she wondered out loud, "Unless Mugs got the ham away from you. Did he?"

Feeling stupid but unable to help herself, she opened the ham and handed down a little piece. The cat grabbed it delicately and swallowed it.

She stared at him. "Did you even chew that?"

Silence. Not even a purr.

She gave him another tiny piece and wrapped up the ham, put it in the fridge and slammed the door shut. She glared at him. "That's it. I have to eat too."

Resolutely she walked to the table and finished packing up the rest of the food. Thaddeus had started working on the lettuce. She ripped off a couple pieces, laid it on the table, packed it up in its bag and collected the bread too. She didn't think he'd gotten to the mayonnaise, but who knew?

She returned with a wet cloth to the table, wiped it down, brushing the crumbs onto her plate. She surveyed the clean area with a smile. "There. That wasn't so hard."

She dumped the contents of the plate into the garbage, then went back to the sink, where she washed her plate. She could almost get used to this. It was kind of boring and tedious work, but it was doable.

And speaking of *doable* and *work*, she needed to phone Mack.

She pulled out his card, dialed his home number and waited until he answered. "I drove past your mom's house today. Are you interested in having the front yard and backyard done? Or just one of them?"

"How bad are they?"

"The front isn't too bad. It'll take a day at the most, I'd think. And it'll take a couple hours a week to maintain it," she said. "The backyard, however, that's a much bigger job. Doesn't look like it's been mowed in quite a while. The front needs to be mowed too. But the back is much worse. The gardens are overgrown and need pruning, etc."

"I honestly haven't been in the backyard in quite a while," he said. "I'll do the mowing. It's my mower anyway.

I usually bring it over. I'll take a look this weekend."

"So I'd estimate the front would take six hours initially. And that would mean trimming the bushes, pulling out the deadwood, pruning back the perennials that are more like weeds and giving it a general clean-over. The weeds should be pulled on a regular basis. You already know that. If you want, we could arrange for me to spend a couple hours every week just to keep on top of it. The backyard, well, I'd have to go in and take a closer look before I can give you a better idea on the time needed."

"When can you start work on the front?"

"This weekend?" It's not like she had anything else to do. Except find out who murdered a man in Nan's garden.

"Okay, we can do that. I'll come over with the mower at the same time."

They decided to meet on Saturday morning at nine. Just before she rang off, she said, "Did you know that the backyard of this property ends at a creek?"

"I took a quick glance over there when I was walking the property," he said. "But it's sealed off."

"No, there is a gate in the fence," she said. "It was a little hard to open, as it's broken, yet I slipped out earlier and found a footbridge that crossed the creek."

"So your backyard is fairly accessible. Is that what you're saying? I'm tied up at the moment, but I'll come by this afternoon to take a quick look. I thought the fence was sealed, so somebody would have to climb over it, in which case the whole thing would likely fall down and leave an obvious trail."

With the call done, she went back upstairs to Nan's— now her—room. She wanted to unpack, but had no idea where to put away Nan's things, currently taking up the closet.

She walked into the spare bedroom and opened its closet. It was stuffed. No surprise there. She grabbed what looked like old winter coats. None of these were her style, and surely Nan didn't need all these. Honestly the coats looked like clothing from the 1940s. She studied the labels, and a couple of them were real fur.

She frowned. Why did Nan have fur coats? Especially at this stage of her life? They looked like they were well cared for. Or had critters gotten into them? Fur was notoriously difficult to look after.

She continued studying the labels, realizing the coats were of seriously good quality. She pulled out her phone to call Nan.

"Nan, you have fur coats in your spare bedroom closet. What do you want me to do with them?" She turned to look at the dozen hanging coats. "Do you have someone I could give them too?"

"Oh, those old things? Why don't you take them to the consignment store and see if you get anything for them."

"Consignment store?" She wasn't sure people did that with clothing. She'd heard of it being done with art and furniture, not so much for clothing.

"Yes. If they accept them to sell, they'll give you a percentage of the money."

"You mean, give *you* a percentage of the money," Doreen corrected. "This is all your stuff here. If you didn't want any of it, why didn't you sell it or give away some of the clothes?"

"Because I knew you needed the money, dear. You go ahead and get what you can for the stuff. In fact," Nan said, "When you're ready to move out some of the clutter, feel free. I was going to, then thought you might enjoy the process. Besides you might be able to get a few dollars from selling some of it. I have everything I want with me right here."

Doreen straightened. She looked around at the roomful of stuff—exactly the same as what the rest of the house looked like—and her eyebrows shot up. "Nan, are you sure?"

Even if Nan said she was sure now that didn't mean she wouldn't change her mind down the road. Better to take it slow and make sure Nan really was ready to let go of her memories. As she opened her mouth to say so, Nan laughed. "I'm serious. Except for you, Mugs, Goliath, and Thaddeus, everything I cherish is in my apartment with me every day."

At that, Doreen's eyes clouded with tears. "I don't know what your finances are like, and I don't want to pry, but neither do I want to take any money that you need for yourself." Then she remembered. "And speaking of money, you never mentioned you were paying on a life insurance policy that has me as the beneficiary. Are you sure you should be doing that?"

"Oh, dear, you're so sweet. I'm fine for money. That policy has been around for decades. I bought it when you were still in school from a nice insurance man here in town. He sold the business years ago, but I did confirm with the new owner that everything was still in place. When I'm gone, you'll be fine. In the meantime, you go ahead and sell anything you want in that house. And check the pockets first. I was really bad about leaving money in pockets." Nan hung up without so much as a goodbye.

Instantly Doreen shoved her hands into the nearest pockets and retrieved several crumpled-up twenty-dollar bills. And, for her right now, that was a gold mine. Excited beyond belief, she systematically went through the pockets of the fur coats, checking both the inside and outside pockets. In each coat she found money. Then she put them on the hangers, giving them a good shake out before rehanging them in the closet in the spare room.

Deciding to be systematic, she took a picture of the fur coat against the closet door. It gave a good idea what condition it was in, then she proceeded to document all the others. She shook her head. "Dear Nan, how the heck did you manage to get away with this all these years?"

But Doreen didn't mind. It was like treasure hunting. And, if there was one thing she could use right now, it was a bit of treasure.

Chapter 17

THAT AFTERNOON DOREEN loaded up her car with Nan's fur coats, several of Doreen's suits and designer shoes she would never likely wear again and other bits and pieces from Nan's spare bedroom closet and drove to the consignment store. She'd already called them and had a conversation about the items she was bringing. The owner was interested but hesitant to say that she'd accept them until she'd seen them. Fair enough.

Doreen parked out front and carried in the items. She didn't quite understand how this worked, but, as the store was empty, she didn't feel quite so bad if she made a blunder in the process.

The shopkeeper's name was Wendy Markham. A robust buxom lady with a brilliant smile. She took one look at the fur coats and exclaimed, "Oh my, those are real."

"Exactly."

Doreen appreciated the woman's reaction. She was afraid Nan's things would be discarded as junk. And that wasn't what Doreen wanted. At the same time, there was no point in keeping these things, cluttering up closet space she could use herself. And, if Nan didn't want them, it was better to put them to good use. Maybe somebody could still appreciate them. Besides, money was money.

"I'll get a few more things from the car." It took her three trips to bring it all in.

By the time she was done, Wendy had sorted through the clothes, placing them into Accepted and Not Accepted piles. Thankfully eighty percent of it went into the Accepted pile. Yet, she worked fast and efficiently as she made her decisions almost instantly.

Wendy said, "It'll take a little bit to figure out prices for the fur coats, but I can tell you right now what kind of prices the suits will bring."

She named off a price that had Doreen's eyebrows rising. That was way less than half of what the suits had cost but still was a tremendous amount of money for her right now. Just to be sure she asked, "And how much of that is commission?"

"I take 30 percent, and you'll get 70."

"That's more than fair. Now, is this too much stuff for you? I have more closets of clothing to go through still."

"I've had a couple really big sales which cleared out my stock," she said. "So why don't you bring me another load, and we'll see how quickly the items move. I have a decent number of return clientele here. With any luck, some of these pieces could go right away. After a piece has been here in the store for sixty days, I discount it. You have the option to take it back if you don't like the discount option."

Doreen smiled. "Discount if you need to. Hopefully not too much will be left by the end of sixty days."

In a much happier frame of mind, she got back in her car and headed home. As an afterthought, she took a left turn toward Mack's mother's house. Doreen considered the amount of money she could earn in return for her hours estimated to do the job at the agreed-upon hourly rate, and it was probably a fair deal. But gardening always entailed more than first envisioned. Tomorrow was only Friday. Her fingers itched to get at Mack's mom's gardens now but would have to wait until Saturday. For now, she must keep working on Nan's closets. She had promised another load for the consignment store today, which was more money in her pocket potentially.

Doreen drove home, headed back upstairs and went through another huge stack of Nan's well-kept clothing, creating a Goodwill pile, a consignment store pile and a Keep pile of a few items she thought maybe she would wear, as they were quite funky and cute and fit her.

By the time the lunch hour had arrived, she was tired. But the car was full with yet another load for Wendy at the consignment store. Doreen decided to drop that off first, then maybe pick up something to eat. She'd take Mugs with her this time.

After the consignment store and dropping off the Goodwill stuff, Doreen headed to a park. With Mugs on a leash, Doreen spied the huge food truck. Such an odd icon, but they served hot coffee during the summer here. She bought a coffee and took Mugs for a long walk. On the way back, she picked up fish and chips to-go, returned to her car, and drove home. As soon as she entered the house, Goliath was all over her.

"Did I forget to feed you this morning?"

But, as she walked into the kitchen, she glanced to the left corner where the broom closet was and could still see food in his bowl. The fish smell in her to-go bag had attracted him. She grabbed a plate, opened the back door, and sat down on the rear veranda with her fish and chips. Thaddeus immediately flew to the nearby railing. She probably shouldn't give him anything fried or too salty. Luckily her fish and chips had been served up on a bed of lettuce. She gave him a wilted leaf. He put it on the railing and pecked at it. Goliath, on the other hand, wasn't interested in the french fry she offered him. He hopped up on the table and batted at her fish.

"I didn't buy enough to share with you guys," she complained but good-naturedly broke off a piece of the white flesh his paw had touched and gave it to the cat. Mugs didn't appear to be bothered that she had fed the other two animals first. He just stared at her. She gave him a french fry, which he sniffed, then grabbed and walked over to the far end of the veranda and lay down. But he ate the fry.

She shook her head. "Who knew all the animals would eat vegetables like that?"

After cleaning up after her meal, she headed back upstairs. She was determined to at least get the spare bedroom sorted out. She had an assortment of money and collectibles from Nan's pockets, which had made this a fun treasure hunt, amassing over $260 so far. And a bundle of change she hadn't even counted. She had brought a kitchen bowl to the bedroom to hold the various little bits—the paper money and the coins, a ring, and a chain. She continued checking the pockets of the rest of the coats, finding another $38.42. A small fortune in itself.

But she had another load to sort through. She sorted the clothes into various boxes, marked Consignment, Goodwill, and Dry Cleaning for the things Doreen would keep. After boxing everything up and making several trips to move the boxes downstairs near the front door, she finally had the spare room closet completely empty. But only the spare room. And only the closet. Still, it was later than she'd planned. So she'd deliver the goods tomorrow.

She focused her attention on the dresser next. The bottom three drawers were full of sweaters. She bagged up several for the consignment store and kept one that appealed to her. In the top drawer she found a novel. Stuck inside, like a bookmark, was a Lifelong Insurance business card. Slowly she set the open book on top of the dresser.

"Is this important?" It showed that the dead man and Nan had connected at some point in time. Then she'd mentioned having checked with the new owner of the insurance company and confirming all was well with her original policy. Doreen flipped through the rest of the book but didn't find anything else inside it. On the back of the card was a time, as if Nan had set up a meeting with the dead man. Doreen set it off to the side.

Letting herself be distracted for a few moments, she finished going through the top drawer, finding scarves, several belts and another $12.00. At this point, she wouldn't be happy until she completely gutted Nan's house, finding all the hidden money. Leaving the book where it was, she sorted and boxed up the rest of the clothes from the dresser, whether to sell at the consignment shop or to donate to Goodwill. She added these boxes to those already near the front door.

She didn't want to load up her car this late in the evening.

Not to mention she had no idea what the crime rate was here but where she used to live, leaving a vehicle full of boxes was asking for someone to break in and steal them.

She'd load up her car tomorrow, right before leaving to

make her deliveries.

As she returned to the spare bedroom, only the night table and the bed were left to inspect. She quickly stripped the linens off the bed, checking out the pillowcases and under the mattress, ensuring Nan had no money stashed underneath. The mattress and box spring were in good shape, intact and didn't have any holes where something could be stuffed inside.

She stared at the box spring on the frame, knowing it would be heavy and awkward to move. But then she decided, if she was going to do this job, she would do it right and proper. She took the top mattress off, leaning it against one wall. With both hands, she grabbed the box spring, lifting it a bit. Finding nothing underneath, she dropped it. But she noticed something was caught underneath. She flipped the box spring on its side this time and found an envelope taped underneath. What on earth had Nan been up to that she'd felt compelled to hide so much stuff?

Doreen rearranged the angle of the box spring so she could reach the envelope, pulling it free to place it atop the dresser before quickly putting the bed back together again. Although she was curious about the envelope, she wanted to finish this room before she went to bed tonight. So she went through the night table and found another $42.00. Glancing at the night table lamp, she picked it up, making sure nothing was underneath the base.

Now with the room back to normal, she picked up her bowl of money and trinkets she had found in the room, the open book with the business card and the envelope. She headed back downstairs.

She picked up her phone and called Mack. "I've been cleaning up Nan's spare room," she told him. "In the top dresser drawer was a book." She looked down at it. "It's a copy of *Moby Dick*. Inside is a Lifelong Insurance business card."

"Interesting," he said. "That means Nan did meet him."

"I don't know that she met him." She then explained what Nan had said to her, adding, "But somehow the business card is in her house, and ten o'clock is written on the back. So it could be from her meeting with him way back when."

"I'll be over there in a few minutes," he said. "And we have to postpone our Saturday clean-up session at Mom's. I've got too much else going on to squeeze that in. I'll reschedule something with you later."

She ended the call, reached for the brown legal envelope taped shut on the back flap. She ripped off the tape and flipped up the flap. She went to pull out all the contents but slowly placed it on the table, suddenly unnerved.

What could possibly be in this envelope that Nan would've taped it underneath a spare bed?

Then Doreen frowned and thought, *What if Nan hadn't taped it there? What if somebody else had?* Doreen stood and paced the kitchen. She had no reason not to see what was in the envelope, but for some reason, she couldn't bring herself to. Realizing Mack would be here any minute, she washed her hands and set up a pot of coffee. It was the least she could do.

"I hope it's a decent cup," she muttered to Mugs, now sitting at her feet. She bent down and gave him a hug. "Tell me what's wrong with the envelope."

He barked.

She nodded. "Yeah, that's about how I feel too." She lifted the envelope and held it for him to sniff. He backed away instantly.

She frowned at his reaction, then held it out for Goliath.

Goliath hissed, and his tail poofed.

"Wow. Okay. So that's a really serious reaction. What about you, Thaddeus?"

Curious to see what the bird would do, she held up the brown envelope to Thaddeus, who immediately took flight, screeching, "Murder in the house. Murder in the house."

Chapter 18

A LITTLE UNNERVED at the animals' reactions, she dropped the envelope on the table and refused to inspect it further. Mack was on his way. He could dang well deal with it. She wasn't superstitious by nature, but something about the reaction from all her animals had her nerves on edge. Of course Thaddeus storming around the house, saying, "Murder in the house. Murder in the house," wasn't making her feel any better.

She again washed her hands and walked over to the coffeemaker and pulled two cups from the cupboard above it. She waited until it finished brewing, then poured one. Mack could pour his when he got here.

She sat down heavily at the table and stared at the envelope. It wasn't like it would reach out and bite her. But Thaddeus was correct—or almost correct about it being murder in the garden—but was it also murder in the house? And how could that be? That envelope had upset everyone. She stared at it. It was just an envelope. What could it possibly contain? And why did it bother her so much?

Still, she never had been a coward in her life. She reached for it and quickly dumped the contents onto the table.

Photographs. Taken in the upstairs bedroom from the looks of the wallpaper. Photographs of a dead man. She shook her head. No. There was no way to prove he was dead. He looked dead, but… he could have been sleeping. If he were dead, there should have been blood, lots of it. Right?

She slowly picked up a picture and stared at the tiny details. Was it really Nan's upstairs spare bedroom? Could she prove that? She turned it over to see a date from thirty years ago. "What the heck? Has this photo been under the bed all this time? Why would Nan do that?" Then it hit her. What if Nan had nothing to do with it? How long had Nan lived here?

Doreen frowned, thinking back. Nan had lived in this house for all of Doreen's life, she thought, but it was hard to remember. She picked up the next picture, a similar shot—same man, same bed, slightly different angle. It showed a wider view of the dresser and the closet. Enough to confirm it was Nan's upstairs spare bedroom.

She picked up the envelope, and something was in the bottom. She gave it a bit of a shake upside down. A crumpled piece of newspaper fell out. She opened it up to find a 1988 article on a missing man, Jeremy Feldspar. The headline stated, "Man Accused of Murdering His Mother with Arsenic Now Missing Himself."

Doreen sat back and stared. "Arsenic and a dead man. Like both the arsenic and the dead man found in the garden." She shook her head. "*This* can't be a coincidence."

Mugs barked then he stood on his back legs and put his front paws on her legs. Given his earlier reaction, she placed the newspaper clipping on the table and gave him a hug and a cuddle.

"It's okay, Mugs. It's okay. I'm not sure what this is all about, but we'll get to the bottom of it."

Thaddeus hopped up on the table and walked across it toward the items there. The bird stared at them with one eye. Then the feathers along the back of his neck ruffled upward.

Not sure what the bird was up to, Doreen quickly repackaged everything into the envelope. As she put the crumpled newspaper page inside, she noticed an odd residue on her fingers. She inspected it closer and froze at the fine white dusting. Her mind immediately jumped to the worst-case scenario.

The trouble was, she had no reason to think that way except for the headline on the newspaper clipping and the arsenic bottle she'd found in the back garden.

Just what the heck was going on? And why hadn't Nan spoken about any of this? Granted Doreen would've been five years old at the time and living with her parents. Still, a murder in your grandmother's guest room would make for an interesting topic to tell many years afterward.

Yet Doreen had never heard anything about a dead man being found in Nan's spare bedroom.

Two dead bodies on Nan's property? Granted, they were thirty years apart, but it did beg the question—were these two cases related? Doreen shook her head, confused and unnerved by her recent findings. She rose, walked to the kitchen sink and carefully washed her hands right up to her elbows several times.

As she finished, the doorbell rang. Thank heavens. That should be Mack. She rushed to the front door and opened it. Her hand went to her chest. "Oh, thank God, you're here!"

Midway over the threshold, he froze and asked, "What's

wrong?"

She took several deep breaths. "You better come in while I explain." She led him to the kitchen where she quickly poured him a coffee. "Sit."

He sat down heavily, his brows creased in the middle. "What's this all about?"

She sat down opposite him and pointed at the envelope. "I found this cleaning out Nan's things in the spare bedroom upstairs."

She launched into an explanation of her day, about the fur coats and the clothing, of Nan's habit of leaving money everywhere. She pointed at the bowl on the table, full of money and things. But as she spoke faster and faster, she could see the confusion on his face.

Finally he held up a hand. "Stop."

She gasped for air, realizing she was barely coherent. She shook her head. "I'm so sorry. I'm so sorry. I'm just really unnerved."

"I can see that," he said. "What does any of that have to do with this envelope?"

She took a deep breath. "Because I found so much odd stuff as I went through everything, and, when I flipped the mattress and the box spring, I saw this." And she held up the envelope for him to see.

His eyebrows shot up.

"I know. But I wanted to make sure I checked *every-thing*," she emphasized. "And taped to the bottom of the box spring was that envelope." She watched as enlightenment whispered into his eyes.

He gazed at the envelope, put down his coffee cup, and said, "What's in it?"

"I think you better check," she said quietly. "I'm really

hoping it's not what I think it is."

He shot her a look as he donned a pair of plastic gloves, reached for the envelope and pulled out the pictures.

That was a much smarter way to retrieve the contents, unlike how she'd just upended it, making a mess. And she noticed a fine dusting of white everywhere. She stood, dampened a paper towel and came back, wiping the table, then used a dry paper towel afterward. "I don't know what this powder is, but it's from the envelope." She sat and stared at him. "Say something." Why wasn't he saying anything?

He stared at her, then focused on the pictures again. "You know what room this is?"

She nodded, her breath shaky as she answered in a low voice, "Yes, the one I was cleaning upstairs."

He nodded slowly. He reached for the brown envelope again and found the crumpled newspaper article inside. He studied that, looked at the man in the photograph and said, "You know something? I think I remember this case." He tapped the newspaper article with his gloved finger. "I certainly remember that headline as the case is one we went over in my training."

"The thing is, as soon as I saw the word *arsenic* in the newspaper article and the pictures of the dead body, I thought of the dead body in the backyard and the empty bottle of arsenic I found in the garden."

He nodded. "Obviously the mind makes a kind of a connection, but we have to be careful not to assume anything."

"How can I not assume?" she cried out. "It's obvious this guy's dead in the picture. If it's the same guy as in the picture, he supposedly killed his own mother with arsenic. And I've got a dead man and a bottle of arsenic in my own garden." And she pointed her hand to the table. "And here is more white powder. I'm terrified that's arsenic."

He froze, staring at the white powder in the envelope. "And you could be right." He got up slowly. "Do you have a vacuum?" He pulled out his cell phone and carefully took pictures of the table, envelope and the floor surrounding where they stood.

She shook her head. "No. I can wipe it up though." Very carefully they moved everything off the table, and she came back with more wet paper towels that she could then throw away. They cleaned up all the powder on the table. She glanced over at Thaddeus. "Thaddeus, go away. You need to get away from this white powder."

He looked at her and said, "Murder in the house. Murder in the house."

"He really has a flair for the dramatic, doesn't he?" Mack asked.

When they finally had it all cleaned up, she turned to him in distress and asked, "Do you think the animals got any?"

"They look clean to me. They're all doing fine. Arsenic is a fast-acting poison, although it can be used for long-term slow killing, as small amounts of it accumulates over time. It's one of the favorite methods of wives getting rid of their husbands."

She stared at him. "You're kidding, right?"

He shook his head. "Poison is very much a woman's tool. I know several cases where the wives slowly poisoned their husbands with arsenic in their lunches. It's supposedly tasteless and slowly builds up in the body to a point that eventually kills them."

"That's horrible." For good measure, she grabbed yet

more paper towels, slightly dampened them, and wiped the table again, taking careful note of the cracks and indentations in the table. Then she dropped to her hands and knees on the floor and scrubbed away.

"I'm pretty sure it's fine now," Mack said.

"*Pretty sure* isn't good enough." But finally even she had to admit there couldn't be more on any of the surfaces here. "Can you get that powder analyzed?"

He nodded. "I'll do that as soon as I leave here." He held up the envelope. "Have you shown this to anybody else?"

She shook her head. "No, I haven't. I don't know anybody else to show it to. And I knew you were coming, so it just made sense to give it to you anyway. I presume the man in the pictures is dead?"

"He *appears* dead." He studied the picture still in his hand. "But, with no visible injury, it's hard to say." He sighed. "You know Nan owned the house thirty years ago, right?"

She stared at her hands and nodded. "I know that." She raised her gaze to his. "But I also know there's no way Nan killed anybody."

"What if he deserved killing?" he asked, his voice quiet, soft. "We're all capable of killing if put in the right position to do so."

She shook her head vehemently. "No," she said softly. "Nan is the gentlest of women. She'd never kill anyone." She studied Thaddeus, now relaxed at the far end of the table. "And would it make any sense at all to keep an envelope with incriminating photos and evidence like that in her own house?"

"I've seen all kinds of strange things people do that don't make any sense," Mack said.

Just then, in a weird, slow humming voice, Thaddeus said, "Murder is everywhere. Murder is everywhere."

Mack departed, business card in hand, soon afterward, leaving Doreen pale but composed by the kitchen table. She wasn't exactly sure where on his suspect list Nan would fall, but Doreen knew her grandmother was the priority for her. No way would she talk to Nan on the phone about this. Doreen wanted to see her reaction, to watch her facial expression. Doreen needed to find out the truth.

And hated the necessity of doing even that.

But it was too late tonight for a visit. This would have to wait until the morning.

Chapter 19

Day 3, Friday

THE FOLLOWING MORNING she quickly made herself some toast and jam to go with her coffee. She walked out the door twenty minutes later.

She wanted to get to Nan first thing. Leaving Goliath sitting on the front railing, completely disinterested in where they were walking, Doreen led the way to Nan's retirement home apartment, Thaddeus riding on her shoulder and Mugs strolling at her side.

With still a block to go, she grabbed her phone and called her grandmother. "Nan, you there?"

"Of course I am, dear," she said in a gentle tone full of exasperation. "Where else would I be?"

"We're walking toward you. We're a couple minutes away," Doreen said with a big smile. It was so hard to believe Nan would be mixed up in anything like murder. She just couldn't be. It wasn't possible.

"Oh, that's delightful. I just made a full pot of tea. I must've known company was coming."

Doreen laughed. "You're a psychic now?"

"Wouldn't that be lovely if I were?"

Doreen shook her head and ended the call, pocketing her phone. She wasn't sure how to broach the subject of the photos. Nan's life was so very different than Doreen's had been. But anybody who had lived as many years as Nan had must see life from a whole different perspective.

Just look at me. In the last six months, everything had changed for her. Imagine if she had survived what Nan had gone through. She'd been married a long time ago, had a son, only to have her husband die soon after. When Nan had married again, her second husband died as well. Then she had decided marriage wasn't for her and had traveled the world. Sure, her son had been Doreen's father. But her parents split up when Doreen was little, her father dying soon after. Yet Doreen's mom had been friends with Nan before she had married Nan's son, and their friendship had continued afterward for Doreen's sake.

Doreen, as a child, had spent a lot of time with Nan. Doreen's mother wasn't the maternal type but enjoyed living a single's tennis-club life. She'd remarried twice since then and had distanced herself a little more each time from her motherhood role, but that was okay because Nan took over, being a true mother to Doreen. When Doreen had gone off on her own, she'd missed Nan.

But, as Doreen had built a life with her husband, it became easier and easier for her to acclimate to her mother's lifestyle. Her new life quickly filled with new people, new experiences—as her husband's ever-increasing control of Doreen's world worked to separate her from everything and everyone from her past, except for those things and people he knew and wanted in her life.

She didn't blame him entirely. She'd been young and naive and so wanting to please. But, over time, her previous life and the people in it had drifted farther away.

Now there was no need to let go. Doreen needed somebody. Nan needed somebody. And they were gravitating toward each other again.

Reaching the corner of Rosemoor's property, she could see Nan sitting in the little garden she had all to herself.

Nan raised her gaze, caught sight of Doreen and waved.

Mugs started to bark.

"Yes, that's Nan." Doreen loved how Mugs had taken to Nan so well.

Of course maybe it was a case that Nan's animals had taken to Doreen, and so her animal had taken to Nan, understanding the loving bond between the two women. Somehow Doreen was already thinking of Thaddeus and Goliath as hers. And this was only the beginning of her third day here, and since her arrival, there had been nothing but chaos. Maybe the animals clung to the familiar face of the person who was in residence. Maybe they didn't give a crap who was there as long as somebody was feeding them.

How fickle animals were. She glanced at Mugs and wondered. "Mugs, if I were gone, would you just take to the next person?"

He barked.

She took that as a yes.

She rolled her eyes, let him off the leash and watched as he ran toward Nan. She stood away from the table and bent to give him a big greeting.

Once again Doreen crossed the grassy lawn, breaking one rule, and also knowing she wasn't allowed to bring the animals here either. Yet she felt less criminal because she was doing something, for once, that was against the rules, yet was doing a lot of good for an eighty-something-year-old lady.

Laughing at her granddaughter's antics and with her arms out, Nan gave Doreen a hug.

Doreen gently hugged her back, with Thaddeus taking the opportunity to shift from one shoulder to the other. Sitting down, Doreen watched as Mugs and Thaddeus claimed Nan's loving attention.

"Where's Goliath?" Nan asked.

"He was lazing on the porch railing when we left."

Nan nodded. "I'll see him next time."

"What's this? A new type of tea?" Doreen sniffed the air experimentally.

"It's brand-new. A friend of mine just came back from China and brought me some authentic Ceylon tea to try."

Doreen didn't have the heart to tell her grandmother that the island named Ceylon was later named Sri Lanka. And the black tea of Ceylon was now grown in India and China as well. But Doreen would appreciate the drink anyway.

Nan poured two teacups full as Thaddeus looked on from her shoulder. "It's lovely to see you again, dear. Has everything calmed down at the house now?"

It was all she could do to hold back an unending stream of questions. "Oh, it's calmed down somewhat," she admitted. "But then something else came up."

"Oh, dear." Nan stared at her in fascination. "I lived in that house for forty years, my dear, and I never had the kind of excitement you're having."

Doreen studied her grandmother and smiled. She could use that opening. "I sorted through the spare bedroom yesterday. I already took a couple loads to the consignment store. Have another ready in the car now."

Nan clapped her hands in joy. "*Aah*, wonderful. It'd be

nice to see some of the clothing go to good use."

"I also took a couple big bags to Goodwill," she confessed. "Wendy wasn't interested in those items."

Nan nodded. "That makes sense. I hope you checked the pockets before you sent everything out." She shook her finger at Doreen. "Remember? I never could keep my pockets empty."

"That's the truth. You could not keep your pockets empty. I found well over $300.00 in all those clothes. Not even counting the change yet."

Nan's face froze for a moment, and then she burst out into joyful laughter. "Well, how lovely." She chuckled again. "You needed money, so there it was. And who knew I had left so much behind."

Doreen instantly felt bad. She leaned forward. "I never thought to bring it to you. It is your money."

Nan lifted a hand and waved it at her. "I told you everything in the house is yours, my dear. I already have enough for my needs."

"And what about your wants?" Doreen asked softly. "Is there anything you *want*? You can't spend your entire life only looking after your needs. Is there anything you want just because it's pretty or makes you smile? What about a book from your favorite author? Or a new bedding set? How about a holiday?"

A quiet silence followed as Nan contemplated… something. Doreen had trouble deciphering the look on her grandmother's face. But she waited.

Nan said in a gentle voice, "My dear, I've already lived well over twice as long as you have. I've had lots of wants taken care of, but now the only thing that matters is making sure your needs are met. I have very few needs in this world."

There was such a sad element attached to that statement. Doreen tried to understand, but it was hard. She settled back and picked up her tea and took a sip. The tea was wonderful, full-bodied, and it was just the perfect drinking temperature. She cupped her hands around the teacup to absorb some of the warmth. "This tea is lovely."

Nan agreed. "It is. I've been enjoying it."

After that they shared little conversation as Doreen contemplated her grandmother's words. She took a deep breath. "Nan, because I found so much stuff hidden all around in your clothing and drawers, I made sure I did a thorough search of the room—cleaning it out, you know?"

Nan nodded and waited.

"I even flipped the mattresses."

Nan stared at her in amazement. "Oh, my goodness. I wouldn't even be strong enough to do that."

And Doreen sat there with that truth staring at her. Of course Nan wouldn't. Even thirty years ago she wouldn't have been able to. Nan was tiny. Doreen doubted Nan could pick up twenty pounds. A man could have handled the mattress, most likely, but that would not be an easy feat for Nan.

Doreen shook her head. "I didn't think of that before."

Nan leaned forward. "Think of what, my dear?"

Doreen settled back and smiled. "I found a brown 9x12 envelope taped to the bottom of the box spring."

"Oh my, this is getting interesting. What was in it?"

Doreen explained about the contents, including the white powder and the newspaper article and the pictures of the dead man from thirty years ago. She studied her grandmother's face intently, looking for any sign of foreknowledge of the package. But Doreen saw nothing but sheer astonishment in Nan's expression.

"What a delightful mystery." She shook her head. "And in my spare bedroom." She sat back with her tea, staring at it for a long moment. Almost as if looking down the tunnel of time and seeing if it would give her the answers she needed. Then she looked up and said, "I wish I had seen the pictures of the man."

"Oh," Doreen said. She quickly pulled her phone from her pocket. "I didn't even tell Mack I did this." She lowered her voice to a hushed tone. "It just seemed important that I remembered the dead man's face." She found the photograph of the man and held it up for Nan to see. "I took a picture of the picture."

"Oh, dear, that sounds very complicated." Nan reached for Doreen's phone and brought it closer, pulling the glasses off her head and putting them on her nose to peer at the picture intently. "He *almost* looks familiar." She lifted her gaze apologetically. "I know my memory isn't quite the way it used to be, but I can't remember ever seeing this man in my house."

Doreen nodded. What could she say? "The thing is, Nan, it was definitely taken at your house. These pictures were of the spare room, with the same curtains, the same wallpaper and the same dresser."

Nan stared at her in surprise, her mouth forming an O. She turned her attention back to the picture. "I just don't understand how that could be."

"Did you go away on a holiday thirty years ago? Were you visiting a friend? Did you let somebody stay in your house for a little while?"

Nonplussed, Nan continued to stare at Doreen. "All of that is possible. But it was thirty years ago, so I really can't be sure of when."

Doreen patted Nan's hand. She didn't want to upset her grandmother. "If you do remember, let me know. Just be aware that Mack is likely to come by with questions."

"Mack?"

"Corporal Mack Moreau. He's the officer investigating the case." Under Nan's prying gaze, Doreen could feel the heat rising up her neck. She shook her head. "No." She made sure to use a strong, firm voice. "There's nothing between us."

Nan nodded slowly, but her gaze twinkled. "Of course not." She settled back and took another sip of her tea. But a smile played around the corner of her lips. "He's a good man. I know his mother. Interesting history there." Then she sealed her lips and went quiet.

Doreen eyed her suspiciously but knew there was no point in pushing her grandmother. She could be stubborn when she wanted to be.

Thaddeus took that moment to jump on the table. He studied the almond cookies that neither of the women had touched, looked over at Nan and said, "Cookie please. Cookie please."

Doreen gave a startled gasp. "How is it this bird has so many phrases in his vocabulary? He continues to amaze me." She glanced at Nan. "Where did you get him from?"

"An old friend brought him over one day years ago, hoping I'd take him in as he'd been abandoned. He had no details on his history, but Thaddeus chose to stay behind, and we've been friends ever since."

"Amazing," Doreen said, eyeing Thaddeus in a different light. "He's very smart."

Thaddeus gave a weird chirp and pecked at the closest

cookie.

"It's not just that he has all these words," Nan said gently, "but the way he puts them together so they make sense. Well, sometimes it's downright freaky."

Chapter 20

"L ADIES?" MACK'S HARD voice cut through their peaceful teatime only to be drowned out by Mugs's sudden barking as he woke up from his nap. Goliath had accompanied Mack on this walk and ignored the dog and jumped into Nan's lap.

Doreen looked at Mack in surprise, but he ignored her to study Nan's face.

Doreen hurriedly stood and pulled up a spare chair. In a bright voice she said, "Join us."

He sat down in the very small chair, making her wince. He glanced at her, even as he scratched Mugs's ear. In a droll voice, he said, "I'm sure it will hold my weight."

She flushed immediately. "Sorry," she muttered.

"Oh, what are you sorry for? Coming here to see Nan before I have a chance to question her?"

"Why shouldn't I be allowed to talk to her? It's not like this has anything to do with the current murder at my place, and it's not like Nan is a murder suspect," Doreen said dismissively. She picked up her tea and took a sip. "Or is she?"

He glared at her. "Every time I turn around in this case,

I am tripping over you. If it isn't at Lifelong Insurance, then it's here at Nan's."

Doreen straightened in outrage. "Well, I'm sure your investigative work entailed more than those two places. And obviously I have to check into anything that might involve Nan. And I did show you the things I found in Nan's house."

"Dear, it's okay." Nan reached over and patted her wrist. "Don't worry about it. Mack's just a little upset that you got here before him."

"A little upset?" She glared at Nan. Mugs, sitting underneath the table, stood up on his back legs, his paws on her knee and growled at her tone. She patted his forehead. "It's all right, Mugs. I'm fine."

"Is he a good guard dog?" Mack asked, a frown on his face as he studied the basset. "They were originally bred for hunting, I believe."

"I have no idea. The guard dog occasion hasn't arisen yet," she said. "He only just realized he could bark. My almost ex-husband frowned on Mugs making noise, so a dog trainer trained him not to bark. But now that it's just us, he's found his voice again." She stroked his long silky ears and smiled at the bag-eyed dog. "Of course Goliath helps in that area too."

"Goliath can take care of himself, that's for sure," Nan said cheerfully. She looked at the teapot and poured another round of tea for all three of them. "Now Thaddeus, he's a different story."

"And why did you not tell me more about Goliath and Thaddeus, Nan?" Doreen asked. "It's one thing to leave me an independent monster-size cat, happy to be inside and outside, but to leave me Thaddeus?"

Nan's laughter trailed across the garden, making both Mack and Doreen smile. "Like we were just saying, Thaddeus is a gem."

On cue Thaddeus jumped up and landed on Nan's shoulder. In his soft crooning voice he said, "Thaddeus is here. Thaddeus is here."

And, in a moment of naked affection, the cat and the bird nestled in closer to Nan.

Doreen stared at the two pets, then shook her head. "How is it you could leave them?"

"I had little choice. Besides, Thaddeus is fickle, my dear. Right now he looks like he is my long-lost friend, and in truth, he is. But he could also be your long-lost friend in five minutes. And I can't have pets here. Thaddeus will outlive me, possibly all of us, so I had to make provisions for him anyway."

Doreen leaned forward. "But you didn't make provisions for him, Nan. You just left him and Goliath behind."

"Nonsense. You were arriving on a specific day. He and Goliath were fine until then as I went back and forth to feed them. And, if I had told you about them, you would have fretted over your delay."

Doreen sat back at that. Just because Nan was correct, it didn't mean Doreen felt like hearing it. Neither did she like to see the quirk of Mack's lips as he held back his smile.

She glared at him. "Didn't you have a reason for coming here?"

He put down his teacup and proceeded to ask Nan the exact same questions that Doreen had.

Nan laughed. "You really should hire Doreen as your assistant. You know that, don't you? She already asked me those same things."

Still, Nan went over the answers she'd given Doreen earlier.

Doreen was fascinated with the case. Quite a twist had been found here, and somehow Nan was involved. Doreen didn't think Nan had anything to do with either murder, so there had to be somebody else. There was really no other explanation.

Mack turned his attention to Doreen. "I had the powder analyzed. It was simple cornstarch. I suspect it was in the envelope to keep the photos from sticking together."

"Well... that mystery at least is solved. I'm glad it wasn't poison," she exclaimed. With a bright smile she finished the last of her tea and stood. She gave Nan a hug and kiss and said, "I'll stop by in another day or two." With Mugs at her side, Goliath at her feet, and Thaddeus now transferred to her shoulder, she turned to Mack. "I'm sure I'll see you again, Mr. Moreau."

In a gruff voice, he said, "I told you to call me Mack."

She smiled. "So you did. Have a good day, Mack, Nan." She walked away, hearing the two of them talking—and heard her name mentioned. Hopefully only good things were discussed because Doreen had been a laughingstock for a lot of people over the last few years. But she trusted Nan. She was the only other person in the world who cared what happened to Doreen, other than herself.

Her mind was consumed with the pictures of the dead man as she walked back to her house slowly.

A library was just around the corner—probably the only way to get the archives on the newspaper articles from thirty years ago—but she would have to leave Mugs, Goliath, and Thaddeus at home. She had the one article in mind, but that didn't mean other papers would have carried the same story.

What she really needed was more history on the death of the first man to die. And, for that, she should've asked Mack.

She pulled out her phone, hit his contact number, and smiled, loving that he'd stayed to visit with Nan after grilling her. When he answered, she asked without preamble, "Did you get any information on the man in the pictures?"

"I haven't gone to the office yet. I'll do that then."

She nodded and smiled at a neighbor, who gave her an odd look and hurried by. As Doreen approached her driveway, she spoke into her phone again. "Let me know what you find, please."

"It's a police matter," he said in exasperation. "I'm not checking in with you at every step."

"But it's probably better if you do," she said. "Otherwise I'll have to get that information myself. And you don't like me doing that." She hung up, cutting him off mid-sputter, and pocketed her phone with a chuckle.

Back at the house, the animals following her, she returned to the spare bedroom for another look around, seeing if she had possibly missed anything. She hadn't even begun to search the walls. Was that an odd thing to consider?

The walls were covered in wallpaper, but paneling appeared to be underneath as seen where the wallpaper had been torn. But how could she tell if something was hidden behind the actual walls? She guessed she wouldn't unless she tore off all the paneling to find the studs beneath. She didn't feel the need to do that. However, feeling foolish but unable to stop herself, she rapped on the nearest wall and continued around the room. It all sounded the same until she got to the closet. She studied the closet, stepped inside and looked around. In the ceiling was a trapdoor leading to the attic.

It appeared to be added to the house as an afterthought.

Just a small three-foot-square opening. From her first look, the cover was just propped there, to be pushed aside once she could reach that high. It wasn't a full-fledged attic access with a pull-down door that had a fold-up ladder affixed to it.

She stepped back out and stared around the room, walking out into the hallway and looking up. Every house had an attic, but wasn't the attic door usually located somewhere in the middle of the house? Where the roof pitch was the highest? That way, someone could stand up inside the attic. Also tradesmen would have access to wiring, piping, ductwork and whatnot strung throughout the attic, amid all the stuff people stored up there too.

Back in the spare bedroom, she eyed the night table but didn't think it would be tall enough for her purposes. Neither was a kitchen chair. Back downstairs, she found a big lantern flashlight. That would help. She clicked it on and off several times to make sure the battery worked. Then she located a small step stool. Its top riser was higher than the kitchen chair seat.

She dragged the light and the stool upstairs into the spare bedroom's closet. With the flashlight in hand, she slowly climbed up the step stool, setting aside the cover to the attic access. With her head and shoulders now popped through into the attic, she turned on the lantern light and slowly searched the space.

Initially it looked empty until she circled completely around and found several boxes. Easily six to eight boxes were stacked between where she was and the outside wall.

Once again, the hunt for treasure overtook her. Small sheets of plywood lay between the rafters to stop people from falling through as they got up here, but they would be a bit of a challenge to navigate. She would have to change clothes before she attempted that.

She walked into her bedroom, quickly put on a pair of her capri length jeans, some tennis shoes and an old T-shirt, courtesy of Nan's closet. Doreen suspected the attic would be full of spiderwebs.

She moved the stepladder closer to the edge of the attic opening and slowly climbed up. Using her arms, she pulled herself into the attic, sitting at the opening, her legs dangling below, and looked around. The attic was empty except for the stack of boxes she had spied earlier. She suspected the contents would be stupid things, like broken Christmas ornaments.

Carefully she crawled on the plywood sheets closer to the boxes. Two were stacked in front of her. She grabbed the bottom one and slowly tugged them both toward her.

Surprisingly heavy, she kept pulling. She needed to know what was in all these boxes. Shaking them first to check for breakables inside, but hearing nothing like that, she then dropped the first two boxes into the closet next to the step stool.

Joining the boxes on the closet floor, she inspected them in the light of the closet, finding no list of contents or other identification marked on any side of either box. She grabbed the corner of the tape sealing the top of the first box and pulled it off. The animals were curious too, as Mugs had joined her in the closet and milled around her feet, with Goliath on the bed glaring and an unusually quiet Thaddeus perched on the dresser.

She pulled out what appeared to be men's clothing. A charcoal gray suit. She shook her head. "Oh, Nan. Where the devil did these come from?"

Doreen searched the pockets of the jacket and pulled out

a twenty-dollar bill, almost proof that this was Nan's work, packing up these clothes in this box. But Nan never would have worn these clothes, so who the heck did they belong to? Inside the breast pocket, Doreen pulled out a business card. The name matched the name in the newspaper article.

Jeremy Feldspar.

She glanced over at Thaddeus. "What's the matter, Thaddeus? Don't have anything to say now?" Normally at moments like this, he had some catchy phrase of doom and gloom. But even now, Thaddeus just stared at her and the clothes and remained silent.

Somehow she found that even worse.

Chapter 21

FOR THE LIFE of her, Doreen couldn't understand why men's clothes were in Nan's attic. Old clothes too. Of course Doreen's mind associated these clothes with the dead man photographed in the spare bedroom. She couldn't be sure.

Doreen refused to believe Nan had anything to do with Jeremy's death.

Just then the doorbell rang. Doreen didn't want anybody to see this stuff, so she closed the bedroom door as she headed downstairs to the front entryway. She opened it to find a middle-aged couple beaming at her. Both were slightly overweight, in their early fifties and dressed like twins with pumpkin-colored T-shirts and khaki pants. She gave a hesitant smile and said, "Hello. May I help you?"

The woman grabbed Doreen's hand. "We're so delighted to meet you. And we're so sorry you've had such a nasty event upon your arrival."

Doreen tried to pull her hand back, but the woman wouldn't let it go. "Do I know you?"

The man gave a hearty laugh. "We're your neighbors to the right." He motioned to the house next door. "We were away the last two days, so we missed a lot of the commotion. But, when we heard, we wanted to come over and welcome you to the neighborhood."

Doreen's eyebrows lifted, and she studied the couple. "Oh, isn't that nice." Yet inside she wondered if that *was* a neighborly thing to do. It just seemed weird. When she was with her husband, nobody would ever do something like this. Of course they couldn't get past the security gates anyway.

The man thrust a tinfoil-covered pan into her free hand and said, "Here. We brought over a dish for you. It's one of our favorites."

She looked at the pan in surprise but felt she had no option but to accept it. "Thank you," she said quietly. "It smells wonderful. It's very kind of you." And it was. She'd seen little kindness these last few months.

He beamed at her. "Well, we're very kind people," he said.

The woman, still gripping Doreen's other hand, said, "Oh my, yes, we certainly are." She turned to look at her husband and added, "I'm sure you'll find everybody here is very friendly."

"So far, that hasn't been my experience," Doreen said in a dry tone. "Then again, it's not every day a dead body is found on your property."

Instantly the two visitors gasped.

"That must have been just terrible for you," the woman cried. At that she blushed, waved her hand, finally releasing Doreen's. "Oh, my dear, I'm so sorry. I'm Cindy. This is my husband, Josh."

Josh stuck out a big mitt to shake hers. "Pleased to meet you."

She nodded and tried to nicely free her hand from his. It was impolite to grab onto her hand and hold it so long. Still, they were being friendly, and she certainly hadn't seen many friendly faces since her arrival. "I'm Doreen," she said. "Nan is my grandmother."

The woman, slightly younger than her partner, clasped her hands in front of her and almost gave a little hop and skip, like a twelve-year-old. "Oh, my dear, that's lovely. Nan is such a sweetie."

At that Doreen smiled naturally for the first time. "She certainly is." She didn't know if she should invite them in, but for some reason, she was loath to do so. She turned to the man and asked, "How long have you lived here?"

"Oh, must be thirty years now, possibly more," he said with a beaming smile. "Best place to live. Nothing ever happens here. It's nice and peaceful."

She avoided pointing out that *something* had happened here and just nodded, figuring they were here when Jeremy Feldspar was in Nan's house. "Interesting. Was Nan here when you moved in?"

They both nodded. "She certainly was. What a colorful character. She was always out and about the city with the neighbors."

Doreen smiled. "I'm learning a lot about my grandmother since coming here. What you know about somebody on one level is a whole different thing when you step into their lives."

Cindy patted Doreen's shoulder. "We're so happy that Nan has you. She shouldn't be alone in the special years of her life."

"She won't be alone now." Doreen looked for a place to put the dish down, but Mugs, having completely inspected the front porch, was now sitting at her side, staring up at the couple. He wasn't being overly friendly, and if she wasn't mistaken, a slight growl came from the back of his throat.

She squatted down slightly and stroked his head. "This is Mugs."

The couple bent down to greet the dog with what must be their usual overexuberance. They must be exhausting to be around for very long. Who had the energy for all that ebullience?

"And what about Nan's other pets? Is Thaddeus still here?" Josh asked.

Instantly the bird was behind her, as if hearing his name. Thaddeus landed on her shoulder. She was startled for a moment but quickly adjusted.

The couple smiled. Josh gently stroked Thaddeus's neck.

"Thaddeus is here. Thaddeus is here."

The couple laughed gaily.

"Isn't he just wonderful?" Cindy said, beaming. "How lucky for Nan that you're here to look after her animals."

"Yes, how very lucky." Doreen tried hard to be polite, but something about these people made her depressed. Surely nobody was nice *all* the time.

Just then Goliath came up the front steps to weave his way through everybody and to join in the melee. Doreen glanced at him and then asked the couple, "Do you have any pets?"

Josh shook his head. "We had, but we lost them a couple years back, and it was just so traumatic we didn't feel we could go through that again."

Doreen nodded. *That* she understood. She wasn't sure what she would do when she lost Mugs.

Cindy stepped back and said, "We've taken up so much

of your time. So sorry if we were bothering you."

Doreen wondered if she had been unfriendly, if she should've invited them in. But they were already halfway down the steps, waving.

"Stop by anytime you want to visit," Josh said. "I work from home most days, so one of us is always around."

Cindy chuckled. "And thankfully I don't have to work. Josh looks after me very well," she said with a big smile. "If you're ever feeling friendly, or just don't want to be alone anymore, come over and have a cup of tea."

With a big wave, the two of them left.

Doreen stood in the front door, feeling like a fool. She'd been raised better than that. In the background she could hear Nan's voice in her head. *What was that all about, dear? Why didn't you invite those nice people in?*

And that was the crux of the problem. They were *too* nice. Maybe it was just her suspicious mind, but it did seem to her as if they had been fishing for information.

She didn't have any information to give them. The thing was, they would know when the house was empty. They would know when Nan was in or out, and if they had wanted to bury the body on the property, there was plenty of time for them to do so between Nan's exodus and Doreen's arrival. Still, these neighbors had come under Doreen's critical review just for being on the spot and having access. So chances were good they'd have moved the body elsewhere for just that reason. Unless of course, they couldn't carry him far or didn't want to get caught with a dead body in their vehicle. Both of which were very valid points too.

Still, she couldn't imagine trying to move a dead adult male body.

She gave herself a shake and walked back inside. "Come

on, Mugs. Let's go in."

With the dog and cat at her heels and Thaddeus on her shoulder, she slowly closed the door. As she did so, she caught sight of a woman on the other side of the cul-de-sac, staring at her. She gave her a half smile. The woman turned around and walked inside, slamming her door.

Well, not everybody was friendly apparently. What did Doreen expect? Since she'd arrived, there had been nothing but kerfuffles at her house. Anybody who wanted peace and quiet probably thought the neighborhood had gone to the dogs with Doreen's arrival.

Unable to help herself, she locked the front door behind her and headed to the kitchen. When she took the tinfoil off the pan, she found fresh-baked buns of some kind. She had to admit they smelled delicious. Were they homemade? Feeling much more endearing toward her neighbors, she picked one, ripped it in half, buttered it and took a big bite. In truth, it was very good.

That was exactly what she needed right now.

She made a cup of tea, buttered a second bun and then took both upstairs. The only reason she could think of for not inviting Josh and Cindy inside was because of the stuff she'd found in the attic. And, yes, she felt guilty now that she'd tasted the wonderful buns.

She still didn't want anybody to know what she'd found. Anyone but Mack. But, before she told him about her latest find, she had to go through all the boxes. Once he got here, he would likely take everything away. And then he wouldn't share any further information with her about them. Although she innately trusted Mack, for whatever reason, still the evidence found in these boxes could initially point more fingers in Nan's direction.

Chapter 22

UPSTAIRS DOREEN WENT back to the job of sorting through the boxes she'd found. Mugs lay contentedly at her side. Of Goliath there was no sign. Thaddeus had been on his roost in the living room as she'd walked through but she suspected he wouldn't be able to resist seeing what she was doing. She methodically went through every item of clothing, checking all the pockets for bits and pieces of paper, business cards, the odd candy and, of course, money. She shook her head to think that so many people left money in their pockets and wondered if she had done so too— *before*.

There was her life *before* the separation and then her life after the separation. She wished she'd saved some of the money that had passed into her hands *before*. But life was life, and it changed. When she'd gone through all the pockets of the men's clothing, she reloaded the two cardboard boxes, stacked them up again, repositioned the stepladder under the attic hatchway and climbed up again.

Carefully crawling on the plywood patches, she slowly dragged the rest of the boxes closer to the attic opening, dropping two more of them to the closet floor. The ones that she'd already repackaged, she had set off to the far side so she wouldn't get them mixed up. These next two boxes held more of the same, men's clothes. Still, if this represented the entirety of one person's life, not a ton was here.

Repackaged, she added these two boxes to the first two she'd gone through, and then brought down the rest of the boxes. It took her several trips because some of them were very heavy. She closed the attic access door and folded up the stepladder, just in case somebody came inside and wondered what she was up to.

"All done, Mugs."

Woof. Then he dropped his head back onto his paws and went to sleep.

She opened the flaps on all four boxes, found another one full of men's clothing and chose to go through that first. This one had outdoor coats, jackets and a sweater. Again a bit of money was in each pocket, plus a couple notes that made no sense and a key.

She stared at the key in amazement. A key to what? It was small, possibly a safe-deposit box key. Almost a mailbox-size key. Certainly not a house key.

She placed the key in the bowl with the money. When she was finished with that box, she closed it and moved it off to the side.

The next box was a little more interesting—books. So maybe these were his personal possessions. She carefully went through them all to find a motley selection of novels and hard-copy books. Everything from a Webster's dictionary to the latest *New York Times* best seller from thirty years earlier. Studying the collection, she frowned. She didn't understand why these had even been kept. She carefully opened and shook each book to make sure nothing important was inside any of them.

When she was done, she had a few more dollar bills, a couple bookmarks that appeared to be more like business cards and that was it. She repackaged the box and set it off to the side.

Now she was down to two boxes. She was hot and dusty and tired. But she knew she had to get through these, just in case somebody came by.

As she had that thought, the doorbell rang. Mugs barking like a loon skittered off the bed and around the corner. She went to the window and looked out to see who was on the front step.

She cautiously went back downstairs. Mugs stood at the front door, barking like a crazy man before she got there. "Mugs, please calm down."

For somebody who'd come here not expecting to know anyone, Doreen was getting way too much traffic through the place. She opened the door to find Mack standing on her front porch, his arms across his chest and a frown on his face. Mugs stopped barking and started whining instead. Somehow he'd taken a liking to the big detective.

"What took you so long?"

She frowned up at him. "I was busy," she retorted. "Sorry if it took me a moment or two to come downstairs."

He looked at her clothing and darned if he didn't hold back a grin.

She stared at her jeans; her trips to the attic had covered her in dust. And likely cobwebs. She brushed her hair back and groaned as her hands were covered in dirt too. "Crap."

"What have you been doing? Going into the attic or something?"

She swallowed her answer, not wanting him to know—

yet—what she had been doing. She opened the door wider. "What do you want now?"

He stepped across the threshold, taking her opening the door as an invitation, though her tone was much less than welcoming.

With a bright cheerful smile he said, "I came to ask a few more questions. But now I'm checking on what you're up to."

She glared at him, feeling her mouth pinch into the same expression after she'd sucked a lemon. "What I am doing is my business."

"Not if it pertains to the murder, or murders, that surround this property," he said with a hard glare. "So, you've been in the attic, from the evidence on your clothing. What have you found?"

She didn't even know how to begin. She wasn't sure she had a choice here. She upped the wattage of her glare. She only needed another hour, and then she'd be done. Darn him anyways.

He laughed.

"Do you have a warrant?" she argued but without any heat.

"Do I need one?" he asked, frustration rippling through his voice.

"I just figured I'd go through it all first. If I found something, I would let you know."

He grabbed her shoulder. "Stop." He gave her a little shake. "Just think about what you are doing. Remember this is a murder investigation? Everything you find concerning this case is information I need to know."

With the animals milling around their legs and generally getting in the way, she slammed the front door shut, put her hands on her hips and said, "I found some boxes in the attic. But I've barely looked through them all yet."

He snorted. "Oh, no. I want to see exactly what you found."

She ran to the staircase and stood on the bottom step, arms across her chest. "Only if I let you. You don't have the right to go upstairs and see what I found."

He picked her up at the waist, turned and put her down beside him. "I can get a warrant if you want. And that'll be nasty because then more officers will come through and make a mess of this place, and they won't care that it was Nan's special possessions or that anything here might be of value to you in one way or another. And the more you try to hide something from me, the more pissed off I get." He glared at her. "Do you understand me?"

She groaned, closed her eyes and said, "Why do you have such crappy timing? I was just getting to the good stuff." She snuck past him and ran up the stairs with him hard on her heels.

"What did you find?"

"Jeremy Feldspar's clothing."

"What?" he roared.

She laughed and darted toward the spare room almost tripping on Mugs as he tried to run past her. "They were all neatly folded and stored in boxes upstairs in the attic. And then I found a box of books with his name on the inside of each one, and I'm down to the last two boxes now."

"Anything interesting in the clothing?" he asked in a hard voice. "I want to see it all. Not just what you think I should see."

She shook her head. At the door to the spare bedroom, she stopped. "So far there hasn't been anything interesting, just little bits of money, little bits of paper, business cards. I went through the clothing pretty intently, and I didn't see anything that had any information pertaining to his death or his life." She pushed open the door, stepped inside and pointed to the boxes on the far side of the room that she had gone through and packed up again. Mugs took advantage of the wider doorway and jumped to retake his spot on the bed beside Goliath who opened one eye then closed it and continued his nap.

"Feel free to look. Everything here on the bed and in that small bowl is what I found in the pockets of his clothes." She turned and pointed to the dresser. "That bowl is tidbits from Nan's clothing. I kept it separate."

He studied the stack of packed-up boxes, turned to look at the bowl in the center of the bed, breezed through its contents—the couple of business cards and some coins—picked up the notepad and realized it was more a shopping list. "Are you sure you checked each item of clothing carefully?"

She nodded. "Those boxes against the wall are clothing, but feel free to help yourself. The last box was full of coats."

He walked over to them, opened the flaps on one of the boxes and pulled out a jacket. He held it up, looked at the style and said, "Definitely older-style clothing."

She nodded. "From the eighties maybe."

"How long has Nan lived here?"

"Since forever. She mentioned being here forty years. But I really don't know the exact year she bought this place. You'd have to ask her."

She watched as he pulled the pockets inside out, and then he did something unusual. He scrunched up the bottom of the jacket, as if looking for something inside the lining. He put the jacket down, pulled out another one and did the exact same thing.

She shrugged and opened the box in front of her. But then he walked over to the light of the window and held the jacket upside down. She walked closer and asked, "What did you find?"

"Something inside the lining."

He turned the jacket inside out and found the seam that had been opened and sewn shut again. He pulled a knife from his pants pocket, quickly cut the stitches, and reached inside.

When he pulled out a sheet of paper, she gasped and said, "Oh my. Somebody went to a lot of trouble to hide that."

He tossed her a hard gaze. "Most killers often do."

"That makes no sense. He was the victim. So why would he go through all the trouble to hide this?"

Mack carefully unfolded the paper. Together they could both see a simple number and also an address.

He glanced at her and she shook her head. "I don't know that address or the number."

He pulled out his phone, punched the address into Google Maps, and it instantly brought up the location—a building in downtown Kelowna. "It's a bank on Bernard Street. And that other number is likely to be his bank account number."

"Or somebody else's account number or a safe-deposit box," she said. "Oh, I found a key." She walked to the bowl and brought it and its contents back to where Mack stood at the window. The key sat among the coins. She picked it up and handed it to him.

He nodded, resting it firmly in his hand and said, "This

is where I'm heading first." He glanced at the box she'd just opened, stepped toward it, looked inside to see books and knickknacks. "I want you to stop right now. I want you to leave this room and not come back in here until I return." When she didn't answer, he added, "Do you hear me?" He glared at her.

She stuck her chin out at him and then considered his point. She'd tossed the suits off as not being of any more value, but he had found something epic that she'd missed.

Her shoulders sagged, and she nodded. "I'll wait for you to come back." She warned, "But I want to be here to go through this with you."

He smiled at her as they headed downstairs. "Put on a pot of coffee, and I'll be back in an hour." He walked out the front door. Mugs milled around on the porch then came inside to slump on the floor beside her.

She watched him get into his vehicle and drive away. Would Mack make it back in an hour? Didn't he need a warrant to access that safe-deposit box? Mack was a good ten minutes away from the bank. So twenty minutes to make the round trip alone. That left him forty minutes, including stopping off to get a warrant first, if needed, and then time at the bank.

If she stayed out of the spare room until Mack returned, he'd be more willing to share his findings with her. Yet, who knew what else she might find elsewhere upstairs while Mack was at the bank?

She walked into the kitchen, washed her hands and splashed some water on her face. Afterward she patted her face dry and wiped her hands on a small towel before putting on a pot of coffee. While he was gone, she made herself a quick sandwich. Her mind was consumed with what could possibly be inside Jeremy's safe-deposit box.

When the phone rang ten minutes later, she knew who it was. "I knew you wouldn't be back in an hour."

Mack's voice came through the phone, hard, clear, concise. "I won't be back for the rest of the afternoon. This led to something quite interesting, and I must chase it down. I'm calling to remind you that no way in hell are you to go back in that room. If you don't give me that promise right now, I will send over a series of officers to collect all that stuff."

She glared into the phone. "I already said I wouldn't." Her voice turned crafty. "Are you going to tell me what you found?

"No," he snapped. "At least not right now. I'll get there as soon as I can."

He hung up, and she put her cell phone on the kitchen table, finishing the rest of her sandwich while deep in thought. Nobody knew the man was actually dead, right? Not for sure. Unless it was the murderer. Not without a body, correct? He was deemed legally dead after he was missing for seven years. What did Jeremy Feldspar have to do with the man in the garden?

It made no sense.

She stood to pour herself a cup of coffee. Facing the table again, she saw Goliath walking along the tabletop, helping himself to the bits of ham and cheese there.

And Thaddeus was busy throwing crumbs to Mugs on the floor.

She smiled. Somehow her trio of furry, fluffy, and feathered friends had become a family.

And her sneaky family knew the exact second when she had turned her back on her food.

Chapter 23

NOT KNOWING HOW much time she had before Mack
returned, she grabbed her coffee and led the way to
the spare room, with her three-animal family following close
behind. She stood in the doorway of the spare bedroom,
remembering her promise. No matter how she looked at it,
she couldn't go in there.

So the boxes would have to come out. Craftily, she studied the layout of the room, then went downstairs and outside
to the back garden where she snatched up the hoe and raced
back upstairs. Those last couple boxes were just close enough
that she could snag them with the hoe and drag them over to
the doorway.

"Ha," she cried out with the flush of success. Now she
could go over the boxes' contents and not break her promise.
Quickly she sorted through the remaining two boxes. They
contained collections of souvenirs, photographs, books, even
an odd pair of shoes tucked on top of everything else. As if
there was no room for them anywhere else. The second box
contained only shoes.

She went through each box, looking for something that
would identify what had happened to Jeremy but found

nothing here. At least nothing *she* could find. Mack might have an entirely different view on that. She put the photos off to one side and stacked the boxes together on another side.

She'd cleaned out the attic but maybe Mack would want to go up on his own, and that was fine with her. He might see something she'd missed.

Back downstairs again she looked at the photos under the bright kitchen light. Names and dates were on the back, like *Rose '79*, and *Jeremy and Tom '76*. All of them appeared to be in their forties back at the time these pictures were taken. Nothing was more recent than 1982, and she didn't recognize any of the people in the images, although the name *Jeremy* sure rang a bell. Possibly Tom and Rose were his siblings. Their approximate ages would seem appropriate for that.

And, if this Jeremy in the 1976 photo was the man who later disappeared in 1988, he would have been about fifty to sixty years old at the time he was last seen, or some eighty to ninety years old today. That put Jeremy roughly in the same age bracket as Nan.

There didn't appear to be any photos of Nan. Doreen didn't know if that was a good thing or a bad thing. She was rather desperate to clear Nan of all wrongdoings. But it was still a little hard to understand how all this stuff had come to be here.

She wanted to go to the library. She glanced at her watch. She wouldn't sit here and wait for Mack. He'd said he wouldn't make it back that afternoon anyway. Surely he would have no problem with her running to the library, looking up any information on this Jeremy Feldspar.

She snatched up her car keys and purse and ran outside,

locking the animals in. "I won't be long," she called out to Mugs.

She turned on the engine and quickly backed out the driveway. She still had boxes of clothes to drop off. She'd have to fit that into her day too. As she swept past the neighbor's house, she saw Cindy waving at her. She caught sight of her too late to react with a wave of her own, and she wasn't sure she wanted to either. Something was very odd about that couple. Was there such a thing as too much sunshine in someone's world?

With all the supposed neighbors forming a crowd in front of her house, few had introduced themselves to Doreen. Just the too-happy couple, Cindy and Josh. Oh, yeah, and Ella had earlier. But Doreen hadn't seen Ella since their first encounter. That was a shame because Ella was at least normal.

At the library, Doreen walked into the massive new-looking building, and, with the librarian's help, she was quickly set up, looking at the old records on microfiche. She went back to the early '70s, the same years as documented in the photos, searching for anything on Jeremy Feldspar in the newspapers.

Then she did a search for her grandmother, from approximately age twenty—her Nan wasn't exactly forthcoming about her actual age—until Jeremy went missing, so covering the thirty years from about 1958 to 1988. She found the odd mention of Nan, who was always very active in community events. So her name came up a couple times. But never in relation to Jeremy. The only time Doreen saw Jeremy's name was in an article about a court case, where he was suspected of killing his mother in the 70s, as mentioned in the newspaper clipping found in the

envelope taped under the spare bed. She read this article thoroughly, just in case it had any additional information. But it appeared to be a rehash of the same material.

She searched other newspapers, hoping to find other mentions of him. But found very little. Back then the local newspaper ran more human-interest stories.

She looked through the rest of the years—the 1970s and early 1980s—but she didn't find anything more on Jeremy or her grandmother. Doreen closed down the machine, picked up her notepad and went to the librarian. "Excuse me. Are there any other resources that would allow me to track down somebody here?"

"Did you check the obituaries?" asked the librarian, Linda Linket, according to her name tag. "We do have a long list of those."

With the librarian's help, Doreen brought up the obituary list and checked through the late eighties and into the late nineties, but no mention of Jeremy was found anywhere.

After thanking the librarian, she got in her vehicle and returned home. As she pulled up, she saw Mack pounding on her front door.

She got out and said, "It's only common sense, but if my vehicle is not here, I'm not here." She climbed the front porch steps to join him.

He glared at her. "Why weren't you here?"

"Because I was at the library, looking for information on Jeremy Feldspar."

He fisted his hands on his hips, and his glare didn't diminish one bit.

She glared back as she unlocked her front door and let him inside. "You can rest easy," she said. "I didn't find anything. And how stupid is that?"

"What did you expect to find? A line saying, *Jeremy Feldspar was murdered by your neighbors?*"

She shot him a look and said in a dark voice, "You wouldn't joke about that if you had met them." She headed to the kitchen, scooping up Goliath as she went. She gave him a great big hug and a cuddle and placed him on the kitchen table. She had left the coffeemaker on. She stared at it and wondered if that was a fire hazard, then shrugged. She hadn't been killed by it yet. She refilled her coffee cup, filling one for Mack. She turned to look at him. "What did you find?"

In a cool voice he said, "Remember this is police business, and it's confidential?"

She stared at him in outrage. "If you want any information from me, I give it to you." In a casual movement, she tossed her notepad on top of the photographs on the table. If he wasn't sharing, well, neither was she.

But she had never been any good at lying.

"What did you find?" he snapped.

She gave him an innocent look and smiled. "What makes you think I found anything?"

He snorted and settled into his chair. "You look guilty as hell."

When Thaddeus hopped up on the kitchen table, Goliath jumped down and stalked off. She stroked Thaddeus's feathered neck, but he cocked an eye at her and said, "Liar. Liar."

She glared at the bird. "I don't need any comments from the peanut gallery, thank you very much."

Mack leaned forward and glared at her. "What did you find?"

She leaned forward and shoved her face into his. "None

of your business."

He let out an exasperated sigh. "Are we back to that again? You really want me to get a warrant, search this place from top to bottom?"

"It might be best," she said. "I keep finding stuff. I don't know if I found all of it or just part of it."

"What did you find? You went through the rest of those boxes, didn't you?" he roared. "After you promised not to go back in there."

She gave him a flat stare and said, "I didn't go in. I pulled the boxes out into the hallway."

He snorted.

She lifted her chin. "Besides, no harm done. They were mostly full of shoes."

"Both?"

"The other was mostly full of knickknacks."

"Anything else?" he asked suspiciously.

Just then Thaddeus walked between the two of them. He gave her that look again, as if waiting for her to open her mouth. She glared at the bird. "You don't know anything."

He made a funny cuckooing sound. She had never heard it come out of him before. Then he did it again. The bird constantly surprised her.

"If only that bird could really talk," Mack said, "I imagine he would have quite the story to tell."

"Especially since so many activities would've been done in and around him while he was here. He would've seen and known what was going on," she admitted.

"Like what you've done today?" Mack snapped. "So, give."

But he was still withholding anything about what he had found in Jeremy's safe-deposit box or about his account at the bank. She opened her mouth when Thaddeus fixed her with that odd glare of his. She raised both hands in surrender. "I can't keep any secrets from that dratted bird. He's against me."

She glared at the two of them, and both just stared back at her.

"Fine." She looked at the notepad and used it to push the photographs toward Mack. "These were inside the second box."

"Photographs," he noted. "Anything of value?"

"I was going to let you have them and decide."

He shot her a look that confirmed he understood her a little more than she liked. He spread out the images carefully, picking one up at a time, studying the features of the people in each photo. He read the names and dates on the back before placing each one down again.

"Before you ask, no, I don't know any of the faces, considering those photos were taken before I was born. And the only name I recognize is *Jeremy*, for obvious reasons."

He nodded. "What if Nan does?"

Doreen shrugged. "I don't know any of the landmarks in the images. For all I know, these could've been taken in Europe."

"I doubt it," he said. "Some of these are from the city beach in Kelowna."

"How can you tell? It could've been any beach anywhere as far as I'm concerned." She sat back and sipped her coffee. "By the way, did you check out my neighbors concerning the body in my back garden?"

He lifted his head and pierced her with that hard gaze of his. "What about your neighbors?"

"It's silly." She shrugged. "But that one couple is just so

dang happy."

That startled a grin out of him. "Is your world so dark you can't appreciate other people being happy?"

"No, they were *too* happy. *Too* bright. *Too* cheerful. *Too* ingratiating. It's not like they came by before, like the other lady—Ella, I believe her name was. She was at least normal."

"You've barely been here three days yet. Isn't there a rule about waiting at least seventy-two hours after a newcomer moves in before you welcome him to the neighborhood? So they have a chance to settle in, unpack some boxes?"

She shot him a flat stare. "I have no idea. Are there rules for things like this?"

"I wouldn't doubt it." He chuckled. "But just because they were extremely friendly, it doesn't make them killers."

"I know," she said morosely. "So far, they are the only ones who were over-the-top friendly."

"Were you friendly back? Did you bring them inside and have tea, spend an hour with them socializing?" He studied her and then shook his head. "Of course not. You probably stayed in the doorway, not even letting them get comfortable on the front porch."

"If I knew there were rules about things like that," she snapped, "then I might have. How was I supposed to know there was a right and wrong way to handle neighbors who were just too darn happy to be comfortable around?"

He stared at her, then despite himself, he laughed. "You might want to consider how that would've been a good way to get information from them. Information about whether Jeremy had ever been here. Information about strangers around the house lately." He settled back after looking at the last picture. "They might have answered your questions. When the police question the neighbors, the officers tend to get those lovely noncommittal kinds of answers. *But,* when a neighbor questions neighbors, well, that's a whole different story."

She stared at him in surprise and with a growing realization. "Well, consider me about to get friendly with my neighbors."

Thaddeus spoke up right then, once again repeating his earlier lines. "Liar. Liar."

It was a heck of a position to be in when even the bird knew her so well.

Chapter 24

Day 4, Saturday

THE NEXT MORNING, Doreen walked out to the garden, considering what to do next. Yesterday had been eventful, but she had just begun to dig into the Jeremy Feldspar case and didn't want to let it go. Checking out the neighbors should be high on her list. But how to approach the problem?

Thaddeus hadn't called her a liar again—then she hadn't lied to anyone since Mack left. It was stupid to let the bird motivate her actions since she was happy to convince herself she was doing this for Nan. Which she really was. The last thing Doreen wanted was to see her beautiful sweet grandmother accused of murder.

Doreen walked out to the garden, where she'd seen several decent flowers. With gloves on and clippers in hand, she carefully cut off a dozen blooms and walked around to the tulips and picked several long stems. She was delighted to see them still flowering.

When she had a collection of cut flowers, she went back inside, grabbed some of the ribbons she'd seen in her grandma's gardening cupboard and made several small bouquets. She planned to walk the neighborhood along the cul-de-sac and at least introduce herself and share some of Nan's garden flowers. Surely that couldn't go over wrong.

She collected the first bouquet and walked to the house on the left. She went up to the front door and knocked. Knowing not everyone loved animals she'd elected to leave the trio at home.

An older gentleman opened the front door and glared at her. "What the hell do you want?"

She studied his face and wondered if she'd seen him in the gawking crowd outside her place. He looked familiar. She glanced at the flowers in her hands. Maybe tulips weren't exactly the best thing to give to a single male. But she was already committed. In a cheerful voice she said, "I wanted to introduce myself. I'm Doreen. Nan is my grandmother, and I'm now living in her house, next door." She handed over the flowers. "These are for you. They are from Nan's garden."

He refused to take the flowers. Instead he crossed his arms, and his demeanor did not change in the least as he stared at her. "And why would I want anything to do with you? Since you moved into the neighborhood, it's gone to hell."

She tamped down her temper. "I hardly had anything to do with that, as I just arrived," she pointed out quietly. "And Nan hasn't been here either for the last few weeks."

"Still, all the police cars coming and going—this used to be a nice neighborhood."

With her hand still out, holding the flowers toward him, she felt foolish. But she still needed information. "Well, at least you could tell me your name, so I can recognize you in the future."

In a hesitant voice he said, "I'm Richard de Genaro."

"And you live here alone?" she prompted.

The wattage of his glare beefed up. "Not that it's any of your business, but my wife lives here with me."

"Oh, lovely. What's her name?" She wanted to back up and run away from the ire that he turned on her.

"Her name is Sicily," he said grudgingly.

She shoved the flowers against his hands and said, "Good. You can give these to Sicily." Figuring she had pushed her luck as far she could, she said, "It was nice to meet you, Richard." And she walked down steps.

She could feel his eyes boring into her back as she walked to her front door. Inside, she slowly closed the door and leaned against it. "Mugs, if you think that was easy, it was not. Next time I have to visit him, I'm taking you. Surely everybody loves dogs."

She walked over to her notepad and wrote down Richard and Sicily de Genaro and their address. That was a hard mouthful. On the other hand, that should also make it easier to find more information about them online because their names were so unique, although each could have multiple spellings. But his attitude had been surly, and he certainly looked like he was quite happy to murder anybody who crossed him. She added Ella and Josh and Cindy to her sheet.

She tucked her little notepad and pencil into her pocket and grabbed the second bunch of flowers, knowing that the surly man would probably be watching her as she walked to the second house on the left. There were six houses in the cul-de-sac, and she planned to hit all of the ones whose owners she had yet to meet.

At the second door, she could hear dogs barking like

crazy inside. A young woman opened the door, looking harried and upset. Two small Maltese looking dogs ran around everyone in a frenzy of barking. The woman held a young child with a reddened scrunched—up face in her arm, which explained why the mother looked like she was having a bad day.

Doreen bent to say hi to the dogs. In a gentle voice, she introduced herself. "I'm the new neighbor. Doreen. Nan is my grandmother, and I moved into her house. I just wanted to stop by and say hi."

The young mother smiled nervously. She glanced out-side, looked over at Nan's house and back again to her. "Nice to meet you. It's been so crazy here since you moved in."

Doreen placed her hand over her chest. "Oh, my good-ness, has it ever. Who knew I'd move into my house and find a body in the backyard?"

The woman shook her head. In a gossipy manner, she leaned forward and said, "Do you know who it is?"

Doreen shook her head. "The police aren't talking. I imagine they've been around to talk to you already, but, outside of collecting as much evidence as they needed, I haven't gotten any information from them."

Disappointment settled on the young woman's face. "Same with me," she said. "I tried to ask them some ques-tions when they came here, but they were pretty closemouthed about the whole issue."

Doreen laughed. "Which just means that everybody in the neighborhood knows already."

The young mother smiled. "Especially Ella Goldman. I'm Brenda, by the way. And this little one here, who's got a bit of a cold and is feeling pretty rough, is Cara. She'll feel better when her daddy gets home from running errands."

Much happier with this meeting, Doreen held out the flowers, letting Cara grab them. "These are from Nan's garden. I thought maybe you would appreciate some fresh— cut flowers."

Brenda smiled at the flowers, then back at Doreen. "Normally I'd invite you in, but she's having such a rough morning."

"Oh, dear, don't worry about it," Doreen said. "I'm just making the effort to introduce myself to everybody."

"You haven't seen my son, Travis, today, have you? I can't keep track of that boy."

Doreen shook her head, frowning.

"He said he met you Thursday. He was up a tree."

"Oh, yes, I did. But I haven't seen him yet today."

"He'll show up for meals. Is that Cindy in your side yard?" she asked, peering around the corner. "I thought I just saw her over on your place earlier." Then she laughed. "I thought I saw Richard, your other neighbor, in your yard a few days ago too. Although he might have been after the dog's ball again. You never see the dog, but Richard often throws the ball over his fence." She shrugged. "No clue what Cindy was doing back there, although Nan used to always share her perennials when it was time to divide them in the fall. She might have been looking to see what perennials Nan had…"

Doreen turned to check but didn't see anybody. "Really? Cindy? Richard?" She couldn't imagine why they'd be in Nan's yard. Still, there wasn't any problem with them being there, particularly if Brenda was right about their reasons.

"Ella lives in that far house, but she was looking along your back fence line. Not sure why she'd be there," Brenda

said, pointing. "But it has been interesting around here, right?"

"It was pretty rough for my first three days here," Doreen admitted, peering into her side yard but couldn't see any sign of Ella. "I don't want people to get the wrong idea about me."

"Oh, my goodness, no. Although we're certainly very curious about what's going on."

As Doreen turned to go, she fostered a bright smile. "As am I." With a little wave at the sick girl, Doreen stepped down the stairs and called out, "Bye now. It was nice meeting you."

Brenda lifted the little girl's hand and waved. She called to the dogs, "Salt and Pepper, get back here. Come on inside."

Back at her house, Doreen sat and wrote down Brenda, Travis, and Cara. She hadn't gotten their last name, had no idea who the husband was, or what he did for a living. She frowned at that. How would she get a second excuse to find out more information? Public records most likely?

Still, she had gotten something, so, if Mack wanted to help, he could probably give her all that information too.

Determined to get this done, she grabbed her third bouquet and walked to the third house on the left. She knocked and waited. Not a sound inside, not a sound outside. The yard was pristine. Either the owners certainly spent a lot of time keeping their garden immaculate or they hired a company to do it. Doreen was impressed regardless.

When she rang the doorbell again, and there was still no answer so she walked back down the steps. Taking a chance, she crossed the cul-de-sac and went to the house at the far side. No point in going home with these flowers if she didn't need to.

It was Ella's house and a good way to see if she was home or skulking around in the back of Doreen's yard. Ella, she was lovely but chatty. As soon as she opened the door, she was off and running.

"Oh, my goodness, I'm delighted you stopped by. It's my day off," the woman gushed. "Nan was such sweetheart. I used to help her with her gardening all the time. I was over there a little bit ago, checking to see how bad it had gotten."

"Nan *is* a sweetheart," Doreen corrected, wondering if Brenda had been wrong about the identity of the person in the backyard. And did it even matter? "She's quite happy and healthy, living at the retirement home not too far from here."

"Oh, good. I should probably walk over and visit with her one day," Ella said. "She was always so full of stories and had such a great sense of humor. And, of course, she set up those betting pools." She shook her head and laughed. "My husband told me, after I lost ten dollars to her one day, to never sign up for one of them again." She held the door open wider. "Do you want to come in and have a nice cup of tea?"

Doreen hesitated and was tempted, but she wasn't exactly sure how that would fit in with her plans. Then she had no choice, as Ella grabbed her arm and tugged her forward.

"Don't be shy. This whole neighborhood is one big family."

And that gave Doreen an opportunity she hadn't expected. "I've been trying to meet a few of them. What can you tell me about the people here?"

Obviously that was the right question. Soon she was seated at the kitchen table, and Ella was bustling about, turning on the teakettle, making a pot of fresh tea. In the meantime, she talked. And talked. And talked.

Apparently Mr. de Genaro used to be in politics. He thought he was above everybody now, even though he was retired. But honestly, according to Ella, he'd been forced out of politics, with a little bit of a shady background in his history. His wife was a sweetheart though. How she ever got stuck with that old prude, Ella didn't know.

And then of course, there was Brenda and her baby. And she had a womanizing husband, Ned. Nasty old guy. Fifteen years her senior and she was his second wife. But Brenda was just a lovely little sweetheart.

The people on the far end were rich snobs. But they were okay when you got to know them. "In the meantime, don't expect them to be friendly," Ella cautioned her.

"So far, I haven't found too many people to be all that friendly," Doreen admitted. "Then again, the events after I arrived wouldn't exactly make anybody overjoyed."

Ella sat down, excitement lighting up her features. "Maybe. This place was boring until you showed up." She laughed.

"Unfortunately I found a finger on my first day here, just a few days ago," Doreen said. "I was supposed to be here earlier because Nan moved out three weeks ago."

Ella shook her head. "True. She was busy setting up her new life. So she wasn't here very much. This community needs somebody like Nan. And I must admit, the last year she hasn't been her usual self. She wasn't doing anywhere near the same amount of betting pools and didn't look as lively." Ella leaned back, her gaze studying Doreen, and added, "Honestly you injected some excitement to this place. And loads of fun."

Doreen silently questioned Ella's definition of *fun*.

Chapter 25

BY THE TIME Doreen finally freed herself from her chatty neighbor, Ella, and returned home, hours had passed, but Doreen definitely knew a lot more about the community. Still not anything pertinent to the case though. Unsettled and full of questions, she decided to walk to Nan's and ask her some more questions—especially about her betting activities. It was very convenient to have her grandmother just a few blocks away. Doreen had to admit to looking forward to the walk.

She put Mugs on a leash, admonished Goliath to get into no trouble while inside alone, then asked Thaddeus, "Do you want to go for a walk?"

Mugs started barking.

Thaddeus called out, "Walk. Walk." His head bobbed up and down and side to side. He jumped onto Mugs's back as she opened the door and locked it behind them.

Halfway to the retirement home, she realized she should probably call before visiting. Maybe Nan had company or had gone out shopping. Doreen quickly grabbed her phone from her purse and called her grandmother. "If you're not busy, I'm coming for tea."

Nan laughed. "Oh, I do like having you close by. I see more of you now than I think I've seen you in your entire lifetime."

Doreen winced. As a reminder of how little time she had spent with her grandmother overall, it was potent.

When she reached Nan's place, Doreen saw Nan carrying the teapot outside for them already. Nan straightened and waved. Doreen and her lively duo walked over and she took a seat at the little table. Mugs lay down at her feet. Thaddeus hopped onto the table and right up Nan's arm. He crooned and rubbed against her cheek.

Stroking his feathers, Nan beamed at her. "This is just lovely. After all the commotion this morning, this is exactly what I needed."

"What commotion?"

Nan shook her head. "Oh, I don't want to bother you."

"What commotion, Nan? I haven't heard anything about it yet." Doreen glanced around. "I thought I saw a cop car in the parking lot, but that could be for any number of reasons here."

"A man went for a walk and didn't come back," Nan said with relish.

"Oh, dear." Despite herself, Doreen winced. The last thing she wanted was the reminder of dead bodies. Her garden still looked like crap, compliments of the last officers who had come to her house. She glanced around. "Is he forgetful? Maybe he just got lost?"

"Around here, anything's possible." Nan patted her hand. "You're a sweetheart, but don't worry about him. He probably won't be back."

Doreen looked sharply at Nan. "What did you say?"

Nan looked confused for a moment, then added, "I'm

sure he'll be back."

Slightly unsettled because Doreen was darn sure that wasn't what Nan had said originally and not knowing why she had said it, Doreen sat back slightly and waited for her grandmother to talk. Perhaps her original wording was a simple mistake. She couldn't know that the old man wouldn't be home anymore.

Could she?

Still worried, Doreen asked carefully, "I presume a search party is out looking for him?"

"Oh, yes. The police are looking for him, and his family is looking too, I should imagine." And she gave Doreen the sweetest, blankest look ever.

Doreen frowned, a shudder rippling inside. Had Nan declined mentally all of a sudden, or was she just preoccupied? And how to tell? "What is his name? Was the man a resident?"

"Oh, no. Robert was a workman here. Nicest man. Always came in to talk to me. Had such lovely stories about the different places he worked in."

An ugly suspicion arose. "Did he mention your house, or ask you anything about what might be in your house?"

Nan looked at her in surprise. "Well, of course we talked about my house. It's not in the heritage zone of Kelowna, but my house has all kinds of unique things about it. Plus I'd lived there for so long."

Nan gave Doreen that breathtaking smile of innocence again that both made Doreen feel better and worse.

"Did he ever work on your deck or in the attic?"

Nan shrugged. "Not that I remember."

Doreen waited, but Nan added nothing further. So Doreen asked again, "But he worked on your deck?"

Nan paused, deep in thought. "He might have built the deck originally, but I don't remember for sure. Why?"

Doreen stared at the grass. Mugs slept at her feet while Thaddeus paced across the table, once again looking for scraps of things to eat. "No reason."

"We talked lots over the years. He's a very nice man."

Doreen nodded. "I'm sorry that he's missing."

Nan said in a very cheerful voice, "I'm sure he'll show up, or at least his body will in a few days."

"You think he's dead?" Doreen asked in a strangled voice.

"He's not here. He's not at home, and he didn't go to work." Nan shrugged. "Sounds like he might be dead."

Glumly Doreen had to admit her grandmother was right. That was often the case. "Well, if he's an older man, then that's possible," she said.

"Oh, dear. No, he's not old. Not even forty yet, I don't think."

Knowing she couldn't handle more of this conversation, Doreen determinedly shifted it to her discussion about the neighbors. "I went around to introduce myself to the neighbors today. Met three more people."

Nan beamed. "Aren't they lovely?"

"Some of them appear to be, yes. Some are talkative. Some are secretive. And some never seem to be home."

"That's people though. No matter where you go, you get a mix of them all." She picked up her tea and gave her granddaughter a sweet smile once again. "You'll fit right in."

"Finding a body didn't make for an easy introduction to the community," she admitted.

"Nonsense. The place is dull and boring. It added some excitement to the area."

"You sure you have no idea who killed him?"

Nan's gaze twinkled at Doreen over the teacup. "No, not at all." She leaned forward. "Do you?"

"No, of course not. I just got into the house. Nan, he was killed several days ago, if not weeks ago. He was killed while you were in the process of moving here, if not before."

"That's so sad." She sipped her tea again and put it back on the saucer. "I was very busy in the days and weeks before this move, and if I wasn't packing up things to bring with me here, I was in my front room watching the telly. Anything could've gone on in the backyard. I wouldn't have known about that."

"Or did you just not want to tell anybody about it?" Doreen leaned forward. "You do know that it's illegal to withhold any information from the police about a case? And it's also illegal to bury a body, even if you didn't kill the person?"

Nan's gaze widened. "Of course I didn't know that. Why would I know that? It's not like I have anything to do with dead bodies. Besides, sweetie, you were living at the house when the body was found." She shook her finger at Doreen. "Make sure you're not involved."

The conversation was making less and less sense and seemed to be sliding more and more off to the side of ridiculous. Doreen worried about her grandmother. "Have you made any friends here?" She was trying to be objective and to change the subject.

"Lots. Several of them are very interested in my hobby."

Doreen perked up. "Now that is good. What hobby are you talking about?"

She smirked. "You know what the hobby is. I had to stop for a long time. But I'm happy to say that I'm playing again."

Doreen cast her mind back and forth as she tried to remember any of Nan's hobbies from the last several decades. But she kept coming up blank. "Why was it you stopped again?"

Nan gave her a droll look. "The police didn't like it."

Doreen stared at her and then remembered Ella's recent words. Doreen closed her eyes and groaned. "Nan, you're gambling again?"

"No, of course not. It's just betting pools. Little stuff, you know? Fun stuff. It's not illegal. I already talked to the cops about it."

"Gambling is bad. Gambling is bad," Thaddeus intoned.

"Oh dear," Nan cried out staring at the now preening bird. "What are you teaching him?"

"Nothing. He picks stuff up all the time. Back to the point, it wasn't illegal before either, or so you told me, years ago I thought," Doreen said. "Why would you do this again?"

"I'm very good at it."

And again into such a bizarre conversation. Doreen leaned forward and asked, "Nan, what are you talking about? There was no need for the police to even know about your gambling before. Unless you were doing something illegal."

"I got in trouble because I was *disruptive* at the casino," she said. "I did have a temper back then, and everyone felt I had a problem. So I had to stop. I'm still not sorry I kicked that man though."

Doreen sat back in shock. "I don't think you ever told me the details about that."

"What can I say? He accused me of cheating, but he was the one cheating. You have to watch out for Walter White.

He owns the hardware store on Springfield. Definitely the sort to stay away from." Nan shrugged. "It's all good now. Besides, everybody should get arrested at least once in their life."

Doreen stared at Nan, shocked.

Her grandmother picked up a cookie from the plate on the table and broke off a piece then broke it again to place small pieces on the table. "Thaddeus here was a godsend. I got him soon after I was arrested. He made me realize just how much I had to change. But that was years ago, my dear. And the loan sharks were really very nice. One of them was sweet on me. Basil Champs. I do love that man."

Oh, my God. Nan had borrowed money from loan sharks? It was much worse than Doreen imagined. Nan's wording and that soft tone of hers had Doreen wondering at this new side to her Nan. She'd always seen her Nan as a sweet old lady. Now it seemed *sweet* wasn't as correct as maybe the term *colorful.* And did she go to the loan shark Basil out of need or out of want? Doreen wondered just how well she knew her grandmother.

"So, if all that was bad, why would you start gambling again now?"

"Well, because I'm not really gambling. It's just betting pools. It's fun."

"So, no real money is involved?" Doreen asked cautiously. "And what kind of stuff are you actually betting on?"

"How long before Robert's body shows up."

Doreen winced. How completely insensitive. "If the police hear about that, they might think you have some insider knowledge that he's dead."

"Of course they will." She gave a crafty grin, taking another piece of cookie and popping it into her mouth. "And the second betting pool is how long before the police solve the case."

"Oh, boy." Doreen shook her head. She stared at her grandmother in fascination. She was learning so much new information about her only living relative. Some of it was a little disturbing. But it *was* like Nan had a whole new lease on life. As if she figured she was too old to pay for the consequences and was just out to have fun. "It almost sounds like you're courting trouble, Nan."

"Not really. I'm harmless. Besides, nobody looks at us old people. Nobody thinks we're constructive or destructive elements. It's kind of irritating."

"I can imagine," Doreen said, her voice soft. "But still, do you want to spend the rest of your years in jail?"

Nan sat back with a thoughtful look on her face. "Only if it was in one of those nice jails. Of course most of them are nice. Especially in Canada. Now some of them in the States, that's a different story. Some of those are rough." She picked up her teacup again. "Would you still visit me there, my dear?"

"Yes, I would still visit, but I don't know how often. It's not like we have a jail close by."

"There is one a few hours away."

"How about you just don't get into trouble to that extent, and you can stay here and have fun with all your friends?"

"Oh, I intend to do just that." She held out a small piece of cookie in her hand. "Did you want some of this?"

Doreen looked at the big piece of cookie on her grandmother's plate and the tiny piece in her hand. "Just give that piece to Thaddeus."

Happily Nan obliged.

"Have you been eating well here?"

"I've been eating just wonderfully. These are Charlie's cookies." She leaned forward and whispered, "He put some of that green stuff in them, you know?"

Doreen's heart stopped and then raced ahead. "Green stuff?" she asked cautiously leaning forward to brush Thaddeus back from the crumbs he was inhaling.

"Yes, they're healthy cookies. He grows the green stuff in his backyard. I have to admit, when I eat them, I feel really good."

Doreen stared openmouthed as her grandmother snapped off another piece of the marijuana cookie and popped it into her mouth. Good Lord, what had gotten into her grandmother now that she lived at Rosemoor?

Chapter 26

HEADING BACK HOME again, Doreen took a different and longer route. Mugs could use the walk, and she could distract herself from her bizarre visit with Nan as Doreen's mind worried on all the little bits and pieces of seemingly unrelated information on the two dead men related to Nan's house that Doreen had gathered from her neighbors.

As for Nan's penchant for marijuana cookies, Doreen couldn't even begin to think about that and shoved it to the back recesses of her mind.

She also couldn't imagine Nan having anything to do with this murder mess, but unless some better evidence showed up, Nan was the most obvious suspect. How depressing was that?

And her two betting pools regarding the missing man, Robert, made her even more suspicious.

Doreen would normally have crossed the river on the small bridge, but she headed the other way, staying on the city-street blocks, going through town and then coming alongside the creek. It was a slow sojourn home letting Mugs happily sniff the trail to his heart's content.

Thaddeus sat on her shoulder suspiciously quiet. She gave him several cautious looks but he appeared to be swaying gently to every movement.

As she stood on the creek pathway, studying the backs of the houses, she realized that this was the same creek leading to the little bridge behind her place also. Farther up was where she'd seen Brenda's boy in the tree on Thursday. She walked the path, hoping she was heading toward home. If so, she'd see her house in a few minutes. It was such a beautiful walk here with the birds and the sunshine. Quiet and peaceful. Up ahead she could see the houses on the cul-de-sac beside her cul-de-sac.

She was almost home.

With Thaddeus giving a running commentary of oddball noises as he sat on her shoulder and Mugs wandering from place to place, Doreen slowly meandered home. It was a different life here. Despite all that had happened since her arrival three days earlier on Wednesday, it was a good life. At least she hoped it would be.

The creek drifted slowly beside her. The water levels were low, but overall enough water kept things flowing smoothly and curbed the smell of wet mud. She was only about ten or maybe fifteen minutes away from Nan's place right now by traveling this route.

She stopped and studied the water. They were coming up to her cul-de-sac, as far she could tell.

Hmm. A pretty place to walk—particularly if someone wanted to stay hidden. Could someone have carried a body that distance?

It would be a heavy load. But a wheelbarrow would make it easier. She studied the ground to find it relatively smooth, without big logs to cross over. But still, it would be taking a heck of a chance of being discovered by pushing a dead body along here in a wheelbarrow. Even though all the properties on her side of the creek had been fenced off from this creek, Travis had been playing on the far side. So there were people around regardless.

Although someone might be seen from the back of the houses across the creek, especially from a second-floor advantage, still any witnesses would have to be looking specifically at the creek path to see this hypothetical wheelbarrow transporting a dead body.

She'd never seen anybody walking back there. But then she'd never been looking. And she had only been here three days, and each one had been pretty time-consuming.

A log was up ahead. She walked over and sat down, happy to enjoy the view in the sunshine. Mugs sniffed around her feet and then lay down beside her. She scratched his back. "Hey, buddy."

He huffed heavily, gave a small bark, then dropped his head on her foot.

"Yeah, you get to roam about, get muddy. It's a good life."

She sat, talking with the animals, lightly stroking Thaddeus's feathers. "We should have brought Goliath with us."

Mugs gave an odd kind of a noise and bolted to his feet. His nose faced upstream, his nostrils flaring. Then he barked. At what, she didn't know. She stared at him. "What's the matter, boy?"

He raced off, pulling on his leash.

She held on tighter and stood. "Okay, let's see what's bothering you."

She didn't have to go very far when she caught sight of something that had her stomach dropping to her feet. She walked closer to make sure, her phone already in her hand. She hit Mack's speed-dial number and waited until he answered.

"What's the matter, Doreen?"

She took a shaky breath. "I found another body."

After a stark silence on the other end, he exploded, "What?"

"I'm at the creek about one hundred yards—maybe fifty yards—from my house. About ten to fifteen minutes away from Nan's retirement home. Apparently a man went missing from there. I think this is him." She took two steps closer. "He's lying in the water. He looks like he's been here for a little while."

"Did you touch the body?"

She shivered. "No. I presume he's dead. I've been sitting on a log here for at least five minutes."

"Sitting?" Mack asked in surprise.

"Not beside the body," she cried out. "That would be terrible... and so very gross." She shook her head. "I was sitting on a log a few yards down the creek when Mugs barked. So I checked it out. The man's wearing jeans and a hoodie jacket, from the looks of it. I don't know. Maybe it's a runner's jacket. He has running shoes on." She turned to stare up the creek, then down a ways. "Maybe it's somebody else. I don't know."

"Don't touch the body. Stay right there. If I come to your house and go through the back gate, will I see you?"

"If you come to my house, go through the back gate and take a left, then carry on down the path, you can't miss me."

"Be there in ten."

She could still hear him on the line.

In a much harder voice he added, "Don't move."

This time she heard the audible *click* as he hung up from the call. She stared at the bright blue sky and sunshine. "Why me?"

Mugs, now that he understood where the smell came from, laid down at her side and proceeded to fall asleep.

Thaddeus, on the other hand, had a whole different thing to say. He stared over her head and screeched at the top of his voice, "Murder in the water. Murder in the water."

"Stop, you silly old bird. You want all the neighbors to know somebody's out here?"

Thaddeus crooned a sorrowful song. Almost like a keening, wailing song that she knew some aboriginal tribes sang for their dead. She looked at him in wonder. "You have hidden depths, Thaddeus. But could you possibly keep it down?" She stood protectively beside the body. Although if anybody else came along, she would look darn suspicious.

With her phone, she took several pictures of the body in the water and the area around it. And, because she had to wait anyway, she looked for any signs of what might have happened to him. Surely Mack would understand that much.

The dirt was a little bit scuffed up at the pathway, although no marks resembled wheelbarrow tracks. She quickly stepped back, took a few more pictures of the scuffled area and searched for a murder weapon. For all she knew, the guy committed suicide, or maybe he'd been drunk and fell in the creek and drowned.

She didn't find anything of interest. But it didn't stop her from taking lots of pictures. She walked up the pathway and took some more pictures, walked to the other side and took even more. She had no idea what she was looking for but figured he'd be up on the matter a little later. Right now she was just protecting the crime scene.

And, for added measure, she took as many pictures of the creek as she could. And the houses on the far side. Who knew if anybody heard or saw anything? This cul-de-sac wasn't where her house was. This was the adjoining one. She hadn't met any of these people yet. Of course, once everyone heard she had found *this* body, there would be no end to the chaos in her world. And the added notoriety to her as the newcomer.

She waited ten minutes, which stretched to fifteen, then to twenty. Just when pulling out her phone on the half-hour mark to call Mack and to give him crap for being so late, she heard a noise on the far side of the creek. She waited, her heart racing. It could be the murderer coming back—if the body in the creek had been murdered.

That didn't stop the thoughts from going through her head.

She kept watch nervously.

Suddenly Mack appeared in front of her. He took one look at her and nodded. "Good. You're still here. Where is the body?"

"I said I'd be here," she snapped, relieved he'd finally arrived. "I kept my word. You, on the other hand, are late." She pointed wordlessly at the creek. "The poor man is there."

They both stared at the man, floating face mostly down with just enough of his face showing to see his open eye, the dirt and water in his mouth. He pivoted to look at her. "Did you touch him?"

She shook her head. "No, you told me not to."

"Have you been standing here in this vicinity for the last ten minutes?"

"*Thirty* minutes. That's how long since I called you. And, yes, I have been here, walking this pathway. I was afraid somebody else would come before you did."

He nodded, his attention returning to the area, then to the body. "I want you to go home, go inside your house, and stay there until I come." He glanced at Mugs and said, "Good job, Mugs."

Mugs barked, walked over to him, looking for a scratch. Mack bent down and gave Mugs what he wanted. Mack glanced at Thaddeus and said to Doreen, "I'm surprised he hasn't popped up with any comments."

She snorted. "He's been crooning some kind of death song for about ten minutes. And then before that, he called out, *Murder in the water. Murder in the water.*"

Mack nodded. "Go home with them both, please. And you're sure that Mugs didn't touch the body or pick up anything else either?"

"Not that I saw. He never went in the water or to the body, never touched or took a bite at anything," she said defensively.

Mack nodded. "I have to check. You know that."

She shrugged. "It'd be nice if you kept my name out of this."

He snorted. "Yeah, in your dreams."

She rolled her eyes at him. "I'll put coffee on. Make sure you get there before the pot turns off." She turned with her animals in tow and headed home.

Chapter 27

BACK IN HER kitchen, Doreen put on the coffee as promised, noticing the dog food bowl was very low on kibble. She couldn't imagine Goliath eating it, but she wasn't about to make Mugs starve regardless. Then realized the cat bowl was empty too. She filled Goliath's bowl and gave both fresh water. Then checked on Thaddeus's food. It was fine thankfully. He was nodding off on his roost.

When the coffee finished, Doreen poured herself a cup and settled on a chair on the back veranda. What a day... That poor man... And what was going on in her world that she'd been the one to find the body?

That kind of stuff tended to stick to a person. She'd need to find a way to change this, or the neighborhood would label her as the village crazy lady who found dead people.

She stared at the old dilapidated fence that hid her view of the creek but also gave her a little bit of privacy from anybody walking on the far side. It also gave them cover from whatever secretive things they might be doing. The path hadn't been heavily used that she could see.

At least Nan shouldn't be a suspect in the latest death.

Right?

Except for her two damn betting pools. Crap.

The three deaths should all be unrelated… with Nan's house as the only tenuous connection.

Doreen sat for a long time when another thought entered her mind. What if the men were related? Maybe by a job, a common goal or having tripped over each other somewhere along the line? Or maybe being in the wrong place? What if the most recent deaths were people related to the dead man from thirty years ago? He would have been old enough to have a family. Any chance it was perhaps Jeremy's children? And the other two bodies were cousins or brothers? Not knowing the ages of the two latest dead bodies wasn't helping Doreen with her musings.

She pulled out her phone and quickly texted Mack. **I didn't see the man's face in the creek. And I don't know the physical features of the man found here on my property. Any chance the two men are related? And how old was each one?**

The response came back quickly. **This is Robert Delaney, general handyman, who worked at the old folks' home where Nan lives.**

Right. Something else to tie Nan into this.

But this man's last name, Delaney, and the dead body from Nan's garden, James Farley, plus the dead man depicted in the thirty-year-old pictures, Jeremy Feldspar, still meant nothing to Doreen. Yet, they didn't have to share the same last name to be related, to support this latest theory of hers. They could've been from the wife's side of the family, or they could've been cousins. They could've even been related on the mother's side—last names changed easier for women after they got married but also for a mom who remarried; her name would've changed too.

She quickly texted him again. **Don't let the names fool you. Make sure there is no blood between these two recently dead men, including any relationship to the man who went missing thirty years ago.**

We know how to do our job.

Short. Succinct... Right. Of course they did.

She had to be grateful for that little bit of sharing. Mack was the investigating detective, and she was somebody who tripped over bodies. Not necessarily a good thing.

Thaddeus crooned at her side. Goliath had somehow found her lap and had curled his not inconsiderable bulk into her arms. And to complete the picture, Mugs slept at her feet, stretched out on his belly froggy style.

"Thaddeus, if you're so smart, why can't you tell us something about these men who were murdered?"

With that thought, she pulled out her phone, shifted Goliath to lie beside her. Then she downloaded the images to her laptop that was parked on the coffee table for a closer look. Yes, she hadn't been mistaken. The man in the creek *had* been murdered, as evidenced by a hole in the side of his head that she could just barely see at the edge of his hoodie. She'd not looked too closely while he'd been stretched out in the water, but it showed up clearly in her photos. Looked like he'd been shot.

Speaking of images, she had none of the body found in her garden. She cringed at the thought of what a decaying body would look like.

But she had seen pictures of him from his insurance ads in the paper. She quickly did a Google search for James Farley and his company. And there was his photo. Then she searched Google for the man they'd just found, Robert

Delaney, bringing up his face on the monitor.

She studied the features of the two dead men, looking for something that would link them. They were both around the same age. She put them each in their forties. Possibly as old as mid-fifties. It was so hard to tell with some people. They were both sitting in the pictures, one heftier than the other. But then one had a more physical job—the handyman. No comparison for muscles and leanness. She kept searching and found profile pictures of both. They both had a bump in the center of their noses. When put side by side like that, there was definitely a resemblance. She saved both photos to show Mack.

And then she brought up the name of the man whose belongings she'd found upstairs—Jeremy Feldspar.

How was she to research wedding records, divorce records, or last known residences? She really needed Mack's help with this. Mack would probably say he needed her to stop interfering. Maybe he was right because, honestly, this was a bit beyond her investigative skills. She had to talk to somebody who had been around for a long time. So far Nan hadn't been a great—or reliable—source of information. Doreen considered her chatty neighbor, Ella. She had shared all about how she had lived in the Mission area for thirty or so years. Just not at the house in this neighborhood.

Then there was the retired guy who hadn't been friendly but was quite possibly someone who would know the old case. She didn't have his phone number, or she'd try calling. She wasn't sure what he'd say if she showed up at his door again. But she was willing to take a chance.

After another cup of coffee, she grabbed her notepad and got up the courage. She walked out her front door and down to the grumpy old man's house, leaving the animals behind.

She knocked on his door. He opened it as if he'd been standing at the front window, watching.

He growled. "What the hell do you want now?"

"I'm doing some research and was hoping you could help. Do you know any of these names or these faces?" She held up her laptop, sporting side-by-side full-face pictures of three men, beside her notepad with the names clearly written out in block printing: Jeremy Feldspar, James Farley, Robert Delaney.

Doreen watched Mr. de Genaro's face.

His gaze went from the pictures to the names and back again; then he stared at her. "Why do you want to know that?"

"Well, one of them is the man found buried in the back garden of my property, so I care. I was wondering if the men were related."

His eyebrows shot up. He shook his head, reached out and tapped one name on her notepad. "I knew this one. He went missing thirty years ago."

"In what way did you know him?"

He shrugged. "We were friends for a while. But he and his wife were into money scams. You know? Buy a property from him, then you find out there's no property to actually buy. The law was after them, as were a lot of angry people too. The fact that he disappeared was no surprise. I would have helped them on their way myself, but I couldn't find them. Jeremy cost me ten grand."

"Ouch. I'm sorry."

He nodded and said, "Jeremy was also accused of murdering his mother, but I never believed that." Frowning, he studied the pictures. "How are they all related?"

"Not sure yet. But I have profile pictures of two men,

one whose dead body was found recently, and they seem to share the same nose." She studied de Genaro's face, seeing the anger, resentment and pain from so long ago. "Can you tell me where Jeremy worked? Who his friends were? If any members of his family still live around here? What about his wife?"

His face twisted in disgust. "That was way back when. I have no idea where any of them are, except for his wife. Her name's Alice. I never could figure out if she was part of it or not. But she's living decent for somebody who never worked a day in her life."

Doreen didn't know if that was a diss on her too because she certainly hadn't worked a day in her life either, not a traditional job anyway. On the other hand, she wasn't living high on the hog now. She was living mostly on her grandmother's charity. And that did prick her pride a bit. "Do you know if she has the same last name?"

"Last I heard, she did. But not sure now. She'd be in her mid- to late seventies. She's living in the same retirement home as Nan."

Inside Doreen cringed. Of course she'd be living there. Everything kept circling back to Nan. An old-timer in this small town. But it'd be nice if one of the darn threads would go in the opposite direction. "Did they have any kids?"

He nodded. "Three or four of them, I think. They were young enough back then that the kids didn't really know what their parents were up to at the time. I don't think the kids were involved in the scams. They were in junior high or so back then."

"Outside of Jeremy just dropping off the earth, did you ever hear any more about what happened?"

Mr. de Genaro shook his head. At least this time his

tone was a whole lot more amiable when he said, "No, I haven't, but I sure would like to. Like I said, for a time, we were friends. If you find out anything, please let me know." On that note, he started to close the door.

She stepped back. "Likewise, if you hear of anything happening with these people, please let me know. I'm just trying to clear any suspicions regarding Nan in all this."

He stared at her for a long moment. "How can anybody possibly think Nan had something to do with this?"

"Oh, I agree. But, since the first body was found in her backyard..." She shrugged. "It does put her in a bad position."

"Fools. The whole lot of them." And the door closed with a bang.

She agreed and returned to her house. As she walked up the driveway, a vehicle came up behind her. She turned to see Mack, smiled and gave him a small wave.

He parked, got out, motioning at the notepad and her laptop in her hands. "Now what have you been up to?"

She gave him a look of complete innocence, but when he narrowed his gaze at her, she knew she had completely failed to convince him. She motioned to the neighboring house. "Richard de Genaro's been around for a long time. He's grumpy and angry, but I figured he might be a source of information."

"On who?"

She held up a photo of Jeremy Feldspar, the missing man from thirty years ago. "Him."

Mack stopped and stared at the photo. Then glanced at the neighbor's house. "Did he know him?"

She nodded. "Apparently Jeremy Feldspar and his wife were involved in a property development scam, and according to de Genaro, a lot of people wanted Feldspar dead."

Mack nodded.

She gasped. "You knew that already, didn't you?"

"I took a look at the old missing person's police file on Jeremy. It's a cold case with boxes of paperwork to go through. I haven't had time for that, but I read the brief on it." He shrugged. "Only so many hours in a day and, so far, you're doing a good job filling those hours with fresh bodies."

"Sorry about that." She winced. "It's not like I'm trying to find them. I'm just at the wrong place at the wrong time. Like moving into Nan's house. If I'd moved in right when she moved out, then likely the first body wouldn't have ended up on her property."

He stopped and grimaced. "Not necessarily."

She stared at the small circle of houses. "When Nan and I first talked about this change of residence, we didn't really lock down the dates. If we both had to live temporarily with each other in the house, we would have. No problem. And, if there was a gap between her moving out and me moving in, Nan was okay with that too."

Doreen spun to look at Mack. "I mean, Nan had been on a waiting list for Rosemoor, but usually someone has to die for a spot to open up at the retirement home. You can't exactly plan to give two weeks' notice for *that* event. Sure, sometimes a family caregiver will take a resident into their home and will give Rosemoor some notice. But those are rare events. So, when a *sudden* opening popped up, Nan took it rather than waiting for the next... opening."

He nodded. "And you got here as soon as you could."

"Something like that. It's not a good idea to leave a house empty for too long. But Nan wasn't all that worried.

Like she said, nothing happens around here, and I was trying to tie up something else before coming."

"The body had been here for at least a couple weeks."

She stared at him and swallowed. "Oh. So while Nan was in transition…"

He nodded. "So what's the chance that, even while Nan lived here, she had no clue?"

"It depends if she had her hearing aids in or not," Doreen explained. "Without them, she'd have heard nothing. And, if she was sleeping, then she really wouldn't have heard anything. Compound that with her moving to the retirement home and all the trips that would have entailed, plus she obviously never went into the backyard for quite a while…"

"So, of course, she had no idea. Likely the location was picked for just that reason."

Doreen froze and stared at the side-by-side pictures on her laptop in her hand. "Or for another more sinister reason?"

Now standing on the front doorstep, he put his hand on her shoulder. "What are you talking about?"

"I can't get past the idea that all the murders are related, that the victims might be related. But, what if the first man, who disappeared thirty years ago, is buried here too? And the body we found in the garden was his son? Maybe the killer wanted to bury him beside his father?" She shook her head and broke into maniacal laughter. "Can you imagine? That would make this property a family burial plot."

Chapter 28

"EASY, TAKE IT easy."

Her wild laughter morphed into sobs. She heard Mack's voice through her tears. She excused herself and ducked into the bathroom while Mugs greeted the newcomer. There she turned on the cold water and splashed her face, patting down the tears. When she was composed enough to face him, she walked into the kitchen, sat down and very quietly said, "I'm sorry."

Mugs nudged his nose against her leg. She reached down to stroke his big ears wondering what Mack must think of her.

He looked at her in surprise. "Why? You've come across two dead bodies, one in your own backyard, and may have found a conspiracy involving the third, all within your first four days here in Mission." He shook his head. "Anybody who's not in law enforcement or the medical profession would have the same kind of reaction."

She nodded, but it didn't help very much. She didn't want to be just anybody. She craved to be somebody special, to be somebody different. She'd been *just a wife* for so long, and now she was an individual person, in her own space. But what did that mean? Who was she? She wasn't sure what to do now in her life. She felt lost in the brand-new scheme of things as her daily events unfolded here in Mission. She could only hope she'd find out who she was soon enough.

She picked up the coffee cup Mack had filled for her and took a big drink. Then she hugged the cup with both hands. "Did you find any connection between the men?"

"Not yet, but if it's there, I'll find it. We do take murder very seriously here."

She nodded. "Mr. de Genaro said Alice Feldspar, Jeremy's wife, is a resident at Rosemoor. Maybe I should ask around at the retirement home or speak to her directly."

"No." He glared at her. "I'll take care of that. What is your problem? Just leave it alone, please."

Doreen glared back. At least she no longer felt like crying. "How can I just sit here and do nothing? The least I can do is talk to people, find out information, and feed it to you. Unless you want me to go off and find the killer myself."

"You just did find out info and feed it to me. The Alice Feldspar lead. And, hell no, I don't want you to go off and find the killer yourself. How would you even know who the killer is at this point? And what would you do? Just walk up to some suspect and ask him if he committed two murders recently? You realize somebody has killed two men in two weeks, possibly the third from as many decades ago.

"If it wasn't you, and it wasn't Nan, chances are it'll be somebody who Nan knows, possibly very well. It could even be somebody who you know. This is a small-town community. Sure, the city itself is big, but this area that we live in, it's small, it's tight, and everybody knows each other. You can't take the chance of pissing off the wrong person. Neither can you take the chance of tipping off the person who did this."

She sat back, disgruntled. Mugs looked up at her from his spot on the floor then dropped his head down again Doreen finally nodded. "Okay."

He stared at her as if waiting to see if she really understood. "Now let's get your police statement started." He pulled out his notepad and pen but also set a handheld tape recorder on the kitchen table and hit the Record button. "What made you go in that direction coming home?"

She frowned at him. "I was just looking for a path along the creek. It's pretty back there. I wasn't looking for the missing man."

"How did you know he was missing?" he asked, a hint of suspicion in his voice.

She gave him a drawn look. "I didn't kill him."

He rolled his eyes. "Just answer the question please."

She nodded. "Nan told me about it."

"And by sheer accident you went in that direction? Just a coincidence that you stumbled over the second body?"

"Absolutely." It sounded a little thin to her ears too.

He studied her for a long moment and then nodded. "Okay, so you went directly from the retirement home toward this creek path?"

She shook her head. She gave him as many of the details as she could remember about the convoluted way she came home. "I was just walking aimlessly, exploring. I don't know the area. I thought I'd walk around and see something new about the town. I came upon the creek, crossed it and kept going. I figured I would end up at home if I kept walking in this direction. I saw the cul-de-sac beside ours." She nodded toward the houses she could see out the back window. The two cul-de-sacs were kind of in a cloverleaf pattern. "I knew I wasn't very far away from home."

"How did you recognize the cul-de-sacs?"

"Only one house in both of these cul-de-sacs has those big Spanish tiles on the roof," she said quietly. "I do observe things, you know."

He wrote down some notes. "So what made you see him in the first place?"

"Mugs."

"Right, the dog."

"But not right away."

He raised his head and looked at her again. "Why not right away?"

"We were sitting on a log maybe ten yards from where the body was. I was enjoying the rest, thinking how beautiful the spot was and how absolutely lovely the town is to live in. That Nan had made a wonderful decision in spending as much of her life here as she had."

"Mugs wasn't bothered?"

Mugs lifted his head at the sound of his name. She stroked his body with her foot and shook her head. "There had been a nice breeze up until then. It came more from across the river. But when a big gust of wind came downriver, then Mugs barked like crazy. Up until then I think he was just tired and sleeping."

"And then what did you do?"

She looked at Mack in surprise. "I stood, and the three of us walked the creek toward home. Mugs was still barking like crazy, and he didn't stop until we approached the body. I could see that the man was dead, just lying there in the water."

Mack finished writing down another note, looked back at her and said, "And then what?"

She raised both hands in frustration. "What do you

mean, *And then what?* I called you. That's what."

"You didn't check out the man's pockets? Did you move him? Touch the man in anyway? Check to see if he was alive?"

She stared at Mack in horror. "He was in the water. Facedown but slightly twisted to the side. Dirt was in his mouth from the water washing around his face. His eyes were open. I didn't think there was any chance he was still alive. And, no, I did not touch him. I did not go through his pockets." She still stared at Mack. "I can't believe you'd ask me that. Check my shoes. They are dry."

Upset, but not letting him get to her any further, she continued, "And then I walked back and forth. I felt like I was being watched, just kind of an odd feeling, like I had to be protective of the body, and I was afraid that somebody would come along before you got there. I had been in that area on Thursday. I had actually found the same path but starting from the house. A boy had climbed one of the big trees. I didn't want him to come along today and see the body." She glared at Mack. "And you said you'd be there in ten minutes. But you were thirty minutes getting there."

It was his turn to roll his eyes at her. "Sorry. I came as fast as I could."

"Yeah, right. What? A dead body wasn't priority enough?"

"I was getting a team together so I wasn't the only one arriving. Also, I had to figure out exactly where you were. Your general directions were not very good." He reached over and shut off the recorder.

"Whatever." She finished her coffee, rising to pick up the pot. "This is becoming quite a habit."

"One I hope you will break."

She froze, coffeepot in hand, and stared at him. "What are you talking about?"

"Your habit of finding dead bodies."

"Oh." Relief washed over her. She waved the coffeepot around slightly. "I was talking about you coming here for coffee is becoming a habit. *A good one to break.*"

He grinned, chuckled and then laughed a great big belly laugh that roared through the kitchen.

She filled his coffee cup. "It's not that funny."

He gasped and tried to regain his breath. "Actually, yes, it is pretty funny. I intended to cut back on my coffee habit. But it's worse now because I'm always here."

"That's not my fault," she protested, but it was hard not to grin. "How about you just solve these murders? That would make my life a lot easier. Although I do have a theory, if you want to hear it?"

"What is it?"

She broached the subject carefully, leaning forward. "You know? I've been giving this a lot of thought. I was thinking about the man who disappeared decades ago. I think somebody in this area probably murdered him, and I think the recently murdered two men were related to him. They were probably looking for his killer."

"Wow. That's quite a theory. Any evidence to back that up?" he asked in a mocking tone but with a smile on his face, letting her know that it wasn't a taunt, more like a casual teasing remark.

"I'm not into conspiracy theories," she said. "Honest. It just seems like all this has to be related. And I thought I saw a family resemblance." She glanced over at her laptop and then back at him. "I have some photos." At his headshake, she got mad. "I did this before you arrived, so you can't get upset with me."

Mugs sat up and woofed.

"It's okay, boy, he's just being difficult."

He glared at her.

She sighed. "Okay. I also sent them to you. Did you get them?"

"No, I didn't. However, I have a lot of messages here. Some of us work for a living, you know?"

"Some of us are trying to find a job so we can make a living, you know?" She grabbed her laptop and brought up the pictures of Robert and James that she had put side by side, in profile. "This is what I found. Do you see the resemblance in these?"

He leaned forward and studied the images. "You know something? You could be right." He glanced at her in surprise.

She beamed. "So I'm not such a foolish old lady after all."

"You're not old at all."

Pleased, she brushed past how he failed to say she wasn't foolish either and said, "What I need is a photo of the man who went missing decades ago. Something in profile that might show features to match these two men."

"There should be some in the archives," he said. "Send those to my email again. I'll check for myself."

She brought up her email program, typed in his email address and sent off the photos as an attachment. When she was done, she sat back. "Can you send me the other photo when you find it?" She added the last bit hurriedly.

He gave her that long stare. "Remember? It's official business."

She gave him a long stare right back. "Remember? I'm

not a suspect."

He chuckled.

"You have to admit I've been some help, haven't I?"

"Maybe. Or maybe you're taking up a lot of official resources, sending me off on a wild goose chase. Maybe you're a Photoshop magician and just made these photos look like this."

She stared at him in shock. "Why would I possibly do that?" She looked at the photos. "Can people do that?"

"Way too often people do that." He glanced at her. "You don't actually think those models on the magazine covers look like that, do you?"

She considered the question. "I never really gave that much thought. But I know my husband believed them to look just like that."

"Ouch. That would be a hard thing to live up to, because it's *not* something you *can* live up to. Those photos aren't real. All those images have been fixed to make the women look better."

She studied him. "But who determines what is *better*?"

He grinned. "Exactly the problem."

Chapter 29

L ATER THAT NIGHT she struggled to fall asleep. Goliath was curled up at her side and Mugs at her feet. Thaddeus roosted happily at the end of her bed. She lay in bed and stared at the ceiling—the ceiling that hid where all the clothing had been kept in boxes. She couldn't ignore the idea that another man might be buried close by. Why else would all his belongings be stored in the attic?

The last thing she needed was to find yet another body. But she couldn't forget the notion. Plus she was learning she didn't like to wait. Especially for answers. And the fact that she was waiting on other people made it much worse. Why couldn't Mack hand over information to her?

"Because he doesn't have any yet, idiot."

She shook her head. She was tempted to go back to her chatty neighbor and ask more questions tomorrow. She sat up in bed and turned on her lamp, then reached for her laptop. She'd searched earlier, looking for a connection between the two men. It'd be easy enough for one to have had a different father with a different surname. But it still didn't answer what the potential connection was to the first man who had gone missing. And she hadn't found very much under his name anywhere.

Theoretically any one of them could have owned property on this cul-de-sac too. And maybe there were more relatives than just the two men. With that thought, she searched for the family of the first dead man found, James Farley, to see if he had any sisters or somebody still living.

She couldn't find anything, but when she searched for family members of the man who she had just found—Robert Delaney—he had an adopted sister, although their parents were both dead.

That was interesting too. But she needed more family information. Stuff that Mack hadn't shared with her.

Frustrated, she finally put everything away and lay down on her bed again. Wide awake.

Mugs was so laid-back that he lay there with his feet in the air, snoozing away. She'd love to sleep a deep sleep like that. But this bed was more conducive to wakefulness than sleepfulness.

Her phone rang just then. Startled, she reached for it and checked the caller ID, surprised to find it was Nan. She glanced at the clock. It was late. "Nan, are you all right?"

"Yes, dear. I just needed to hear your voice."

Doreen didn't know what to say about that. "Well, I'm glad you called. I'm just lying here, unable to go to sleep."

"Well, rumors are circulating here, something about you finding yet another body?"

Doreen winced. "Oh, dear, I was hoping you wouldn't hear about that."

"It's true?" Nan's voice rose in shock. "Doreen!"

"I didn't mean to," she said hurriedly. "After visiting you, I went a different way home, and I found a body in the creek."

"Whose body?" Nan asked suspiciously. "This really isn't helping your reputation in the town, you know, my dear?"

Doreen rolled her eyes. "Nan, I didn't do it on purpose." She could hear Nan's heavy sigh come through the phone.

"No, of course you didn't. I'm sorry, dear. Could you tell me what time it was you found the body?"

Doreen stared at her phone, nonplussed. "Nan, you want the exact time?"

"Yes. We had a pool on how long before the body was found. Some of the bets are really close. I need to know who the winner is."

Doreen rested her back against the headboard. "Nan, I thought you were teasing when you first told me that." Besides, she had been really gobbling up those marijuana cookies at the time too. "You didn't really have a betting pool on when somebody would find the body, did you? That's morbid."

"Well, we didn't know for sure he would be dead when he was found. And you found him, didn't you?"

"Yes." She frowned. "Nan, how do you know I found the missing handyman?"

"You just said so, dear."

Yes, just now. But Doreen cast her mind back on their conversations to remember if she had mentioned the handyman specifically earlier.

"Not that it matters, dear. Everyone is talking about it." Nan went gaily onto the next subject, completely unrelated. "How's Thaddeus?"

Doreen brushed her hair off her face, wondering just what kind of marijuana-induced haze Nan was in. "Thaddeus is fine, Nan." She stared at the bird perched at the end of the bed. "Why?"

"Well, he does have a good nose. So, if you had him with you, it's no surprise that you found our missing person." Her voice perked up as she added, "Oh, my goodness, it's actually a great thing. Maybe we can use you and Thaddeus and Mugs to hunt down lost people."

"No," Doreen cried out. "No, Nan. Stop. That's really not how I want people to look at me."

"Well, it's better than people thinking you murdered all these men."

Nan was nothing if not blunt.

"You could put yourself in my position and realize they might think *you* murdered all these men," Doreen said slowly. "Nan, I found the bodies. I didn't turn them into bodies."

Nan laughed. "Of course not, dear. I was just teasing. So back to when you found him again. Can you remember exactly what time it was?"

"I phoned the authorities. I probably have a record of the call, so hold on." Doreen looked back at her recent phone calls to when she had contacted Mack. When she came back on the phone, she said, "I think it was around 3:15."

"You *think*? You do understand that it's kind of important to know these things. People get quite irate if we don't have exact information."

"I *know* it was around 3:15," Doreen snapped. She couldn't believe Nan was doing this. "Nan, would you please stop betting on things like this? It's very upsetting."

"Well, we need something to do. Rosemoor's a small place where nothing much happens, and we have lots of time on our hands. We bet on lots of things. It just happened to be that Robert Delaney's disappearance was one somebody suggested. We didn't know he would end up dead, did we?" Nan paused for a moment and said, "Doreen, I hate to say it, but you sound awfully tired. You really should go to sleep. It's after eleven, my dear."

On that note she hung up, leaving Doreen to stare at her phone in surprise.

"And how am I supposed to sleep now?" she asked of the empty room. "Nan's setting up a betting pool as to when a dead person is to be found?" She shook her head. "Oh, I feel like I fell down the rabbit hole."

Thaddeus straightened a bit. "Body in a rabbit hole. Body in a rabbit hole."

She glared at the bird as Goliath rolled out and used his claws on her belly to get comfortable and Mugs kicked out at her feet to make more room. "No, there is no body in the rabbit hole."

He cocked his head at her and squawked, "Are you sure? Are you sure?"

She groaned, lying down in her bed, pulling the covers over her head. She just wanted this to be all over.

Chapter 30

Day 5, Sunday

WHEN SHE WOKE the next morning, she was surprisingly rested and in a relaxed state of mind. She sat up and stretched. Mugs wasn't on the bed—he was lying in the open doorway to her bedroom, stretched out on his back with his feet in the air again.

She smiled. "Mugs, are you still alive?"

He rolled over, his tongue flopping with his movement. But he didn't bark. There was no sign of Goliath or Thaddeus.

She hopped out of bed and headed to the shower. When she dried off and dressed for the day, she went downstairs to start her coffee and to feed her furry and feathered family. Waiting for the pot to finish dripping, she sat at the kitchen table and opened her laptop to check her email. She found an email from Mack, which made her brighten. When she clicked on it, she read, *No news yet. Still working.*

Her shoulders slumped. She had been so sure some good news would appear somewhere along the line. At least he had responded. It was always worse waiting.

With her first cup of coffee and her animals in tow, she

stepped onto the back veranda and surveyed the massive garden. Now that the dead body was gone, she really needed to get something done out here. With all the chaos going on, Mack had postponed any work in his mother's garden. But there was no reason Doreen couldn't get started on Nan's garden.

She walked through the backyard while Thaddeus strutted behind her, thankfully silent. Mugs was rolling in something. Too late to stop him now. With a groan, Doreen expected that he'd probably need a bath afterward. Surprisingly Goliath was acting well behaved and calm.

The weeds were *heavily* overgrown here in the backyard. Doreen shook her head. Even the *planned* additions to the garden had gone awry. Irises had grown into massive clumps, and other bulbs were mixed in with each other. The hyacinths were done, and the tulips were almost done. There could be bulbs planted all throughout the place. Nan had been nothing if not passionate about bulbs. Doreen would have to sit down, draw out her plan for the garden, so she could relocate a lot of these bulbs. That way, they'd have more room to grow.

A whole bed designated for the bulbs would be nice, especially if she could coordinate the colors, putting in summer-blooming shrubs for when the bulbs were done. As she looked at the yard, she realized there'd once been grass in the middle. It needed either new sod or some topsoil and seed.

As she walked along, she thought maybe just an application of nitrogen would help it. Most of the garden could be salvaged, but it would take a massive amount of labor. *Her* labor.

With her now empty coffee cup in her hand, she walked

around to the front yard, drawing the animals with her. A few hours a day would bring this garden back into shape. Nan had poured her love into the small front garden, and it showed.

Out of the corner of her eye, she thought she saw a woman at the side of her house. Wondering if it could be that nosy Ella, Doreen headed that way, where mostly moss and ferns grew in the shade. She didn't see anybody there but found the ground was spongy. Soft. She wondered if there was a water leak in the area. It seemed really damp. But then she spied the neighbors' hose, dripping steadily in a stream toward her place.

That explained that. She tossed the end of the hose back on the neighbors' lawn and then returned to her backyard for one last look—finding no sign of Ella—and Doreen decided that she'd get started on her gardens today. She went inside, made some toast, and ate it as she formulated a plan for her morning.

She went upstairs to put on her work jeans—the comfy and durable ones from Nan's closet that looked like capri pants on her since she was a good five inches taller than Nan. Afterward she grabbed a pair of Nan's garden gloves off the back veranda. With what tools she could find, she headed out to the front garden. Less work to be done here. Then she'd work in the back garden a little bit too.

She happily got down on her knees in the dirt and grass and quickly pulled up the weeds out front, waving at several of the neighbors who appeared outside for no other purpose than to see what she was doing. To Mugs she said, "They're probably looking to see if I find another body."

Mugs barked, then gave her an open-mouthed tongue-licking grin.

She glared at him. "That wasn't meant to be funny."

With Thaddeus settled on the front porch railing and Goliath asleep on one of the porch steps, Doreen spent the next couple hours pulling weeds, trimming shrubs and generally getting a handle on Nan's front garden. Doreen glanced up to see her chatty neighbor walking toward her. Ella had a smile on her face. Doreen settled back on her heels and smiled. "Good morning, Ella."

Ella's smile widened. "Good morning. I see you're cleaning up Nan's garden."

Doreen wanted to make a snide comment about that being obvious but held back. She was just hot and cranky. Then Mugs growled low in the back of his throat. "Hush, it's fine, Mugs." He sat down beside her but didn't relax. He really was taking to the guard dog role. Even Thaddeus flew onto a rock at Mugs side. And as if to not be outdone, Goliath stretched out on the grass, his tail twitching in short sharp snaps.

As the neighbor woman approached, Ella said, "I heard you found another dead body."

Something was off in her tone. Doreen studied her and gave a small nod. "I did, indeed. But don't make it sound like I do this as a habit. I'd be happy to never find another one ever."

Immediately Ella made a sympathetic face. And yet, again, something was off.

Doreen lowered her head, spotted some lady's mantle and gave it a yank. The herb was helpful in some cases but had a tendency to take over if given half a chance.

"Some people are just unlucky," Ella said cheerfully.

"Yes, like these two men apparently." Doreen studied Ella's face. "Maybe you knew him?" She watched carefully as she mentioned Robert Delaney's name. And caught a flicker in that steady gaze of Ella's.

Ella made a mock shudder and shook her head. "No. Thankfully I didn't."

Doreen nodded but didn't believe Ella's carefully schooled expression. "He worked at the retirement home," Doreen said. "Actually he worked several places as a bit of a handyman. I've been looking into his life and finding out all kinds of things." She shouldn't say things like that, but she couldn't help it. Something about this woman made her want to prick that complacent expression on Ella's face.

"Oh, dear. I'm sorry to hear that. It couldn't be pleasant to have been the one to find him." She gave another physical shudder. "I won't take that path again."

Doreen looked at the garden again, her mind caught on the fact that Ella knew where the man had been found. "Do you go down there often? Maybe you saw something that would be helpful to the police."

"Oh, I couldn't talk to the police," Ella cried out in horror. "That's just too unnerving."

"I talk to them all the time." Doreen studied Ella's face for a moment. "I didn't tell you that he was found in the creek."

Ella stopped and stared. "Didn't you? Well, somebody did. It's all over town." Ella stepped backward, her nervous gaze zipping from Doreen to the garden and back. "That's another reason I couldn't possibly talk to the police. I'm always spitting out the wrong information because I don't hear quite as well as I used to." She apologized, backing up several more steps.

Doreen watched as Ella retreated again. "Who were you talking to about it?"

Ella stopped—something about her gaze hardened. She snapped, "I'm sure I don't remember. People like to gossip. Nobody can resist a chance to spread the news." And she stormed off.

"I just bet they do," Doreen said to the animals that all watched the woman rush away. She pulled out her phone and dialed Mack's number, watching as Ella reached her house.

"Yes, Doreen," he said cautiously.

She frowned into the phone. "Is that any way to talk to me? I am trying to help, you know?"

After a short silence, he exploded, "What have you done now?"

She gasped. "That's so unfair. I didn't do anything."

"Then why are you calling?"

"I just spoke with Ella, my chatty neighbor. She already knew that the body was found in the creek by my house. How does everybody know so fast?"

"One of the greatest mysteries of life is how fast gossip travels," he said drily. "Remember how you were behind other houses? Somebody may have seen you."

"She didn't tell me who she heard it from."

Mack's end of the phone went silent.

She pressed further. "She's acting really nervous. I think she knows a whole lot more than she's telling." Doreen sat back on her haunches as something occurred to her. "And something's familiar about her face. Maybe she's related to the two men."

"Now hold on a minute," Mack protested. "We don't even know if the men are related yet."

"Well, get on it," she moaned. "Her name would be different because she is married. She could be the sister. I'm working in the front garden right now, so why don't you come by in a couple hours? You can go over and talk to her then."

"I'm running an investigation here. Stop interfering," he retorted.

"Fine." She smiled. "I'll see if she does anything suspicious."

"No," he said, alarm in his voice. "Leave her alone. I don't want her to get any more suspicious, just in case she is involved. Back away until I can talk to her. I need you to butt out of my case and stay out." When she didn't respond, he added, "We are trained to deal with murderers. You are not."

She didn't like it, but it made sense. "Okay, fine."

"I mean it."

"I heard you," she said in exasperation. She ended the call and finished weeding the flower bed. Yet, her mind was consumed. Now she wanted to research this lovely chatty neighbor of hers and see what she had been up to. Because Doreen was sure Ella was up to something. Now to figure out what.

Unable to leave it another second, she hurried inside, the animals excited at the change of pace. After washing her hands, she put on a cup of tea, sat down at the table and turned on her laptop, grabbing her notepad of information on the case so far. Thank God, she had had the foresight to make notes of all her conversations with the neighbors. She typed in her chatty neighbor's name—Ella Goldman, per Brenda—and brought up as much of her history as she could locate on Google.

What did people do to get information in the old days?

Instantly pages popped up. "There she is," Doreen said

aloud.

Sipping her tea, Doreen read through the various articles. The first revealed when Ella got married, another one when her mother had died. Somewhere in the obscure paragraphs of still another article about some charity work Ella had done was a mention that she was adopted.

Doreen sat back and studied that for a long moment. *Adopted.* She went back to the article and read it again. It didn't say by who or when. Doreen knew those distinctions mattered because she herself had been adopted by her mother's second husband.

He'd been a good man with strong beliefs about right and wrong.

There was no way for Doreen to determine the circumstances surrounding Ella's knowledge of the latest dead man. Maybe it was just a fluke. Or maybe Ella was a liar.

Looking through various articles, Doreen learned Ella had lived in Kelowna all her life. Another said she'd been married twice. Her first husband had died from a heart attack a few years after they were married. To Doreen, that alone was suspicious. Of course, she was *looking* for reasons to be suspicious. "A heart attack? How old a man was he?" It had been her first husband after all. He could have been too young to have a heart attack.

Ella had ended up with the house, vehicles and whatever money her first husband had left behind, as was normal in most marriages. She'd done very well for herself in the end. That in itself didn't mean she'd done something to him. It could mean that she just had some compensation to help her deal with the loss.

Mugs barked. Doreen stood, grabbed her tea and walked to the front room. Someone was at the front door, but no one had knocked. Doreen walked over to the living room window in time to see her neighbor Ella walk across her front yard.

Was her neighbor going for a walk? Why would she be at the front door and not knock? Doreen wasn't sure *what* was wrong, but things felt all kinds of wrong.

Hidden behind the curtains, she watched what her neighbor would do. Ella was up to something, most likely seeing if Doreen was home. They had just spoken to each other earlier this morning. And Doreen's car remained out front. Why wouldn't Doreen be home? On a hunch she waited and watched as her neighbor walked up Doreen's driveway and around the side of her house. Ella's hands were empty, and she was smiling. What was Ella up to?

Doreen picked up her phone and called Mack.

"Now what?" he said in exasperation.

"It's the same neighbor. She's back in my yard, walking about, acting weird. I think she's trying to figure out if I'm home, which of course, I am since my car is here."

Silence followed on the other end.

He was still there from the staticky sounds, like she was losing the connection. "I'm not making this up."

Resigned, he said, "No, it's too crazy for you to have made it up."

Just then she heard the doorknob on the front door turn. "Somebody's trying to open the front door," she whispered.

"What?" he asked in alarm. "Are you sure?"

"Yes, I'm sure. I have to go." She ended the call, pocketed it and watched as Mugs, barking, ran toward the front door. Using his commotion to distract the woman, Doreen headed up the stairs to the first landing on the staircase. From there she waited, listening to find out what the woman would do.

Ella entered Doreen's house. "Nice dog. Aren't you a nice dog?"

Mugs wasn't having anything to do with Ella. He barked and barked and barked.

There was no sign of Goliath. But that was fairly typical. If there was work to be done, Goliath was gone.

Thaddeus, on the other hand, screeched.

The woman cried out. "Oh, my God! She has a zoo in here."

The woman raced throughout the living room, and Doreen could hear sounds of drawers opening. The only thing in the living room with a drawer was the coffee table. What was Ella searching for? Doreen's laptop and handwritten notes were on the kitchen table. She wondered if she should grab them. If Ella opened the laptop, she would see what Doreen had been looking at—Ella's history. And that wasn't anything Doreen wanted her chatty and possibly insane neighbor to know about.

However, while the woman was in the living room, Doreen could sneak into the kitchen. Taking a chance, she quietly took the stairs, thankful she was barefoot. In the kitchen, she snagged her laptop, turned. And stopped.

Her neighbor faced her with a feral smile, raising her hand.

Doreen's jaw dropped. "Is that a gun?" Her gaze locked on the barrel pointed in her direction.

"Oh, my God!" Ella yelled. "Are you that stupid? You really are the typical dumb blonde, aren't you? Of course it's a gun."

Doreen raised her gaze, seeing the anger and determination in the woman's eyes. "Why do you have a gun? And why are you pointing it at me? What are you doing in my kitchen? That's breaking and entering."

"No, it isn't. The door wasn't locked," she said. "Idiot. This may be entering illegally, but I didn't break in."

Doreen stared at her, stood stock-still, her mind racing to pull the pieces together. And then it clicked. "You shot the man in my garden."

"I didn't shoot anyone," the woman snapped.

But Ella wasn't anywhere near as convincing now as she had been earlier. Doreen shook her head. "What did he ever do to you? That man was harmless."

"He was my brother. He was also an asshole."

"Oh, my God! You killed your own brother?" Doreen gasped. "He was family."

Ella glared at her. "No, I didn't kill him. My brother did."

"What?" Doreen was too shocked to make sense of that. "So how did he end up in Nan's garden?"

"I told him to get rid of the body. But he's an idiot and buried it on your property."

Doreen felt shaky. Her legs had turned to rubber. "Why did he kill him?" she asked in a faint voice. This was too bizarre.

"It was an accident. They had a fight over a woman they both wanted. Robert punched James hard in the nose, and it killed him. Shoved his nose right into his brain. Robert came to me afterward for help, and we worked out what to do. But, instead of burying him out in the woods, like I suggested, he said he knew a place that had been recently turned over."

"Of course... He's a handyman. It wasn't by chance that he asked Nan if she wanted him to do some gardening work in the backyard. Put in a small extension to the deck so she could walk down easier. It's been a huge mess, and he knew it was bothering her."

Ella nodded. "She told him that she wouldn't bother as you'd be coming soon, and you'd take care of it. He'd seen her digging a few months ago though and figured it would be the easiest place to hide the body, but he was an idiot. You have to bury a body way deeper than that."

"Six feet," Doreen said. "Six feet to stop the dogs from smelling it."

"Well, my brother was lazy. He's always been lazy." Ella shook her head. "Now I have to do everything myself to fix this."

Doreen looked at her. "Well, you didn't bury your brother six feet deep either. How can you blame Robert for being lazy when you did the same thing? Hell, you didn't even bury him. You left him to rot in the creek." She paused and fixed Ella with a direct question. "You did kill him, right?"

The woman waved her gun hand, brushing away the question, as if taking a life was just that simple. "It doesn't matter. What matters right now is that I need your notes, and I need to know who you may have said something to."

"Why would you want my notes?"

The woman shot her a look. "Oh, for the love of God. Are you really that stupid?"

Doreen bristled. "Are you really that crazy to keep insulting me? I put up with that crap from my husband for a long time," she snapped. "I don't have to take it from you too."

"I can't imagine why he stayed married to you." She snorted, waving her gun around. "Then I read about the divorce online. Saw pictures of him and his new much younger girlfriend. You should have realized what was happening. Once you hit forty, you're automatically replaced."

Doreen glared at her. "I'm not forty."

The woman smirked. "Okay, so in your case, thirty-five, and he was done early. How is that any better?"

"This is a ridiculous conversation. You can't shoot me. How would you explain my death? And, if the same gun was used to shoot your brother, the police will connect all the murders," she said, hoping to keep Ella talking long enough to give Mack time to get here.

"Of course it won't be related. I'll shoot you in such a way that it looks like you shot yourself." Ella's gaze turned crafty. "Overwhelmed with guilt for having shot my brother."

Doreen's jaw dropped. "I didn't kill your brother."

Ella rolled her eyes. "No, but the cops don't know that. See? They'll get all the evidence together, proving that you shot him, and then you came home and shot yourself. After all, you're depressed and despondent about losing your lifestyle and your husband."

Glumly Doreen wondered if that would work. Surely Mack would see she had no motivation for these killings. Would Mack fight for her cause? Would he understand she wasn't that stupid and how he had been tipped off that Doreen was suspicious of Ella first? Or would he not care, as it would nicely close several cases for him?

Hopefully he was already on his way here right now.

Suddenly she remembered the insurance office. "Was that you making a mess at James Farley's insurance office too?"

"No, that was my stupid brother. Tried to make it look like a robbery and kidnapping or some such thing."

Mugs sniffed around the woman's legs. Thaddeus was in the corner of the kitchen. Doreen could see him walking back and forth in obvious distress, his head bobbing up and down, his wings flapping as he looked around. Somewhere in the mix was Goliath. What Doreen really needed was a sneak attack from Mugs or Goliath or Thaddeus or all three. Something to distract this woman so Doreen could grab the gun.

She looked down at Mugs and said in a determined voice, "Attack, Mugs."

Mugs jumped toward Doreen, barking.

"Not me, Mugs, her."

Ella chuckled. "You're such a mess. Your dog doesn't know what that means."

But a streak of orange flew into the kitchen as Goliath raced forward, dodging between Ella's legs. Ella shrieked, stumbling a bit, and grabbed the doorjamb to stop herself from falling.

Mugs turned, barking at Goliath, chasing him back out of the room again. Both of them bumped into Ella as she tried to right herself and to also get out of the way of the animals.

It gave Doreen her chance. She stepped forward and kicked the crazy woman's legs out from under her. As she went down, Doreen knocked the gun out of Ella's hand and smacked her hard across the face with her closed fist. It wasn't really a punch, but considering she still had rings on her fingers, it would do major damage to the woman's cheek, and that wasn't all bad in this particular situation.

With Ella down on the hallway floor just outside the

kitchen, Doreen sat on her. She looked around for something to hold her here but found nothing to use.

Ella arched her back and tried to dislodge Doreen. When that didn't work, Ella scratched Doreen's arms and screamed, "Get off me."

Meanwhile Mugs barked like crazy, Goliath howled and Thaddeus flew about the kitchen.

Doreen shook her head and grabbed one of the great big books sitting in a stack on the floor off to the side—another of Nan's perpetual collection of useless things, *until now*—and smacked Ella over the head with it. It shouldn't have been a hard blow, but her eyeballs rolled into the back of her head, and she collapsed, unconscious.

Just then both the front and back doors burst open, and cops streamed toward her. She held up her hands and pointed at the floor where Ella's gun had landed. Mack picked up the gun and asked, "What just happened?"

Slowly, as the cops holstered their guns, Doreen stood. "The man in the creek was her brother. She shot him, as far as I can tell, because he didn't bury their other brother deep enough in Nan's garden." The cops looked at her, then at the woman unconscious on the floor and back at Doreen. "If you can believe anything Ella says, Robert Delaney accidentally killed James Farley. Then Ella killed Robert Delaney because he messed up the burying part of James's body." Doreen smirked. "Talk about family love."

Mack shook his head. "Can't you stay out of trouble for five minutes?"

She glared at him. "I'd be happy to."

"So there is no connection with these recent murders to the things found upstairs?" Mack asked, frowning.

"I didn't really get a chance to ask her about the rest, but

I think these three siblings were Jeremy Feldspar's children."

"You think they killed him?" Mack asked, raising his eyebrows.

One of the policemen had Ella's arms behind her back, cuffing them together. She opened her eyes while still on the floor. "No, our mother did."

Doreen crouched beside her. "Why?"

"Because he was having an affair with Nan. Mother and Father had had a fight. When Father came to stay at Nan's house, Mother came over and killed him while he was sleeping."

"And where is the body?"

Ella just stared at her.

Doreen looked at the back garden, particularly the vibrant long patch of azaleas. "Never mind. I think I know where he is."

Tears came to Ella's eyes. "I've lived with that for so long. And everything we've done since then just seemed to make it worse. All we could do to protect Mother was hide the body. So when Robert buried James here, probably to be close to our father, I knew that the earlier murder would come out. I was so mad at him. At his stupidity. I couldn't let that happen."

"You didn't have to shoot me," Doreen protested. "I didn't have anything to do with this mess."

"I was so frustrated about everything going wrong that I didn't know what else to do. You seemed to be everywhere all the time. Digging into stuff that you shouldn't be into. Then you found my brothers' bodies. James's first and Robert's shortly afterward. I figured, if I could make it look like you killed Robert, you'd be the prime suspect for James's death."

Doreen said, "So you hid all your father's clothing in the attic here? Was that to point fingers at Nan? Did she even know about that?"

Ella shrugged. "I've no idea. I don't know what she thought when he left her house and never returned."

Doreen shook her head. "For all I know, Nan had no interactions with Jeremy Feldspar. He may have even been in her house without Nan's knowledge or permission."

"Mother was sure they were having an affair. She found him sleeping here."

"*Here*, yes. But in the spare bedroom."

Ella's gaze widened. She stared at Doreen in horror.

Doreen nodded. "He was probably just taking time away from your mother while going through a tough spot in their relationship. For years, when Nan was younger, she came and went on a regular basis, traveling a lot around the world. He probably knew she wasn't home most of the time. Maybe he was even looking after the place for her. I do know that he was in the spare room. He wasn't in Nan's bedroom."

At that Ella burst into tears.

Doreen stood and walked to the kitchen table and collapsed in a chair. She stared at her now cold tea. "All this death for nothing."

One of the cops beside her said, "So often we find that is the case."

She turned back to Ella. "How did your mother kill him?"

Ella was still sobbing as the men hauled her to her feet. "She poisoned him. She came over here, supposedly to tell him that they could work things out, and she put arsenic in his tea."

"And his mother? Your grandmother? Did your father

kill her?"

That sent Ella's sobs to a louder pitch. Finally she sniffled back the tears enough to answer. "That's why Mother chose arsenic. He'd killed his own mother that way." Her sobbing resumed.

Doreen watched from the front porch as the police led Ella to the waiting cop car.

At her side, Mack said, "That's what we found in the safe-deposit box at the bank. A signed confession from Jeremy. He said he'd hated her all those years ago for the way she'd treated his father. He'd idealized the man and his mother ran around on him constantly. He'd watched his father take it for as long as he could then he took his own life. Jeremy then took her life. He'd written the confession and saved it all these years. Maybe to clear his conscience or maybe waiting for a time for his conscious to bug him enough to give it to someone. But we found it, and now we can close four cases at the same time."

The satisfaction in his voice made her laugh. "See? I wasn't such a hindrance after all." Doreen pointed at the look on his face. "Maybe it's time for a good cup of coffee."

"Maybe you would prefer tea?" Mack asked with a wicked grin.

Doreen shuddered. "Maybe never again. Jeremy's tea was poisoned, and his wife buries him in the azaleas and tosses the empty arsenic bottle in there with him."

Mack laughed. "Murder is often a simple affair."

"Arsenic in the azaleas." She shook her head. "What a way for the story to end."

USA TODAY BESTSELLING AUTHOR
DALE MAYER

Bones in the. Begonias

Lovely Lethal Gardens 2

Chapter 1

In the Mission, Kelowna, BC
Thursday, Not Quite One Week Later ...

DOREEN MONTGOMERY STOOD in the open doorway to her kitchen. *Her kitchen.* There was just something about settling into this house finally, with the chaos under control and something like normality entering her life ... Well, as long as "normality" could include her three very unique and personable pets. It was weird, but the phrase, *settling into this house*, to her, meant having a cup of coffee or tea whenever she wanted it, going to bed when she was ready, and sitting in the garden because she wanted to. And, boy, did she want all that. Even better, somedays she could take a step out her front door without being accosted by somebody wanting more details on the recently solved murders.

Somehow she'd become a celebrity in the small town of Kelowna. But she really didn't want that role. At least it took the townsfolk's focus off her status as a penniless thirty-five-year-old *almost* divorcée, living in her grandmother's home.

Yet Doreen was determined to handle her new life, sans chefs and gardeners and maids and chauffeurs. Doreen could handle most of that herself, except for one thing. Doreen couldn't cook. Which was why she had to face down this most terrifying thing of all things in her kitchen. She strode forward to fill Nan's teakettle and placed it on *the stove*—the appliance she had a hate-hate relationship with. She turned the dial to light the gas, but, of course, there was no blue flame. However, immediately she could smell gas wafting toward her nose.

She snapped off the dial and glared. "You're not a stove. You're a diabolical demon. I don't understand how you work, what makes you work, and why the hell anybody would want something like you in the house," she announced to anyone nearby. The only ones listening were Mugs, her pedigreed basset hound—content to lay on the floor out of the way—and Thaddeus, Nan's huge beautiful blue-gray parrot with long red tail feathers, currently walking on the kitchen table, hoping for food scraps. "I've already fed you this morning, Thaddeus." Doreen shook her head. She should have never let him eat there. Now she'd never be able to keep him off her breakfast table.

Goliath took that moment of calm to appear, racing around the kitchen, through Doreen's legs, and out again into the living room area.

"Goliath!" Doreen yelled, righting herself. "Stop doing that, or you'll end up hurting me and you too." Goliath was the gigantic golden Maine coon cat—the size of a bobcat— that came with the house. Goliath, being Goliath, was disruptive, picking any inopportune moment he could possibly find, yet sleeping the rest of the time. Initially Doreen had considered Goliath's races through the house were in pursuit of a mouse—heaven forbid—but Doreen had never seen one or any evidence of one inside. She decided this was Goliath's "normal" behavior.

Sighing, Doreen glared again at her stove. *Is it too much to ask for hot water for my tea?* Other people managed to produce incredible meals by using one of these things.

And then there was Doreen.

Her stove was a black gas-powered devil. Yet she was determined to not let it get the better of her. Again she reached forward to turn on the gas and then froze. She couldn't do it. What if something was wrong with the gas line? What if something really was broken? At least that gave her an excuse to stop her half-assed attempts at cooking. She grinned at that thought.

Feeling like it was a cop-out but grateful nonetheless, she picked up the electric teakettle she'd found in the back of Nan's pantry when Doreen had first arrived, filled it with water, and plugged it in. Then she pushed the button on its side and waited for the water to heat up. *That's the best way to make tea anyway.* She comforted herself with that thought as her gaze returned to the stove. "Damn thing."

Right behind her popped up a voice. "Damn thing. Damn thing."

Talking parrots should require an owner's manual—and circumspect owners. She turned and shook her finger at Thaddeus. "Don't you repeat that."

"Damn thing. Damn thing. Damn thing."

She stared at the African Grey parrot with her hands on her hips, worried that now Thaddeus would swear at the most awkward moments. Like with every other terrible thing he'd learned to say since she'd arrived.

Another *first.* Doreen was free to swear now. Free to say anything she wanted. Throwing off the shackles of her marriage had also freed her tongue. Maybe not such a good thing. She did have an image to uphold. She wasn't exactly sure what that image was yet, but it was here somewhere, and she was supposed to uphold it. Nan's image had been tarnished for a little bit with the recent murder cases. But Doreen had cleared Nan's name, and that was what counted.

Such a sense of peace flowed through Doreen now, as if she'd somehow successfully passed a major test, probably one of many as she made this major life transition.

Mugs waddled over and rubbed against her thigh, giving a bark.

"I haven't forgotten you, you silly boy." Doreen bent to give him a quick ear rub. When he barked again, now sitting at her feet, giving her that woeful look, she reminded him, "I've already fed you too."

As the teakettle bubbled beside her, she opened the kitchen's back door and stepped onto the long flowing veranda along the rear of the house. The dark slash beside the second set of veranda steps at the far end, where one of the bodies had been dug out, was still a raw insult to the garden that should have been here. And, of course, the rest of the garden was even worse. She wanted to wander and plan and design how and what she could do with this space, but, since she had no money, it was hard to imagine any workable options at this time. At least she had no pressure to do all of it now.

That brought back memories—when she had been only a decoration on a rich man's arm—how she'd directed gardeners to do what she wanted, regardless of the cost. As she stared at her massive backyard space, nonstop ideas filtered in. She smiled with delight, then walked back inside, grabbed her pad of paper and a pencil, and was about to step outside again when she realized the teakettle was still on.

That had never bothered her before, but now she couldn't leave the house while any appliance was running. The thought of having this house—her home—burn to the ground was too unnerving. She'd only recently settled into having something of *her* own and couldn't bear to lose it.

Making tea for herself over the past couple days had been an eye-opening experience. She used to get fancy lattes with beautiful patterns on the top without realizing they came from a five-thousand-dollar machine and a skilled barista. What she could do with five thousand dollars right now. ... She cringed every time she thought about the seemingly insignificant cost of one of those fancy lattes that she'd consumed on a daily basis when married. A humble cup of home-brewed tea was a simple pleasure now, those fancy coffees an indulgence. Something she could no longer afford.

She waited until the teakettle fully boiled, then dropped a tea bag into a large chipped mug Nan had left behind and poured the boiling water atop it. Checking the fridge, she was relieved to find a little bit of milk left inside an open carton.

She opened the top, took a whiff, and grinned. It was still sweet. She poured a splash into her tea, put the carton back into the fridge, picked up her cup, and said to Mugs, "Are you ready to go outside?"

Mugs barked joyfully at the trigger word.

The door was already open, but she propped it to stay that way with one of the chairs off the veranda. Mugs ran forward, his great big saggy facial jowls wobbling and shaking with every step. Thaddeus flew overhead—although how the bird could fly, Doreen didn't know. When she had first arrived, he didn't fly much. Now he did a half-soaring and half–free fall to the ground. But he did it very elegantly. Or at least it would be elegant if the words pouring out of his mouth weren't "Damn thing. Damn thing."

Why did he have to repeat himself? She had heard him the first time ... unfortunately.

Goliath raced past again, his tail in the air.

Apparently this was a family outing.

She chuckled. It was a beautiful day, and everything felt ... right.

She wandered the far back area of the property, her entourage in tow. The paperwork still had to be processed to legally transfer the house, compliments of her grandmother, into Doreen's name. Nan had chosen to move into a nearby seniors' home and had left her house to Doreen. She'd been absolutely stunned and heartened by Nan's generosity at a time when Doreen had been desperately in need of a place to call home and a pillow to lay her head on at night.

Thaddeus flew down and landed on her shoulder. Doreen stroked the beautiful bird's head. "Good bird." But Thaddeus didn't repeat that. *Figures.*

Now she wandered the backyard, taking delight in the garden, knowing it was hers forever. Even though overwhelmed with weeds, the garden held so much potential. Seeing several small trees in the mix, Doreen walked closer and gasped. "Fruit trees," she cried out in joy. Bending down to avoid the unruly branches, she studied the leaves and identified an Italian plum, maybe an apricot too, and one she wasn't sure of—possibly a cherry tree.

Fruit trees were a delightful addition to her garden. This place could shine with a little effort—everything outside came alive in her mind as she contemplated the improvements she could make.

Doreen heard muffled grunts and stopped to see what Mugs was digging up. Thankfully it was just dirt this time.

Gardening was Doreen's one and only talent. But designing a garden that *somebody else* would implement was a whole different story than making it happen by her own elbow grease. She didn't know the last time she'd held a shovel in her hand. She wasn't at all sure how much physical strength would be required to clean up this backyard. Plus she'd signed on to do some gardening for Mack's mother, hopefully for some much-needed money. Just the reminder of the local detective who'd helped her navigate the nightmare of finding several bodies in her garden last week made her chuckle.

He was a very interesting man ...

And likely thought she was nuts. Then it had been a crazy week, her first week living in one of the oldest neighborhoods in Kelowna Mission, so she could hardly blame him.

Mack had helped her through this trying time. He had been a godsend when the bodies had showed up at her place. Not that the dead bodies were her fault by any means, but somehow she happened to trip over them. Or maybe she should blame Goliath. Or Mugs. They had both helped ... or hindered. Then there was Thaddeus ...

She frowned as she watched her brood, especially the dog sniffing deep into the brush. "Mugs, don't you dare find any more bodies," she warned. "We've had more than enough corpses in our world."

Mugs gave a heavy *woof* and continued to waddle forward, the grass splitting wide to let his girth through. She grinned. He had been with her for five years already. She had inherited both Goliath and Thaddeus from Nan, as part and parcel with her house. Goliath had an attitude. He came and went on his own and still demanded that she look after him when he did show up. Kind of like her soon-to-be ex-husband. Only Goliath had had his tomcat ways fixed, and her almost ex-husband had not.

She chuckled at that. "That's what we should have done. We should have had him fixed. Then he wouldn't have brought home another arm ornament and booted me out."

Regardless, she was better off without him. Now all she had to do was figure out how to make money. At least enough to keep the electricity on in the house and food in the fridge. It was proving to be a bigger challenge than she'd realized.

But that wasn't today's problem. She walked over to the dilapidated fence, built out of several different materials, each of them finding their own unique way of partially crumbling to the ground. It might keep out some people, but it sure as hell wouldn't keep out anybody who didn't want to stay out.

She wished she could afford brand-new fencing all the way around the property because that would be the place to start. Structural work first, then do the prettier stuff. In this case, she wasn't sure how to do the structural stuff, especially on a shoestring budget.

She walked to the rickety, now-broken gate—Mugs behind her, Thaddeus still on her shoulder, Goliath off somewhere—unlooped the wire from the post, and pulled it open. She stepped outside to the path and the pretty creek that ran behind her property. She didn't want the fence along here at all. Most of it was past saving anyway.

About 140 feet of the creek's footage area was a beautiful sight to see from her backyard, much more so than a dilapidated fence. She looked closer at the creek, not sure to call it a creek or a river. Right now it was more of a babbling brook. But she imagined, later this spring, it could get a little bit uglier. Still, the creek's bank had a decent slope, so flooding shouldn't be much of a problem. She spotted a place where she could set up a little flagstone patio to sit and to enjoy the water.

Thaddeus flew from her shoulder to land near the water, strutting around, looking hopefully for fish and bugs.

No defined pathway was on this side of the creek, and everybody else's property was fenced off from the creek too. She thought that was such a shame. The creek offered a beautiful, peaceful view.

She walked back to her rearmost fence, put her pad of paper and teacup down on a rock, then grasped a fence post and shook it to see how strong it was. Instantly the fence made a low groaning sound and bent over sideways. She jumped back, crying out, "Oh, no."

But whatever she'd done had been too much for the old wood. Several of the fence panels toppled to the side, creating a bigger mess than she'd intended. Mugs came closer, but she shooed him away. "No, Mugs. Stay back. You could hurt yourself on a nail."

As she retreated into her backyard, coaxing Mugs with her, and stared toward the babbling brook, she laughed. "It might not be the way I had planned to do this, Mugs, but the end result is beautiful. It really opened up the view." She took Mugs's silence to be acquiescence.

Some really nice overhanging willows were on the far side of the brook, and her property had other trees dotted along the remains of her back fence. She had a small bridge just at the other end of the property that she could access. In fact, it was a beautiful scene.

Enthused by what she'd accidentally started, she returned to the remainder of her fence and gave it a shake. And, sure enough, three-quarters of the rest of the creekside fence fell to the ground, almost grateful to give up the effort to stand any longer.

With a big smile, she walked to the last piece of this section, all wire fencing with iron rods deep into the ground. She pushed and pulled on the first iron rod, hoping it would be loose too. The first one was, but the second one wasn't. She managed to lift up one and watched as most of the wire fencing fell into a big snarly mess around the next pole still standing. What she really needed was a handyman to finish pulling out the fence and to haul it off, but she didn't have one. That brought back unwanted memories of last week's events. The only handyman she had known of in town had been murdered.

With a shake of her head, she returned to the problem at hand. She wasn't sure how much yard debris she could transport in her small Honda. A truck would be helpful to make a trip to the dump. She wondered what it would take to get somebody big and strong to come give her a hand.

On that thought, Mack came to mind. Again. The detective was well over six foot—his shoulders were almost as broad as he was tall. He was a big mountain of a man. But, so far, he'd been very gentle and kind to her. Although she exasperated him more than anything.

But all for the right reasons …

Chapter 2

UNFORTUNATELY DOREEN WASN'T sure Mack believed that though. Nor had he believed her at first about the dead bodies. It took closing an old cold case and several more current cases before he did. So, all in all, Mack should be thanking her. Maybe he should even be paying her for her assistance. She brightened for a moment, contemplating the idea of a fat check coming from the local Royal Canadian Mounted Police and then shook her head.

"Not going to happen."

She shrugged. It was her current reality. And, for whatever it was worth, she was a whole lot happier now than when she had been a plastic Barbie who never worried about money.

She stared at the scratch on her palm, blood already welling up. She should have worn gardening gloves. No point looking at her damaged nails. Besides, she couldn't see them for the dirt.

"Doreen?"

She spun around and yelled, "I'm in the back!" She turned toward the felled wire fence and sighed. This would make a mess of her hands. And possibly her back. She headed to her teacup, scooped it off the rock, and took a sip. When she heard footsteps, she pivoted to see Mack walking toward her, holding Goliath while scratching his furry head, and talking to Mugs who had run to greet him. She set down her cup and beamed. There was just something about Mack …

Mack grinned, setting the cat free on the grass, giving Mugs a smile and a quick ear rub. "Leave you alone for a week and look at you. You're ripping the place apart."

She laughed. "Well, someone had to," she said with a smile.

Thaddeus decided to join them now, landing inside the backyard.

"Hey, boy," Mack said, waiting for the bird to walk to him for a quick pat on the head.

All three animals clustered nearby to watch the big man.

"What brings you by?" Doreen asked.

He pointed to the front of the house. "Is that crowd bothering you?"

She shrugged. "The notoriety is definitely different. Can't say I'm accustomed to it. However, the stress is easing slightly."

"Well, you are accustomed to notoriety, just not necessarily at this level."

She winced at the reminder of her wealthy now-estranged husband and the number of times she'd been photographed as his partner at one do or another. She nodded. "Point to you. Doesn't necessarily mean I like the sensationalism though."

He motioned to the fence. "Did you mean to take that down?"

She glared at him. "Does it look like I did it by accident?"

He laughed. "With you, anything's possible." He walked over and tested the corner post. "This won't stand for long either." He looked at the long and rambling busted-up fence on the side edge of her property shared with one neighbor and the big fancy fence butted up against it that was her neighbor's. "Are you going to remove this side too?"

"Is there any reason I can't and just use the neighbor's fence?"

He shrugged. "That's what I'd do."

With a big fat smile, she asked, "Can you pull out the last of those posts?" She was almost rubbing her hands together in joy at the thought of getting rid of this huge eyesore. Having this much of the ragtag fencing down had opened up so much of the creek's natural beauty that she couldn't wait to get rid of the rest of her creekside fence.

It seemingly took him nothing but the same effort to lift a cup of coffee, and he had the huge iron post up and out of the ground.

She couldn't even rock the pole slightly.

"It's a big mess back here," Mack said. "For now, the only good place to drag this old fencing is in the middle of the backyard. It'll take some of this plant stuff here with it."

"That *plant stuff* you're talking about happens to be perennial bushes that I would like to keep."

He glared at her but twisted so he had the post with both hands, pulled it higher over his head, and dragged what he could toward the center of her backyard where it ended up in a big heap on the lawn. "You'll need some good wire cutters to clip this into manageable pieces."

"What I need is a truck to make a trip to the dump," she announced. "I can't get very much in my car at one time."

"After you work on Mom's garden project, we'll probably make a trip to the dump, depending on how much yard waste we need to get rid of at Mom's house and how much new compost we may need to add. We can always take some of your yard debris at the same time."

She beamed. "Now that would be lovely." Then she frowned. "I don't think I have any tools that will cut up this wire fencing."

"I don't know. Nan had a whole pile of them in the hall closet."

Doreen glanced at him in surprise and then remembered the hall closet full of an odd assortment of things. "You could be right. I'll go check." She started toward the house before suddenly turning and calling out, "Careful! Don't hurt those plants!"

He shot her a look but continued to struggle with the posts.

Leaving him standing there, tugging at more fencing, trying to pull it up without damaging the plants, she headed inside to the closet. Once there, she wasn't exactly sure what wire cutters looked like. She found a hammer though—she needed that to pull out the nails in the wooden boards on the fallen pieces of fencing.

She grabbed what looked like two pairs of something—possibly what she needed—and, with the hammer, raced back outside. As she reached Mack, she held them up and said, "Ta-da."

He took one look, and his smile fell away. He started to laugh.

"What's wrong with that?"

He pointed to one and said, "Those are fancy toenail clippers for a dog."

She stared at them and then over at Mugs, who gave her a look that could have said, "Don't you dare."

She shook her head. "I've never seen any like this."

"It certainly won't cut wire. Now these, on the other hand," he said, taking the other pair that looked like weird shears to her, "will probably do it." He tested them on the center post he had pulled out. Instantly the wire snapped under his grip. He went to the main rod, cutting the wire off there and said, "Now do that to every one of those posts and separate the wire so you can roll it into a bundle."

She nodded eagerly. "I can do that." While she'd been searching for tools, he'd pulled out the rest of the main posts. Some of the plants were likely damaged, but she would spend the afternoon cutting this fencing monstrosity into something easier to handle. She smiled. "You can see how much better it looks already."

He turned and studied her massive backyard all the way to the creek and nodded. "You're right. Just getting rid of that ugly nightmare has opened it up beautifully. But you don't want a fence at the back?"

She shook her head. "No, I want to see the creek. It's beautiful." She led him to where she'd been standing earlier. "I think I would put a patio in here."

"Don't let the government know about that," he warned. "This is a riparian zone. You're not allowed to do anything without a mess of permits."

She lifted her eyebrows. "Permits? It's my land. Why can't I put down some flagstones?"

He shrugged. "All I can tell you is, you'll probably need a permit to do even that much."

She frowned, disgruntled. The last thing she wanted was anybody to stop her gardening fun. "I can just make it gravel then. I don't know. That's not a top priority. I have this lovely bank and a small path and the bridge. Although old, it's solid." Except for where she'd put her foot through one of the boards last week.

The bridge theoretically could be used by anyone, but she'd never seen anybody walking that creekside path, as it was quite overgrown and not very popular. But, for Mugs, it was a great way to get exercise. He could use it.

Just then Thaddeus hopped onto the pad of paper on the rock, sending it and her pencil flying into her teacup. The teacup fell with a crash to the rocks below, and Thaddeus hopped farther away from the damage. But, of course, in his high piercing voice, he called out, "Damn thing. Damn thing."

"Oh, Thaddeus, why do you say that?" She walked over, collected the busted pieces of china and the pad of paper, now covered in tea. It was her fault. She shouldn't have put it here. But she had no table or outdoor chairs at this spot that she could have otherwise used.

"I see you're teaching him more words." Mack kept his voice carefully bland.

She sent him a suspicious look. "Not intentionally."

He chuckled. "I'm pretty sure that damn bird will pick up everything you don't want him to."

Thaddeus looked at Mack with beady eyes, tilted his head to one side, and said, "Damn bird. Damn bird. Damn bird."

She groaned. "Watch what you say around him."

Mack held out his hands. "Me? I'm not the one who taught him the first phrase."

"But now you have taught him the second one," she snapped. "Before we know it, he'll know all the curse words and shock the neighbors."

"I think you've already shocked the neighbors," Mack said with a grin. "Finding bodies, capturing a murderer, and solving a case that has been cold for a long time all definitely counts as shocking the neighbors."

She blushed at the admiration in his tone. "Well, I did my best. Besides, you needed my help."

"I did *not* need your help," he blustered. "I have been a detective for a long time, solving crimes well before you ever came here."

"Yes, but you didn't solve this one, did you?" She couldn't help teasing him.

"Well, how was I to know you had a body hidden on your property?"

She shrugged. "At least *we* solved it," she said, magnanimously adding, "the two of us together."

He hesitated, tilted his head in her direction. "Okay, I'll give you that. We did that one together."

She beamed. "Now that Thaddeus has emptied my tea and broken my cup, do you want to go inside and have a cup of tea?"

He shook his head. "I'll take a rain check on that. I stopped by to ask if you could come to my mother's house. She's got a patch of begonias she's fretting about. I don't know if you can fix them. But, while we're there, we could discuss what to do and when."

Doreen donned her expert gardener face. "Of course I know how to deal with ailing begonias. I have begonias here that need to get into the ground. They were dug out when your department came and removed the body. The first one."

He nodded. "And since I mentioned that begonias had

been pulled out here, my mother has been fretting over the begonias in her garden."

"When do you want to go?"

He hesitated. "I don't want her to worry, so would you mind coming with me now, just to take a quick look? We'll come up with a plan on what we can do with them."

Excited, Doreen said, "Absolutely. Let's go."

They walked around to the driveway. Ignoring the people standing and staring outside her house, not saying a word to anyone, Doreen hopped into his truck, Mugs trying to follow her. "Okay if Mugs rides with us?"

Only it wasn't just Mugs as Goliath raced toward them, Thaddeus squawking from the porch before soaring in their direction.

"Everyone? Really?" Mack sighed and allowed time for Doreen to pick up her menagerie. When they were all in the vehicle, he reversed out of her driveway and drove the five minutes to his mother's house. It was close enough to walk, but then they would have been accosted by all the curious onlookers.

As they got out of his vehicle, he said, "She should be napping still. I left her ready to go to sleep and came straight to your place." They slipped around to the back, and he pointed out a large patch that wasn't doing very well.

Doreen sighed. "If these are begonias, they've definitely seen better days." She wandered the large six-foot-plus patch and then bent down on her hands and knees, plunging her fingers into the dirt, checking and testing the soil. "I'm not exactly sure what's wrong with them. Is there a shovel handy?"

He brought over a small spade. She dug in close to the roots on the first bush, pulling up some of the dirt so she could see the root system. After scooping away several spades full, she stopped, brushed off some of the dirt against the tubers, and took a closer look. "They're definitely not happy. How often are they getting water?"

"There are sprinklers and soaker hoses on timers. So they should be getting plenty."

She nodded and shifted her spade back a little bit, so she could pull out more dirt. Some perlite was all around the base of the plant, but the black dirt was decent. Although plenty of clay was here too, it appeared to be absorbing enough water. As she pulled up another handful, she froze.

Mack bent down beside her. "What's the matter?"

She plucked up something white, dropping it in his hand. She turned to look at him. "Is this what I think it is?"

He frowned, shook his head, but his mouth opened, and then he froze. "I sure as hell hope not."

"It would be fitting," she said in a dark tone.

"How?" he barked, his gaze on what was in his hand.

She snickered. "Bones in the begonias, anyone?"

Chapter 3

M ACK GLARED AT her. "That's not funny."
        Doreen slapped her hands over her mouth to
hold back the giggles and stared at Mack. "Then tell me it's
not human."

The glum look on his face said it all. "I can't say that."

She peered closer. "That could be a raccoon bone. It
could be a bone from a squirrel. There's no way we can say
it's human right now."

He reached into his pocket, pulled out a small bag, and
stuffed the bone in there. "There is one way. I'll take it to the
lab. But they'll need a few days."

"Good," she said shortly. "I need more than a week between bodies, please."

At that, he gave her a sideways look and grinned. The
grin quickly turned into an infectious laugh.

She stared at him, feeling her own sense of humor returning. "The only funny thing I see about this is the fact
that, this time, it's your mother's property."

Instantly his laughter cut off. He glared at her. "That's
not funny."

She smiled sweetly. "No, but it's true." She stood,

glanced around. "And your mom has a lovely garden back here. If there are bones in the begonias, well, maybe it's not her fault either." She glanced at him. "How long has she lived here?"

He frowned. "I was born and raised here. And she was here probably soon after she married my father." He turned his gaze to the house. "I don't exactly know how many years ago though. Fiftyish?"

"Might be time to find out." Ignoring him, she walked the length of the begonia bed, then surveyed the whole backyard garden. "Everything is healthy but the begonias. So we can transplant them to another location, turn this particular plot of soil over, enrich it with some peat moss, fertilizer, and some perlite—maybe new soil, depending on the last time your mother boosted this area. Then plant a different perennial there."

Willing to change the subject, he turned to the rest of the garden. "Where would you put the begonias?"

"Begonias love sun." She turned in a slow circle, study- ing the garden that ran the perimeter of the backyard. "There's a lot of sun on that back fence over there." She walked closer and studied the big daisy bushes in the spot she had in mind. "Daisies will grow in poorer conditions. We could do a switch. Move the daisies to where the begonias are."

She contemplated the idea as she glanced around at a few other bushes. "You've also got a big spot here." She walked to a patch of bare garden beside some azaleas and what looked like a big rhododendron. "You can always split up the daisies and pop one in here and scatter them around the yard. They throw a nice touch of white color throughout the summer."

"I'll talk to my mother about that."

Doreen nodded. "You do that. In the meantime, when you decide what you want to do, you can give me a call. We'll walk home, except I guess Goliath will do what he wants to do." She gave Mack a cheerful finger wave and headed out the backyard gate. "Come on, Mugs and Thaddeus. We've done enough damage here."

Thaddeus walked toward her, calling out, "Damn bone. Damn bone."

She sighed. "That's not quite what we said, Thaddeus."

Thaddeus tilted his head to the side as he started forward.

She held the gate open for him, and, before he passed through, a golden streak raced through the opening. It almost sent poor Thaddeus tumbling. "Goliath, remember your manners."

Goliath stopped, turned, gave Doreen a malevolent look, and slowly loped forward.

She bent and caught Thaddeus. "How about a ride, big guy?" She popped Thaddeus on her shoulder.

He leaned forward and stroked his head along her cheek. "Thank you. Thank you."

She laughed. "That was appropriate. Who taught you to talk anyway?"

"Miss Nan. Miss Nan."

Instantly Doreen felt homesick. "Well, we can go the long way home and stop to visit her, if you want. Or maybe go to town after a cup of tea?"

With a nod of Thaddeus's head at her second suggestion, she opted for heading home.

As she carried on past the fence, she cast a glance behind her to see Mack standing in his mother's backyard, his hands on his hips as he watched her with her trio maneuver toward the creek path. She waved again. He waved back, but she caught the odd look on his face. Whether it was because he heard her talking to the bird or because of the begonias and whatever they'd found, she didn't know.

Surely by now he'd be used to her though, so she voted for the bone she found in the begonia bed being what upset him. It would certainly keep her attention for a while. Maybe longer than a while actually. As she made her way to her backyard to walk around the partially dismantled fence, her animals dispersed, and she stopped and stared. "We've made a bigger mess than ever. What are we going to do about that?"

"Hey," a bright cheery voice called from the side of her house.

Doreen turned to frown at the stranger coming toward her. "May I help you?" she asked politely. She was almost more determined to get a new fence up across the front, including the driveway, than she was worried about taking this one apart. Since the media had found out about the murder cases, they'd been all over her property.

The woman extended a hand, but she was a little too perfectly coiffed to make Doreen happy. She'd seen women like her a lot over the years. This one had entered her backyard without an invitation, making her someone Doreen *really* didn't want to talk to.

Yet manners always came to the forefront. Her soon-to-be ex-husband had drilled that into her all the time. It didn't matter if she liked somebody or not. *Smile and use those manners to your advantage.* She plastered her bright society smile on her face and shook the woman's hand.

"My name is Sibyl. I'm here from the Kelowna newspaper. You've been giving all kinds of interviews to the big television and newspaper reporters, but you haven't done an exclusive for us yet."

Doreen bared her teeth. "And I won't either. And now that you've identified who you are, you can please remove yourself from my property."

The smile fell from the woman's face. "Oh, dear. I didn't mean to upset you."

"There's a reason why I've been avoiding the crowd in the front. It's called *I don't want to talk to anybody anymore about this*." Doreen crossed her arms over her chest and tapped her fingers on her arm. "So please turn around and leave."

"Well, maybe I'll just ask you about the fact that our lovely police detective, Mack Moreau, is over here a lot still." The woman's tone turned insinuating and slimy.

Doreen tilted her head and pulled out her phone. "And he'll be here in two seconds flat to arrest you for trespassing."

The woman took a mock step back and raised her hands. "Oh, dear. Aren't you feisty?"

The thing was, Doreen wasn't kidding. As much as she wanted to fit into the community and to make this place her home, the last thing she wanted was to be hounded by reporters. She lifted the phone to her ear and said, "Mack, I've got a lady here …" She repeated the woman's name and the newspaper she mentioned she worked for. "She's making insinuations about your visits to my place and won't leave my property. Please come and remove her."

Mugs walked closer to the reporter and sniffed her shoe.

The woman jumped away and just missed Mugs lifting his leg where she'd been standing. "No, no, no. Don't tell him that."

Doreen snorted as she stared at Sibyl. "Why the hell wouldn't I?"

And there she'd done it again. She'd only ever sworn since moving here. Not good. Yet another part of her loved it. The freedom to swear and to not have anybody chastise her publicly for it? … Priceless.

"Well, I didn't mean to upset you," the woman said as she backed up hurriedly.

"Really?" Doreen said. "I got the impression that not only did you try to insinuate yourself into my life and to pry information from me but you also were slurring Mack's character, not to mention mine. And that's called slander." At that, she laughed inside. She'd heard her almost ex-husband say something almost identical to that at a party one time. She never thought that one of his party tidbits would be useful, but apparently this one was.

The woman quickly retreated, waved at her gently, and said, "How about I come back another day when you're feeling better."

"How about another decade when I no longer live here? And I'm feeling just fine, thanks," Doreen snapped.

The woman turned and dashed around to the front of the house, almost tripping as Goliath dashed in front of her path.

Had he done that on purpose? *I hope so.*

At that point, she heard Mack's voice in her ear. "Wow, I don't think I've ever heard you act like that before."

And, to her mortification, she actually had dialed Mack. She'd just dialed half the digits, or so she thought. Instead she had completed the call, and Mack had been listening in on her conversation as she had yelled at the reporter. "Mack, I don't know what's happening to me," she said, bewilderment in her voice. "This has been such a circus."

His voice softened. "Take it easy. You have good reason to be irate. Let me know if she comes back, and I'll have a talk with her."

"Well, if she comes back, I'm likely to set one of the animals on her. Mugs didn't like her. But I don't think she even noticed when he deliberately lifted his leg."

"He didn't pee on her, did he?" Mack's voice was raised in a fascinated horror.

"No, more's the pity." She shook her head. "The woman moved because of what I said. She doesn't realize how lucky she truly is."

Mack laughed. "You and those animals. Are you okay now?"

"I was okay before. I didn't mean to dial your number. I was using the phone more as a prop to get her to behave. But I accidentally completed the call. I'm sorry you had to hear that. I'm really not as incapable of taking care of myself as I might seem."

"You're doing very well. Have a little self-confidence and trust in some of us, and you'll be fine." And just like that he hung up the phone.

She smiled and straightened her shoulders. Mack was right. She *was* doing much better. Hell, she'd helped him solve several murder cases. And that was huge. Maybe, if she could do it again, she'd get some respect from people around here and not just a macabre fascination. It pissed her off that the woman had been so bold and nervy as to come into Doreen's backyard. Doreen wondered what her rights were as a homeowner.

She wandered around to the side of the house and stared out toward the front yard. The woman was there with her cameraman. And they were taking pictures of the front of her house. She understood from Mack that she could not do a whole lot about that. But damned if she would let them on her property.

She walked into the kitchen, locating a large piece of corrugated cardboard by the laundry. She picked it up, grabbed a permanent marker, and wrote NO TRESPASSING on the front, and then, on the bottom, she wrote TRES-PASSERS WILL BE PROSECUTED. Walking back outside, she then grabbed one of the fence posts Mack had pulled out. An I-beam, he had called it.

She walked to the garden right at the front of the property, ignoring the cameras that clicked and whirled in her face. Several people called out to her. She ignored them all. Thaddeus joined her as she punched the cardboard through the post twice so the sign would stay up, then pushed the vertical metal post into the edge of the soft garden bed. Then she twisted it so people could see her sign. Without saying another word, she turned and walked to her front porch.

The people standing there gasped and said, "Well, I never."

She stiffened her back and kept on marching, Thaddeus flew ahead to meet her at the door. Mugs wasn't with her—he'd stayed in the garage. Smart dog. He didn't like the nosy crowds any more than she did. Of Goliath, there was no sign.

She walked up to the front door and said, "Good riddance."

As she stepped inside, Thaddeus turned and called out to the crowd, "Good riddance. Good riddance."

She gasped, ran inside with Thaddeus at her heels, and slammed the front door shut.

Chapter 4

B ACK INSIDE SHE headed for her kitchen and her trusty *electric* teakettle.

Her soon-to-be ex-husband always headed for the bottle when he found a situation stressful. When she'd lived with him, she'd always gone to her room to get away. Tea had never been part of the equation. But now it was the solace she needed. And given what she'd been through, it was very necessary. Besides, it could be much worse. It wasn't like she was pouring alcohol into her tea. Although, if she'd had any around, she might today. But with money so tight, she had none to spare for such an indulgent item.

She put the teakettle back on, glaring at the stove. If only she could figure out how that thing was supposed to work properly. She knew all about cooking shows and cooking videos and stuff, but somehow, whenever she tried a recipe, it ended up being a big mess or only half done. And she just didn't understand how it was all supposed to go together. She wondered about taking a cooking class, but again there was the money issue. On top of that, she didn't want anybody to know how absolutely inept she was in the kitchen.

Nan had told Doreen that boiling eggs was simple, just a pot of water and eggs. But she had yet to try it. Partially because of the damn stove. She couldn't seem to get it to light properly. She should have mentioned it to Mack.

She pulled out her phone, intending to call him, but realized how much she'd been leaning on him lately. That wasn't fair to him. As long as she had an electric teakettle, she could plug that in and have tea and broth. She also had a microwave and was learning to use that.

With another cup of tea she headed back outside to the rear garden. As soon as she stepped out the kitchen door, she saw the mess from the fence. She sighed, but was distracted as Mugs ran straight for the open edge along the creek. "Mugs, you stay on the property," she warned.

Mugs turned to look at her. And then, ignoring her, wandered to the other side of the gate. The gate still stood, which was foolish because the fence around it was gone.

Stepping back into the house, she rummaged in Nan's messy front hall closet and found a pair of gardening gloves. They weren't very thick, but they would do for the moment.

Taking her tea, she walked back outside again and sat on a big rock. With the clippers, she cut apart the wire fencing. She laid the poles neatly on one side, then, with manageable pieces of the wire fencing, stretched them out and stacked them up. It was hot, dusty work. But it was honest work, and she appreciated that. It was also unpaid work. And that sucked big-time.

However, the weather was perfect for gardening work.

By the time she straightened and rubbed her lower back, several hours had passed. Still, she'd accomplished something. Even if only to unearth a rubber block, an old silt screen she couldn't even begin to understand why Nan had, and a chipped pottery mug. She turned to look around to locate all her animals. Mugs had stretched out on the grass beside her, snoring. Goliath had taken a perch on top of the rock where she'd put her cup earlier. Of Thaddeus, she had no sign. She frowned and looked around. "Thaddeus? Thaddeus?" No answer. "Mugs, where's the bird?"

Mugs didn't even open an eye.

"Well, you're no help."

She stepped away from the fence line and turned around and laughed. She'd found Thaddeus. He sat on top of the neighbor's fence. He'd chosen the corner fence post hidden behind an overgrowth of bushes and had perched there, surveying the world around him.

"How come you didn't answer when you were called, Thaddeus?"

He turned, fixed her with a gimlet eye, and then immediately swiveled his head back in the direction he'd been staring. Curious, she walked closer, picking her way through the overgrown garden to see what the bird had found.

She peered around the neighbor's fence, staring at the beautiful creek, and asked Thaddeus, "What are you looking at?"

In a voice that she hadn't heard before, Thaddeus said, "Old bones. Old bones."

She groaned. "You have a horrible turn of phrase. You know that, right?"

He made a weird cry and flew off the fence post. But Thaddeus wasn't meant to fly anymore. Not only was one of his wings gimped but apparently the wing feathers were supposed to stay clipped so he couldn't fly. She hadn't done anything about it, but Nan had, although she had warned Doreen that he didn't fly well anyway.

As she watched, Thaddeus made a half-crash landing at the edge of the brook, the long grass flattening beneath him.

She hated the thought that immediately came to mind. Seeing one dead body in the creek was more than enough for anybody. She headed over to see what Thaddeus was up to. He sat perched on a rock and just stared.

With her heart sinking, she walked closer. "What's the matter, Thaddeus?"

Mugs, suddenly awake, barked and raced up behind her.

"I wasn't going for a walk, Mugs."

But Mugs ignored her and raced ahead to where Thaddeus sat. Mugs parked his butt with surprising force beside the parrot.

She laughed. "Well, it's not like you're a pointer or a search-and-rescue dog giving me signals. So I don't know what the heck your problem is." In fact, she'd never seen Mugs act like he had since they'd arrived here at Nan's house.

She glanced back, but Goliath appeared completely unconcerned about their antics. In fact, his eyes were closed. She took the last few steps out to the edge of the creek and studied the water. "See? Nothing's there, guys."

But the dog and the bird weren't listening. She took several more steps down the creek way, but she couldn't see anything wrong or out of place. She smiled with relief. That was a good thing. She'd had her full share of dead bodies already.

The longer she looked, the better she felt. She motioned to Mugs. "Come on, Mugs. Let's go home."

Of course, she was already home, only a few feet past her property line. But still Mugs stared at the water, and so did Thaddeus.

She groaned and decided to play the game too. She walked over to stand directly behind them and asked, "What are you looking at?"

Just then an orange streak ripped past her, and Goliath appeared. Somehow he'd woken up, maybe realizing he was all alone. He approached the creek from a few feet up the path and hopped onto a rock in the middle.

"You like water?" Doreen asked in disbelief.

Goliath shot her a look.

She wasn't sure what she was supposed to make of it. It was a cross between *Don't be a stupid idiot* and *Of course I love water. All cats do. NOT.*

She shook her head at her fanciful thoughts until Goliath also stared down at the water. Now all three of them, from different spots, were focused on a point in the middle. She groaned. "I don't know what the hell you guys are looking at. Not sure I want to either."

Nevertheless she grabbed a stick and poked the creek bed, which only had a couple inches of water in it at this spot. But, even as she poked it, the silt moved, and the water picked up the sand and carried it down the creek. And left the spot just underneath clean. And damn if she didn't find something white and ... creepy.

Was that another bone? "That doesn't mean it's a human bone," she muttered, swallowing hard. "No reason to suspect anything *human* is here. It could be a raccoon bone. It could be a squirrel bone. Hell, it could be a rock."

Yet seeing it reminded her of the other bone she'd found in Mack's mom's begonia bed. Even though it hadn't been confirmed as a human bone, Doreen worried that it was.

But here? ... She had to know for sure. She took off her shoes and socks and stepped into the water. And cried out,

"Holy crap, that's cold."

She leaned down and brushed away whatever was half covering the item. As she picked it up, she laughed. "See? It's not a bone at all, you guys."

It was a small ivory case. With a lid. It was beautiful. She studied it and gave a crow of delight. Pretty etchings were on the side. "Will you look at this?" She tried to open the lid, but it was sealed or stuck. She flipped it around, looked at it, had no way to see what was inside—and didn't want to shake the box for fear of breaking up whatever could be hidden there, if anything—but she did find a name on the underside.

"*Betty Miles*," she said out loud. She turned to the animals and said, "Nice discovery, guys. Maybe we could find this Betty Miles online and notify her. She probably wants us to return her property."

As she stood admiring the little white box, a gruff voice from the other side of the fence beside her called over, "Who are you talking to?"

Doreen winced and fell silent. Then finally she gave it up and said, "I'm talking to Mugs, the dog."

"Well, what the hell are you talking about that murdered girl for?"

Doreen fell silent. She stared at the name on the little white box and then at the fence, where she couldn't see her neighbor standing on the other side. "What murdered girl?"

"Betty Miles," her neighbor said in a querulous voice. "Isn't that the name you just said?"

The neighborhood had made a point of fencing the entire back of the creek so they couldn't even see the water. She didn't understand why anyone would do that. "Yes, that's the name. But I don't know anything about her."

"Not many people talk about her anymore," her neighbor said.

Doreen wasn't sure if the speaker was the husband, who she had met, or his wife. He was an older man. So Doreen suspected his wife was elderly too. There was just enough crankiness to the voice that it could be either one.

"At the time, there was a big media storm about it all," the neighbor said in disgust, this time sounding more feminine. "Something like what's going on out in front of our houses now. Ever since you found those damn bodies, there's been no peace and quiet here."

Doreen winced. "Yes, you're right. I'm sorry about that."

"No point being sorry. Just don't do it again. Maybe these people will finally realize nothing is here to see, and they will take off. Can't happen soon enough."

She decided it must be the man from next door. There was just something *male* about the way he said those last words. "Hopefully they'll leave soon." She hesitated and then asked, "What can you tell me about this Betty Miles?"

"I'm not telling you nothing. You'll just go off on another wild goose chase and bring the media back down on top of us. Like I need that."

The voice faded away, as if he walked toward his house.

"Well, can you tell me how long ago she was murdered?" Doreen called out.

"At least thirty years. One of the most famous cold cases around here."

"Where did she live?"

"Not too far from here, in the poorer section of the Mission. We were all interviewed by the cops because of that. Damn nuisance, the whole thing was."

"Nobody ever found out who killed her?"

"I didn't say that, did I? You want to know something, then you figure it out." And the voice fell silent.

But Doreen grinned. Solving a cold case was way better than working on her fence and digging into her overgrown garden. Something about a murder mystery caught her attention and held it. She couldn't wait to get inside and find out more.

Chapter 5

CARRYING HER FIND, Doreen nudged Mugs and Goliath and Thaddeus back inside. She couldn't wait to get to her computer and search for Betty Miles. Doreen was all about the fun of figuring out this mystery.

Inside she carefully placed the fancy box on the kitchen table. It was both clean and dirty. She laughed. "How can something be both, Doreen?"

But it was. The creek had kept it mostly clean. But, over time, the creases of the carvings had filled with sediment that filled the river. She wasn't sure if that was dirt all through it or something else. She grabbed her cell phone and took several photos of the box. She was learning. Once Mack knew about this, he'd be over here in a heartbeat, and she'd never see the box again.

Moving around it until she had photographs of all sides, she transferred all the images to her laptop. With that done, she got up and put on the electric teakettle. Only to remember she'd left her tea cup outside. She dashed outside to retrieve it as the water boiled.

As she walked back inside Mugs raced in at her heels thinking the run was good fun. The kettle wasn't ready yet though. While she waited, she looked online for the cold case that her neighbor had talked about. She frowned, thinking about her neighbor's voice. And the trouble was, that voice coming from behind the fence was androgynous. Doreen couldn't tell who she'd been talking to earlier today. It had been querulous and cranky, as if nothing was ever good enough for ... *it*. And she hated to use that term when *it* referred to a person, but she really didn't have a clue if the neighbor speaking to her today had been male or female. And that was a mystery in itself.

She grinned. *Another one.* Perfect.

When she ran her query through the search engine, all kinds of links came up. She read each one to find out that a Betty Miles had disappeared close to thirty years ago, like her neighbor had said. She'd been a troubled teen, running away from home several times. When she had disappeared the last time, everybody had thought she'd just run away again.

But, when she never came back, Betty's mother got worried. She filed a missing person's report, but apparently nobody had ever heard from or had ever seen Betty Miles again.

There was no evidence to indicate foul play, so the police hadn't been too bothered about it until, about one year later, an arm with a hand attached had shown up in a creek, also close to this part of the Mission area. Doreen leaned closer to the screen, studying the article in front of her. "Just an arm? That's bizarre."

She quickly read through the article, looking for more information, but it was typical journalism that took one salient fact and blew it into complete online articles that really had nothing new to add. And most of these articles were scanned in, rehashed years later.

Only the single arm and hand were ever found. They'd been xrayed after the ring was identified as having been given to her by her best friend. As it happened Betty Miles's middle finger on that hand had been broken and healed crooked.

"Does that count as a body?" Doreen mused aloud.

With no further evidence, the case ran cold. At the time there was a lot of sensationalism surrounding a series of murders in California where the victims had all been dismembered as well. Various parts had been tossed into garbage bags and then thrown all up and down the highways.

Doreen sat back and considered that. "Why grab a victim here in Canada only to spread the remains in California? Plus the local police didn't find Betty's arm in a garbage bag but tossed, or buried, in a nearby creek. So somebody cut up Betty and threw her body parts wherever he thought they wouldn't be found. And obviously one of his choices hadn't been well chosen."

As the teakettle whistled, she realized she had automatically assumed the killer was male.

She almost tripped over Mugs, who stared at her balefully. She glanced at him and said, "Sorry, Mugs. I know it's not your fault you're male. But really, most murders are committed by men."

She continued to talk to the dog as she dropped a teabag into her cup and filled it with hot water. If Doreen hadn't busted the teapot earlier this week, she would be making a complete pot of tea. She had to chuckle. Right now she was working her way through breaking Nan's chipped mugs. Why Nan had decided to keep a cupboard full of the darn things, Doreen didn't know. But having broken three already, she would have to find her own source of chipped mugs in a few weeks. Or maybe she could afford to buy a new one without a chip for a change.

With a fresh cup of tea, now with milk in it, she sat down at the table to continue her reading. "Fascinating stuff." And some of it she needed to keep track of.

She got up, found a notepad and a pen, and sat back down at the table. She titled the notepad with the teenager's name and then wrote down *Found arm and hand, detached after death—xrays confirmed identity.* And then Doreen added the fancy box found in the creek, just for her own notes.

She winced. Mack would have a heyday when he found out she had removed the ivory box from the creek, and she hadn't taken any photographs of where it lay in the creek itself. She sighed. "I really suck at this job." At the word *job*, she winced again. She glanced at Mugs, still staring at her. "Hey, I've got enough money to buy your dog food with Nan's pocket change, so it's all good. I'll find work at some point. Don't you worry."

Mugs gave her a soulful look, interested in something a little more than her words to reassure him.

She got up, walked to the cupboard missing its door, and peered in his food bowl. It was empty. With Mugs at her heels, his tail wagging, snuffling the ground around his bowl, she filled it up again. She spent a moment cuddling the big guy. Mugs was good for a lot of things, and giving comfort was one of them. She didn't know what she'd do without him. He'd been her mainstay, her calm center when her world had flipped so badly through her separation and now the pending divorce.

As she straightened up, her back screamed at her from the heavy garden work she had done earlier. She winced, grabbing the counter, finding Goliath there, staring down at her. She shook her head. "Oh, no you don't. You got food already today."

Meow.

"No, no, no. Mugs's bowl was empty. You ate his food, didn't you?" She turned and walked toward the table only to have Goliath run along the countertop, jump down, and wrap himself around her legs, almost tripping her. She groaned, reached down, scooped him up, and cried out, "You're heavy. You've gained weight since I've gotten here."

His big guttural engine kicked in, and he rubbed his head against her chin.

She chuckled. "I'm not that much of a sucker."

But he rubbed his head against her chin again and again. Then she heard his tummy growl. Horrified, she walked over to his bowls to find his dry food was gone too. She shook her head. "What is wrong with me? Normally I would never have forgotten to feed you guys." She frowned and looked from one bowl to the next. "Did you two just eat out of each other's bowls or something?"

It didn't matter because, according to Goliath, he was going to starve if she didn't feed him *right now.* She put him down, scooped up some dry kibble, and poured it into his bowl. Immediately he dropped his head in and feasted.

She stepped back. "Doreen, you've got to be losing it. You've never missed a day feeding these animals yet."

More than a little troubled, she returned to her seat at the table. Thaddeus wandered from one bowl to the other bowl. But he couldn't get his head into either. Both the dog and the cat were busy plowing through the food she'd given them.

She watched Thaddeus for a moment. "Thaddeus, did I feed you?"

Immediately his head turned, and he stared at her with a beady gaze. "Thaddeus. Thaddeus."

"I know you're Thaddeus. That doesn't tell me if you're hungry or not."

"Thaddeus hungry. Thaddeus hungry. Thaddeus hungry."

She groaned. "Of course you are. More to the point, you're only saying that you are so you don't lose out. I highly doubt any of you are starving."

She got up and walked over to the big hall closet where she kept the bird food. Thaddeus watched her, striding along behind her, his tail dragging on the floor. She didn't understand why he did that. She would look it up later, but it seemed that she never got on top of all of her questions to research when it came to the animals. She always got sidetracked by something else. It was a little disconcerting. She pulled out a handful of bird seed and returned to the kitchen table. She plunked down his food on top, watching as he dug in. "There. All animals fed. Do any of you care about me? I don't think I've eaten in hours."

On cue her stomach growled.

"Life never used to be this difficult."

She was torn between getting food for herself and doing more research. Finally she gave up, walked the few steps to the fridge, and opened it. But, if she didn't want sandwiches, it would be eggs for her. And that wasn't something she cooked very well yet. That was why the eggs were still there—like a taunting specter in front of her. She slammed the fridge door shut again. So it would be cheese and crackers again, which she gathered together on a plate. She found some cucumber and cut that up on the side. She stared at the simple meal and sighed.

"Remember when we had steak and lobster with red wine?"

None of the animals gave a darn about answering her. Such was her life now too.

Resuming her research again, her phone rang. She glanced down at the small screen. It was Mack. He seemed to have a sixth sense when she was looking into stuff she shouldn't be. Shaking off the misplaced guilt, she answered his call with an overly cheerful voice. "Hey, Mack. What's up?"

"What are you up to?"

She could hear the worry in his voice. *Silence.* "Nothing," she hurriedly reassured him. *How could he know?*

"Now I know you're up to something," he declared. "I'll be there in five minutes."

Chapter 6

S HE GROANED AND slammed down her phone. How could he possibly know? He didn't have to rush over, but he would because he was suspicious and wary of her. However, it was a good excuse to have Mack make some coffee while he was here. He was the best at making coffee she'd ever met. She could make a decent cup, but still, he had a special touch. It was frustrating because it was the same damn coffeemaker and the same damn coffee that she used. But when he did it, ... magic happened.

Like everything else that happened in the kitchen, other people seemed to have a special touch. Or maybe she was missing it. Either way her self-confidence was nonexistent when it came to food preparation of any kind. She continued to surf on the internet and sipped her tea until Mack arrived.

As soon as she heard him pull into the driveway, she slammed down the lid of her laptop. She got up and walked to the front door, opened it, and studied the crowd outside. A few vehicles and only one TV station van were here now. Maybe the crowd had finally gotten bored and had left to find other more amusing pursuits.

Mack waved at her as he closed the door to his vehicle.

He walked up her driveway, his stride determined and forceful. She liked that about him. He never hesitated. He always seemed to know what he was doing and why. Whereas, for her, life was just one big question mark.

He stepped onto the front porch. "Looks like the crowds are finally dispersing."

"Good," she snapped. "They can go bug someone else for a while."

He just grinned, motioned her inside, then stepped in behind her, shutting the door. "Did you put on coffee?"

"No, I didn't. You can put it on yourself."

He laughed, not fooled in the least. "You still haven't figured it out, have you?"

She flushed and looked at him with a sideways glance. "That's not fair. I make coffee every morning."

"Yeah, chances are, you aren't putting in enough grounds," he said.

She stood beside him and watched as he measured the water, poured it into the back of the maker, and then brought out her small grinder to grind the beans and afterward to put them into the coffee filter.

She shrugged. "I do exactly the same thing."

"*Maybe.* And maybe I'm just gifted."

Because it was too close to her earlier thought, she wouldn't give him the satisfaction of agreeing. "Any results from the lab on that bone we found in your mother's garden?"

Mack snorted. "It's too soon for any results, Doreen."

She walked over to the table and sat back down again, opening the lid on her laptop. But then she realized he would ask questions about what she was looking up. So she pushed the lid closed again. He slowly turned, glanced at her, at the laptop, back at her guilty face, and gave her a long serious look. "What are you up to?"

She gave him an innocent look that didn't fool him in the least. She shrugged and sat back, picking up her cup to drink the remains of her tea. "Why do I have to be up to anything?"

"You look guilty as hell," he snapped.

She pinched her lips closed and glared at him. It didn't matter how good-looking he was, he was still irritating.

He shoved his hands in his pockets, leaned against the counter, looking like a *GQ* model worthy of the front cover, even without trying.

She didn't know how he did that. Her former husband had to work at it. He had these fancy lotions and creams and hair sprays and conditioners to style his hair—more than Doreen used even back then—and his suits were always dry cleaned. Mack probably ran his fingers through his hair once he was awake and called it good enough. He wore jeans, shirt, and a blazer, and he looked just fine—rugged and handsome and fit. It was a natural look, and he wore it well.

But he waited and waited, his gaze going to the animals, now collecting around him. "They didn't come and say hi or bark when I came in."

"They were eating." She said it as if that was enough of an explanation.

He shot her a look. "So?" He bent down and scratched Mugs on the back of the head. "This guy is a hell of a watchdog. Why wasn't he barking?"

"Because he recognized your vehicle, your footsteps, and your voice," she said grudgingly. "They all do now."

He nodded, as if that made sense. "I sure hope they continue to be guard dogs—or guard animals, I should say—

when I'm not around." The coffee finished brewing, and he poured two cups, bringing them to the table.

"He has been barking and causing chaos with all the reporters outside. I just hope they leave me alone soon." She lifted her cup and blew on her coffee, but it was too hot to drink.

"Looks like you're getting there," he said with a smirk. "Only one news vehicle now."

She nodded.

As he straightened in his chair, he caught sight of the tea towel she had quickly tossed over the small box. He frowned and, without asking, lifted the towel.

"Hey," she said. "Mind your own business."

He shot her a look. "With you, whatever you do ends up being my business." He nodded down at the box. "Whose is that?"

She didn't answer. She just stared at him, her eyes wide.

"Interesting," he said. "The minute you react like that, I know something major is going on." He picked it up and studied it. "It's pretty."

"Yes, it is."

"Whose is it?" he repeated.

She shrugged, testing her coffee. *Perfect.* "I found it, so it's mine."

And then he flipped it and saw the name underneath. His eyebrows shot up, and his jaw dropped. Slowly, ever-so-slowly, he turned and stared at her. His shoulders sagged. He sat at the table and took a swallow of his coffee as he continued to eye her.

"What?" She flushed but didn't say anything more.

"Doreen, talk to me," he ordered on a low growl.

Something about a man with authority in his voice made

her give up all her secrets. "I found it in the creek."

"Where?"

"Just past my place," she explained. "Actually the animals found it. I went over to take a look at what they were all staring at, and I found it in the water."

"The animals found it?" He turned to look at Mugs, Goliath, and Thaddeus. "Which ones?"

"I think Thaddeus first saw it from his perch on the neighbor's fence. Then Mugs finally woke up and barked at it until Goliath joined in. That's when I got really curious, saw something white, and dug around in the creek."

He studied her for a long moment and then gave a hearty sigh. "You better show me."

"Why? It's just a nice little box." But she hurried to drink more of her coffee before leaving the house.

"And, if I open your laptop, I won't find the name *Betty Miles* in your search bar or research up on the screen related to her, will I?"

She flushed, dropping her gaze to the notepad in front of her.

He nodded. "That's what I thought." He motioned toward the back door. "Let's go."

She glared at him but hopped up, opened the door, and called all the animals. "Mack wants to see the location for the box you found today, guys. Come on."

Mugs ran out, barking cheerfully. Goliath sauntered past as if orders were beneath him, and he was only accompanying them because he felt like it. Thaddeus, on the other hand, flew to her shoulder and cheered them on with a war cry in her ear. She led the way to the back of the property.

"You made a great start with the fence," Mack said. "Hard work, isn't it?"

"Yes, it is," she confessed. "I was working until the animals started acting up. Then I found the box and came back in. Why did you call me?"

"Instinct," he said bluntly. "It told me to get over here before you got yourself into more trouble. Apparently I'm already too late."

She snorted. "I don't think even your instincts can keep me out of trouble."

He laughed out loud. "Isn't that the truth?"

They'd reached the back of the property.

He stopped for a moment and smiled. "I can't believe everybody has this creek view fenced off. It's beautiful."

She turned enthusiastically. "See? That's what I thought. Especially since my fence was just a nightmare."

They both turned to look at the mess of fallen wood and iron poles and wire. He motioned at the stack she had managed to cut up. "You've done more than I thought you would."

She shrugged. "I still have a lot of work left." She turned and stepped behind her neighbor's fence. She motioned at it. "You know who lives there?"

"I met them when I was investigating the murders last week," Mack said. "I thought you'd met him."

"I did. I just wondered if his wife was really there."

"I haven't met her. Why?"

"Because I thought I talked to her today. But then I couldn't decide if it was a her or a him." She took a few more steps, studying the creek, trying to place her animals as they were earlier today. Mugs had gone to the outcropping.

And, as she thought about that, Mugs moseyed past her to the outcropping, parking his butt in the same position it had been in earlier. Goliath sauntered around to the far side.

"I think they were at opposite sides of the outcropping earlier today. But their placement was similar to this."

Thaddeus, still on her shoulders, made a funny *caw* sound and flew down to sit beside Goliath.

She motioned to where the creek had pooled in the circle between the animals. "The box was in here."

Mack looked at her as if he didn't believe her.

She held out her hands. "It was, honest."

He raised an eyebrow, looked at the animals, and stepped forward. "How did you get into the creek?"

"I went in barefoot," she explained. She glanced at his expensive shoes and socks and jeans. "Too bad you can't go in and see if anything else is there."

"Did you see anything else?" he asked.

She shook her head. "No, I didn't. I saw the box, picked it up, and brought it out."

"Not quite," her neighbor from the other side of the fence said. "You also asked questions about the Betty Miles's case."

She glared at the fence in front of her. "I'm not exactly sure who I'm speaking to," Doreen snapped, "but you're the one who volunteered the information."

The voice on the other side jeered. "Semantics, semantics. You're the one who was curious."

"Yes, I am. But you can go back in your house anytime now," she called out.

"Don't have to. It's my yard," the voice snapped. But it did seem to get fainter.

She waited another few moments and then whispered to Mack, "Do you think he's gone?"

Mack, being over six feet fall, stepped up on the outcropping beside the dog, where he could better see over the fence, and then shrugged. "I can't see anybody."

"Good," she said. "I didn't realize having neighbors meant having people in your business all the time."

He sighed. "This is hardly being intrusive." He motioned back at the water. "You want to point out exactly where the box was?"

She stepped out of her sandals and said, "I'll do one better than pointing it out. I'll show you exactly where it was." She stepped into the water and gasped. "How can it be so cold?"

"It's glacier water, coming down from the mountains."

She shot him a look. "Are you serious? This is actually from a glacier, like, as in ice cubes?"

"No ice cubes here," he said patiently. "It's water, remember? Not frozen over—at least not yet."

She shrugged. "Still, there should be ice cubes at this temperature." She leaned forward and studied the water, then pointed. "Yes, see that indent from the box being here?"

"No, not really. The creek has filled the void." He squatted at the bank, beside her, and studied it. "You want to shift that ground a little bit and see if anything else is in there?"

She shook her head. "Not really. It's cold. Remember?"

"Of course you want to because I see something silvery. If you don't want to get it, I will." He rested one hand on the ground and stretched out his other arm. Right in front of her, his hand disappeared into the cold water and into the space where the box had rested. He stuck his fingers right into the dirty sand and rock. "Aha."

"What?"

"I found something." And pulled his hand back out. In his palm was something shiny, metal, and very old looking.

Chapter 7

M ACK WOULDN'T SHOW her the ring, and trying to
rush him to the kitchen so she could take a look
faster was like trying to push a grizzly bear with hemor-
rhoids. He kept snarling at her to stop prodding him. She
groaned when he finally turned the corner to her property,
and she danced around him, nudging the cat and dog ahead
of her. Mugs barked in excitement so much that he went in
circles instead of gaining any distance, and Goliath just
sauntered like he didn't care what anyone else did. He'd get
there in his own time—kind of like Mack. Thaddeus was his
usual talkative self but making no sense. "Body in the water.
Body in the water."

"*No*, Thaddeus. There was no body in the water," she
said. "We didn't find any bones or a body. Nothing to do
with a human body. Nada."

Thaddeus cocked his head at her and started his stiff-
legged walk forward. "Body in the water. Body in the water."

She raised both hands in exasperation. "Okay, so *my*
body fell in the water. Why can't you say things once and
then never again?" she scolded the bird as she walked
forward. But she kept an eye on Mack. He studied the ring

in his hand and took his sweet time about it. She stopped, waited until he caught up, slipped her arm through his, and tried to speed him up toward the kitchen. "I don't know why you won't let me see until we're inside," she grumbled. "I saw enough to know it must be a ring, but I want a closer look at it."

He slanted his gaze down at her and grinned.

She rolled her eyes. "That look of yours ..."

"What look?" he protested.

From the dancing laughter in his eyes, he knew exactly what she was talking about. She sighed. They were almost at the bottom of the deck steps. She stopped as she looked at the disturbed dirt in her garden. "Your men should have replanted my garden," she announced. "Look at the mess they left me."

He snorted. "Good luck with that."

"You guys are the ones who made the mess," she said as she stomped across the deck and then up the few risers leading to the porch and to the kitchen door. "Why shouldn't your men have to clean it up?"

"You had a body hidden in your garden," he said with exaggerated calm. "That's not our fault."

"Well, they could have taken better care when they removed the body. Besides, I wasn't responsible for the body, so why should I be responsible for the mess you and your men made?"

He sighed, put his hands on his hips, motioned at the door behind her, and said, "Are you *not* going in now? You've been pushing me the whole way back from the creek, and, now that we're finally here, you're blocking my entrance."

She glared at him but stepped inside. Instantly the aroma of fresh coffee hit her nose. She laughed. "There's enough for me to have a second cup." She raced over to the pot and poured herself a cup.

He leaned against the doorway and just stared at her.

She frowned. "What?"

He shrugged. "If I don't get any coffee, I don't have to show you what I found."

"That's blackmail. There's a law against that. Besides, *now*, if I give you coffee, I'm bribing you, and that's illegal too."

He snorted. "I think you're a little confused over the value of coffee."

She raised her hands, palms up. "I don't know what to call it. The bottom line is, you won't let me see the ring."

He motioned toward the coffeepot. She walked to the table, grabbed his cup, and refilled it. That finished the pot. She placed both cups on the table.

Mack sat, taking a sip of his coffee.

"Now may I take a look, please?" she asked with careful enunciation.

He laughed and placed it carefully on the table.

She gasped when she saw the bright red shine. "Is that a ruby ring?"

"Yes, it is."

"I didn't see the ruby earlier." Now that it was on the table, she could see it clearly. She picked it up, studying the old Victorian-type setting and the massive ruby in the center. She held it up to the light, letting it shine and twinkle. "It's real, isn't it?"

He shrugged. "The experts will determine that. I don't know enough about gemology to understand if it's real or just a really good fake."

She studied the setting. "It's also real silver." She rubbed the inside, feeling for an inscription. And something was written there, but it was hard to see. Everything was filled in with dirt. She handed it to him. "May I clean up the inside with some silver cleaner?"

He nodded. "If you have some."

"Nan left some. Apparently at one time she had a silver tea service."

She rummaged in the front closet, the catchall for everything. There she found a small black jar and grabbed a couple blue cloths and returned to the table. She sat down, opened the jar, dipped her cloth-wrapped finger into it, then held her hand out for the ring. He gave it to her. "I wonder how long it was there."

"I don't know. I wonder if it was inside the box." He motioned at the one she had found, sitting off to the side of the table.

She considered the placement of both of them in the creek and nodded. "It's possible." She wished she'd taken a closer look in the creek and had found the ring herself. She cleaned the inside of the band, taking special care to clear out the dirt from the lettering. When it was clean, she tried to read it and then shook her head. "Either my eyes aren't what they used to be, or that's really hard to decipher."

He took a look, then held the ring higher, directly underneath the light over her kitchen table. When he moved it to one angle or the other, he said, "I can't read it, but it looks like initials of some sort. Likely the original owner's initials."

She smiled. "It's antique looking. Depending on its age, it's probably a real ruby."

He handed it back to her.

"Is it okay if I clean the rest of it?"

He considered the ring in her hand for a moment and then nodded. "Depending on how long it was in the creek, any forensic evidence could have been washed away."

"What aren't you telling me?" she asked. When he refused to answer her, she offered her own opinion. "You recognized this ring, didn't you?" She gave him another moment to share with her, but, when he didn't, she huffed out a sigh. "Fine. Be that way." She polished it, and the band brightened to a warm silver. She handed it back to him with a sigh. "That's a lovely piece."

"It is."

Something in his voice made it sound like he wasn't terribly enthralled about the concept. She glanced over at him. "The hand originally found was also adorned with a lovely piece. Would she have had two expensive rings? Her girlfriend gave her the one but two…?"

"We can't know for sure *she* had it," he corrected without making any attempt to misunderstand who Doreen was talking about. "No jumping to conclusions."

"No, but, considering it was found beside a box with her name on it, it could have been her grandmother's ring," Doreen said slowly. "Any family member might have passed that on to a much-younger family member."

He nodded, but, from the look on his face, he wasn't happy with her suggestion.

"Was there anything like this in her cold case file? Any photos of her that might have an image of this ring?"

He tapped the table as he studied the ring. "No idea. But I will go to the office and take a look."

"You do that." She closed the jar of silver cleaner, threw the cloth into the garbage, and took the cleaner back to the closet. When she returned, he was still sitting at her table and

319

now held the ivory box in his hand. Her heart sank. "You're taking it away, aren't you?"

He glanced at her and nodded. "If it doesn't have anything to do with the cold case, you can have it back. But you know how this works. If it's related to a case, I take it in as evidence."

She crossed her arms over her chest and pouted. "I just thought it was really pretty."

"It *is* really pretty."

All of a sudden she wanted him to leave. If she couldn't keep the box—and she knew it was irrational to expect to do so—she would head back to the creek and see if she could find something else. Something else she wouldn't tell him about. Two trips that found two things. As far as she was concerned, that meant there was likely more to be found in the creek.

Then he blew it.

"I'll come back in the morning. I want to return to that same place." He shot her a hard gaze. "No more digging in the creek looking for more items."

She stared at him. Immovable at her table. Would he ever get up and go to his office?

He nodded slowly. "I know exactly what you were thinking. You're probably waiting for me to leave, so you can head back out there. And honestly it makes sense. In two trips we found two things. But that doesn't make either of these items yours."

"I'll take a receipt for them though, please," she snapped.

He smiled. "You can have a receipt for the box. But I found the ring."

She sat down back in her chair, pulling her coffee toward her. "That's just mean."

"It's valuable," he said gently.

She nodded. "I know. Why do you think I wanted to keep it?"

"What would you do with it?"

She stared at him in surprise. "Sell it and buy food."

She had said it so simply that he sat back in shock. After a long moment, he asked slowly, "Are you that short on money?"

Sorry she had brought it up, she mumbled something, hoping he'd just forget about it.

But he wouldn't forget about it. "If you really need work, I'm sure somebody in town is hiring."

"I'm planning to pass out résumés," she said tiredly, "but I'll wait a few more days. It's pretty embarrassing when nobody gives a damn about what's on your résumé. They just want to ask questions about the recently solved murder cases from last week."

He winced. "Yeah, I can see that. All these murders don't make you the most employable person, does it?"

She shook her head. "I'll be fine for a week or two, as long as no more bills show up in the mail." She ran her hand over her forehead.

Reading the mail was starting to unnerve her. Who knew there was so much to pay on a monthly basis?

She still had some of the money she'd found by going through Nan's clothes. What Doreen really hoped for was to get something from the commission of the sale of Nan's old clothes. She needed to contact Wendy, the store owner, and see if there had been any progress on that. She'd do that soon.

Doreen looked around the kitchen. "I'll go through the house and see if I can sell something. Nan has several antiques here that could be worth some serious money." She picked up her coffee mug and took a sip. It still tasted mighty fine. She took a bigger sip before setting it down.

He watched her over the rim of his mug. "So you want to do my mother's begonia garden …"

Straightening, she studied his face. She hated to think he'd do this out of pity, but she needed the money. Her pride was a small price to pay for a full stomach. Besides, he'd been talking about her helping out in his mother's garden for a while long before her confessing to being so broke. Hopeful, she asked, "Did your mother decide to go ahead with fixing the begonia bed?"

"I talked to my mom, and she wants the begonias moved to another spot and something new put in the empty bed."

"That would be good," Doreen said. "The begonias would be much happier." She tilted her head to the side, remembering the look of the dirt there. "But you'll have to bring in something to nourish that bed. Otherwise anything we plant will struggle."

"It's not a very big garden. I can pick up a few bags of topsoil, maybe a bag of peat moss to hold in some moisture. I'll stop at the local gardening store on my way home, maybe tomorrow or the next day."

"When do you want me to start?" Inside, she was delighted. She didn't know what he would pay her, but fifty dollars right now was fifty dollars, and she needed every dollar she could get her hands on. She wasn't used to paying bills. These several days had been a brutal awakening as to how life really worked. And how it was for people without any money. There were gas bills and electric bills and phone bills. If you were lucky at the end of the day, there was money left over to buy food.

More often than not she'd had nothing left over.

"You'd save a lot of money if you would cook for yourself," he said gently.

She shot him a resentful look. "I would, if I didn't have to deal with the devil himself to do that."

He frowned at her and glanced around the kitchen, as if questioning what she was talking about. "What do you mean?"

She snorted and pointed at the stove. "That thing. It's the very devil. Every time I try to do anything with it, it fills the room with a horrible gas smell. I'd be sick before I could even cook something. Better to go hungry than fight with that nightmare."

Chapter 8

MACK STARED AT her in disbelief, a strangled sound escaping despite his best attempts to hold it back. But that quickly became a chuckle, and, before long, the room filled with a big rolling sound as he laughed.

She stood and glared at him. "You can leave if you're just going to laugh at me," she snapped. But she doubted he even heard her, his laughing was so loud. She stomped her feet in frustration, making him howl all the more. "What is your problem?"

He dropped his chin to his chest, still chuckling. Finally, after several big gasping breaths, he raised his head and said, "It's a stove. It's not the devil incarnate. It is *a stove.*"

She sniffed and raised her nose in the air. "To you, it's a stove. To me it's something designed to torment honest citizens all over the world."

He tried to contain the mirth once again bubbling up.

She shook her finger at him. "If you dare laugh at me again …"

His face worked in all kinds of directions as he tried to hold it in.

Finally she slumped down at the table into her chair

again. "It's not funny," she said in disgust. "You have no idea how many times I've tried to work that stove."

He leaned forward. "You could take a cooking class."

"Do you think they teach these basics, like how to turn on the damn thing?" She narrowed her gaze as his eyes widened, and his shoulders shook, and his face turned bright red as he tried not to crack up once more. She crossed her arms. "Oh, what the hell. Go ahead and make fun of me. That's what my soon-to-be ex-husband always did."

That stopped his laughter as fast as anything. "Did you not cook growing up?"

She shook her head. "My mother wouldn't cook at all. We lived on takeout."

He stared at her in horror. "What?"

She nodded. "It was either takeout or we had a house-keeper who cooked. I never was in the kitchen. All throughout my marriage we had chefs, and I wasn't allowed to do anything. I couldn't even get my own tea."

It was his turn to sit back and stare. "I can't imagine a life like that."

"Well, I can't imagine a life like everybody else must have had. It seems like I was raised in an entirely different way from the rest of the world. I married into a similar atmosphere and now find myself completely flummoxed by the basics."

He glanced around the kitchen, then back at her, a spec-ulative look on his face. "How are you surviving if you can't cook?"

She shrugged. "I can make cheese and crackers."

His jaw dropped.

She waved a hand at him. "Okay, it's not that bad. I can make a sandwich."

"And what else?"

She glared at him. "Anything that comes out of a can or a jar that doesn't require cooking. Takeout is my best friend. But even more so is the deli. I eat a lot of bread and peanut butter lately." She stared morosely at the table. "I feel like I must have something in common with starving students. They always talk about Ramen noodles and peanut butter sandwiches."

In a deceptively calm voice he said, "Ramen noodles have to be cooked."

She stared at him in outrage. "Really? I've been eating them dry out of the package."

And that did it. He almost fell off his chair to the floor as he howled.

Pissed off at herself and at him, and frustrated by the whole world for making something so simple so complicated, she picked up her coffee and headed to the back deck. She'd be damned if she would sit here and let him laugh at her.

Still, if she were rational and detached from the whole thing, it *would* be funny as hell, providing it happened to somebody else. The fact that it was her, *that* was a whole different story. As she walked in the backyard onto the grass, or what was supposed to be grass, she tried to focus on the broken fence in front of her and the weeds in the garden.

It all seemed like too much. She should be eating well to do this kind of physical work. And she'd lied, as she couldn't afford takeout. It was too expensive. Her last grocery shopping had been fruits and veggies for a salad, and some hearty bread. She could at least have those with cheese.

"I'm sorry," Mack said from behind her.

Her shoulders stiffened and then relaxed. "Whatever. I'm glad it made somebody's day."

"I could show you, if you want."

She froze. She didn't know how to take his offer. Was he being genuinely helpful, or did he just want his funny bone tickled every time he came over? Because she knew he'd find her inability to do anything in the kitchen amusing. She didn't have anything left but her pride, and that hadn't gotten her anywhere so far. She turned to look at him, studying the sincerity in his face. "Show me what?"

"Well, we could start with lighting the stove," he said with a big smile.

She glared at him but was cutting her nose off to spite her face if she said no. "And I want you to show me how you make the coffee. Mine never tastes the same."

He nodded solemnly. "You wrote it down before, didn't you?"

She frowned. "I did, but it doesn't taste like yours when I make it."

Back in the house, she snatched up her pad of paper where she'd been taking notes on the Betty Miles case.

He caught sight of the name at the top and glared at her. "No digging into cold cases."

"The thing about cold cases," she snapped back, "is that nobody gives a damn. They're cold. They're old. They're gone and forgotten."

"Nobody has forgotten Betty Miles." He waved a hand over her kitchen table. "Look. You just came up with the name on the box, and your neighbor popped up, heard you, and told you about the girl. It was a big case at the time. Nobody has forgotten about her."

She shrugged. "In which case, nobody should object to me taking a look around to see if I can find anything, should they?"

He glared at her. Now she felt better.

"And why was she so infamous? She was just a teenager."

"She was. She was a troubled teen. But a lot of very expensive jewelry disappeared around the same time, and there were suspicions it was all connected. But all of the threads fell apart. The prosecutor couldn't pull together enough evidence to charge anyone."

"So she became known as the thief as well?"

"She was a local, and there was a lot of press about the missing jewels, so she became quite infamous. The fact that she'd been dismembered, and we'd only found one arm, just added to it."

"And we are sure it's her?"

"Yes." He pulled the ring from his pocket. "I'll check and see if this is one of the missing pieces of jewelry from back then."

Her eyes lit up. "You suspected that right away, didn't you?"

"No, not necessarily."

She sniffed. "Liar."

He glared at her. "Is that anything to say to somebody who's willing to help you?"

Immediately she felt bad. He *was* trying to help her. In fact, ever since they'd met, although he was brusque and gruff, he'd been very good at helping her out. "So why don't we go back to the creek and see if there's more jewelry?"

"Because it's a waste of time if this isn't connected to the case."

"That means you have pictures you can check?"

"The pieces were all insured. So, with any luck, there should be pictures, yes." He pointed at the stove. "Let me at least show you how to turn that on."

She smiled, happy that maybe he could help her with that much.

"But let's start with this." He showed her the coffee ca-rafe and where he filled the water up to.

She read the line that said *six cups*. She carefully put that in her notes. She had been filling the entire carafe.

"Fill the water to here. Pour it into the back." He pulled out the used coffee grounds and dumped them in the trash.

She wanted to say something about him mocking her for not knowing something so basic as to where the water went in a coffeemaker, then realized not being able to turn on a stove was pretty damn basic. So she should just shut up and take notes in case her brain decided to have a fast one day, and she couldn't remember what the hell she was doing again. She wrote down his instructions as he explained how much coffee to grind, how to know how much coffee she was grinding, and how to pour it all into the new filter.

Then he gave her instructions on cleaning the coffee grinder.

She stared at the small hopper in horror. "You mean, I have to clean that thing?"

He slid her a sidelong glance. "You don't do it all that often. But every six months would be a good idea."

She shrugged, made a note on the page, but mentally thought, *Nope, not going to happen*. Still, she was turning over a new leaf and trying to do everything herself, so, if cleaning out a coffee grinder was doing that, then fine.

Then he moved on to the stove. "Come take a look at this."

Obediently she stood beside him, the pad of paper and a pen in her hand.

"See this?" He pointed at all the knobs in the front.

She nodded. It really hurt her ego to have somebody explain this to her.

"This one's for the back left burner. This one is for the back right. This is for the front right. This one is for the front left."

She looked at the knobs. "How do you know that?"

He glanced at her in surprise. "That's what these letters mean down here."

The letters were so worn off she couldn't see them. In fact, she wasn't sure she'd ever seen them. "How did you know that?" She waved at the stove knobs. "There's nothing left to read on this thing."

He stared at her. "In this case it's common sense because I've used stoves a lot. But you're right. All the letters and numbers of the dials have been completely worn down to nothing." He frowned. "It would be a good idea for you to get something more modern."

"Like I'm going to spend money on a second devil when I can't even use the first one," she scoffed.

He chuckled. "Now, when you turn this knob, the gas will come up. It should light automatically."

Instinctively she backed up as he turned the knob, and instantly the smell of gas wafted up her nose. But no lighting happened. There was no flame. There was nothing at all.

A frown formed on his face. He turned off the burner and turned on the second one that went to the back burner. Again the same thing.

"So?"

He turned it off and opened the doors on the side of the oven. "If it doesn't light automatically, then she must have a lighter here for it."

"A lighter?"

He nodded. "A lighter. Something that will ignite the gas to a blue flame."

She stared at him in horror. "As in *flame* flames? Like fire? Real fire? Inside the house?"

He turned to look at her and, once again, broke down laughing.

Chapter 9

An hour later ...

A S SHE WALKED to the creek after her cold dinner of salad and crackers, a cup of tea in her hand, she pondered how she would have known the stove wasn't working properly if Mack hadn't tried. There really wasn't any way to know unless she understood the workings of a stove. He told her not to turn it on again until she had somebody come and check it out.

She had frowned. "I don't have money to fix that."

He gave her a harsh look. "And you don't have the money if this thing blows up. It's ancient. None of the lighters work, and I wouldn't trust the gas either. It comes on too strong, too fast. It probably just needs to be checked out. Don't worry about it. The repairman is a friend of mine. I don't think he'll charge you very much."

Her gut clenched at the *not very much*. That was relative. It varied from person to person, but, in her case, there really was no variance. *Any* money was too much money.

She stood at the creek for a long moment, unsettled. And then thought of Nan. Doreen hadn't seen Nan today. Buoyed at the thought of seeing her grandmother and hearing Nan's quirky stories, Doreen pulled out her cell phone and called her. "Hey, Nan. Have you had dinner?"

"I sure have. Are you coming to visit me and have a cup of tea?" Nan invited her over.

She stared at the tea in her hand and smiled. "Absolutely. You okay if I bring the animals?"

"I'd be heartbroken if you didn't," Nan declared.

With that, Doreen left her chipped teacup on a nearby rock, crossed over the creek on the bridge, Mugs and Goliath moving ahead of her, and Thaddeus, being stubborn, waddling behind. She led her menagerie down the opposite side of the creek toward Nan's place.

It was a bit of a roundabout way, but it was much nicer than going through town. Not that Nan lived very far away. This route just tacked on five minutes. But it was five minutes along the creek, so who could argue with that?

She passed *the spot* and tried not to look where she'd found the dead man last week. It was hard to believe it had only been a handful of days ago. "Come on, Mugs," she called out to the basset hound, who dragged his nose along the ground as he appeared to sniff every critter's scent that might have gone this way.

He was a good guard dog. But, more than that, he was a wonderful companion. He'd helped her keep her sanity when her marriage had splintered. Who'd have thought that this pet would be such a comfort to her?

She turned to look at Thaddeus and frowned. "Thaddeus? Thaddeus!"

Worried, she retraced her steps. "Where are you, Thaddeus?"

"Thaddeus is here. Thaddeus is here."

With relief she watched as he wandered toward her from

the underbelly of a tree. "Thaddeus, you can't just roam around free like that," she said worriedly. The bird appeared to be completely unconcerned. "Don't you know it's dangerous for you to be out here alone?"

He stopped and stared at her. "Thaddeus up. Thaddeus up."

She frowned. Normally he didn't request to come on her shoulder—he just flew up. She patted her shoulder, and he opened his wings. But he didn't seem able to hop. Startled, worried, she walked toward him and scooped him up. That was when she saw the blood on his foot. "What have you done?"

She wasn't sure what he got caught in, but something small had ripped his skin. Cooing to him gently, she turned and walked toward Mugs and Goliath. "It's just a little scratch. You should be okay."

As she wandered toward Nan's, Thaddeus gently cooed along Doreen's neck and brushed against her cheek.

She smiled and reached up to stroke him. "I wasn't so sure about having you originally, but I'm really glad you're part of my family now," she said in a low voice, kissing his shoulder.

As if he understood, he dropped his head against her cheek and just held it there for a long moment.

With a happy sigh, and feeling more contentment than she had all day, she walked the last block toward Nan's place. As they approached, Nan was already seated outside on the patio, waiting for them. Mugs barked and raced across the grass.

Doreen winced. She'd been told many times by the rude gardener here how she was not to walk on the grass. But no stepping stones or even a walking path led to Nan's corner apartment, so Doreen had to cross on the grass. The only way for her to avoid it was to walk all the way to the front of the complex and enter the building, where no animals were allowed. She shrugged and once again did what she was told not to do and stepped on the grass. But she did it just as fast as she could.

Before long she was seated at the little bistro of a table Nan had. She smiled as her grandmother joyously welcomed a big greeting from both Goliath and Mugs. Nan looked over at Doreen and beamed. "I think it's the best thing ever that you moved to town, my dear."

"That's just so you can keep your pets close."

Nan chuckled. "Well, I certainly have lots of friends here. At my age, this is a lovely place to be. The house was getting to be a bit too much work. I do miss the animals though." She reached across the table with a tiny bit of bread in her fingers. "Thaddeus, are you hungry?"

Thaddeus hopped off Doreen's shoulder and waddled across the table.

Nan immediately noticed the blood. "Oh, dear, what did he do?"

"I'm not sure," Doreen said. "He went into the under-brush when we were on the path. When he came back out, he had this scratch on his skin there."

Nan sighed. "He does think he's a dog and should be allowed to go wherever he wants."

"And Goliath thinks he's people, and Mugs thinks he's the king of the pack," Doreen finished for her grandmother with a laugh. "That's all right. They've become a family for me, and I appreciate that."

With a smile of satisfaction Nan sat back. "Good," she said firmly. "That's what you need."

"I really appreciate you giving me a place to stay," Doreen said. "I am having trouble with the stove though."

Nan looked at her with a frown. "What kind of trouble?"

Doreen shrugged. She didn't want to say too much. Nan knew Doreen couldn't cook, but that didn't mean she understood the depths of Doreen's ignorance. "Couldn't get it to light."

Nan nodded sagely. "It could be fussy."

"That's not what I call it," she said with a smirk. "I think it's a little more than that. Mack said that I need to get it checked out before trying to use it again."

"If you have to, you can always get a secondhand stove."

But she must have seen Doreen's grimace at the mention of buying anything because Nan leaned forward and said, "Are you out of money again?"

"That's not fair," Doreen said. "There's no *again* about it. I haven't made any money since I arrived, remember? But after all that mess last week, I doubt anybody wants to hire me. Instead of blending in, I've become infamous," she said, like it was a joke. The trouble was, there was a lot of truth to that statement. It wasn't what she had intended. But it was what had happened.

Nan waved her hand in a dismissive gesture. "Don't you worry about those folks. You've done the town a huge service. Just look at all the murders you've solved."

Doreen smiled. "Well, it's nice to contribute in some way. But I wish there had been a monetary reward for it. And, no, I didn't do it to get a reward. But the money would have come in handy."

"What about the clothing you took to the consignment store? Did you ever talk to Wendy, see what is selling?"

Doreen shook her head. "It was on my list to do today, and I completely forgot about it. I've been working on that old fence at the creek," she said on a laugh. "I never got around to calling her."

Nan stared at her. "You took down the whole fence?"

Doreen shook her head. "You know the one neighbor has a really nice fence, and there was that old fence on the property on the left side. So I decided I didn't want the fence along the back blocking the creek because it really was broken and ugly looking. And that one side fence wasn't necessary, with the neighbor's nice new fence."

Nan laughed at that. "No doubt the place needs some work. But you won't be able to do it all yourself," she warned.

"I know. Mack stopped by. Then he helped me pull up the big iron stakes from the back corner." She picked up her teacup and took a sip. When silence fell across the table, she glanced at Nan, drawing her eyebrows together. "Are you okay?" She studied the odd look on Nan's face.

Then suddenly her grandmother's face cleared, and she smiled a bright sunny smile. "Of course I'm okay. I think it's delightful that Mack came to help."

"He didn't come to help," Doreen said firmly. "I'm to do some gardening at his mother's place. So he came to talk to me about that job."

Nan's face lit up in delight. "Well, that would be wonderful. That's something you've always loved to do and could be a way to make money."

Doreen nodded. "It's just they need to pay me. I was thinking I could get a job at the gardening center, when it opens up."

"And I could put in a good word for you. Isabel runs

that place, and her grandpa, Joshua, he's here with me."

Doreen studied Nan for a long moment. "What do you mean, he's here with you?" she asked delicately.

Nan looked surprised and then burst out into bright laughter. "Well, he's not *with* me, silly." She laughed again. "I mean, he lives here at this residence with everybody else. He's much older than I am. I think he's at least eighty-eight."

It was all Doreen could do to hide her smile as she heard that. Nan was going on seventy-five. To think anybody in the retirement-age category was *much older*, … it was cute.

"Well, that might be a good thing then. If you get a chance to say something, I'd appreciate it," Doreen said as she took another sip of her tea and sighed happily. "My life is so much different now."

"Good," Nan said firmly. "It needed to be different. You were just a shell of a woman back then."

Nan had said many things like that before. Most of the time Doreen had brushed it off. But she was starting to understand what Nan meant. Back when Doreen was married, she wasn't allowed to have any of her own thoughts. She couldn't put forth any suggestions as to what to do or how to solve a problem, and, anything she did say, her ex-husband would toss off as being ludicrous. It had really demoralized her to realize she had nothing of value to contribute.

He hadn't wanted her to contribute. That had been part of the problem. He'd been all about being the lord of the house, and everybody else was below him. He also was a sexist, and women were good for very few things. Unfortunately for her, Doreen's self-confidence had quietly eroded with the constant criticisms over the way she dressed or the fact she hadn't done her nails properly or that she didn't look as well presented as somebody else's wife.

And, if she opened her mouth about anything business oriented, he'd mock her.

It had been a struggle to maintain appearances yet be quiet, just the way he wanted her to be. She'd presented this pretty face to the outside world, but inside her had been nothing.

Nan was right. Doreen had been a walking shell.

Chapter 10

I T WAS LOVELY to have her grandmother so close. Nan had lived here for so long that she knew everyone who lived in the Mission area of Kelowna.

Doreen studied Nan's face over her teacup for a long moment and then impulsively asked, "Do you know anything about Betty Miles?"

Nan was so startled by the question that she almost dropped her teacup. "Oh my. I haven't heard that name in forever."

Doreen leaned closer. "But you have heard it?"

"Of course I have," Nan said with a bright smile. "Anybody who lived in Kelowna back then knew the story."

"What story?"

Nan took a moment to collect her thoughts. She sipped her tea quietly while Doreen shuffled impatiently in her seat.

There was no point in pushing Nan. As she would often say, *There were few rights one had at her age, and doing things in her own time, in her own way, well, that was one of them.*

Finally Nan settled back, at the same time she took another sip of tea. She looked up with a twinkle in her eye. "Is there a reason why you're asking?"

Surprised, Doreen studied her grandmother and then shrugged. "Maybe."

Nan's laughter pealed out. Mugs lifted his head to see what the disturbance was. Seeing nothing going on, he dropped his head back on his paws. Thaddeus hopped onto the table and walked over to Nan. She smiled and gently stroked his feathers. "Are you keeping an eye on her, Thaddeus?"

Thaddeus bobbed his head up and down, up and down.

Nan laughed. "I always thought this bird could understand exactly what we say."

"He has the darnedest timing," Doreen exclaimed.

"So, before I tell you about Betty Miles, why don't you tell me what brought this on?"

Doreen winced. She probably shouldn't have brought it up. Particularly since Nan wasn't one to be fooled easily. "I found an ivory box in the creek." She smiled at the look of confusion on Nan's face. "It had the name Betty Miles carved into the bottom."

Bewildered, Nan looked at her and said, "It's a far stretch to go from an ivory box in the creek to a murder from thirty years ago."

Doreen laughed. "And I wouldn't have known that name from Eve's, except for your neighbor."

Nan leaned forward. "Left or right?"

"Left."

"The husband or the wife?"

At that, Doreen was stumped. "I don't know. I've met the husband. I've never met the wife. I honestly couldn't tell if the voice behind the fence was male or female."

With a look of satisfaction Nan settled back and smiled. "So it isn't just me. I've never seen her either. Or at least not in many years. And anytime I spoke to one of them on the phone, I never could tell if it was her or her husband."

"So do we know for sure she lives there? Or that she's even still alive?"

"I have no idea. It's all I could do to figure out anything about my neighbors without appearing too intrusive. I figured you'd be better at it."

Doreen snorted. "I'm not very subtle. My former husband had hoped I'd be good at ferreting out information, but I failed at it miserably. That was something he didn't understand, as information was his stock in trade—and he felt gossip and information gathering were intrinsically female traits. But apparently, now that I'm free and clear, I don't really give a damn about being subtle." Then she slapped a hand over her mouth at the swear word.

Nan's laughter rippled through the small patio area again.

Doreen looked around, wondering how many other people heard her and if people would come out of the old folks' home to see what Nan was up to. But it was a private patio, so they shouldn't.

Nan leaned forward and patted Doreen's hand. "I'm really proud of you."

Doreen shook her head. "I wouldn't be, if I were you. I still can't work that stove."

"Did Mack get it fixed?"

"No, there hasn't been any time." She stared at Nan suspiciously. "I didn't tell you Mack was getting it fixed."

"No, but Josie—she's one of the assistants here—her stepbrother works at the police department with Mack. The stepbrother heard Mack had gone to your place."

Doreen rolled her eyes. "The gossip in this town is worse

than anything I've ever seen before."

Instead of being upset, Nan nodded her head in agreement. "And this place here is a wonderful source of all gossip," she said. She leaned forward and, in a conspiratorial whisper, added, "I know you don't know everybody in town—or even in your neighborhood yet—but plenty of the females hereabouts want to snag a husband. Many have thrown themselves Mack's way. Yet Mack has no girlfriend, you know?"

In spite of all her good intentions, Doreen couldn't stop the color washing up her neck. She shook her head. "Nan, we're not going there."

Nan sat back comfortably. "That's okay. You don't have to. All the gossip already has."

Astonished, Doreen could feel her jaw dropping. "You're not discussing Mack and me, are you?" Nan gave her a wide-eyed innocent look that Doreen didn't trust for one minute. "No, Nan. Don't do that."

"I don't have to," Nan said with a bright and cheerful smile. She picked up her teapot and refilled their cups. "Just thought you should know people are thinking about the two of you."

"He was over all the time because of the murders last week. And I still have reporters and pestering neighbors gathered on my front lawn. I wish everybody would just forget who I am."

"No, my dear." Again Nan laughed. "That's so not happening."

Doreen glared at her grandmother.

"Look at you. The first chance you get, you put your nose into another cold case."

"That's not fair," Doreen protested. But she had to admit that, once she'd had the taste for solving these cases, it did get into her blood. "I just asked you if you knew the name."

"You asked me about the case as well." Nan took a sip, then she set down her teacup.

Doreen struggled to remember if she *had* asked Nan about the case. Nan was so very good at twisting words around and adding a slight change to the context that Doreen wasn't exactly sure anymore if she had asked about the case or not. She was pretty sure she hadn't, but no way would she argue that point with Nan.

"Body in the creek. Body in the creek," Thaddeus cackled.

Doreen stared at him. "We didn't find a body in the creek."

Immediately Thaddeus turned and pinned her with that gimlet eye.

"Okay, we didn't find a body in the creek in the last few days," she quickly amended. How the hell could that bird know when she was lying? But, in truth, she'd honestly forgotten about *that* body. She was a little overwhelmed with the thought of another body. Not that she'd found anything like that.

Nan looked at her with a bright light in her eyes.

Doreen groaned. "Thaddeus was with me when we found the ivory box, and he was with me when the neighbor was talking about Betty Miles."

"I'm loving the fact that Thaddeus and you have bonded so well." Nan glanced to see Goliath stalking a bird in her garden. "Even Goliath seems to have taken to his new ownership quite well."

"That's because it's a zoo at my place," Doreen said in

345

DALE MAYER

exasperation. "They eat each other's food. They get into *my* food. They're in my bed. The cat and the bird are on my kitchen table. Mugs can't jump that high, or he would join them too. They are just all over the place." Nan tried hard to hold back a grin, but Doreen caught sight of it regardless. She glared at her grandmother. "You're being impossible today."

At that, Nan laughed again. "You do bring such joy to my life."

Instantly Doreen felt bad. She cupped Nan's frail papery-thin-skinned hand with her own. "You've been a godsend to me."

Nan squeezed her fingers. "Likewise."

The two women shared a glance of complete understanding. Then Doreen settled back again. "And you still haven't said anything about Betty Miles."

With a chuckle, Nan sat back as well, lifted one foot, and rested it on the side of the garden bed, crossing the other over it at the ankle. "Because it's a little complicated, and we don't know a whole lot."

"What do you know?"

"Betty was a difficult teen who got into trouble a lot. She came from a broken home, living in a poor section of town. She went missing, so nobody thought much of it because she was always running away from home. That's what most thought. And, along with that thought, they said, 'Good riddance.'" Nan shrugged. "I didn't know her very well, but I certainly heard all the gossip. I didn't have the same opinion because I didn't know her. I just thought it was difficult to understand other people's actions without knowing more about the person. It's not something I'd have done, but we're all different."

346

"What difficulties?" As Doreen well knew, motivation went a long way in determining what somebody did and what somebody would do with their life. "What happened that sent her off the rails like that?"

"Her parents separated or got divorced or just stopped living together. Thirty years ago, divorce wasn't terribly common, not like it is today."

They both thought about the current state of marriage and the lack of long-lived matrimonial bliss.

"But regardless of their marital status, it wasn't an ugly parting of the way," Nan added slowly. "Or so it appeared on the outside."

"Teens do tend to act out when their parents break up. This running away event seems to be a strong reaction though, so maybe it wasn't as amicable as everyone thought."

"Exactly. That's what I thought at the time too," Nan exclaimed. "Nothing seemed to justify all that she was doing."

"What exactly was she doing?"

"Well, she was breaking and entering into places. With some small-time thieves. She had multiple boyfriends, so was acting out in that way too. She was always shoplifting in the mall."

Doreen frowned. "Sounds like she needed some help."

"True, but often, when a teen needs help, they don't get it. When they take that step down the criminal path, everybody just washes their hands of them. Society should have done something to help Betty before it became that bad."

Doreen agreed. "So, what got her killed?"

"Well, that's the thing. We never heard from her or anything about her for weeks and weeks. Most of us forgot about her. And then that arm washed up in the creek about a year after Betty disappeared. High floodwaters brought it up. It was after the spring thaw, and you know that creek can get quite a bit higher, don't you, dear?" Nan leaned forward. "You might want to move some of those garden beds back some because, every springtime, that water seeps in under the fence line. The backyard can get soaked from rising ground-water in the bad years."

Doreen shook her head at the quick change in conversa-tion. "I'll keep that in mind." She frowned. "You never mentioned that before."

"We never talked about bodies floating down the creek in high water before," Nan stated.

"True. When I get back, I'll take a look at where the high-water lines are."

"In order to do that, you should get the fence back up. The water marks are on it." Nan smiled at her with a twinkle in her eyes. "Just saying ..."

Doreen crossed her arms over her chest. "So what else do you know?"

"Not much. Nobody knew who the arm belonged to for the longest time. Until they did the xrays and confirmed it was Betty. And, of course, when they finally ran an article in the newspaper, that brought up some information from the locals. And finally led to Betty's best friend, Hannah, identifying the ring."

Nan nodded. "Exactly. Betty was a wild child. She'd been caught shoplifting, given several warnings, and let off. But, after she went on to rob a couple, she was fingerprinted and was waiting for her court case when she disappeared. Everyone thought she had just booked it out of town. So far, after all these years, the rest of her hasn't shown up either."

"Well," Doreen said, "wherever the rest of her is, she's likely buried locally. I highly doubt they would have buried the trunk of her body, which is much heavier and more difficult to get rid of, too far away."

Nan looked at her granddaughter in surprise. "Now that's a very interesting thought. You do realize she was very tiny?"

"How tiny?"

Nan pursed her lips and looked off in the distance. "As I recall, she was one of those tiny petite girls, not even five feet tall."

"Well, the police obviously have all that information."

"You should ask Mack about it," Nan said enthusiastically. When Doreen turned her dark gaze on her, Nan sobered slightly. She held out her hand, palm up. "You can't expect me not to be happy to hear you might have a relationship in the offing."

"No, the last thing I want is a relationship," Doreen said firmly. "He's helped me out—that's all."

"Doesn't matter if you want it ... or not. Sometimes it just happens."

Doreen asked with alacrity in her voice, "And did *you* have lots of relationships over the last thirty years?"

Nan chuckled. "Oh, no you don't. My personal life has been an open book. You've seen a couple of the men who came and went, or at least I told you about them. But I never found anybody who I wanted to spend every day of the year with."

"Does that bother you? That you never found true love?"

Nan's laughter pealed across the patio again. "Of course not. I found true love over and over and over again," she said with a wide grin. "What I didn't find was anybody who I wanted to get up with every morning and who would cook for me every day of the week and do the laundry every day of the week and make the bed—because he didn't exist. Or at least I haven't found him yet."

At that, Doreen had to laugh. "How very *Modern Woman* of you."

Nan nodded. "I was always ahead of my time." She leaned forward and linked her fingers together. "So, tell me what else you found."

"I told you. I found this ivory box with the name written on the bottom side."

"And yet, you and Mack were seen in the creek."

Doreen frowned at her. "How do you know that?"

"Because somebody here saw you, or somebody's family member saw you."

"We didn't see anybody at the house or at the creek," Doreen said.

"You have always got to expect you're being watched by somebody in this town."

Doreen tucked away that tidbit of information. "Good to know."

"You're evading the question," Nan said gently.

"Not so much evading as I know Mack didn't want me to say anything. But, close to the same spot, we found a piece of jewelry. Again, we don't know whose it is. It could have been from something completely unrelated."

"Interesting," Nan said. "Because one of Betty's best friends, Hannah, was rumored to have given her a ring before she went missing. And even more interesting is that you seem to always be at the right spot at the right time."

Chapter 11

DOREEN SHOOK HER head. "That's not true at all," she protested. She stood and placed the small chair out of the way, where Nan normally kept it. "But, on that note, it's time for us to head home."

Nan smiled. She shifted her hand in her pocket and pulled out something, reaching to give it to Doreen.

Doreen frowned as her grandmother palmed something small in Doreen's hand.

Nan waved her off. "Don't look at it now. You can look at it later."

Shrugging, Doreen put it in her pocket, picked up Thaddeus, propped him on her shoulder, and put a leash on Mugs's collar. "Goliath, come on. It's time to go home."

He opened one eye and looked at her, let the eyelid drop and stretched out farther.

She groaned. "How come Goliath isn't trained like the other two?"

"Oh, he *is* trained, and he's trained you," Nan said on a laugh.

Doreen looked both ways before she walked across the grass to the edge of the road, with Thaddeus and Mugs.

Goliath, once he realized he was being left behind, bolted up and passed them.

Nan stood and waited until they crossed the street, then called out, "It was lovely to see you today."

Doreen turned and smiled. "It's always lovely to see you." And with a wave she moved her odd family up the street toward the creek.

On any given day, she'd much rather walk the path behind all the houses that led to the creek than to travel the streets. It was also much safer, considering Goliath wasn't leashed. Just the thought of trying to put that behemoth on a leash and get him to walk obediently beside her made her grin. "I should put you on a leash, shouldn't I, Goliath?"

He ignored her, like he always did. It took them several minutes to get to the end of the block and then around the corner to head toward the path that would eventually take her to the creek. But it was still a beautiful day. Yet it was late, as she'd stayed longer at Nan's than she had planned to. But that was okay. She had nothing taking up her time anymore.

Doreen grabbed her cell phone from her pocket and dialed Mack's number. "Hey, Mack. When do you want me to move your mother's begonia patch?"

"*Uhm*, how about this weekend?"

His voice sounded distracted, as if she'd caught him at a bad moment. "This is Thursday already, isn't it?" She smiled.

"Yes. So, the day after tomorrow I can meet you there. Is nine in the morning a good time?"

"Sure, but I can do it without you. That is, if you trust me to handle your mom's garden. And can we actually work in the garden? Or is it off limits after what we found yesterday?"

"I don't think that was a human bone, so yes, and I trust you to handle Mom's garden, no problem." His tone was more active, as if he'd switched his attention from whatever was on his desk to his phone call. "It's you I can't trust."

"Hey!" she gasped in outrage.

He chuckled. "Meaning, I can't trust you *not* to get into trouble. And, if you'll be at my mom's house, I'd prefer you didn't get into trouble there. I'm trying to keep her world nice and peaceful."

"Well, I wouldn't do anything on purpose." Still frowning, she checked the traffic as she crossed the last street. "Although I'm convinced that was a human bone we found there. And probably one of Betty's."

"Don't go jumping to conclusions. We should have the lab results back in another day or two."

Once on the other side, Mugs wanted to race around free. She bent down and unclipped the leash from his collar. "Can I bring the animals?"

"I don't see any reason why not. It's probably better if you do. Otherwise they'll just follow you on their own."

"True enough," she said. "We're walking back from Nan's now. Your mom's house is not very far."

"Nothing is very far away in that corner of town," he said drily. "Make sure you get home without finding anything unusual, okay?"

"Okay," she said amiably. "And, if I do find something odd, I just won't tell you about it. That will make you feel better." She hit the End Call button on her phone and dropped it into her pocket, grinning like a fool.

At least her life held more laughter now. And more love, come to think of it. Especially with Nan around the corner and her three pets at home. It was lovely to spend so much time with her grandmother. Doreen didn't realize how much she'd missed having family in her life all these years. Only as her marriage broke apart did she understand just how isolated she'd become. That had been the way her former husband had wanted it. And she apparently had been a willing victim to all his ploys. Or a blind dupe ...

As she looked back on it, it made her angry to see how much she'd lost over the years. Would it have hurt him to let her see Nan more often? Of course it wouldn't have. But he didn't like sharing. And would it have hurt her to stand up to him more often? Maybe, but it would have been better for her *and* Nan in general.

Doreen turned the corner onto the path behind all the properties that led to the creek. The path was barely walkable since it was so overgrown with greenery. She idly contemplated what it would take to cut it back but then realized more people would use it, and she didn't really want that. She liked having the place to herself.

She could cross the creek at a couple places with the low water levels, and, given a choice, she always wanted to be on the far side, away from the properties. It was nice to know that this chunk of nature was just a few steps away from civilization.

She whistled as she walked. She might not have any money, and she might not have a job, yet she smiled a whole lot more than she'd ever smiled before. She shoved her hands into her pockets, her fingers wrapping around the small roll Nan had given her. She pulled it out and frowned. "Nan ..."

Nan had slipped her a one-hundred-dollar bill rolled up tight. Doreen carefully unrolled it, disconcerted, and yet smiling. "Thanks, Nan. I could use the money. I really wish you didn't feel like you had to do this though." It was such a kindhearted gesture on Nan's part that it almost brought tears to Doreen's eyes.

She didn't remember Nan being so generous in the previous years, but then Doreen hadn't needed the money while married. Now, of course, one hundred dollars was huge. It could pay bills and buy food.

Just the thought of food made her want to head back into town to pick up something more substantial for her meals. Cheese and crackers wouldn't hold her for long. What she really needed was to deal with the devil stove.

She picked up her cell phone and quickly dialed Nan. When there was no answer, she left a message saying, "Thank you so much for the gift, Nan. I really appreciate it. I wish you didn't need to help me, but, considering the facts of my new reality, I do need it right now. So, it's much appreciated."

Doreen walked the rest of the path, delighted with the extra bright ray of sunshine in her world.

As she got back to her property, she crossed the small bridge and ambled through her backyard. The sight of the downed fence made her wince. "I should have done more work cutting this apart today."

But she hadn't. She'd allowed herself to get distracted. She was too tired now to deal with it, plus the sun would be setting soon. As she walked up to her house, she realized somebody was inside. Her heart froze. She quickly ducked around to the side of the property. Mugs, sensing something going on, took one glance at the back door and growled. She knew how he felt.

"What kind of watchdog are you, Mugs? You were supposed to tell me *before* I found out."

But, of course, he ignored her. This time he raced furiously to the kitchen door. Well, if she'd wanted to stay quiet and not let anybody know she'd arrived, that just went out the window.

Thaddeus ruffled his feathers against her shoulder. She could tell from the look in his eyes that he wasn't happy either. Of Goliath, there was no sign. *Figures. When trouble was brewing, he's not anywhere to be found.*

She sneaked around to the front of the house and stopped when she saw an appliance repair van. Was this guy looking at her stove? And who had let him in?

Frowning, she stepped up to the front door and walked inside with Thaddeus, shutting the door and leaving Mugs outside, barking at the back door still. She carried on right through to the kitchen to find her stove pulled out all the way. A small wiry man lay on the floor beside and behind her oven. Thankfully she could hear noises from the back of the stove and knew he wasn't dead.

She stopped and said, "Hello?"

A head popped up. A monkey of a man smiled a great big grin that split his face in two.

She responded in kind. "Did you just walk in?" she asked him.

He nodded. "Of course. I had Mack's permission," he said. "You weren't home, and I figured you really needed this fixed, so I didn't want to wait." He frowned. "I didn't take nothing."

She stared at him. "I'm just surprised and still adjusting to small-town ways."

Mugs continued his guard-dog barking at the rear kitchen door. Then Thaddeus strutted in, peering at the stranger.

The repairman must not have thought either was unusual as he nodded to her and continued with their conversation. "Most everyone lets me come into their houses, even if they're not home. Mrs. Bee from two blocks over, she has me in regular. I'm pretty darn sure she expects me to clean the stove every time I'm there. So she calls me in to give it a quick tune-up, so she doesn't have to clean it. And Mr. Argon, over on the far side of town, he has me come in for his fridge on a regular basis. They leave messages, asking me to come by whenever. I pop around when I have a few moments. Most of the time they're not home."

He spoke in such a confident tone that she had no doubt he told the truth. She shook her head. "I spent a lot of years in Vancouver."

His face twisted up in a grimace. "That's a deadly place, that is. You need not only locks but you need dead bolts. Couldn't imagine being a repairman in a place like that."

Thaddeus walked right up to the repairman. Absentmindedly he stroked Thaddeus softly. This acknowledgment must have placated the bird for he flew off to check for any birdseed or table scraps on the kitchen table.

"You need security clearance to get into houses there." The repairman shook his head and plunged back down behind the stove, his voice wafting out from the space. "So, your stove is almost dead," he said.

She walked closer, staring at the thing in front of her. "*Almost* dead?" She hated to ask, but she hadn't been aware it was alive in the first place. She knew Mack would be having a heyday with her right now.

"Yeah. You need to get a new one. I might be able to keep this thing going a little longer, but I wouldn't count on it."

"And just when I was figuring out how to use it," she

said humorously. "I haven't the money to replace it."

"Of course," he said in a surprise comment. "Most of us don't. Repairs never happen at convenient times."

She tried to figure out what he meant or if he was just trying to make her feel better.

He stood. "I've got one in the store you can have for a hundred bucks."

She thought for a long moment. "Did you give Nan a similar quote sometime in the last year?"

He nodded. "A couple times. I told her that she was getting to the point where it couldn't be used anymore. But she always shook her head and said, *It'll be fine.*"

"It'll be fine. It'll be fine," Thaddeus repeated, strutting atop the table.

Doreen shook her head at the bird, but at least Mugs had stopped his barking at the back door. "And I gather we've run out of the *It'll be fine* comments?"

He laughed. "We ran out a while ago. In actual fact, you shouldn't be using this at all. But, if you really don't have the money, maybe you could do without a stove for a while longer." He glanced around the kitchen. "But ... this room's pretty clean, so I can see you're not really into kitchen gadgets."

She wasn't at all sure what *clean* meant in this context or what it had to do with kitchen gadgets. When she raised an eyebrow in question, he motioned at the long bare countertops.

"You don't have all your counters cluttered full of mixers and bread makers and rice cookers," he said by way of explanation. "So you probably need the stove to cook with."

She knew about a few of those things, and some of them appeared to be self-explanatory, but honestly they were almost appealing because, if something could cook rice, and she didn't have to get involved in it, she was all for it. She loved rice. "How much would some of that stuff cost?"

He looked at her in surprise. "Well, secondhand, quite cheap. You'd probably get a rice cooker for five bucks."

She stared at him. "Someplace local?"

He nodded enthusiastically. "A couple good thrift stores are in town. But you should come to my shop and take a look at what's available there first, so you know it works when you buy stuff used. My wife sells most of that refurbished stuff, so the stock changes all the time. I have a couple guys who work in the shop, repairing small appliances. I'm the only one who goes around to fix big appliances in people's houses though."

"I'd just as soon have the one you mentioned. What would it cost to have you deliver and install one of those"— she waved her hand at the demon appliance—"things?"

The laughter in his eyes deepened. But now a curious light was in there too. As if she was adding to his list of curiosities in turn.

"I'll include installation in the cost of the stove for you."

She nodded. "Thank you. But I need to pay you for your time today as well, correct?"

He shook his head. "Nah, I needed to come and see how bad this was. I've been telling Nan for years this one was dangerous. But she didn't want an electric one. Said she didn't trust those new gadgets."

Doreen had no idea why an electric stove would be considered a new gadget. Electricity had been around for a long time. And it had to be way safer than an actual fire underneath a pot on a stove. That was too unbelievable. Yet that pretty well described Nan.

Doreen really had to do something about this horrible thing. "How long would it take to replace this one?"

The repairman frowned for a few moments, as if contemplating his schedule. "If you don't need it today, I can probably bring it on Saturday. I need to make sure it's still available and that my wife didn't sell it."

"Maybe, when you get back to the shop, you can take a look and let me know."

He nodded. He was fiddling with something in the back, and then all of a sudden he nearly whispered, "Oops. Yeah, this isn't going to work anymore." He held up some rigid cable-looking thing. "The attachment on this end is bad news."

"Bad news. Bad news," Thaddeus added.

The repairman frowned at the cable, then the oven. "I really don't want you using it again."

She wasn't going to say she hadn't used it yet. "What about the gas?"

"No problem," he said. "I'm a licensed gas fitter. I'll shut this down here. I think you're probably better off with an electric stove, unless you really want another gas stove, but they are more money. Of course we need the 220 power for an electric stove," he muttered half under his breath. He hopped over the corner of the counter, now standing on the same side of the stove where she was, and carefully maneuvered it back into position.

"Isn't that kind of useless? You just pushed it back, and you'll have to pull it out when you bring another one."

He looked at her in surprise and shrugged. "I move these suckers all day long. Doesn't make any difference. I thought it would be easier on you if you didn't have to walk around it while you haven't yet made your dinner tonight."

She nodded as if she understood what he was saying. And she did, if she followed his logic. He couldn't possibly know she really didn't do anything in the kitchen.

He collected his tools scattered near the devil stove. "I'll give you a shout when I can get back again. Maybe at that time you can decide what you want to do."

"I want the secondhand electronic one. Any chance we can do it for one hundred dollars, taxes and delivery and installation included? Oh, and carting off this old one?" Now Doreen knew why Nan had given her the money tonight.

He tilted his head, hesitated, studying the stove. "What the hell. Yeah, I can do it for that. But it has to be the stove I fixed. And, if my wife has sold it, then I don't know where to get one for you right now," he warned. "We also need to run a new electric line for the stove."

"How much for that?" she asked hesitantly.

"Not sure but it shouldn't be much. In these older homes, the breaker panel is usually in the basement or crawl space," he said with a smile.

She nodded as relief flooded her stomach. In her current reality, she could do without the demon gas stove. But she probably needed one to eat properly, according to Mack. And surely it was cheaper than takeout and a whole lot better for her to eat at home too. Plus the electric stove wouldn't scare her, so she might want to use it.

The foods of her past were a long way away, but, if she could make a simple decent soup, it would help her feel like she'd accomplished something and was broadening her menu choices.

Within minutes the repairman had packed up his bag and walked out the front door. Doreen followed him and relayed her thanks again. She found Mugs waiting quietly on the front porch. Obviously he had given up on her opening the back door for him. She left the front door open for him as she stood on the front porch steps, realizing the crowds were gone. She glanced over at the repairman. "Was anybody out here when you drove in?"

He frowned up at her. "Where?"

She waved a hand toward the front yard, where all the lookie-loos had been. "In the driveway and up along the road, standing and staring at my place?"

He studied her as if she'd lost her mind.

Maybe he hadn't heard the news about the recently solved murders. Some people refused to read newspapers, saying it's all bad news and how they can get the highlights with a ten-second glance via the internet. Unfortunately Doreen couldn't avoid the dead bodies she had found last week. Or the nosy reporters and gossiping neighbors thereafter.

"No, can't say there has been." He smiled. "Wait for my call." And he left.

If he drove off out of the driveway a little too fast, maybe it was to be expected. He probably thought she was loony tunes. Then again, he'd been trying to get Nan to replace that stove for years. So he understood exactly how free-spirited Nan was and would likely think Doreen was exactly the same.

Then a big yellow cat bolted out of nowhere and into the house. Goliath was back. Doreen sighed. *And* this *is my new life.*

As she turned to enter her home, a middle-aged woman walked up her driveway. She had a fierce determination in her step, as if she'd seen Doreen standing here. Doreen frowned at her, but it didn't seem to stop the woman. She came charging up the front steps where Doreen stood, numbly looking on. "May I help you?"

"Yes. You can stop asking questions about Betty Miles." The woman reached up and smacked Doreen hard across the face. Then she turned and left.

Doreen stood in the open doorway, her hand to her cheek, tears in the corner of her eyes, staring at the retreating indignant woman. She was middle-aged, plump, dressed in an old-fashioned skirt. Her shoulder-length hair bobbed with every step. "What the hell was that for?" she whispered. But Mugs and Thaddeus and Goliath had no answers.

Chapter 12

DOREEN SLAMMED THE front door shut, her cheek still stinging. Through the living room window, she stared at the woman storming off, trying to get an idea of who she was and what had been her problem. The stranger continued to the end of the cul-de-sac, turned left, and kept going. Her back was stiff with righteous indignation, and her footsteps were clipped, her arms swinging at her side as she plowed forward. Likely half of Doreen's neighbors saw the altercation or at least the woman's angry departure.

So much in Doreen's life sucked right now. For what had been a lovely start to the day, this was an ugly ending.

She walked back into the kitchen, realizing all her joy at having one hundred dollars to spend was gone too. She should probably be grateful the repairman had accepted the deal—or at least verbally. That didn't mean he still had the refurbished one available, but she hoped so. The thought of having a broken gas stove was even more terrifying. What if the gas leaked? She understood he said something about being a gas fitter, but that meant nothing to her.

And there was the unknown cost for the wiring. She winced and put it out of her mind.

She did know how to make a good cup of coffee though, if she could follow the instructions Mack had given her. And right now, after that undeserved slap, she could use a cup. She found her notepad with the instructions and carefully tried to make a pot of coffee based on Mack's newest detailed steps.

She walked to the fridge, opened it, winced, and closed it. There was seriously nothing to look at inside. No cheese meant crackers with peanut butter. She headed over to the cupboard. Even the animals ate better than she did. She sat down with her meal at the otherwise empty dining table.

Her phone rang just then. She glanced at the Caller ID and growled. "What do you want?" she answered.

After a seemingly surprised silence on the other end, Mack asked, "Is there something you should be telling me?"

She slumped her chin onto her free hand and propped herself up on the table. "I figured that's why you were calling. The news must have traveled to you already."

"What news?" he snapped.

She kicked her feet up on the next chair and leaned back. "Some stranger walked up to me while I was at the front door, saying goodbye to your repairman friend, and she told me to stop asking questions about Betty Miles, and she whacked me hard across the face." She heard Mack's harsh intake of breath.

"Are you okay?"

Kudos to him for being concerned about her safety first and foremost. That was part of what made him such a nice man. "Yes. It still stings though. I don't know why she did it. I don't even know who she was."

"Can you describe her?"

"Matronly, probably thirty or forty pounds overweight,

maybe mid-forties, wearing a skirt, blouse, and a long cardigan." She shrugged. "I can't tell you much more than that."

"That describes a good one-quarter of the population of Kelowna." He laughed.

"Only there's nothing funny about this," she said in a morose tone. "It was a terrible shock."

"You want to press charges?" Mack asked, serious all of a sudden.

"No, she was obviously very distraught. I just don't know about what."

"If she told you to stop asking questions about Betty Miles, chances are she's related to Betty in some way."

"But Betty went missing thirty years ago, Mack."

"If she's a family member or was a good friend or some-body who was caught up in that investigation, the passage of thirty years doesn't matter. It still hurts today," he said quietly. "I know, for you, it's a fun puzzle to solve, some-thing to distract you from the ills in your own world, but you're raking up old ground that can cause pain to any number of people."

"I hadn't thought of that," she said quietly, turning her attention to the darkening sky outside her kitchen window. Just then the coffeemaker beeped. She hopped to her feet. "I'm hoping I made a decent cup of coffee. I followed your instructions."

"Good. It sounds like you could use a cup right now."

"Yeah, not to mention the fact that the gas stove can't be fixed."

"Ouch," he said. "That sucks. Did he give you a cost estimate on a replacement?"

"He said he had an older secondhand electric one—if his

wife didn't sell it—and he would handle everything, including installation and hauling away my old one, for one hundred bucks."

"That's cheap, *really* cheap," Mack said in surprise. "Normally I trust him, but that sounds very cheap. Maybe I should give him a call and see if that electric stove is okay."

"How dangerous could it be? I thought the gas stove was bad enough. I don't even want to be in the kitchen right now. What if the gas is leaking?" She could hear the rumble of Mack's laughter as it left his chest. She frowned at him through the phone as she poured a cup of coffee and held it close, sniffing it. "I get that I always say stupid things, but it's really not fair that you get to be amused when I'm not."

"Sorry, it's just the way you say things that makes me smile."

"So, what's so funny in this case?"

"He's a gas fitter. He would have capped off the gas line, and you'll be safe there. Considering the age of that house, maybe an electric stove is safer. But, then again, I don't know what the wiring looks like."

"Wiring?" She turned to look at the kitchen. "I know it's an old house. So you're saying the wiring is not safe either?"

"I'm not saying anything of the kind," he said hurriedly. "Don't worry about that now."

She took an experimental sip of her coffee. Not bad. She had only made two cups' worth, in case it didn't turn out right. Plus she couldn't expect to drink more and sleep tonight. She wouldn't mention all that to Mack as he'd just laugh at her again. "Now I get to worry about strangers walking up to my house and smacking me across the face," she grumbled. "And how would she have known I was asking questions?"

"You know what the Mission's gossip is like, especially with your current notoriety."

"It was just the two of us talking, although I did talk with Nan today."

"There you have it," he said in exasperation. "That old folks' home is the worst for gossip."

"And gambling. Although I haven't heard Nan mentioning any of that this week."

"I'm surprised she mentioned it at all. Did she tell you that I had to warn her to stop?"

"Officially? As in, she did something illegal?" She shook her head. "That doesn't sound like Nan."

"How about making bets on some people's love lives? Or making bets on who'll have a baby first? Or making bets on when somebody is going to die?"

"Okay, taking bets about people dying is not nice. But those about babies being born are just having some fun."

"That's all fine and dandy, until she acts like a bookie out of that old folks' home."

At that, Doreen sat back and thought about it; then she giggled. And giggled until she was laughing to the point that tears ran down her face. "Oh, my goodness. I can *so* see her doing that."

"Exactly. And when people lose, they get upset. And, while Nan's raking in the money, other people are losing their money, and that's when people get mad and complain."

"I rather imagine that any money she makes will be used to help others somehow," she said with a smile. "Like she gave me one hundred bucks today."

"Yeah, but that was probably because she heard your gas stove was out of commission."

"I doubt she needed to hear anything," Doreen said.

"She didn't have to. She already knew. Apparently your repairman has been telling her for years how she should get a new stove. He said he mentioned the hundred-dollar repair estimate to her several years in a row." She frowned. "Do I have to give you the hundred dollars because it might be Nan's ill-gotten gains?"

He chuckled. "No, you don't have to give me the money."

"Good. I need more to cover the repairman's fees for wiring as it is." She brought the circle of conversation right back around again. "By the way, why did you call?"

"To see if you stayed out of trouble this afternoon. But I gather you didn't. And also to hear what Willie said."

"Who is Willie?"

"The repairman," Mack said in exasperation. Then changed the subject entirely. "Did you find anything out about Betty Miles?"

"Oh, so now you want to know what I might have found out?"

"Doreen," he said in warning. "Don't start."

She raised both hands in frustration, even though he couldn't see it. "Only what Nan told me. Just that she was a runaway teen, blah, blah, blah, blah."

He chuckled. "So, in other words, all the same stuff you already knew."

"Yes. I'll see what the library has to say. They should have the newspapers from back then still on microfiche."

"Is it really that important to you?"

"I'm curious. I feel like I found a piece of her history," she said quietly. "And I don't think things like that should be forgotten. She's never been found, has she? Just her arm? Right? Nobody's been charged with her murder?"

"No, yes, and no. But that doesn't mean the case is closed. No unsolved murder case is ever closed. At least we're presuming she was murdered."

"She certainly didn't cut off her own arm," Doreen said sarcastically. "But I guess what you're saying is, she might have died in an accident."

"Or by natural causes. And someone wanted to hide her death. We can't assume anything at this stage."

"Well, if I find anything at the library, I'll tell you. But, in the meantime, it'd be great if you could look into the cold case and see what details are there. Like about that ring." She took a long swallow her coffee.

"That much I did already," he said.

"You mean, you found something, and you didn't say anything?"

"I'm the detective. You're the busybody, remember?"

But it was said without rancor. "Maybe, but, just to clarify, I was a help last time. I could be a help this time."

"There is no *this time*," he argued.

"Are you going to tell me what you found?" She poured herself the last of her coffee. She would completely ignore everything he said about staying off the case. If there was one thing in her life she needed right now, it was something to do. Something that brought her a sense of satisfaction— something interesting and something exciting. She'd had enough of her soon-to-be ex-husband's *exciting* business dinner parties for a long time. All she wanted now was something that was fun. She felt like she should join a knitting club, where everybody could sit around and discuss the evidence. But she wouldn't. She didn't even know how to knit. And she didn't know anybody else who would care to delve into these murder mysteries with her—other than

Nan.

"The ring," Mack said. "There's one mentioned in one of the thefts at the time, and the description matches the ring I found."

"Meaning, it's connected. Do you think Betty might have stolen it?"

"It was a very sophisticated theft. If she was involved, she certainly wasn't the only one."

"But," Doreen added, "Nan said there was gossip about how Betty's best friend, Hannah, had given Betty a pretty fancy ring."

"That's hearsay, Doreen. Don't put much stock in it."

"Still, if Hannah gave the ring to Betty, then Betty wasn't involved in the jewelry thefts."

"We're following up on some leads to see where the evidence takes us."

"So you'll tell me what you find out?"

"*Active investigation*, Doreen," Mack said and hung up.

Chapter 13

Friday …

THE NEXT MORNING Doreen got up after a night full of crazy dreams of people slapping her for no reason. Her cheek hurt just enough that she wondered how many times she'd slapped herself to make it seem more real—or to wake herself up from one of those horrible nightmares.

As she showered and dressed—with all the animals joining her in the bathroom, which she noted with a headshake—she couldn't stop thinking about the crazy woman who'd walked all the way over to slap Doreen across the face. She could almost hear the neighbors in her cul-de-sac snickering. Not that she could see them. … They were too smart for that. As if she hadn't had a rough-enough couple of weeks, but to have something like this happen … As much as she wanted nobody to have seen it, she knew that was an impossibility. According to Nan, nothing was a secret here—at least for long. Doreen was inclined to agree with her grandmother.

But, if that was the case, why had nobody seen what happened to Betty Miles? Because, if the nothing-goes-unnoticed logic applied today, it applied even more so thirty years ago. Today people were much less inclined to talk to their neighbors.

Thirty years ago, neighbors were a much closer-knit group. They did things together; they were concerned, watched out for each other's kids. There was an innocence back then. But now, with the internet, newspapers, media personnel, and everyday horror stories about pedophiles and serial killers and kidnappings, people were even more cautious, kept to themselves more. That was a disconcerting thought. And it brought up yet another wave of disappointment in her own life.

She had never had children. She wasn't sure if she ever would, but her biological time clock certainly ticked away without any prospective father in sight. And, no, she wasn't going there with Mack. She could have children at her age and later, but, by the time she got married and had a baby, she'd be that much older. Besides, what kind of a mother couldn't even cook?

Shaking her head and getting back to the present, she still had no answers to this current puzzle. She walked downstairs, the animals in tow because they all wanted to be fed. She had figured out that if she fed all three at the same time, there were less issues of the cat eating the dog's food or the bird eating the cat's *and* the dog's food or ... Plus separating their eating bowls helped.

So Doreen put three of Nan's leftover teacups in the hall closet within each pet's bag of food. She scooped up one of each, carried it to the kitchen, and dispensed them as quickly as she could, returning the teacup scoops to the closet.

Now she could think in relative peace as she returned to the kitchen. This was all so stupid. If only she knew why the woman was so angry at her. It wasn't like Doreen had asked anybody, other than Nan, about Betty Miles. If the woman was family or friends with the deceased, you would think she'd want closure.

Doreen's gaze caught the stove, still sitting here, staring at her—dare she say, mocking her? She shook her head. What she really needed was a good night's sleep, not one filled with the stranger slapping her over and over.

Groaning over her cycle of never-ending thoughts with no clear answers, Doreen finally sat down with her laptop as the first coffee dripped for the day. She stared at the clock in horror. Already nine on a Friday morning. It wasn't like she had anything to do today that made getting up at any particular time important, but somehow it *was* important.

She'd had it drilled into her, year after year, that she had to get up early in the morning and be perfectly coifed for the day. Per her controlling ex. And here she sat, in a pair of comfortable plaid cotton pants and a T-shirt haphazardly thrown over her head. She hadn't even brushed her wet hair.

She turned to gaze out the window and thought of how far she'd come. She just wasn't sure if it was in the right direction. Her life was so vastly different than what it had been. However, considering where she'd ended up, she'd take this anytime.

As she got up and poured her first cup of coffee, her phone rang. She glanced down at it. Seeing it was Mack, the corners of her mouth turned down. She wasn't sure she wanted to deal with him right away. Still, for him to call at this hour, especially when they had already spoken late last night, maybe he had some news. "Good morning, Mack."

"You waited to answer it. I figured you were still asleep."

She laughed. "That's not happening. However, I did sleep in for the first time ever that I can remember." She waited a minute for him to say what he was calling about. When he didn't, she nudged him. "Still, it's a little early for you to be calling."

"Did you hear from the stove guy?"

Startled, she realized she hadn't. "No, he didn't call yesterday after he left. Should I give him a call this morning?" She glanced around her kitchen to see where she had dropped his card. There was no sign of it. She frowned. "Now if only I could remember where I put his card."

"On the kitchen table most likely," Mack said with a laugh. "But I know the number by heart. Have you got a pen?"

"Yes." She grabbed the nearby pad of paper. He reeled off the number, and she wrote it down. "Okay, got it. Thanks."

"And are you still on for nine tomorrow for the begonias?"

She nodded, realized he couldn't see her, and said, "Yes, nine is fine."

"And you'll be up and ready on time? A couple cups of coffee in you by then?"

She snorted. "I think this is the first time in my life I've ever slept in," she said, confused. "I can't tell if I like it or not."

"Whenever you break a long-time habit like that, the guilt can be overwhelming."

"But why should there be any?" She didn't understand, but he was right—she felt guilty.

"There shouldn't be. Once you adjust to this new lifestyle, you'll get used to it."

"I'm not sure that's a good idea." She brushed the tousled hair off her forehead. "Do you have any news?"

"If you mean about Betty Miles, the answer is no. I don't really expect to get any with the case being thirty years old."

"Sure, but to a woman who smacks me across the face, it's obviously not old at all."

"Now all we have to do is find out who it was and ask her why she felt so strongly about this," Mack said gently. "But, if you don't know who it is, how am I supposed to talk to her?"

Doreen sat back in her chair and stared morosely at the laptop. "I should have run after her, shouldn't I?"

"Not necessarily," Mack said hurriedly. "That could have made her even more violent."

"*Ugh*. That's not something I want to think about." She could just imagine what the neighbors would say if she'd had a wrestling match on her front lawn.

"Anyway, call the stove guy and see what's happening. I'll talk to you later." And he rang off.

She thought she'd heard somebody talking to him in the background, realizing he'd probably called from work. Not the easiest job in the world being a police detective in the RCMP Serious Crimes Division, but at least it had to pay a whole lot better than what she was doing, which was exactly nothing. One could hardly count charity cases of gardening for Mack's mother as being regular employment. Yet it was something. And the money from Nan would pay for a stove.

Thinking of which, she grabbed the phone again and called her grandmother. "Thanks for the money to pay for a new stove, Nan," she said without a salutation.

"Good morning to you too, Doreen. And you already left your thank-you message on my voicemail machine. No need to repeat yourself," she said in a gentle voice. "Did you have a good night?"

"No, I didn't. I kept dreaming about people hitting me."

Her grandmother gasped sympathetically. "That's terrible, sweetie. You really should have a nice cup of chamomile tea before you go to sleep at night."

Doreen rolled her eyes. "Sure. I'll add that on my list of things to buy out of my nonexistent money," she said, then groaned. "Sorry, Nan. I guess I got up on the wrong side of the bed too."

"Bad nights will do that to you. Why would you think people were hitting you?"

Realizing Nan might know something about this woman, Doreen explained what had happened yesterday. "Now, if only I knew who she was, Mack could talk to her."

"Interesting," Nan exclaimed. "You certainly have livened things up in this town, my dear."

"That wasn't what I was planning on doing. I was hoping to fit in and to become one of the nice lovely little villagers, living here in the Mission, where nothing ever happens."

Nan's laughter pealed through the phone.

"Do you have any idea who she could be?"

"Not from the description you gave me, but let me think about it." Nan's tone was slower, more thoughtful. "I wonder if any of the neighbors saw what happened."

"According to you, somebody always sees."

"You're right. That's exactly the way it works," she said. "Thanks for giving me something to work on today." And, with that, her grandmother hung up.

Doreen dropped her cell phone on the table and checked on her animals. From her seat at the kitchen table, she could see Thaddeus atop his perch in the living room, and Goliath had left the kitchen for parts unknown, which was normal for the cat. But Mugs rested at her feet as she drank the last of the coffee in her cup. She got up and poured another cup. With Mugs at her heels, she opened the back door and stepped out into the sunshine.

The weather in Kelowna was normally beautiful. There were a few hot spells in the summer and a few cold spells in the winter, but, compared to living in other parts of Canada—back East or up north or enduring the heavy rains of down South—this was lovely. She walked around the garden, noting the downed fence that still had to be dealt with in the middle of her yard and realized today might be a good day to tackle more of that. At least then, if Mack came around with his truck, he could make a trip to the dump for her, if he didn't mind. With that she chewed on her lip, worrying there would be a price attached to her dump run.

She'd like to think it was free, but it seemed nothing in life was free anymore. Her stomach grumbling, she went inside and checked out the contents of the cupboards. She knew it was bad when the leftover dog food looked appealing. She pulled out the last of her crackers. She still had some peanut butter, so that was enough for breakfast, but she was ravenous. All the salad and sandwich fixings were gone, although she did have a couple of apples left. Rummaging through one of the kitchen drawers, she found several granola bars.

She would have to make that trip to the grocery soon. As she eyed the contents of the pantry, it looked as if she could survive today, and Mack would pay her tomorrow. Hopefully. But they hadn't discussed that issue yet. She was pleased she still had some of the money she had found when sorting through Nan's clothes. That was for real emergencies. Like food.

But her stomach grumbled as she contemplated her breakfast. She sat down and scarfed an entire plate of crackers and peanut butter, then cut up an apple. After that she went for her third cup of coffee. With it, she sat outside on the deck steps and ate a granola bar. When she finished, she went inside to put her coffee cup in the sink and propped open the back door, so the animals could go in and out as she worked in the backyard. She grabbed Nan's work gloves and headed to the garage for the wheelbarrow to deconstruct the remainder of the downed fence.

She worked steadily all morning. When her phone rang, she stopped, wiping the sweat off her brow, and saw it was almost noon.

It was Willie, the stove guy. "I'm out front with my buddy. I have the replacement stove here too. Are you home?"

Delighted, she told him, "Yes. I'm in the backyard working. I'll come around to the front." She hung up and raced around in time to see a panel truck backing up her driveway.

Willie hopped out of the driver's seat with another man getting out on the other side. They both smiled at her. "I decided I might as well do this on my way to another job." Willie motioned at the stranger. "This is Barry. He's an electrician and will give me a hand installing the new line."

She smiled. "Much appreciated."

At least it would be if she knew how to use the darn thing and could afford to pay both men working on this. But electric was a whole lot easier than gas. Isn't it? She was sure of it, since she could handle an electric teakettle and an electric coffeemaker. An electric stove was just a step up, right?

She watched in amazement as the two men manhandled the large heavy item onto some sort of a small hand-maneuvering wheeled thingy, and then they got it up the front steps. She stayed out of the way as much as she could, but Mugs wasn't quite so easy to deal with, in their way and underfoot. Finally she ended up calling him back to the kitchen door, so the two men could pull the old stove into the center of the kitchen and put in the new one.

Then both men worked under the deck until Willie called out to her, "Okay, wiring is done." He sighed as he climbed onto the deck. "Unfortunately Barry doesn't have the right breakers for the stove." He headed back inside, checked out the back of the new stove, and then turned toward her. "Are you okay if I come back tomorrow with the parts needed for the rest of it?"

She nodded. "That's fine."

He left the stove partially out for easy access when they returned. With a wave and a honk, he took off, leaving her alone with two stoves, neither one usable. At least the gas one was mostly out of the way. And the newer one was jutting out in the kitchen, but what did she care? She didn't need to be on that side of the room anyway. Unless she was curious about her new stove.

Wiring? Breakers? She leaned over the back of the stove to find part of the wall open, with wires, one in particular, sticking out with its end cut open. Also some metal plate was over something else on that wall. She presumed that was where the gas line had been cut off. She wondered if that meant she didn't have a gas bill to pay anymore. How stupid that she didn't even know this stuff.

Returning to her backyard to something she did under-stand and could work with on her own, she surveyed her handiwork. She'd accomplished a fair bit. Only she was hungry again.

Thaddeus walked on top of a stack of fence posts she had managed to get out of the ground. He shook his head, looked up at her, and said, "Thaddeus hungry. Thaddeus hungry."

She snorted. "You're hungry? The real problem is, I'm hungry."

There was no help for it. She had to go to the grocery store and get some food. She nudged the animals back inside, washed her hands and face, and quickly straightened up her hair. After she grabbed her keys, she hopped into the car and drove the few blocks to the grocery store. On a normal day she would have walked, but today she needed a whole lot more than what she could carry home.

She grabbed a cart and walked through the store. She picked up fresh fruit, more crackers, bread, peanut butter, cheese, and the list went on. She stopped halfway through her shopping and stared at her purchases, worried about the cost so far.

She did a mental calculation, figured she was close to maxing out her budget for an entire week, and quickly walked to the meat counter to look at what was on sale. Which didn't matter because she still couldn't cook anything anyway, even if the new stove was hooked up. She headed to the deli section. There she picked up some chicken and some ham on sale. Finally she walked toward the clerks and checked out.

She winced when she realized she was over her budget by a good forty-five dollars. She paid the bill and headed to her car.

While she was unloading the groceries into her car, she

caught sight of the same woman who'd slapped her. Doreen stared in surprise as the woman got into a small gray car and pulled slowly away. She was just enough ahead that Doreen could see the license plate. She wrote it down on her receipt and, with a smile of satisfaction, got into her car. Instead of driving home before calling, she dialed Mack right away. "I saw her," she said excitedly.

With exaggerated patience in his tone, Mack asked, "You saw who?"

"The woman who slapped me," she cried out. "I'm at the grocery store, and she just pulled away, but I got her license plate." She rambled off the tag.

"Well, hold on a minute. I need a pen. Now give it to me again slowly."

She repeated the letters and numbers. "Do you think you can track her down now?"

"Maybe. You leave this to me. Congratulations for not talking to her."

"I would have, but she really surprised me, showing up like that." She laughed. "But I did good, getting the license plate, didn't I?"

"You did at that. Now go home and get some real food into you." There was a pause before he said, "You did buy food, didn't you?"

"Of course I did," she said indignantly.

"There's no *of course* about it. You're always starving. You need to eat more."

"I would buy some meat, but I still don't have a working stove."

"Would you know how to cook it anyway?"

"No, but I'm willing to try."

"Why don't you have a stove? When did Willie say he'd

come?"

She explained the problem, adding, "Maybe by tomorrow night I'll have a working stove."

"And what's the first thing you'll make?"

She stopped, thought about it, and then said, "I haven't a clue." She laughed out loud. "Go back to work. One of us needs to be employed." She hung up on him, grinning like crazy at the thought of Mack finding out who had slapped her.

Chapter 14

DOREEN UNLOADED HER groceries and stopped for lunch. Feeling better now, she could get more done. Although she didn't want to, Doreen was determined to get the downed fence cleaned up. Most of it was stacked, but she had more to do. She pocketed her wire cutters, grabbed her gloves and her cup of tea, and headed back outside. Mugs immediately headed to the garden, digging and rooting through the dirt. Goliath found a big rock, hopped on top, and curled up to go to sleep. Thaddeus, on the other hand, was bugging her. He insisted on riding on her shoulder, even as she bent to pick up piece after piece after piece of wood, wire, junk, and nails.

"Thaddeus, can't you find some other place to sit?"

And damn if that the bird didn't call out, "No. No."

She sighed. "How come you can be so amiable and easy to get along with most times, and then there are times like right now?"

He made a funny sound, almost like a trill. She likened it to laughter. She glared at him. "It's not fair. Everybody is laughing at me. You're not allowed to laugh at me too." Trying to ignore him, she bent down for one of the last few pieces of rotten wood and added it to the appropriate stack. She should probably carry all this stuff out to the front driveway, so it could be loaded from there to take to the dump.

But that looked like a heck of a lot of work. Still, she didn't have to do very much at a time. If she could get one stack to the front yard, that would help. She chose the rotten wood because it was the lightest. When she had the wheelbarrow full, she realized it would take at least three if not four more full loads. She picked up the wheelbarrow by its handles, determined to make this work. It took a lot of effort to get through the rough backyard, but, when she made it onto the path that ran alongside the house, it was much easier.

She dumped all the wood onto a tarp on the paved drive. She didn't know if the tarp was necessary, and she certainly wasn't capable of lifting it full of wood, but it might keep her driveway relatively clean of nails and excess dirt. She came back and did it again and then again. By the time she was done with the rotten wood, she was exhausted.

She called out to Mugs, "Come on, Mugs. Let's go for a walk by the creek."

Woof. And Mugs ran toward her. His jowls and ears flapped in the wind.

She laughed, loving the look on his face. Too bad she hadn't brought her camera ... Although she did have a camera on her cell phone. By the time she got it up, the dog already stood beside her, his tail wagging so hard it might come off any second. She chuckled and turned to look at Goliath. "Goliath, you coming with us?"

Goliath didn't even raise an eyebrow.

Figures. And Thaddeus, ... no way to get rid of him, so

with just Mugs and Thaddeus, she walked to the end of her yard and along the path behind her neighbors.

She knew Mack wouldn't be impressed, but how was she *not* supposed to return to the spot where he'd found the ring and she'd found the ivory box? For all she knew, third time was the charm, and they'd find something else.

She shivered. *Let it not be a body part, please.*

With that thought uppermost in her mind, she studied the creek carefully. She was relieved when she couldn't see anything untoward. She found the spot where they'd been on the previous day. With a look toward her neighbor's fence—completely closed off from the creek and with no knotholes for the neighbor to see through—Doreen crouched beside the creek. She could see the indent where the ivory box had been, but the creek bed was slowly filling it back up again. She pulled her sleeve higher and reached into the icy-cold water.

All she found was rock and sand. Moving slightly to the side, she checked where the ring had been. And again found nothing unusual. Frowning, she widened her search and kept on digging. Again *nothing*.

She sat back on her heels and glared. "I was so sure something would be here," she muttered.

"Well, it serves you right."

She gave a squawk. And Thaddeus squawked in her ear. She lost her footing, desperately tried to catch her balance but ended up in the creek. She let out a shriek as the cold water soaked her jeans. She twisted to glare at Mack standing there with a grin on his face.

He struggled not to laugh out loud, but he lost the battle. Still chuckling, he stepped forward and reached out a hand.

She stared at it suspiciously. "So why would you want to help me now?" She frowned at him. "You're the one responsible for the predicament I'm in."

He gave her a look of sheer astonishment. "What did I have to do with anything? I didn't push you in. You're the one who fell in." He reached down, grabbed her under her arms, and plucked her up so she stood in the creek.

She glared at him again as he noted her soaking-wet clothing and smirked. "Do you have any idea how cold this is?"

He shrugged. "I had my hand in there yesterday. But I can't say I'm ready to go for a swim. It is a bit too cold for that yet."

"So you think this is funny?" she muttered.

He nodded. "As a matter of fact, I do."

She shook her head, then wrung some excess water out of her pants. "You know what? I'm so fed up with everybody laughing at me. Even Thaddeus laughed." At that point Thaddeus was no longer on her shoulder. "Damn bird flew away. Probably to stay dry." She turned to look for him, finding him in the middle of the creek, stuck on a big rock. "Thaddeus, hold on. I'm coming."

He tilted his head to the side.

When he went to open his mouth, she said, "Don't you say it."

"Body in the water. Body in the water. Body in the water."

She groaned. "You just had to say that, didn't you?" She extended her hand for Thaddeus to walk up her arm, and he grabbed onto her wrist and slowly made it to her shoulder. By now her shoes were pretty well ruined, and she was knee-deep in icy-cold water. She slowly turned to make it back to the shore, where Mack waited.

Mugs was there, watching the show. She saw with disgust that Goliath had even arrived. Suddenly Goliath took several pounces to the left and raced up to the bank on one of the jutting-out pieces. There was a fallen tree branch, which he hopped on and sped down the end toward the water.

"Goliath, don't," she cried out. But the cat wasn't listening.

Expecting the worst—that he would head into the water himself—she raced over, trying hard not to fall with the current and the slippery rocks. But, as she got closer, he stared at something intently in the water.

"Mack, please tell me nothing is down there that I won't want to see."

"Shouldn't be anything there. My team checked out this area pretty thoroughly the other day," Mack said. "He probably just sees a minnow or a frog."

"A minnow?"

"Sure, the creek is alive with all kinds of wildlife. Goliath is a predator at heart."

Given the look in Goliath's gaze, she figured Mack had to be right. But she wouldn't be happy until Goliath was back away from the water. Cats hated water, so she didn't understand why Goliath was so darn close to the stuff. As she stepped closer, her gaze caught sight of something white in the creek. She froze, her mind cataloguing what it was. She shook her head. "It can't be."

Mack raced toward her. "What?"

She turned to look up at him. "Please tell me it's not so?"

Mack quickly shifted until he stood on an outcropping

from the creek, staring into the water. "I can't see anything."

She judged the distance from the tree branch that had fallen into the creek. It was a good six feet from where he stood. "I'm not sure you can see it from there. But I don't think that branch will hold you. Wait." She took another step forward and almost fell as the rock underneath her foot gave way. She gasped as she partially went down. Thaddeus opened his wings, hitting her in the face. "Calm down, Thaddeus. Calm down. I'm fine."

"Are you?" Mack asked.

At least he wasn't laughing at her anymore. She tried to grasp the branch to get upright again. "It's definitely deeper here," she said, as if something had created a pool beneath the branch in the outcropping. She studied the creek bed for a long moment, looking for whatever it was that had caught her eye. It was small—at least she thought it was. With her steps into the area, she had created a surge of silt rising up, dirtying the water. "I saw it right here."

Mack crouched down using the branch for support, the two of them only four feet apart now as they stared into the creek around her. "Any idea what it was?"

"Small and white," she said briskly.

"That covers a lot of things."

She shifted the branch off her slightly and thought she saw something white pop to the surface. She reached out and snagged it. "Got it." Mack held out his hand, and she just glared at him. "You can see it after I take a look," she snapped. "There's got to be some benefit for me being soaking wet and freezing cold."

She opened her hand and eyed the item in the flat of her palm. Her stomach knotted. She slammed her fist closed and held it out for Mack.

He had to stretch most of the way across the four feet separating them, using the branch for support.

Part of her really wanted to see the branch give away and watch him fall on his face into this ice-cold creek. But, given what was in her hand, that was not a good idea. She dropped the thing into his outstretched palm and waited for his thoughts.

"What the heck?"

She gave him a terrified look. "It's human, isn't it?"

He frowned. "I can't say that it is for sure. It could be all kinds of things."

But she knew. Inside she knew. "You have to get it tested. And did you hear back from what we found in your mom's garden?" She looked down at the area where she'd seen the white thing originally. Now that the creek bed was a little clearer, she could see more. And what she saw wasn't exactly awe inspiring. "You want to get my shovel for me?"

He stood. "Are you saying there's more?"

She gave him a grim look. "Get the shovel, and let me see what this is."

He headed to the garden, and she waited, figuring out the best way to get this up without destroying anything. She was not sure exactly what she had found.

When he returned, he took off his shoes and socks and rolled up his pant legs. He stepped around the area they were looking at until he came beside her. She pointed downward and heard him whisper under his breath.

"Shit, that better not be what I think it is." He shifted to the side. "Move out of the way, will you?"

She moved to the other side of the branch, just in case something shifted enough to float down creek. The last thing she wanted to do was catch any more pieces, but the alternative could be much worse.

He maneuvered the shovel under the item and gently lifted it to the surface. As it broke free, there was no doubt. It was a set of bones. Almost completely skeletonized. Slightly misshapen but unmistakable.

"It's a hand," Doreen said. She wanted to throw up in the creek but knew Mack would yell at her for contaminating the scene, not to mention no one down creek would appreciate her addition to the water flow. However, it was just too much to consider. When she'd found a man drowned in the creek, that was one thing. But this was a hand, just a hand.

"I think something else is here too." He lifted the shovelful of hand bones and gently put them on dry land. When he reached back in the water, something floated away. He lifted up two small bones, each about eight to ten inches long. He raised them gently and put them on the creekbank too. "We'll search this whole area. I shouldn't even move those, but I was afraid the current would take them away."

"What are they?"

"Arm bones. Looks like we found another arm."

She stared at him. "What's the chance that the second arm came from a different person?"

He shot her look. "What's the chance of you finding another murdered body within a week?"

That shut her up—for a moment. "It's her bones, isn't it?"

He shrugged. "It's way too early to guess. I hope it is more of her. Because to think we found a second dismembered body is too ugly to contemplate." He pulled his phone from his pocket and organized his team.

She looked at her clothes, completely covered in creek

water, knowing this place was about to be overrun with law enforcement. She took a step back, forgot about the deeper hole, and fell in. She cried out, causing Mack to turn toward her as she floated ever-so-slightly downstream. She grabbed hold of the branch to stop from going farther. And damn if the branch didn't shift, and a whole mess of the bank fell away.

"Stop," Mack roared. "We have to preserve what we can."

She wanted to laugh and cry at the same time. "It's amazing that those bones—if they are Betty's—have been here for thirty years. So what are the odds that anything else could possibly be left here? Wouldn't it have floated downstream with the late spring flooding each year?" she asked, regaining her footing.

She left the branch where it was but knew chances were good that the branch wouldn't shift any more, especially as she wasn't tugging on it. But she had set the water to churning. Then she thought of the silt screen she'd found in the back of her garden. She stumbled to the shore farther ahead, crawled out, and walked the few feet to her garden, squelching mud and water with every step. Grabbing the silt screen, she went a little farther downstream—a good six feet from the fallen tree branch near where they'd seen the hand—and placed the screen in the stream. So, if anything had come loose, it should be trapped by the screen.

He looked at her in surprise and then nodded approvingly. "That's a great idea."

"It could be too late for anything now. I should have thought of it first."

"Yeah, sure, when you went in the first time or the second?" And then he laughed.

She glared at him. "You're the only one I know who can laugh over dead bodies."

He wiped away his smile and gave her a clipped nod. "You're right. That's completely inappropriate to laugh about."

The river swirled around them, and she glanced at the hand bones. "I wonder how long it's been here." She was sorry for pricking his humor. He wasn't laughing at the dead body—he certainly had respect for the situation. He'd been laughing at her. And, for once, she didn't mind in the least. "Any chance I can go home and stay out of this?" she asked with hope.

He slid her a sideways look and gave a very definitive headshake.

Her shoulders sagged. "How about I go home and get changed?" In the distance she could hear emergency vehicles. She groaned. "It'll put me on the front page of the paper again, won't it?"

"Well, you do live in an area with a dubious past."

"I had nothing to do with this," she cried out. "Anybody could have found that ivory box. And you found the ring."

"And then you had to come back and take another look, even though I told you that I had a team coming."

She pointed upstream. "But that's where the box and the ring were. Would you have found this?"

He looked in the distance and then said, "I would hope so. But maybe, when you fell in, you dislodged the dirt and brought the bones to the surface." He shrugged. "No way to know."

"Right. So, in other words, I'm not in trouble. You just wish I wasn't here at all."

"I wish you would follow orders for once."

"You could tell me to go inside and get changed," she said brightly. "I promise I'll follow those directions."

He glared at her. "If I have to stand in here and freeze because of you, then you can stand in here and freeze too," he declared. "Besides the water is warming up. The sun is out, and it's a nice spring afternoon."

"I don't care how warm it is outside. This is still glacier-fed creek water."

He grinned. "Very true."

Before she had a chance to say anything more, voices called from her backyard.

Mack turned, cupped his mouth, and yelled, "Come to the edge of the backyard."

As she and Mack watched, several officers rounded the corner. They stopped, took one look, and then raced toward them. "What did you find?"

"Did you call the coroner?"

One of the officers nodded. "He's on his way." The man crouched near the shovel, noting the silt screen farther down creek, then considered their finds so far gathered on the bank. "A hand? An arm?"

Mack nodded. "Looks like it."

The two officers walked to where Doreen was. "Are more remains down here?"

She shrugged. "I have no idea. But we disturbed the creek bed, so a few pieces could have floated down creek." She nodded toward Mack. "He has a finger bone in his hand too. I put the silt screen here to stop anything else from going too far."

After that, chaos once again filled her yard. She glanced at Mack. "Now that the troops have arrived, surely I can leave the creek."

All business now, he nodded. "Yeah. Go in and get warm."

She extricated herself from the water without any help. As she walked toward her house, Mugs' barking added to the chaos.

Mack called behind her, "Make sure you take the animals too."

She nodded. "But I don't see Goliath."

One of the officers standing with Mack said, "Where did you put the finger bone?"

Mack pointed to the shovel that held the hand. "It should be right there."

Walking away, she heard them discussing the fact that the finger bone had gone missing. She scrunched her shoulders and lowered her head. She had a bad feeling about that.

"Doreen," Mack called, "check Goliath and Mugs for the finger bone."

"Will do." She shook her head. "But you know that I can't keep track of those two at all times."

Suddenly there was a ruffle of feathers, and Thaddeus decided walking was too dangerous. He flew up to her shoulder and sat there, his claws digging into her flesh. "Cold. Cold. Cold."

She reached out and gently stroked his feathers. "You're right. I'm very cold."

"Thaddeus cold. Thaddeus cold."

She groaned. "So you are, little one. Your feathers are wet too, aren't they?"

Up ahead Mugs raced forward and backward as more people streamed around her house. She caught one of the officers and pointed to two people standing at the corner of her backyard, recognizing Sibyl and her cameraman. *Again.* "That's the press. Get them off my property. You don't want them here at all."

When the reporters realized they'd been caught, the pair backed away.

She called out, "If you come back on my property again, Sibyl, I'll prosecute."

They shot her a dirty look and stepped around the corner of the house, Goliath running into her sight from the opposite direction. *Good, I hope he tripped them.* She turned to the officer. "You get somebody up front, and you post them there. You make sure nobody steps foot on my place. Do you hear me?"

The officer frowned at her and turned to Mack. Whatever Mack said obviously satisfied the officer because he nodded, pulled out his phone, and said, "We'll take care of it."

At least her temper had eased the chill taking over her body. She stormed into the house, and, with all three animals inside, she slammed and locked the door tight. Then she walked carefully, throwing a couple kitchen towels on the floor to get her to the bottom of the stairs without leaving a trail of water behind.

She gave up trying to keep the dripping to a minimum, grabbed the towels, and ran upstairs. In the bathroom she quickly stripped down and hopped into the shower. It took several minutes of standing under the hot spray before she finally warmed up.

She couldn't believe they had found more bones. The last thing she'd wanted was to find another body. Thankfully this was a whole lot better for her to handle. Ancient bones were just white, looked like dried sticks in a way. That they'd been human at one time was disheartening, but those old bones were a lot easier to deal with than the blood and tissue found on the bones of a more recent corpse.

Was it weird that she knew this much about decaying bones after so few days here in the Mission? But, the more she thought about this, the better she felt about her new-found knowledge. *After all, Mack needs to know this stuff. And I'm like his ... partner. Right?*

Sighing at her insights, she quickly shampooed her hair, then did it a second time before she stepped from the shower and dried off. There was just something about having been in the creek with those bones right there, much less with minnows and frogs and whatnot in the water. She found dry clothes, dressed, and then grabbed all the wet clothing she'd brought into the house. Back downstairs, on her way to put the wet things in the washer, she noted the size of the crowd gathered out front. She peered through the front door window. Sure enough, the crowd completely filled the cul-de-sac.

The coroner's vehicle was parked partially in her drive-way and partially in the street, with several other RCMP vehicles around, all because she had a tarp full of wood scraps taking up much of her driveway space. At least fifty people were out there, and, *of course*, the press had set up cameras and had microphones, ready to nail anybody who came or went.

"How did they find out so fast? Dammit." She headed to the utility room off the kitchen to put her wet clothes on to wash, then pulled out her cell phone and found she had several missed calls. "Good. I don't need to talk to anybody." But just then the phone rang in her hand. It was Nan. With a heavy sigh Doreen walked into the kitchen and hit Talk.

"Hello, Nan."

"Oh, my dear, you are just livening up this town like nothing else." Her grandmother sounded thrilled.

"I really wish I wasn't." Doreen picked up the electric teakettle and, with the phone against her shoulder, walked to the sink and filled it. "Honestly this has nothing to do with me."

"That's not what everybody is talking about though," Nan said excitedly. "So, give me the details."

"I can't. You'll just share them with everybody else."

There was an awkward silence on the other end.

Doreen sighed. "You know that's how this works, Nan. I've got police everywhere. I've got press everywhere. And every bloody neighbor for miles around is standing out in the front yard."

"Are they ruining the grass?" Nan cried out.

"No, I had the police push them back off the property." That was a small white lie. Because, so far, she had seen some had crept onto the front lawn again. "As soon as I'm allowed to tell you anything, I will."

"Well, the news is, you found a body."

"I did not find a body," Doreen protested. "I don't walk around every day and find bodies, you know. C'mon, Nan."

"Well, a lot of people went missing over the years. And, since you've been in town, it seems like you're right in the thick of it all."

"But they don't think I did it, do they?" she wailed.

Nan's laughter trailed through the phone. "Oh, my dear, of course not. You're not old enough, for one. And, for two, you haven't been here for a long time."

"Maybe I killed them thirty years ago, and I've now come back to find the bodies and to make good on my deeds from back then."

More laughter filled the phone.

Doreen grinned. "Okay, that was a bit far-fetched."

"Just a little. So, if you didn't find a body, what did you find?"

"Part of a body but don't you dare tell anyone." And Doreen hung up the phone.

She knew it wouldn't do any good. Nan would tell everybody. At least it was a bit of truth and no details. Doreen stood on her back deck, waiting for the teakettle to whistle. She was so cold inside and out that she wondered if she'd ever get warm. The shower had helped, but seeing the gathered crowd out front had her warm glow leaving again.

The police would need to dredge the places in the creek where she'd found the ivory box and where Mack had found the ring and now where the bones had been unearthed. If there was an arm, there could be so much more.

And then she thought about how the bank had been built up, and some of it had washed away. What the police really needed to do was take that bank back a full foot. See what else could be buried there. Of course they couldn't do that. It would compromise the ecosystem or some other such nonsense. Everybody had an excuse for everything.

Still, she didn't want to be the one who got into trouble with the government about this riparian zone that Mack had warned her about. Surely a murder investigation trumped a zoning issue, right? And, yes, she had found the box, which led to the other finds ... But this was hopefully solving a murder from thirty years ago. That was the bigger picture. In her mind at least.

The teakettle finally whistled behind her. She turned, headed back inside, and made a cup of tea.

She wondered if Mack needed a cup. Of course he did. He'd been standing in the creek this whole time. But, if she were to offer him some tea, in front of his team and the coroner and the nosy onlookers, that would put Mack in the middle of something she didn't want to thrust him into. Right now, he was all business. A whole different story than his teasing from earlier. She didn't know what kind of relationship they had going, but she didn't want to mess it up. As long as she kept finding bodies, or body parts, it was a great excuse to keep him around. How sad was that?

With her teacup in hand, she wandered into the living room to see how bad the crowd was outside. They had surged forward, over her front yard, and the two people she'd ordered off earlier were right at the head of it. She put down her tea, grabbed her camera, and stepped outside, taking pictures, focusing on the ones in the front on her land. They had knocked down her No Trespassing sign too.

She called out to them, "I have a lawyer who will be in contact with you."

Fortunately the crowd backed off her property. The cop turned to look at her and grinned. She gave him a small smile, took a picture of him, then stepped inside the house. She'd be damned if she'd let them run all over her place again. She'd been the hottest story in town last week. The last thing she expected was to be the hottest story in town *this* week too.

She returned to her tea, sat on the big comfy couch, and put up her feet. Goliath jumped on her and kneaded her lap before turning in a circle and collapsing, as if Doreen had nothing better to do than to be a comfortable pillow for him.

As she stroked his long back, she realized maybe that was a good purpose in life after all. There were a lot worse things than having pets that loved to be with you.

Mugs, true to form, jumped up with his front paws on her lap for her to cuddle him for a few minutes, then walked over to lay down on his dog bed. He was just as happy down there as he was on the couch with her.

He and Goliath got along amazingly well, considering. Every once in a while, Mugs still chased Goliath; and, every once in a while, Goliath seemed to deliberately taunt Mugs. But, when it came to times of crisis, they were both very calm and very patient. They would be back to their normal behavior tomorrow morning. If not sooner …

By then, maybe some of this media hype would have died down again. She worried that was a very long and distant hope. Now that she'd found a second body—no, make that pieces of her fourth dead body—in less than a couple of weeks, she knew she'd never live it down. So much for her hopes of a *nice* new beginning by moving.

Thaddeus walked into the living room, hopped up on the couch beside her, and then walked up onto her shoulder. He brushed his beak against her cheek. She smiled and tilted her head into his gentle strokes. "Thanks, sweetie. I'm okay, Thaddeus. It's just been a very frustrating day."

He cooed in her ear, and she sank back, enjoying her first really contented moment as a family. The outside circumstances left a lot to be desired. But inside? Well, her world could be a whole lot worse than it was. She smiled, picked up her tea, and relaxed.

Chapter 15

Saturday ...

DOREEN GOT UP the next morning bright and early, put on her gloves while the coffee dripped, and headed out to the backyard. It was thankfully empty. Which she couldn't say about her front yard, still filled with people. She had no idea how long the police had stayed last night. Neither did she care. They had a job to do and would do it, regardless of the length of time it took. But they didn't seem to be here right now. She just hoped her appointment with Mack wouldn't be affected by all this.

With the wheelbarrow in hand, she burned through her restless energy, still hanging on after a bad night. She moved the cut-up wire around to the front, ignoring the crowd. She hadn't heard from Mack and still had no idea if he would be on time or a little bit later this morning or if he'd come at all, given yesterday's events. She wanted to get some work done on her own garden before she headed to his mom's. She was excited at the idea, mostly because she needed the money, but also to see how this could work as a career direction. If she got in a few hours today, then she hoped that Mack might pay her today.

Having overspent her grocery budget yesterday, she had to find a way to replenish that money. No income coming in sucked. Half an hour later, she walked inside through the back door into the kitchen, snagged a cup of coffee, and sat down at the kitchen table, waiting for the sweat to evaporate off her back and face. She had moved all the wire to the front yard.

Thankfully, with her last load, Doreen noted how the nosy neighbors had left. Was that Mack's doing?

Regardless, now she had two stacks of refuse for the dump on her driveway, one of wire and the other of rotten wood. She still had all the metal poles to move. But her efforts had made a massive difference already, as the backyard looked quite decent. By rights, the entire backyard should be scraped clean to the dirt, underground irrigation put in, topsoil put down, then she could plant her garden. If she added decent nutrition-based fertilizer, she'd have a thriving backyard.

She didn't think Nan's place had any irrigation anywhere, and that was a problem. Doreen should look around, see if she could get secondhand soaker hoses to weave through the beds.

As she finished her second cup of coffee, her phone rang. Willie's number appeared on her screen. "Hi, Willie."

"Hi, are you there right now? I'm heading up to the lake country in a little bit. I was going to run by and hook that stove up for you on the way. If that would work, I've got the breaker with me."

"That would be great. I have an appointment at nine," she said, adding a little self-importance to her tone. "It takes about ten minutes to get there, but, if you could come now, and it doesn't take you very long, that would be perfect."

"Okay. Me and my son will see you in about ten minutes," he said, then hung up.

She pocketed her cell phone, put down her empty cup, and walked outside again. The wheelbarrow wouldn't work so well for the poles. She'd carry them one by one.

She was dragging the last two large ones from the back-yard to the front when Willie pulled up. He hopped out, his son too, and took a look at all the old broken-down fencing material and said, "Wow, that's a lot of junk."

"Isn't it though?" She smiled up at him. "Now if only I had a decent way to get rid of it all before the neighbors start to complain about the mess."

"Dump run," Willie said in a sing-song voice. "I end up doing those on a regular basis. Once I take that old stove away, it will have to go somewhere."

She gazed at him with a crafty look. "So what would it take to have you haul all this with it?"

He frowned. "I don't have my dump-run vehicle today. Didn't think to bring it to haul away your old stove." He glanced at his panel van and back at her. "If you don't mind me leaving the gas stove right here beside the rest of your fencing stuff, tomorrow I can load it all up and take it to the dump. You don't have very much here. If I put the other appliances I have to haul out on the flatbed truck first, we should be good to go."

Her face lit up with joy. "If you could do that, that would be awesome. Thank you." Mack had said he might be able to haul some away too. So maybe, between the two men, she'd get rid of it all.

He nodded. "It's really a pain to have stuff like this hanging around. The wood will be full of bugs." He mo-tioned at her small car. "You don't want to put wire and rotten wood with nails into a vehicle like that."

She nodded. "I noticed the bugs."

He nodded agreeably, motioned for his son to follow him and headed inside. He had a couple boxes in his hands, which she presumed were breakers or something.

She walked around to the backyard and made sure it was all picked up, loaded another wheelbarrow full of little bits and pieces, took it to the front, dumped it on the tarp, and then took the wheelbarrow back around again. As she walked into the kitchen, she checked the clock. Almost eight-thirty. She needed to leave soon.

Willie had just wiggled the new stove into position. Standing upright, he said, "It turns on and looks good."

"And the gas lines have been capped off properly?" she asked. She couldn't help but remember Mack's comment about the gas dangers.

Willie nodded. "You're safe and secure. This is properly wired up. You'll have to put some money into the house wiring at some point, but it was done right originally. Only the codes have changed in the last fifty years. So, whenever you renovate, be prepared for the fact that the electrical bill will be a little higher than you had planned."

He put the old stove on what he called a hand truck, and, with his son's help, moved it to the pile in the front driveway.

She watched as her stack of trash grew bigger. "You sure you can come and get this tomorrow?" She couldn't imagine what all the neighbors would say if she had a junkyard like this around long. Her ex-husband would have had a fit. He would have the man back within the hour to get it all gone. But then her ex hated disorder of any kind.

"No problem," Willie said with a big smile. With that,

the two men hopped into the van and drove away.

She looked at her watch, walked into the kitchen, and washed her hands. Then she grabbed some yogurt and granola that she had gotten on her last grocery trip for a quick breakfast today. With that polished off way too fast, she could almost hear her ex-husband's admonishing voice about proper manners as she placed the bowl in the sink, ran some water in it, grabbed her gloves, and walked out the kitchen door. No way she wouldn't walk to Mack's mom's house. It was only a couple cul-de-sacs over. And she could take the creek path. Provided the police hadn't crossed the area off with yellow tape. Although she didn't think that was possible since it was Mother Nature's space. Surely they couldn't block it all off.

She called for Mugs, who came racing and barking toward her, as Goliath strolled into view. Thaddeus took up his position on her shoulder, and she realized the entire family would go to work with her. Goliath led the way. She went around the corner of her property and stopped. Mack was there with two policemen. She frowned up at him.

He grinned.

"I was just going to your mom's house," she said.

He nodded. "I'll walk with you." He gave a couple more instructions to the two officers, then turned and led the way.

When they were out of earshot, she asked, "Are you here to stop me from digging in the creek?"

He tossed her a surprised look. "No. Of course not. I left men here this morning, working, so no way would they have let you do that."

"Oh." She didn't dare admit she had planned to at least look at the area to see if anything had surfaced overnight.

His smirk said he knew exactly what she was thinking.

The morning was beautiful, and she'd already gotten some work done. Although she'd forgotten to pay Willie. "Willie was here this morning. He hooked up the stove. But he didn't ask for the money."

Mack looked at her in surprise. "He might send you an invoice. Does he have your email address?"

She thought about that. "I don't know."

"He'll probably request an e-transfer."

Her heart stopped. "An e-transfer?" She sighed. "Just give it to me straight. What do I have to do?"

He led her through the process of sending money online to Willie through the banks.

"I didn't even know that was possible. What if I don't have the money in the account?"

"How were you planning on paying him?"

She shrugged. "Cash. But I have to pay Barry too somehow for the electrical work he did."

"Call Willie to see when he'll be in the area next, or you could drop it off at the office."

"He's coming back tomorrow because he didn't bring his big truck to take away the old stove. Plus he has a bunch of other stuff to haul to the dump, and he said he would take the fencing I had piled out front too."

"That's very generous of him."

"It is. I've got it all stacked up in the driveway so he can easily load it."

"Did you already get everything moved to the front yard?" he asked in astonishment.

She nodded. "I've been working on it since yesterday."

The five of them walked toward the cul-de-sac where Mack's mother lived, down the path to the road, where it widened into a big circle. What a sight they must have made.

His mom's place was in the middle. They headed into the backyard, and Doreen took a good look at the begonia bed again.

"This bed has definitely suffered. Because we don't know why, you should boost the nutrients in it." She glanced around at the hilly beds, watching as her brood checked out this backyard with curiosity. "If you don't want to bring in any new topsoil, you could quite probably steal enough from some of these beds."

He looked at the beds. "But that'll disturb all the plants there, right?"

She nodded. "Yes, and I don't really know what bulbs she's got buried in there. Once you start digging around, you'll damage the roots."

"I can bring the pickup by with a load of topsoil," he said. "It's not that big a deal."

She smiled. "It isn't for you. For somebody like me, with no truck and no muscle, it is."

He laughed. "I think you have more muscle than you know. You moved all that fencing material."

She smiled. "I did, didn't I? Do you have a tarp? I can start laying out the begonias and getting them moved over. It's early in the season, but, because they aren't doing much here, we'll trim the old roots back to the tuber and put them in their new bed. They won't do much this year, but they'll be very thankful for it next year."

"Next year. Next year. Next year."

Doreen smiled at the bird, shaking her head. She never knew just what he would say, just what he would pick up.

Together she and Mack walked to the large garden shed. Mack pulled out a spade for her and a shovel for him. Next he found a big tarp, and they spread it down beside the

409

begonias.

Instantly Goliath appeared midjump and landed on the tarp, loving the sound it made. After Doreen's heart started beating again, she enjoyed watching her huge cat play with his tail, like he was a kitten again. Mugs sat nearby, staring. He probably thought Goliath was strange too.

"Never a dull moment," Mack said.

Doreen wondered if he was talking only about her pets or was she thrown into the mix too. As she stared at the spot where they had dug into the begonias the first time here, she said, "You never did tell me about that bone."

"What bone?"

She motioned at the begonia bed. "The one we found here."

"Did I say it was a bone?"

"You did."

He shrugged and went back to work.

"Or have you not found out yet? The lab should be able to tell almost immediately if it's human or not."

"I've been a little busy. I haven't checked on the results." He dug in the bed where they would move the begonias. Goliath and Mugs helped by digging their own holes.

"I don't think the animals can dig deep enough to do any harm to the begonias." Then she nodded. "Maybe you should call the lab."

He shooed away the animals before stabbing the shovel into the dirt beside her and asked, "Why?"

She glanced up at him and shrugged. "Because what if it's human? We just found an arm and a hand near my place. What if that was a toe bone or a foot bone here at your mom's?"

He stared at her in astonishment. "So, because we found

an arm in the creek, you think my mother's garden bed will have a foot?" With shock and laughter in his voice, he said, "Better get back to the gardening job. Leave the police work to me."

"Okay, fine. So it's a little far-fetched. But you have to admit it is interesting."

"What's interesting?" He wasn't giving an inch, but he had stopped to pet Goliath and Mugs.

They were eating up the attention. Apparently Thaddeus got jealous and waddled over. Mack stroked the bird's head, murmuring something to him.

"Think about it," Doreen said to Mack. "What are the odds we'd find another human bone?"

"Considering it's you …" He let his voice trail off.

At this point the animals decided it was time to run wild in this backyard.

She snorted and carefully picked up another large group of begonia bulbs. The bulbs themselves looked healthy. But the roots were small, stunted. She laid them carefully on the tarp, though Goliath seemed intent on rearranging them but gently so she kept on working. She looked at the bed. "Do you think I'll always see a six-foot-long garden bed and think a body is buried in it?"

He laughed. "I wouldn't be at all surprised."

Doreen watched as her trio suspiciously calmed down, lying together near the garden. She frowned, wondered what was up. "Any updates on the ring by the way?"

He was back to shoveling. "No, none."

Just then the kitchen door opened, and Mack's mother walked out. Considering Mack's size, his mother was tiny. She probably didn't even reach four feet ten.

Doreen waved. "Good morning. I'm Doreen, and I'm

here with Mack," she said by way of explanation.

The woman stared at her in surprise, then shifted to see Mack walking toward her. She didn't seem to mind the strange animals in her yard. Or maybe she hadn't seen them yet.

"Good morning, Mom. How are you feeling?"

The frail-looking older woman had a shawl wrapped around her shoulders. But she gave him a bright smile. "I'm feeling much better, thank you." She turned to Doreen again. "You're the body lady."

Doreen's jaw dropped. "I'm who?" She'd half expected to get some kind of a nickname but wasn't at all sure she liked this one.

Mack turned to his mother. "Mom, this is Doreen. She's the *gardening* lady," he said with firm emphasis.

His mother chuckled. "That's what *you* call her." She smiled at Doreen. "I'm glad you like gardening. Considering the amount of bodies you're finding, I'd have thought it might have turned you off the hobby."

Doreen gave her a bright smile back. "The fact is, it's made me more intrigued." She motioned at the garden around her. "You've spent a lot of time and love on this garden."

Mack's mother nodded. "Call me Millicent. And, yes, I have indeed. It was a shared hobby with my husband. It makes me sad that I can't come outside and do the same work anymore."

"I understand. I'm now living in Nan's house. And, of course, it was the same thing for her. I have my work cut out to get her gardens back to the glory days they were."

"Oh my, you're Nan's granddaughter." Millicent clasped her hands together in delight.

Doreen looked at her and sighed. "I gather you know my grandmother?"

Millicent laughed. "Of course I do. Everybody knows Nan."

That's what Doreen had been afraid of. Now the real question was, was that a good thing or a bad thing?

Mack patted his mother's shoulder and said, "Mom, why don't you go inside where it's warm?"

She waved him off. "It's lovely out here."

"But you haven't been feeling well, have you? We don't want you to catch cold."

She looked at him and smiled. "I know you're trying to keep me safe, but it's really lovely out here. And I do love gardening."

Doreen understood. It would be hard for her too. It had always been hard for her to let others do the gardening she wanted to do. "Well, maybe if you had a hot drink, and you sat in the sun close by, you could watch us," she suggested.

Millicent ignored Mack's look. "That's a lovely idea. I'll make a pot of tea, and then I'll come out."

Doreen smiled and returned to her digging as Millicent hurried back inside. Doreen heard her animals getting frisky again but didn't dare look up because Doreen was intent on ignoring Mack too, even though he loomed over her.

"You really didn't need to invite her out here, you know? The reason we're here doing the work is so she doesn't."

"If she sits and watches, she'll feel like she's more in control and not like we're taking over her garden," Doreen said quietly. "A garden becomes a living thing. She's attached to it. Her memories from years past are here. To have someone else doing things in her garden without her knowing about it will be very painful and intrusive, like it's no longer her garden." She sensed his surprise. She turned to look up at him. "Letting her sit here surely can't be harmful, can it?"

"She's not allowed to get her hands dirty," he warned.

Doreen nodded. "Fine." She pulled up another big pile of begonia roots, but she felt something hard underneath. "I'm surprised rocks are in here. This bed's been established for a long time."

"Maybe that's why the bed isn't doing very well," he said. "Although I don't see any rocks. It's all dirt."

She stuck her spade back underneath and hit something solid. She turned to look at him. "Really?"

"You're making me paranoid these days." He stooped beside her.

"I don't think we're paranoid. Just wary."

He rolled his eyes and helped to remove the loose soil.

The animals, again curious, huddled together with them.

Depending on the climate, begonias were usually removed every winter. But these bushes hadn't been pulled out in decades. So they had a massive connected root system. Moving gently, Doreen and Mack cleared a spot a good foot long.

"I'm surprised so many bulbs are here," Mack noted.

"Another reason why the tubers need to be divided and moved," she said. "When they're growing in on top of each other like this, the bed gets too crowded, and the plants have to fight for nutrients."

He got the bigger shovel, and, using his heavy boot, he pushed the shovel into the area where she had hit something hard. He hit the same thing. He lifted the shovel so he could brush some of the dirt off the top of whatever it was. Within minutes he had a larger area opened up, and Doreen scrambled to pull out the begonias as he loosened the dirt.

Typical male. Everything done fast but without too much care.

She had removed a pile of rocks too. "Why the devil would rocks be in here and dirt thrown on top?" She frowned. "They seem to cover this section here. Like a small cairn."

"Don't say that word," he said in an ominous tone.

She frowned. "*Cairn?*"

"Cairn. Cairn. Cairn," Thaddeus added.

"Yeah. They're created by heaping rocks over bodies to keep animals from getting at them."

Doreen looked at the relatively small pile and laughed. "If it's a body, it's a cat or small dog. And, either way, the rocks must be removed before we can put any plants back in here."

He brought over the wheelbarrow and removed the rocks. Goliath jumped in the hole, for all the good he did. Each rock was a good six to eight inches across. Then Mugs jumped in. She lifted both of them out, gave Mack a hand removing the rocks, then froze at the sight of a wooden box. "Did your mom ever have cats?"

He shook his head. "No, she's allergic to them."

"By the size of this box, a pet is probably buried here."

With the rocks gone, he loosened one portion of the long box, but the end was all rotted and shifted. When he lifted the box, all the wood fell away, leaving something inside the hole.

She dropped to her knees as the air sucked out of her chest. She tried to find oxygen, but it just wasn't there. She sat back on her heels and gasped, like a fish.

A hand slapped her on the back. "Breathe," Mack ordered.

She took a great big gulp of fresh air and nodded. "I'm fine," she gasped. "I'm fine."

"Good for you," Mack said morosely. "Because I sure as hell am not."

The dog, the cat, and the bird stood at the edge of the hole. Together the humans and the animals stared at the item in the box. It was close to two feet in length, maybe a hair smaller. And what Doreen could see appeared to be bones—foot bones. "Are you sure you don't want to check with the lab now to make sure that the bone we found the other day wasn't human?"

He groaned. "And only one foot is here. That means, we're still missing the other one."

She pointed to the bones. "It's missing several bones, especially the big toe."

He nodded.

At that moment she turned to look at Mugs sitting nearby with a big grin on his face and something small and white between his front paws. "Don't look now, but it looks like Mugs found it."

Chapter 16

MACK INSISTED ON his mother staying inside as he made the necessary phone calls.

Doreen pulled out the rest of the begonias, knowing the officers would do it anyway, and, in doing so, they would hurt the bulbs just as they had damaged her own.

Now that the box was uncovered, the animals had gone off to find other adventures.

"Doreen, get away from there," Mack roared at her.

She twisted and said, "They'll dig it up anyway. I might as well save Millicent's begonias first."

He glared at her. In the background she could hear his mother persuading him to let Doreen continue. The fact of the matter was, Doreen hadn't stopped. She was almost done. And no wonder that section of the garden hadn't been doing very well. It wasn't like the bones themselves would have hurt anything. As long as there was no disease in the flesh, then it shouldn't have impacted the bed. Except the rocks on the rotten box had stopped the roots from reaching the nutrients in the soil. It would have been better if there had been no box involved. Then the plants could have feasted on the rotting flesh. Obviously the begonias weren't terribly happy with the injustice done here.

When she thought she had the last of the begonias dug up, she straightened and groaned, putting her hand on her lower back. Then she grabbed one edge of the tarp with all the tubers and dragged it off to the side of the garden where she would replant them. The craziness would start soon enough. They had to get the bone away from Mugs too, but he wasn't being very cooperative.

She figured, if she got a chance to sidle up to him quietly and to distract him, she could take the bone back. When the cops got here, they'd want to tie up Mugs until they got the evidence from him. Mugs didn't appear to be chewing it, more like protecting the bone. And she could appreciate that.

Finally, with the begonia tarp over on the opposite side by the neighbor's fence where the bulbs would be replanted, she walked toward Mugs. As she casually bent to pick up her spade, she scooped the bone from between his paws. Mugs barked at her. She bent down and gently stroked him behind his ears. "It's fine, buddy. But Mack needs this."

Mugs barked and barked again. She got up and took a few steps back. Something about this bone really bothered him. Then again, something about this bone really bothered her too. It seemed so small, forlorn. She stared at it, not sure which bone it was, but it appeared to be something connected to the toe or the longer foot bones. She'd seen images of feet but not enough to identify the individual bones. She turned toward the flower bed and just stared at it.

With her cell phone she took several pictures because she knew Mack wouldn't let her get any later. When she pocketed her phone, she headed toward the house, where he stood on the deck, talking into his phone, glaring at her.

He cupped the mouthpiece of his phone and said to her, "I saw you take pictures."

She shrugged. "I am the one who found it after all." She held out the bone. "Here, and you're welcome, by the way."

He looked into her hand and nodded. "You got it away from him?"

"Yeah, he wasn't chewing on it. It was between his paws. I know it probably sounds foolish, but it's like he was protecting it."

Mack sighed. "With your critters, who knows?" He pulled a little baggie from his pocket and held it out as she gently dropped the bone into it.

"Doesn't it seem odd how nice they act around your mother?"

"Odd?"

"Yeah. Like they are on their best behavior when she comes out here."

Mack only gave her a one-shoulder shrug.

"Animals can sense emotions. Some can sense disease. I've been reading about it on the internet. Maybe my animals realize Millicent needs a calm environment, to heal, to get better."

"With your critters, who knows?" Mack repeated with a little grin.

She motioned at his pocket. "Do you always have little bags stuffed in there? Just in case you find evidence of crimes?"

"Ordinarily not. But when I'm hanging around you, then definitely."

"How's your mother handling this?"

He sealed the baggie and tucked in into his pocket. "She's not. She's quite upset."

"Do I get to come in and have a cup of tea, or am I supposed to go home and stay out of the way?"

"Come in and have a cup of tea. It might make her feel better."

In the background Doreen heard his mom call out, "Doreen, please do come in for tea. I'm so sorry. I forgot my manners."

She motioned at her animals and asked Mack, "I know she's allergic to cats, but what about a dog and a bird? How would your mother react to them?"

Millicent's head popped out around the corner. "That's right. You have a dog and a cat, don't you?"

Thaddeus took that moment to land on Doreen's shoulder.

The older woman's eyes widened. "Oh my. I thought he was just an odd bird on the fence over there."

Doreen laughed. "How about we sit out here on the deck? That way they won't come into your house and get hair everywhere." Doreen then whispered to Mack, "It will make it more normal for her."

Millicent nodded gratefully. "Mack, show her to the table. I'll bring out the tea."

Mack rubbed his temple. "You realize this is hardly a teatime activity, right?"

Doreen dropped her voice again. "Not that there's anything normal here, as, yet again, we did find a body part. Still, if we're lucky, it's part of the same body."

He stared at her. "I hope it's the same, but this doesn't make sense. Why? Why here?"

"I was thinking about that. Any chance that everyone here used the same landscaper back then? Maybe he cut up Betty, or assorted dead bodies, and buried them in various gardens?"

Mack stepped back ever-so-slightly. "You heard Mom say that she and Dad did all the work all the time. You're not suggesting my father had anything to do with this?"

She laughed at the suspicion in his voice. "No, of course not. But, if it was anybody else's garden, you wouldn't even question the suggestion."

"True enough. But it *is* my mom's garden."

Doreen nodded, turned, and chose her seat at the deck table so she'd have a bird's-eye view when the policemen arrived. She called out to Mack, surveying the most recent crime scene, "Maybe they won't damage as much of your mother's garden with you standing here, watching over them." She gave him a flat smile. "I'm sure they'll be a little more careful than they were at my place."

He groaned. "You'll never let that go, will you?"

She shook her head. "Why would I? Your guys left a hell of a mess at my place."

Millicent stepped outside the house, carrying a teapot and cups and cookies all on a platter.

Mack quickly intercepted her and took the serving dish, following her to the deck.

Mack's mother sat beside Doreen and patted Doreen's hand, grinning. "Like I said, the body lady."

Doreen shook her head. "Not by choice."

"Some people just have a nose for that stuff. Did you ever consider being a detective, like Mack?"

Mack joined the ladies at the table, frowning at Doreen.

Doreen chuckled. "I think your son would be horrified to have me join the police force."

Mack sat quietly, shaking his head.

"Why would you think that?" Millicent asked.

"I'm fairly unorthodox in my methodology," she said with a smile to Mack. *Unorthodox* was putting it mildly. And the fact was, Mack was horrified if she went anywhere close to any of his cases. She hadn't exactly proven to be very good at anything but finding bodies.

"But it seems like this is definitely your forte. You should just wander around Kelowna and see what you find," Millicent said.

"I don't think we're allowed to do that," Doreen said with a smile, trying to ignore Mack, who glared back at her. Doreen motioned at the garden bed. "When did you put in the begonias?"

Millicent frowned as she cast her mind back over the years. "The begonias have been there at least twenty-five or twenty-six, maybe thirty, years now," she said slowly. "I'd have to find my gardening journals to know exactly."

"What was there before the begonias?"

"Very old heirloom roses," Millicent said thoughtfully. "But they had such horrible big thorns. And they weren't doing all that well. When we pulled out the first one, it's like it had no roots at all."

"And how long had they been there?" Doreen could hear Mack's mind turning as he listened to her questioning his mom. But, as far as Doreen was concerned, this was just two gardeners discussing plants and how they adapted to being moved.

"That's why we were moving them. Because they'd been there since forever. I really don't know how long, and they seemed to bloom for years and years and years, and then they started to fade. I was talking about getting somebody in to take out all the roses for us. Every time we went close to them, they would rip our clothing, and Harold would end up with scratches, even though we wore gloves when we pulled them up," Millicent said.

"And so you took them out and planted the begonias?" Doreen smiled. "At least begonias are very mild in temperament."

Millicent laughed. "They are indeed. They don't scratch or tear at us at all." She leaned a little closer. "And they have such beautiful colors. Some of those were dinnerplate begonias. I do wish I had known you were out here earlier because I could have told you which ones were which."

Doreen wrinkled up her face as she studied the tarp full of begonias. "Oh, dear."

Millicent followed her gaze to the big tarp. "Yes, I can see that we'll have quite the surprise when they bloom again."

Doreen laughed. "And maybe it'll be a good surprise."

"Absolutely."

"I'm surprised you can leave them in the garden over winter."

"We brought them in for a long time. But then I'd forget to put them out in the spring again. It just seems like time went so quickly when raising a family, and we were both working all the time. I eventually put them in and thought, *What the heck? If they survive, they survive. And if they don't, well ...*" She laughed. "Of course, I did end up covering them with mulch as best I could. And, to my surprise, they kept coming back."

"Did you ever add more topsoil?" Doreen wanted to know exactly what had happened to the beds over time. There was a fair bit of dirt on them, and yet, the begonias had been a shallow planting, like added on top of another planting. As she studied the bed itself, she noticed it was slightly higher than the one beside it.

Millicent nodded. "Yes, indeed. We used to bring in all kinds of topsoil and top-dress the lawns. Anything extra we would throw on the gardens. We put mulch in every couple of years." She waved her hand. "It's really hard to remember all the details. We spent fifty years in the house, and it all blends together."

"How wonderful that you kept journals though," Doreen said with a smile. "I've never thought to do that."

Millicent bounded to her feet, showing more energy than she had so far. "I'll go get them." And she raced away.

Doreen slid her gaze toward Mack, surprised he no longer glared at her. "Do you remember anything about what happened to that garden?"

"I've been sitting here, listening to her reminisce about it," he said quietly. "But I can't say that I have any clear-cut memories myself. I do remember the roses though."

"Why do you remember the roses?"

"Because they were vicious." He pulled up his shirt sleeve and showed her a scar across the back of his hand. "This happened with one of them. They had thorns an inch long, I swear. They were barbed at the end. Triple hooks that, once you got caught, it just tore you to shreds."

"Of course. That's a defense mechanism to protect them," she explained.

"Well, it didn't help them when Dad came along and ripped them out by the roots. And the begonias were planted in their place. It's hard to say when that wooden box was put in there. With the wood rotting, it's got to be at least twenty years ago."

"Or not. It's received steady watering," she reminded him. "You're not on the creek, so we can't assume the creek bed rose and soaked it. Did they put underground irrigation in here?"

"No, we planned to but after my father passed away, we never quite got there. They had a system all organized with sprinklers and timers. She was happy with that system in place. There was no point in changing it. I suppose we could look at it now. The garden is really too much for Mom to look after at her age. So that might be a good answer. Although it would be expensive." He frowned pondering the thought. "We'd need to plan it all before we did much digging."

"And considering beds and digging," Doreen continued, "it's hard to say when that box would have deteriorated. Somebody will need to do the forensic work on it and see if it can be dated."

"The labs will do that," he said, "but, if we're talking about the same body, then it's obviously closer to thirty years ago."

She really wanted it to be another body part for poor Betty Miles. Because, if they now had a different body, that was just too unbelievable. "If it is her, then we have a lot more pieces to find. The good news is, it's not a huge foot," she whispered. She could hear Millicent returning.

He shook his head. "We don't know anything yet. There could be a ten-year span between these two body parts, and their cases could be totally unrelated."

She shot him a hard look. "Two dismembered bodies in the same town—not only the same town but basically the same location?"

He glared at her. "It's not the same location at all. There's at least a mile between them."

She snorted. "A half mile as a crow flies. If that. Probably closer."

"But we don't know where the arm in the creek may have washed down from," he reminded her. "In the latter part of spring, that creek is not a nice little quiet babbling brook, like it is now. It ends up being a raging river. The snow on the river melts and all the tributaries flow into this river."

"Oh," she said. "I hadn't considered that."

"Exactly. Remember we are the police."

"Right, and I'm just the body lady."

Chapter 17

WHEN MILLICENT RETURNED with two journals in her hands, she also came with two policemen. They both shook hands with Mack and slid sidelong glances Doreen's way.

She held out her hands, palms up. "What can I say? Yes, I found more body parts."

Their eyebrows rose, but they stayed quiet. Just like her animals did when Millicent was around.

With a sigh of disgust, she sat back and picked up her tea. She was figuring out how to slide the journals her way so she could take a look, but Millicent still held them in her arms. Finally, Mack got up and walked away with the officers.

When the three men were back in the garden, Millicent sat and opened one of the journals. "This is the first twenty years of my marriage," she said with a big happy smile. "There are lovely memories in here." She turned some pages, her smile warming at what she found there.

"Sounds like they are more about your life shared with your husband than just about gardening," Doreen pointed out with a soft smile. After Millicent's faint nod, Doreen asked, "So the other one would be the more recent years?"

Millicent nodded. "Yes. That would be the next fifteen or so years. I didn't write anything hardly at all in the last few years since Harold died. I guess my heart hasn't been in it anymore."

Doreen slipped her hand toward the second journal. "May I?"

Millicent nodded. "Sure. Go ahead."

Doreen snatched it up and opened it. She flipped through the middle pages to see what kind of notes were in it. Indeed, Millicent had noted the daylight, the sunshine, the frost, trimming the hedges, even about pulling the begonias. But Doreen wasn't at the first few pages. Realizing what she was doing would be out of sync with the time line, she quickly flipped to the front of the book and read. She wasn't sure how long it would be before Mack understood what she had in her hand. When he did, he wouldn't let Doreen keep it; she knew that much.

"You've done a lovely job keeping track of everything," Doreen said in admiration. And she wasn't just saying that to be nice.

Very detailed reports were here of when Millicent and Harold had put in extra mulch and topsoil or when they did the trimming and how they cut and thinned, when they divided the glade. There were a lot of details, including the date of the first frost and the heat in summer.

Doreen flipped through the days, looking for an entry that might point to something relevant to the lower leg they found. There didn't appear to be very much. Plus the dates were from thirty-five years ago. Betty Miles had disappeared only thirty years ago.

Doreen flipped through more pages, trying not to look

obvious that she sought a particular time frame. When she got toward the end of the journal, she slowed down and read a little more intently. "Oh, here it says you went to Europe for two weeks." Doreen looked up with a smile. "That must have been a lovely trip."

Millicent launched into a detailed recital of everything they'd done on the trip.

At one point, Doreen, feeling the pressure of time, interrupted Millicent. "It must have been hard to leave your garden."

Millicent laughed. "Yes, indeed. But we had the timers for the irrigation, so it really didn't matter much."

"So nobody had to come do any work? Smart," she said admiringly. "That's very smart." She wondered if Nan had considered anything like that over the years. Obviously not because no underground irrigation was at Doreen's place. "That would have been pretty new thinking back then."

"I think my husband took garden hoses and drilled holes into them. Then we buried them, so everything would get water all around. We only had to set a timer to turn it on and off. Now underground irrigation is very expensive. But garden hoses and timers were cheap."

Doreen sat back with a smile. "That's something I might do at my house too. I could manage some garden hoses and just drill holes into them." Her mind fired with ideas, but she had to pull herself back a little. "It's nice that you didn't need anybody to water your garden. I feel bad asking somebody to do things like that."

"The neighbors were always around, but we didn't really get along with some of them back then," Millicent confided. "In fact, for a while, we had a terrible neighbor. He was nothing but trouble. He was always yelling and having parties, and, after the parties, it seemed like he got angrier and angrier. But then I think he was just a mean drunk. My husband and I didn't have very much to do with him."

"What happened to him?"

"I honestly don't know." She stared out over the gardens where the officers stood, looking down at the wooden box. "I think he moved away, but it was a long time ago." She glanced back at Doreen. "Getting old is terrible. When your memory starts to go it seems like the answers are so close, and then, all of a sudden, they're just whisked away. You don't have any say in that, and you want to yell, 'Stop! Give me just another minute with that information, so I can understand it.'" She smiled. "But it never happens."

Doreen felt sorry for Millicent, but there wasn't a whole lot Doreen could do to help. "At least you did lots of traveling with your husband."

"Every year," Millicent said. "Sometimes twice a year. And because we had the garden set up the way we did, we never had to have a full-time caretaker. Just someone to come in and check that everything was working properly. Of course, that was once we got it set up. We didn't have Mack until we had been married for ten years. So, before Mack was born, we used to pay someone to look after the place while we were gone."

"And, of course, the only way into the backyard was on the side, where you have the gate, right?"

"*Now* that's true, but originally we didn't have gates. The neighborhood changed though. It just seems like more crime is everywhere, and the older I got, I felt a little less secure. Once my husband died, Mack put in the gates on the sides for me."

"So they are new?"

"Well, newish?" Millicent laughed. "They were put in the last seven or eight years, yes."

All Doreen could think about was that, as soon as any-body knew the couple was gone on their annual holiday, it would be easy to come in and bury a body in the garden. Doreen flipped through the journal and said, "You went in June and in August that year also?" She tapped the diary. "It looks like you even wrote that down in here."

Millicent smiled. "Yes, those were great years. We did a lot of traveling after Mack left for college." She stood and said, "I better get more cups. The police are coming over again." And she walked inside.

Doreen grabbed her cell phone and took pictures of various pages of the latest journal. Just as Mack was about to come up the deck steps, he turned to talk to one officer a little longer. She smiled and heard Millicent returning. But Doreen had a lot of pages to cover, or maybe, with any luck, the information and the dates she needed were on the photos she just took. Because, if she could line that up with Betty Miles's disappearance, it was possible Doreen had something to back up her earlier theory that she had shared with Mack. He had been the one to say, *with the wood rotting, it's got to be at least twenty years ago*, but not really. If the bed with the rotting wood box in it had had underground irrigation, like a hose, close to it, it would rot much faster. That would also explain why one end had rotted quicker than the rest because that end would have been closer to the hose. Anything that stood in pooled water would deteriorate much faster.

She popped her cell phone back into her pocket, then saw Millicent again outside, handing out tea to the officers, keeping Mack distracted, so Doreen slipped her phone out of her pocket again and took several more pictures of the second journal, flipping through the pages until halfway into the book.

Millicent rejoined her at the deck table, gave a hefty sigh, and glanced toward Doreen. "Does it bother you?" she asked.

Doreen looked up at her. "Does what bother me?" She'd almost gotten through the whole second diary. But not through the first diary near Millicent's seat at the table. There could be at least one more diary—maybe two to cover the whole fifty years Millicent had lived and gardened here.

"Finding bodies?" Millicent asked.

"No, it doesn't bother me." Doreen thought about that for a long moment. "I guess that doesn't say very much about me. But I think it's much better to find the bodies and to bring these people home than it is to not find them and to know the families never got closure."

"Good. I'm glad you understand." Millicent looked at her. And a big smile dawned across her face. "I do like the way you think."

Doreen smiled and waggled the book in her hand. "This journal stops about thirty-five years ago."

A frown creased Millicent's forehead. "Really?"

Doreen held it open toward the end to show the dates, which were thirty-five years earlier.

"Oh, interesting. That's right. I do have another one in exactly the same color." She flipped the other journal open. She smiled. "I have the first one. You have the second one. I'll go look for the third." She hurried inside.

Doreen snagged her camera and took more pictures. It could all be for naught. Since the journals weren't that long, and it was just a quick flash from her cell phone, she got through all of the second journal quickly. And then she heard Mack's voice.

"Okay, you guys get on with that, and I'll make sure my mother is all right. We want to keep this as low key as possible. So full blackout on the media."

She closed the second journal just as he came up the deck steps with a hard snap of his boot heels. She glared at him. "Sure, don't worry about Doreen being upset by the authorities' treatment of her gardens but make sure your mother isn't disturbed by all this police interference."

He gave her a hard look. "I really don't need more of this crap right now, you know?"

She sighed. "That's fine. Your mom has gone to get another journal. She forgot there was a third."

He reached out his hand, palm up. Quietly, without arguing, she picked up the second journal and gave it to him. He looked at her in surprise.

"Either there's nothing in it, or you've got something else up your sleeve, because I never expected you to hand it over quite so easily."

She gave him a look of pure innocence and a big smile. "You would take it either way."

He glared at her suspiciously and snagged up the first volume too. "And I'll be taking the third one when my mother returns," he said firmly.

Doreen shrugged. "That's fine. I should be going home anyway." She stood. Turning back to Mack, she said. "I'd love to hear an update, but I know you won't give me one." She then remembered why she'd been here in the first place. "I need to get those begonias in the garden before long. If you still want me to ..."

He frowned as he looked at the dug-up begonias on the tarp and then over at the other side of the garden. "Yes, if you don't mind. Maybe even later this afternoon, but I don't know …" His voice petered out.

She brightened. "I can do that. How about I come back alone, if you're too busy? Or, if the officers are still working here, I can return tomorrow and get most of the begonias in then."

He smiled and nodded. "Thanks. Tomorrow might be better."

She smiled back. "No problem." She headed into the house and caught Millicent going through a bookshelf. "It was so nice to meet you, Millicent. Thank you for the tea and for sharing your gardening tips with me. I'm leaving now so the police can do their thing. But, if they get done early enough today, I'll come back this afternoon and get your begonias into their new bed. Although Mack thinks tomorrow is more likely."

Millicent beamed. "Thank you so much. You are a lovely body lady."

On that note Doreen laughed and walked out the front door, calling the animals to her.

Chapter 18

WALKING INTO HER house that afternoon, Doreen was a little stunned at the different look the electric stove gave to her kitchen. With glowing chrome and glass, the contemporary looking stove was a little daunting for the very old-fashioned room. She was sure Nan would completely disapprove. On the other hand, Nan wasn't cooking here.

Then neither was Doreen. But this stove gave her hope. It was exciting to see it. She studied the knobs on the front, deciphering the codes on each as to which knob controlled which burner. But, when it got into Bake and Broil as options, along with Convection, she got really confused.

"He said this was an old one?" she muttered to Mugs. She crouched down, opening the oven door to stare at the clean interior. "It doesn't look old at all. In fact, this looks like a brand-new model. Not only brand-new but the latest cutting-edge thing."

Mugs snuffled all along the outside rim of the oven door in agreement. Or maybe he dreamed about wonderful dishes that could possibly come out of it as he recognized what an oven was for. Unlike her. She'd never had that opportunity to see food go in and come out, other than on TV cooking shows. It was hard to imagine how much she'd missed in life. And yet, nobody else would think it was anything to miss. Still, she stared at the oven door with pride. It was a lovely thing to behold.

Now, if she could make it sing, she'd really be doing well. Except, she had an absolutely terrible singing voice. But there was the internet, and she was handy at research.

"But first, I need a nap, so I can work later. Come on, boys. Want to take a nap with me?"

She couldn't fall asleep right away, but, when she did, she slept fitfully over the next few hours. She wanted a solid two hours of uninterrupted quality sleep. But she didn't get that. Her brain wouldn't stop working. She had a lot on her mind too as she got up and headed downstairs. She put on a pot of coffee, wondering if she could afford her new coffee habit. Now that she could make it here by herself anytime she wanted it, she was inhaling the stuff.

As she looked through the fridge, she heard a knock on her door, and Mugs went crazy. Frowning, Doreen walked to the living room and peered out through the curtains. Thankfully the inquisitive crowd was no longer around her house. This time the new finds of old bones had Mack dealing with that lovely interfering-neighbor syndrome at his mother's house.

A pizza delivery guy stood on her porch.

She opened the door. "Hi. I think you're lost."

Mugs sniffed around the young man, then, jumping on his back legs, reaching up to smell the pizza in the delivery guy's hand.

He looked at her in confusion, checked the address on the slip, and held it up for her to see.

She read it off and nodded. "Yes, this is my address. Any

idea who ordered this?"

He shrugged. "No, I don't." He thrust the pizza toward her.

"Well, I'll take it, but I don't have any money to pay for it," she explained, slightly embarrassed and not sure how to handle the situation.

"Already paid for," he mumbled. And, as if she'd already pushed his ability to communicate without a cell phone or some electronic device in his hand, he backed away from her.

She smiled brightly. "Okay then, thanks."

He nodded and disappeared into his beat-up small blue car he had parked in front of her house. She thought it was a Volkswagen bug from the 1970s, but she wouldn't count on it. She'd never been able to correctly date vehicles or men.

She carried the pizza box into the kitchen, putting it on the table. Thaddeus jumped up on the table beside her and sniffed at it. When he pecked at the cardboard, she brushed him back gently. "This isn't critter food. This is people food," she admonished him.

Mugs barked at the edge of the table. She turned and patted him on the head. "You're a good boy, but you don't need pizza either."

He didn't seem to listen—he just kept barking. While she dealt with Mugs, Thaddeus pecked at the cardboard again. No sooner had she brushed him away than Goliath decided he would have better luck than those two. He hopped on the table and batted at the top of the box.

She looked at the three of them in astonishment. "What the heck? Are you guys that hungry?"

She checked their food bowls, and, sure enough, all were empty. Mortified at her own lack of insight into the animals' world and castigating herself for having forgotten to feed them, she filled their bowls, and they grudgingly all left the tantalizing aroma of pizza on the table to eat their individual servings.

And they must've been hungry because they wolfed it down and then returned quickly to her kitchen table.

In the meantime, she poured herself a cup of coffee and sat at the table. She wondered who had paid for this treat. But she really appreciated it. She couldn't remember the last time she'd had pizza. She lifted the lid, carefully letting the hot steam escape. The pizza had everything on it but the kitchen sink. She stared at it in astonishment. "How can you possibly pick up a piece when it's so overloaded?"

She couldn't imagine holding a slice, even with both hands. It would fall to pieces, which would just entice Goliath and Thaddeus to be on her table. She walked to the cupboard, pulled out a plate, then opened a drawer for a knife and fork. A lot of people would be horrified at what she was about to do. But she really wanted to eat, not to retrieve the random pizza toppings from the table or to fight for them with Goliath and Thaddeus.

She scooped up the largest of the pieces, feeling smug that she didn't have to be polite and take the smallest one. "Smallest be damned today. I want to eat every last piece."

Just as she got it onto her plate, her phone rang. She glanced at her cell atop the table. *Mack.* She dropped her knife and fork, picking up the phone. "Mack, what did you find out?"

"Most people say, *Hi, Mack. How are you? Having a nice day?*" he said in a sardonic voice. "In your case, all you ever want to hear about is any development on the cases."

"You can hardly blame me," she said. The pizza in front of her went a long way to keeping her mood upbeat, regardless of what Mack said. "I do have this bad habit of tripping over bodies."

"Yes, you do," he said.

She could hear the fatigue in his voice. "You still at your mom's house?"

"No, I just got back to the office."

She frowned. "Make sure you eat," she admonished.

He chuckled. "It's one of the reasons why I'm calling."

She stared at the pizza cooling on her plate and frowned. "Why?"

"Did you get my gift?"

She stared again at the pizza, and it clicked. "You sent the pizza?"

"I did indeed. And, if you haven't eaten it all, I thought I'd stop by when I left the office."

"It depends on when you're leaving the office." She laughed. "I'm pretty hungry."

"I'm leaving in five. I'll be there in ten." And he hung up.

She sat back with a fat smile and turned to Mugs. "This is a really nice thing he did."

Mugs barked, and she plucked what looked like a piece of sausage off the top of the pizza and held it out for him. It disappeared instantly. When she returned to the piece on her plate, she found Goliath trying to snag a piece of cheese hanging off. She smacked him gently. He bounced back and gave her a disgusted look. She smiled.

"I'll get you a piece of cheese of your own. Hold on." She ripped off some of the stringy cheese and placed it in front of him. Just as she did that, Thaddeus attacked a green pepper.

"What's wrong with you guys today?" she cried out. Finally she divvied up a little bit more between the three of them, then turned to her own piece and took her first bite. Her mouth was filled with wonderful hot spicy sausage and a mess of different vegetables and cheeses.

Her palate wasn't used to pizza. She'd only ever had it a couple times in her life, and most of that was since she'd left her ex-husband. Technically her soon-to-be ex, but that entailed too many words and too much time spent on him.

She was now addicted to pizza, but it was another expensive habit to maintain. She was only halfway through her first piece, taking her time, chewing and savoring the delicious treat, when she heard heavy noises at the front door. She got up to open the door for Mack, but he'd already entered before she ever reached it.

He smiled and said, "Did you leave me any?"

"I'm still working on my first piece." She smiled. "Thank you. It was a lovely surprise."

"Good." He raised his eyebrows. "But you didn't have to wait for me."

She shrugged. "I didn't. I was savoring it," she admitted.

He nodded in understanding. "How many times have you had pizza?"

"Hard to remember exactly," she said. "But less than the number of fingers on one hand."

He stopped and stared at her. "Seriously?"

She nodded. "My ex-husband considered it peasant food. Along with hot dogs and burgers and beer." She laughed at the look on Mack's face. "One of the first things I did after I left him was to have every one of those things. Probably just to spite him."

She returned to the kitchen, Mack following. He waited for her to sit down and then he joined her at the table and looked at her plate with the knife and fork and swallowed hard.

She glared at him. "No laughing. You might have bought me the pizza, but I don't have to share if you're gonna be mean."

He shook his head. "I'm too darn hungry to be mean." He snagged the second-largest piece, lifted it to his mouth, and took a great big bite.

She returned to her piece with a happy smile. When he coughed and cleared his throat, she glanced at him to see him nodding toward the pizza box.

And, sure enough, Thaddeus and Goliath were helping themselves again. She sighed, put down her knife and fork, found little pieces for each of them and put them on the table near each animal.

Mack stared at them. "You know most people don't let their animals on the table while they're eating, right?"

"No, I didn't know that," she admitted. "I think I have free-range animals."

He studied her for a long moment, as if not understanding.

She explained. "As in, they're free to range wherever. I have very little control over them."

"I think you have pretty darn good control over them," he said, chuckling. "But they also have very good control over you."

"This"—she waved at her animals—"is because I feel guilty. I forgot to feed them earlier. When I did feed them a little while ago, they inhaled their own food in its entirety and then went after the pizza. I'm sure they've been starving all day."

His lips twitched. "I doubt they are starving," he said.

"They look in very healthy shape."

"Well, that may be," she snapped, "but I'm the one who messed up. So I'm sharing."

He nodded solemnly and snagged another piece.

She watched as he took another bite. "How can you eat so fast?"

"I don't waste time talking," he muttered.

She looked at her barely touched piece, nodding. "Good point." She proceeded to polish off her slice. She reached into the pizza box and grabbed the next largest slice and put it on her plate. Then seeing Mack was almost finished with his second piece, she snagged up her third and put it on her plate too.

He laughed. "Now you're learning."

With a mocking glare she grabbed the pizza box and moved it to her side of the table. "I am."

He chuckled again.

Inside she smiled. He didn't look anywhere near so tired now. The trouble was, the minute she picked up her knife and fork, he reached across the table, his arms way longer than hers, and moved the box to the far side of the table, where she couldn't possibly reach it.

"Hey, that's not fair," she protested.

"Nope, it isn't. But apparently you're one piece ahead of me."

"I am not."

"Are too," he said, motioning to the two pieces on her plate. He snagged his third and proceeded to eat while she picked up her knife and fork again.

But her eyes were bigger than her stomach. She managed eating two and a half pieces and then wasn't sure she could finish the other half. But it tasted so damn good. Mack had gone after a fourth and had left her the last piece. She shook her head. "I think I need a break."

"Does that mean you're full?" he asked.

She stared at him. "You can't still eat more, can you?"

He just waited.

She rolled her eyes at him. "Fine, go ahead." He had paid for it, after all.

He snatched the last piece in seconds. And then he looked at her plate.

She glared at him. "I can probably finish this in a little bit. I just need a sip of coffee and a chance to rest."

"*Rest?*"

"Eating, it tires me out."

He looked at her to see if she was serious. Then shook his head. "If you'd eat a little more often, your body would become accustomed to it, and food wouldn't be such a shock to your system."

She shrugged. "Believe it or not, I bought food this week, so I have something in the house to cook."

"Right, *cook*," he exclaimed. He pushed his chair back, got up, and examined the new stove. In a quick and easy move, he shifted the stove forward and checked behind it. "Oh, good. He's capped off the gas nicely, and Barry put in the correct wiring. Nice jobs." He nodded approvingly, shoved the stove back, as if it was a little Lego block.

She'd already tried to move it once, but no way could she budge it. His inherent strength was something so natural and so easy for him that he didn't even recognize it was so special, and yet, for her, almost any effort seemed to be more than she could handle.

He studied the front of the stove and turned to look at her. "How much did you pay for this?"

She shrugged. "One hundred dollars. Which I haven't paid him yet. Nor do I have Barry's bill." That worried her. She hopped to her feet and walked to where Mack stood. "Do you think he'll charge me more?"

"Are you sure he decided it was one hundred?"

She nodded. "That's what he said." But even now she doubted herself. Unnerved, she said, "He'll have to take it back if he wants more. I don't have any more."

He closed his fingers over her hands.

She had bunched them together so hard that her knuckles had turned white.

"Let's see what he says first."

She nodded, returned to the table, picked up her cup, and refilled it with coffee at the counter.

He reached for an empty cup from the cupboard and filled it with the thick rich brew. "Hey, this is fresh coffee." He lifted it to his nose and inhaled. "Smells good."

She smiled. "I've been making it the way you told me to."

"Good. Too often people make it too weak, and they end up with coffee tasting like dishwater," he said with a smile. He took a sip and then a second. He nodded. "Nice."

She beamed. She'd done it. Sure, it had been his recipe, and she'd tweaked it again to make it work—but she'd done it, and in a kitchen no less.

Chapter 19

A S SOON AS they were done with their coffee, Doreen asked, "So what can you tell me about the case?"

"Not much. Obviously it's a human foot and lower leg. No, we haven't confirmed if it's male or female. It's with the coroner right now. They'll run DNA."

"Do you have any other cases with missing lower legs and feet?"

"We're searching through the cold case files. But nothing yet."

"And what about solved cases?"

He looked at her in surprise. "Meaning?"

"Meaning, a case that was closed but where potentially not all of a body was recovered or even where no body was recovered."

He frowned. "I haven't gone looking into the closed cases. Generally they aren't closed if we're still missing pieces."

"But you have closed cases where there was no body?"

"I know of some cases across Canada," he said cautiously. "But I can't recollect any here in town."

She studied him for a long moment. "Might be worth another search."

"It's in progress. In the meantime, you can tell me what you found in my mother's journals."

He had said it so calmly, so smoothly, that she didn't understand for a moment. And then she laughed. "I didn't find anything. That's the problem. She has three journals, and they'll take a little bit to go through." She sipped her coffee.

"I need to know you will share any information you might have found. That way, I won't have to charge you with interfering in an ongoing investigation or taking photographs of the evidence."

She shook her head. "That won't wash. I haven't interfered in any way. In fact, I've helped." She quickly moved to the next topic. "What about the creek bed?"

He shook his head. "Nothing new."

"So far a lower leg and a foot less than half a mile from a severed hand."

"Severed hand and forearm," he corrected.

She nodded. "I hope they are from the same body. I think the foot was too small to be a man's. I understand Betty was small."

"Again, no way to know at this point. The coroner will make that decision, and, if he can't, they'll bring an anthropologist from the coast."

She frowned. "I guess each specialty is quite different, aren't they? Bodies with flesh for the coroner. Bodies without flesh for anthropologists?"

"I'm not sure it's quite so clear-cut and simple, but yes."

"How often do you bring in specialists from Vancouver?"

"Considering Kelowna has a very low crime rate with less than three murders in a year, I would imagine not very often. I've been with the police force seventeen years, and I can only think of a half-dozen cases where we've had to."

She nodded. "So one every other year on average."

"It depends. We had several people hiking who never returned. They were declared missing several years later, but it's not like the case was closed. Then we had a particularly heavy thaw, a fast melt, and their bodies floated down in one of the creeks. They still had on their backpacks and hiking boots. But not a whole lot was left of the flesh. They had been frozen, so we needed outside help to determine how long those bodies had been there. The DNA confirmed who they were, but that had taken a lot longer than we'd like to see, in terms of notification."

"I can understand that. But they probably had IDs on them."

He nodded. "They did. But we didn't have anybody locally who understood the time it took to decompose under those severe mountain temperatures. I believe these hikers had been missing for a good seven years."

She winced. "Their poor families."

"Exactly. So, even if I cross a line a bit more to bring in a specialist, we're happy to do it for the families. If it gets us confirmed IDs and some kind of a time line as to what went on, then that's a bonus."

"Did you track where the creek flowed to find out where the hikers went missing from?"

"No, in that case we had a massive snowmelt coming down. They could have come from halfway up the mountains. There was no way to know, and we don't have the resources to pinpoint something like that."

"This is all really fascinating. I wish I could have a career involved in that."

He looked at her in surprise. "You really like this stuff, don't you?"

She nodded. "I do. But, at my age, I can't say I want to go back to school and get a degree that will take five, six, or seven years to complete, and then start a new career fresh when everybody will be looking at me, asking, *Why aren't you retiring?*"

"You're not that old."

She shook her head. "No, I'm not, but I feel like I am some days."

He chuckled. "We all do." He stood. "I'm heading home. I'm tired, and I need to get some sleep."

She rose, walking to the front door with him. "Thank you again for the pizza." She meant it sincerely. "I wasn't looking forward to a cold dinner."

He nodded. "I figured you wouldn't have learned how to use the stove yet. We both had a rough day." He turned and glanced at her. "Are you okay tomorrow to finish the garden? Even solo?"

She winced. "I told Millicent I would, didn't I? I was supposed to check if I could do the work this afternoon."

"It doesn't matter. I couldn't let you in anyway. The officers were taking soil samples and photographs and doing all kinds of crap in my mom's backyard. It went way longer than we expected. It's still not done. I told her that you weren't allowed back, so she understood."

Doreen leaned against the doorjamb. "Still, I shouldn't have forgotten."

"What did you do when you got home?"

She frowned and motioned toward her bedroom upstairs. "I fell asleep. Or tried to."

He chuckled. "Good. Now you've eaten, so have a good

evening, get some more sleep, and I'll meet you at the garden tomorrow morning."

"If I wasn't allowed today when the team wasn't finished, not even when you left, what if I'm not allowed back tomorrow?" she said with a head shake. "I don't want to disappoint your mother."

"How about I call you before ten and let you know if everybody's finished?" With that note, he lifted his hand in a wave and headed to his vehicle.

As she stood there, she watched several neighbors and other people, suspiciously new faces, walking their dogs in a very slow motion around the cul-de-sac. She didn't recognize half of them. What were they all doing here? But, ... of course, the news would have already spread.

She might have stayed inside, but no one else had.

Chapter 20

Saturday Evening ...

AS SOON AS Mack left, she went back inside the house, cleaned up the few dishes they'd used, made sure all the animals were inside, and grabbed her car keys. It was a Saturday. It was late, but the library should still be open.

She had to admit she really enjoyed the fact that, in a small town like this, it took no time to go from point A to point B. Had it not been getting dark, she would have liked to walk to the library, helping to digest her nearly three pieces of pizza. But instead she got in the car and drove there tonight.

Some things were more than a few blocks away, but nothing that she needed was more than a ten-minute drive from her home. She pulled onto the main road, took a right, and turned into a very large parking lot that serviced not only the library but a skating rink, a fitness center with a swimming pool, and a restaurant. Parking on the library side of the lot, she got out and walked up to the front door. She checked the times they were open and realized they closed at nine o'clock. She didn't have much time, but curiosity drove her forward. Who knew what she could learn in the next half hour or so? She walked inside and smiled at the librarian.

The woman rose to her feet. "Are you all right?"

Doreen looked at her, glanced around to see if the librarian was questioning somebody else, but she seemed to have spoken to Doreen. "Yes, of course. Why wouldn't I be?"

The librarian had gray hair tucked into a tight bun, wore a white blouse and a light-gray A-line skirt that seemed part of some dress code very typical of her age group. Her name tag read Martha Cummins. She placed her hand on her throat and said, "Well, my dear, you found more than one dead body last week. Are you sure you have recovered?"

Doreen looked at Martha with surprise. It was all Doreen could do to hold back her smirk. If Martha only knew about the body parts Doreen had found recently. But she managed to nod gravely. "Yes. Thanks, Martha. I'm here for some reading material."

The librarian nodded in understanding. "I don't think I'd sleep again. You run along now and find some books. The library is closing in forty minutes."

With a smile, Doreen walked over to the microfiche machine instead, but she took a roundabout way so the librarian wouldn't see where Doreen went. It wasn't that she was trying to hide, but, well, she really didn't want people to know she was looking up the history of Kelowna. But, for things that had happened thirty years ago, it was the right place to get some information.

She brought up the old newspaper articles on the Betty Miles case. Doreen could save it as a PDF, and it would be a quick process to attach the file to her email message to herself, so she could read all of this while at home. Even though it was an easier process than she had expected, it still took time.

She scanned through several years' worth and then did a search for the teenager's name. Doreen quickly saved as many articles to a PDF as she could, in the time allowed.

When done, she hopped up, walked to the fiction section and grabbed two of her favorite thrillers. Then she walked to the librarian and smiled. "I found a couple things," she said hesitantly.

The librarian put her glasses on her nose and stared at the titles. She shook her head and clucked her tongue. "I don't think these will help you sleep."

Doreen looked at them doubtfully and said, "Well, I'm a little desperate at the moment." She handed over her library card. "I'll give them a try. Maybe I won't be able to read them at night. But maybe, when I'm sitting out in the sunshine, they'll grab my attention."

The librarian checked out her books.

It was five to nine. With a wave Doreen said, "Thanks so much." She stepped outside. The sun had set, leaving the parking lot dark, but the surrounding businesses were still lit up nicely, spilling light into the parking area. She found her car easily enough.

A large group of noisy people were off to the side, just outside the restaurant. The skating rink and fitness center were popular with the locals. In her case, neither were in her budget.

She got into her car and slowly drove home. Once there, she grabbed her books and headed inside. As she walked in, her cell phone rang. She glanced down at the screen and saw it was Nan. "Hi, Nan. I'm fine."

"I know you're fine, but I want to hear all about it."

Doreen groaned. "How about we meet at a restaurant for breakfast instead?"

"No," Nan said firmly. "We're not meeting anywhere because you don't have money to go out. But I can drum up some breakfast here for you instead. How about at ten?"

"Good. I'll see you in the morning." Then she gasped. "Oh, no. I can't. I'm working at Mack's mother's garden tomorrow. I'll call you in the morning to set up a later time."

"You get some sleep, you hear? And keep me in the loop if anything happens. I need exact details, remember?"

Nan never changed. Still Doreen felt a little guilty. Nan had always been generous and kind, and here it seemed like Doreen didn't have time for her grandmother. Doreen *was* tired; she hadn't lied in that respect, but she certainly wasn't going to bed yet. Not when she had all these PDFs to read. Then again she considered Nan's words and worried about the bets she and her cronies were placing. Thankfully it was all in fun. She couldn't help wondering what the current bet was. Murder for sure, but was it when the case would be solved? Or who would solve it first?

"It's too late for a cup of coffee," she said, glancing around the kitchen. "What was it Nan said the other day? Something about chamomile tea?" Doreen rummaged through the drawers and cupboards and finally found several boxes of tea, some oddly shaped. She pulled them out and studied each and every one. "Nan, these are all herbal teas. Why do you have so many?"

Doreen lined them up on the counter, so she could take a better look. Six boxes of different herbal teas, things like chamomile and even mint. Then some were mixes, like Sleepytime. She liked the sound of that one.

She turned on the electric teakettle. When it whistled, she poured herself a cup of Sleepytime tea and put all the boxes back where she'd found them. She'd glanced at them earlier but hadn't really inspected them or knew how they could benefit her.

Nan's cupboards were full of stuff like this, but Doreen didn't know exactly what to do with any of it. Taking her cup of tea, she walked to the kitchen table and sat down in front of her laptop. She turned it on and waited for her email to load, all the PDFs slowly showing up soon afterward.

Goliath hopped into her lap, his engine already kicked in, and he kneaded her thighs. She gently stroked the huge cat. "I didn't expect to like you so well," she muttered against his fur. "But it appears I'm a cat person too."

She wrapped her arms around him and gave him a hug. He was big enough that she could gently squeeze him without any fear of hurting him. And he didn't seem to mind a bit. His claws never came out. Instead he leaned into her chest as if he needed the comfort as much as she did. She smiled and just held him, enjoying this softer side to him.

Until Mugs got jealous. He barked right behind Goliath. Instinctively Doreen tensed, waiting for the cat's claws to come out. Instead Goliath's tail just twitched back and forth, the tip smacking Mugs in the face every time. But, being Mugs, he never backed away. Instead his face took each swat. *Swat. Swat.*

She looked at him and giggled. "Mugs, you *could* move."

He looked at her, his jaw working, and all the while the cat's tail swished in his face. She grinned and reached a hand toward Mugs. He came closer, sniffling her hand, and she sat there, holding the cat close and scratching Mugs's ears. "It's a good thing Thaddeus isn't feeling left out."

But she shouldn't have spoken so soon. Thaddeus flew up and landed on her shoulder. He rubbed his beak up and down her cheek. She smiled, feeling an overwhelming sense of love for her unique family.

"Okay, so this life might not have a pure white dining service and spa dates, but neither does it have cold empty beds and indifferent silences at the dining room table." She smiled. They sat and cuddled for a long moment. Then she lifted her hand to sip her tea.

Thaddeus tilted his head into the teacup with her. And darned if he didn't take a big drink.

She gasped. "It's hot."

But she'd obviously been cuddling the animals long enough for it to cool. Thaddeus dunked his head back in her teacup and took another drink.

She laughed. "So this is my life. I'm a piece of furniture for the cat. I'm a scratching machine for the dog and somebody who makes tea for the bird. No wonder I couldn't figure things out. I was having this identity crisis. I was looking for a job that *actually* paid," she complained good-naturedly to the animals who couldn't give a darn if she was paid or not. As long as they were looked after ... It was hard to be upset at the animals because they brought her so much joy that she hadn't expected. "How could Nan possibly have left you all behind?"

She knew Nan hadn't wanted to. And maybe it had been part of Nan's ultimate setup to suck Doreen into finding the joys of having animals in her world. She'd had Mugs these last five years, but he was held at a distance due to her ex-husband. Of course she'd let Mugs on the bed when her ex hadn't known about it.

One time he found dog hair on the bed, and poor Mugs had been sent outside. He'd been bathed and brushed and sent to the spa, just to make sure he was clean before her ex-husband would let Mugs back in the house. And all the bedding had been changed and her room vacuumed.

Back then her room was vacuumed daily. She wanted a little clutter, but the minute she put something down, a maid always came along, picked it up, and put it away properly. Even when outside in the garden, she wasn't allowed to touch anything. The gardeners would walk over to see what they could do to make her life easier.

What she really wanted to do was scream for them all to disappear and to let her put her fingers in the dirt. She'd been aching to do some gardening on her own. But every time she picked up a plant pot and tried to do something, everything was taken away from her.

She sighed as she recalled those long and lonely years. "I really was a fool. I should have left way earlier."

At that, Thaddeus tilted his head and looked at her as if to say, *You just realizing that now?*

She shook her head at him. He shook his head back at her. "Oh, no you don't," she said. "No imitating me."

"Imitating me. Imitating me."

She rolled her eyes. And then froze because it looked like Thaddeus was trying to roll his eyes too. The giggle started deep and it rolled up, hitting every vertebra of her spine. As it burst free of her chest, she could feel something inside her breaking free—something releasing—something old and ugly dropping away from her shoulders.

And she laughed heartily. Goliath, offended that his bed vibrated, hopped down and gave her a dirty look, his tail twitching in the air as he jumped onto an empty chair beside her. But she couldn't stop laughing.

Thaddeus, as if figuring out what she was doing, made some weird sounds that came darn close to laughter. And that just made her howl all the more.

When she finally calmed down, she realized she didn't need to be looking at all this research tonight. She could review it in the morning. It would be much better if she went to bed. She was tired but happy, and she thought she could get a good night's sleep for once, having had a lovely hot meal of pizza, followed more recently by hot tea. What about a hot shower too?

With that uppermost in her mind, she picked up Thaddeus, scooped up Goliath, much against his will, and, calling Mugs, she and her family headed upstairs.

In her bathroom she stepped into the hot shower, scrubbed down, then shampooed her hair twice. When done, she dried off and got dressed for bed. She grabbed one of the thrillers she'd picked up from the library. With the lights on and the rest of the house locked down for the night, she snuggled under the covers.

Mugs lay with her on the bed, Thaddeus beside her on the headboard, and Goliath on her lap as she started to read.

She was only a few chapters in when she realized the story was about body dismemberment. Fascinated, she dove in until she couldn't keep her eyes open, and she fell asleep with the lights on.

Chapter 21

Sunday ...

T HE RINGING PHONE woke Doreen the next morning. Groggily she sat up, glanced at the clock beside her and gasped in horror. "Oh, my goodness. It's already a quarter to ten." She bolted out of bed, grabbed her phone in time to answer it. "Mack?"

"What's the matter? Did you sleep in?"

She winced. "Yeah, maybe." She brushed her hair off her forehead and stared outside. It was a gray, cloudy day. Unlike the day before with the sun shining all afternoon. "It's not very nice out, but, if we're doing physical work, it's probably better this way."

"That's the spirit," he said heartily. "I forgot to plan for Willie collecting all that stuff from your front driveway. You have to pay him as well."

"Oh, dear. I forgot too." She was still in her pajamas. She raced to the closet, and, while talking to Mack, she quickly dressed. In the distance she could hear a big truck approaching. "Someone's coming now. With any luck that's Willie."

"Give me a call when you're done."

Promising to do that, she hung up and raced downstairs to put on coffee. No way could she garden without coffee first.

As soon as it was dripping, she headed out to the front yard, and there was Willie, backing up a big old flatbed truck with several appliances on it. She went back inside to her purse, pulled out the one-hundred-dollar bill Nan had given her, and walked outside again.

He waved good-naturedly, and he and his son loaded up the old stove. Then he walked toward her with a piece of paper in his hand. "Forgot to leave you this. It's an invoice. Barry owed me a favor, so no charge for his services."

Nervous, her heart in her throat, she glanced down at it. With relief she realized the bottom price tag was, indeed, one hundred dollars. She smiled at him broadly. "I think you gave me more than a fair deal on this."

He shrugged, a little embarrassed. "Couldn't have you cooking with that old thing in there. Besides, I got a lot of these going through the store. It won't hurt me to give one away at cost. And you having helped the community and all, finding those poor men ..."

That was unexpected and much appreciated. "Thank you." She handed him the hundred-dollar bill she held in her hand.

He nodded, pocketed it, and helped his son load up the rest of the dump stuff.

"You're okay with taking all that to the dump?" she asked anxiously. In the back of her mind she was afraid he would turn around and ask for ten bucks more.

He just tossed a hand in the air and waved at her.

She smiled. "Thank you again." She went in her house, closing the door. She danced down the hallway at the great deal she'd gotten on the stove, even if she didn't know how to use it yet. Everybody loved a bargain, and, in her situation, she loved it even more. In a way, it was like she got paid to help the police last week by getting this wonderful stove.

As the coffee finished dripping, she grabbed a cup and went back to check on Willie and his son. They were just loading up the last bit. She watched as they flipped up some weird sides to the flatbed and closed up a piece along the back of it. Both men got into the cab and drove away.

What a smart truck. It could be a flatbed or a pickup truck. Well, not so much a pickup, as it was definitely bigger than that. Still admiring the truck, she folded her tarp and tucked it away in the garage.

Satisfied that everything was back to normal, she turned and walked back into the kitchen. Her half piece of pizza was in a baggie on the kitchen ledge. She ate it cold, mumbling to Mugs sitting there looking at her anxiously, "Should have made Mack leave me the last piece too, for breakfast."

With the final bite in her mouth, she washed it down with coffee. Then fed the animals. When done, she poured a second cup, then called Mack back. "Willie was just here. He collected the old stove and all the stuff so far from my garden. He gave me an invoice and stuck to the original price." The last bit was said with surprise in her voice. "I couldn't believe it. The invoice was for the hundred dollars." And she rushed to add, "He said Barry owed him a favor, so no charge there either."

Mack gave a big whistle on the other end of the phone. "Lucky you."

"Yeah." She still grinned in delight. "When do you want me over there?"

"Have you eaten?"

"Yes, of course I have," she fudged, if the half piece of pizza counted. "I'm having my second cup of coffee."

"Put another cup in a travel mug and come on over. If we get at it, you could be done early afternoon. You can go home and have the rest of the afternoon to yourself."

"Sure. Sounds good." As she put her cell phone on the kitchen table, she spoke into the air. "Mack, remember I don't have a job. I get every afternoon to myself." With that, they ended their call.

But he made a good suggestion about a travel mug. She'd seen one somewhere. She walked to the front hall catch-all closet. She found a windbreaker and grabbed it since the weather looked ugly outside. Then she pulled out several travel mugs. One looked relatively clean. She took it to the sink, washed it, and filled it with coffee. It nicely emptied the pot. She put on her gardening shoes, grabbed the windbreaker, found her gloves, and led her menagerie out the back door.

"Let's go, everyone. We're heading off to Millicent's garden again today."

The animals obediently fell into line, always happy to go on an adventure. She had to admit lately that there'd been a lot of them. Coming around the back corner of her property, she could see no sign of activity at the creek, thankfully.

By the time she arrived at Millicent's backyard, it appeared to be completely empty too. No police anywhere in sight.

She didn't want to disturb anybody, so she headed to the garden where the begonias had been. She peered around in the dirt, but the wooden box was gone, and it looked like they had dug a few feet around it but obviously hadn't found anything more, or at least there was nothing to show they had found anything.

Pulling on her gloves, she walked toward the bed where the begonias would live now. Definitely some weeding needed to be done. Not to mention the new bed was full of daisies from what she could see.

As she dug, she had to work around a plethora of daffodil bulbs and tulip bulbs. The begonias would fit in here nicely, but they definitely needed more dirt.

Mack walked outside just then. "I didn't hear you arrive."

She shrugged. "I didn't want to bother you." She motioned at the bed. "It's already full of spring bulbs and daisies."

Mack frowned. "Right. I remember that. Of course. That's why the bed looked mostly empty. What do you want to do with them?"

She shrugged. "We could do borders. There's an awful lot of bulbs, but I don't know what colors they are."

Millicent arrived on the deck. "There you are, bone lady. How are you this morning?"

Doreen didn't correct her. She'd gone from *body lady* to *bone lady*. Neither was appealing, but, at the same time, the nickname could be much worse. And *bone* was better than *body*. She smiled and waved. "I'm doing well. How are you?"

Millicent shrugged. "Now that all those strangers are gone from my yard, I'm much better."

Doreen chuckled. "I hear you there. Where would you like all these spring bulbs? If we put the begonias here, it'll be crowded. This bed appears to be full already. Daffodils, tulips, crocuses, ... not to mention daisies ..." The words escaped her for the moment, but Millicent spoke loudly.

"My hyacinths are in there too." She frowned. "They

probably should be thinned out anyway. We haven't touched that bed in years. It's got to be completely overgrown."

Doreen looked at Mack and whispered, "It would have been nice to know that first."

He shrugged. "Where would you like to put them?" he asked his mother.

Millicent called out, "Give me a minute, and I'll come down."

After that, they spent several hours discussing good and bad options. Doreen wouldn't be finished here today. Now that she had to move and replant all the bulbs already in this other bed, she set up a plan with Millicent to get to work today and then several more days during the coming week. With that in mind, she spent many hours digging up bulbs. When she looked up, Mack was long gone.

And there was no sign of Millicent. Doreen walked to the front to see if anybody was home, but the vehicles were gone.

Shrugging, she decided to call it a day. Besides, she wanted to return to the creek and see if anything had surfaced there.

As she walked past the begonia bed, she stopped, glanced back at the house, and then walked to where the box had been. They couldn't replant anything in this bed until Mack picked up more gardening materials for it.

The beds needed topsoil for a start. And she didn't think that was on his list for today. Although maybe that was where they'd gone now. But he hadn't said anything to her. As far as she could see, she was alone. She had dug out the bed yesterday before the police ruined the begonias but couldn't do more until Millicent returned. Leaving the shovel and the spade in the garden bed, she headed toward the stream. She should have brought a shovel with her. But the police officers had already gone over the creek pretty intensely. Still, she stopped at the spot where she and Mack had found the pretty ivory box and the ring, then walked to the spot where she'd found the hand.

"It absolutely makes no sense to have two parts from different bodies here."

Shrugging, she headed home. "Come on, guys. Let's go. We have some research we need to do." Back at home, she put on the electric teakettle, ready to sit down with her laptop to read through the library articles. Her stomach grumbled. She got up and snagged an apple from the fridge.

As she read and munched, she wrote down notes: the time frame that Betty had been here, when she'd gone missing, what her family had been doing. Doreen had learned very quickly that, in the criminal world, one always had to look at the family first. Some of that information was going to need to come from Mack. He's the only one who could check for any criminal records of other family men. Then again he would tell her to butt out.

Still, she jotted down a note to get Mack to cross-reference the family members. She kept looking but couldn't find much else on Betty's parents.

Doreen studied her notes. Two jewel heists at the same time had to be connected. If it was the girl's handiwork, Doreen didn't blame Betty. She was just a young kid, obviously under the influence of somebody older and wiser. But was it her father? Or her mother? Or someone else?

And where were the other family members? Doreen had found a mention of an older brother, Randolph, but that was all. And she couldn't find any background on him. If he was smart, he'd left town and created a life away from his criminal family's publicity. But where was Betty's mother? Doreen did a quick internet search for a Miles living in Kelowna and found no hits.

But it did bring up the earlier slapping incident in her mind. Who the hell was the woman who had walked up on Doreen's property and then hit her?

As she got upset about that all over again, Mack called. "You never did tell me the name of the woman who hit me," she stated without any greeting.

"*Hi, Mack. How are you, Mack?*" he said. "Remember social Ps and Qs and general niceties?"

"Screw that. I spent fourteen years in a rotten marriage with all those social niceties, largely insincerely exchanged too. How about the truth for a change?"

He laughed. "I didn't tell you because I figured you'd immediately talk to her."

"I do have that right," she said quietly. "She accosted me on my own property."

"I know. I will have a talk with her. But *I* want to do it, not you."

"Why can't I?"

"Because she was Betty Miles's best friend."

"Wow." Doreen sat back, not sure what to say. She turned to face her laptop. "So it was Hannah. That's fantastic."

"Why is that fantastic?" Mack asked cautiously.

She laughed. "Because now maybe we can get some answers. I've been going over all these articles from back then. Did you know Betty Miles's father was a robber?"

Mack was silent on the other end. "I think there was something criminal in his history, but I don't remember the details."

"According to the news articles from thirty years ago, Betty was carrying certain jewels on her when she left. That was per her father. Her mother said she didn't know anything about it, and then, two years later, her father was charged and convicted of a robbery."

"But he robbed the place where he worked, if I remember it correctly," Mack said. "He filed the report for the insurance."

"Sure, but he owned his business," Doreen argued.

"And it was a *jewelry* store," Mack added.

This time she got dead silence.

She grinned. "Gotcha."

Chapter 22

Tuesday ...

FOR THE NEXT two days, things were quiet—absolutely nothing happened as far as finding dead bodies or even parts of dead bodies. All Doreen did was research, garden in her yard or Millicent's, plus visited with Nan. They had that breakfast together as promised. This afternoon, Doreen thought, maybe the world would leave her alone now. She wasn't overwhelmed with reporters anymore. If she could avoid being seen at Millicent's house, then the media wouldn't make the connection between her and the newest body parts. At least she hoped. But then Mack's orders to do a press blackout about the bones found at his mom's house must have included the arm and hand found in the creek, as Doreen had seen no mention in the press about any of those finds. And that was really helpful too, as far as Doreen's infamous reputation was concerned.

Not that she believed this gossipy town wasn't going to get a hold of this juicy news—regardless of the blackout. Just the presence of the police would get the grapevine buzzing.

Which reminded her ... She pulled out her phone and sent Mack a text. **Still looking for the name of the woman**

who attacked me. Did you talk to her?

The response was instant. He called Doreen to say, "Not yet. Forget about her."

"No. The next time I see her, I *am* going to talk to her. So it's in your best interests to give me the name now."

This time, when the answer came, it was in a much lower voice. "Hannah Theroux. Don't do anything criminal." And he hung up.

Doreen walked to her laptop, put down the ever-present cup of coffee that had become her at-home addiction that she could barely afford, and typed in the name. Hannah Theroux was part of one of the founding families of the area. They'd been here since … She tried to do the math and gave up. She went with *forever* and grinned at that.

"In that case they should know damn near everything I need to find out."

Mugs growled beside her. She looked down at him. His hackles rose as he stared at the back door. "What's the matter, Mugs? What do you see?"

Mugs jumped to his feet and barked. She never quite understood that philosophy. If she didn't say anything, he would normally sit here, content to growl a little in the back of his throat. But the minute she told him it was nothing, he became an aggravated guard dog.

With everything else that had been going on in this crazy world of hers, she wouldn't ignore Mugs's warning. She stood and glanced out the window, then opened the back door and stepped out. Mugs raced into the backyard. "Mugs! Mugs, get back here," she shouted.

Mugs ignored her. He was intent on whatever it was he saw. Unfortunately she couldn't see anything. As she stepped down the few steps of the deck and walked across the yard,

Mugs disappeared around the corner in the direction where they'd found the body part. And that immediately made her suspicious.

She sneaked up to the side of the fence and peered around the corner. Sure enough, there was a reporter, the same woman who had been in her front yard. Doreen gasped.

The woman turned, caught sight of Doreen, and cried out, "There you are."

Doreen shook her head. "What are you doing back here?"

The woman gave her a fat smile. "Not trespassing. This is city property." She motioned at Mugs. "I see your dog is as well-trained as you are."

Doreen's back stiffened. "Excuse me? In what ways am I not well trained? And what kind of comment is that coming from you?" She pulled her cell phone from her pocket and hit Video.

The woman snorted. "You won't give us the time of day for an interview."

"So that means you can insult me?"

The cameraman nudged the reporter, but Sibyl wasn't listening to him. She finally had a chance to talk to Doreen, and she wouldn't let this opportunity pass. "Ever since you arrived, you've been nothing but a headache in this town."

"The headaches were here long before I got here, and you are welcome, by the way. Because, other than this, you'd be left covering the annual bake sale for beagles."

The woman stiffened. From the look of laughter in her cameraman's face, Doreen realized it probably was the truth.

The reporter sniffed. "If you wouldn't terrorize the innocent residents of this town, it would be a lot easier to talk to you. But, as it is, you're one pain in the ass." The woman lifted her nose and glared.

Doreen studied Sibyl for a long moment. "You never gave me your last name."

"And I won't give it to you now."

She hadn't caught sight of the woman for very long, but there was a definite ... "You're a Theroux, aren't you?"

The woman's face paled. The cameraman looked surprised.

"I see the resemblance. So was that your mother or your sister or an aunt who assaulted me?"

The woman shouted, "Nobody assaulted you. And certainly none of my family."

Doreen leaned a little closer. "Are you sure about that?"

The woman paled even further. She turned to look at her cameraman. "Let's go, Robert. Nothing to be seen here."

"And stay away from here. Do a story about Hannah Theroux—who I'll be talking to my lawyers about—going to jail."

The woman trembled. "Hannah? You were talking to Hannah?"

"No, I was not talking to Hannah. She attacked me. Came to my house and smacked me across the face. I am sure you loved that. Maybe you even put her up to it."

The woman shook her head, her hands gripping and ungripping the microphone in her hand. What the hell did she need a microphone for?

But Doreen was much too wary of reporters. "And, if you're recording this, I'll definitely have my lawyers come after you too."

Robert held up his hand. "Camera isn't on."

"Doesn't mean audio isn't," Doreen said, pointing at the

microphone.

"We're allowed to do audio. We keep the town up-to-date with all the news. You never know what tidbits will end up being important."

"Doesn't mean I give you my permission to use anything I say or do either," Doreen said. "Do you give your permission?"

"Of course. I am always on TV and in the news." She tossed her hair back, making Doreen laugh.

"And, if you had anything to do with Hannah's attack, believe me, I'll make sure your name is included in my statement to the media and to my lawyer."

The reporter shook her head. "I don't know what you're talking about." She tried to step back, but Robert was in the way. She turned and shoved him. "Robert, I said we are leaving."

"Strategic retreat," Doreen taunted. "That's all right. I know who you are now."

The woman shot her a look, but it held fear more than anything else.

Doreen had to wonder just what the hell was going on here. As soon as they were out of sight, she called Mugs back and headed inside again. She sat down to continue her research when her phone rang.

"I don't want you going after Hannah Theroux," Mack said without a preamble.

"What about the stupid reporter? Can I go after her?"

"Was she at your place again?" he asked in curiosity. "I already warned the press to stay away."

"She was at the creek just a minute ago. Where we found the hand."

"Interesting," he said, his voice thoughtful. "I wonder

who told her something was there."

"You can bet it wasn't me. But there was something about her. I accused her of being a Theroux. She turned very white."

"Now that you mention it," Mack said slowly, "I think she is part of the Theroux family. She married and changed her name, but I think she might be Hannah's niece."

"I don't know how old Hannah was. I was thinking early forties, maybe mid-forties."

"I think she's forty-six or forty-sevenish now."

"That would make sense. The reporter isn't older than twenty-five, I don't think. She got pretty upset when I suggested she do something about Hannah attacking me." She heard Mack's long-drawn-out sigh on the other end.

"Did you have to go there?"

"She insulted me. She was nothing but rude. I have taken just about enough abuse from that family," she said curtly. "If you want to hear the audio of the conversation we had, you can come over and listen to it. I got it on record." And she hung up. Inside she smiled. Then Goliath hopped up on the table and lay on her keyboard.

"No. Get off the keyboard. What is it about cats and keyboards?" She'd never had a problem before, but, all of a sudden, Goliath realized the keyboard held greater interest than him in her eyes. She picked him up and cuddled him. "Honest, I love you. But I need access to my keyboard."

His huge guttural engine kicked in, and he rubbed against her. She looked down at the laptop to see he'd switch the pages. She didn't even know how he managed to do that.

She leaned forward to read the page he'd brought her to. And wouldn't you know it? Something to do with the Theroux family. Doreen shifted Goliath in her arms so she could study the page. Apparently the family had been here for several hundred years. Their original homesteaders had water rights to Mission Creek—blah, blah, blah, blah. Hannah Theroux was one of two daughters. She'd gone through a rough period when her best friend had disappeared.

Doreen continued to read, finding tiny bits of information threaded through the interviews, but nothing really concrete was there. Until she got to the last line. *Hannah Theroux was the last person to see Betty Miles alive.*

Doreen sat back. "*Well.* Now I really want to talk to her."

She searched where Hannah currently lived and frowned. She didn't appear to have an address Doreen could find in the Mission. She searched for other family members and came up with two more, including a sister.

She looked up the sister's house number and street name, plus got a phone number. As soon as she dialed, a woman answered. "Yes, I was looking for Hannah, please."

"Why?" came the curt tone on the other end.

Doreen's eyebrows rose. "I wanted to speak to her."

"Well, it's not going to happen, so give it up." And she hung up on Doreen.

Very interesting. She really should have gotten out of the vehicle and talked to Hannah at the grocery store. Although the woman most likely would have driven away. Doreen should have followed her while she had the chance. If Hannah was the last one to see Betty Miles, then it made sense that Hannah didn't want it all dredged back up again. She probably went through hell back then.

Doreen frowned again. There had to be more to this. She kept digging. While the internet was mighty huge, it was slim on viable information.

Then she went back to the PDFs she'd sent from the library. She printed off all the articles, wasting several dollars' worth of paper and ink, but, at the moment, it seemed that important. With a stack of paper in hand, she grabbed her coffee cup and headed into the living room to study the information. She brought a highlighter and her notepad and pen with her.

She found several mentions of Hannah. But, as Doreen came to recognize, the mention of Hannah added sensationalism to the article. Anything that brought involvement of the prominent founding family would be news.

The girls had gone out in the evening and had come back in high spirits and drunk. Doreen nodded. "In other words, normal teenage girls." As Doreen continued to read, according to Hannah, this behavior on Betty's part never stopped. She got wilder and wilder. Although Hannah got drunk just as often as Betty did. But—toward the end—they weren't getting drunk together.

"So, at what point were you no longer best friends?" Doreen asked quietly to the empty room. "And why?"

She jotted down more notes, realizing she needed the case files from Mack. Or at least to have him double-check some of this information. Seemed like there was a three-month period where Hannah and Betty weren't hanging out as much.

If anybody knew what Betty was up to, it would be Hannah. But it was unlikely Hannah would discuss her friend's disappearance.

Particularly not with Doreen …

Chapter 23

WHEN THE DOORBELL rang two hours later, Doreen didn't give any thought as to who it might be. She got up and opened the door to find Mack, his arms crossed over his chest, glaring at her.

She raised her eyebrows. "Is this an official visit? It's unlike you to wait for an invitation to come in," she said in a dry tone.

He brushed past her and went into the kitchen, his gaze going to the coffeepot. He smiled and poured himself a cup.

"Well, that's more like the Mack I'm used to," she said.

He didn't say anything until he finished pouring his cup of coffee, then turned and leaned against the counter, where he studied her. "What are you doing recording conversations?" he asked in a very quiet tone.

Her jaw dropped. "You don't care about somebody hitting me, but you care that I recorded a conversation?" She turned to her small table and sat down, crossing her arms over her chest. "Well, you sure have your priorities straight, don't you?"

"I said I would talk to her."

Doreen nodded. "And did you?"

"I can't find her," he admitted. "She's not answering her door, and neither is the family where she is staying."

"And, of course, you contacted the reporter to find out?"

"No, not yet." He motioned at her phone. "Play the recording."

She swiped the screen, found the audio and video, and then hit Play. He listened quietly as the reporter's voice filled the phone. She watched his face as he frowned and tilted his head to the side, as if making sense of it. When the voices finally died away, she said, "See?"

He shrugged. "It's not like she admitted to killing anybody," he said in a half-joking tone.

Only Doreen wasn't ready to be appeased. "No, she might not have. But I am not taking this kind of torment from her family. I didn't do anything, and neither did I deserve to get smacked."

He nodded. "You're right. But I would like you to leave the family alone right now."

"And why is that?"

He didn't say anything.

She stared at his face for a long moment, figuring out why he would ask her to do that. And then she got it. She bolted upright. "You found something that ties into the case, didn't you?"

He glared at her.

She gave him a flat smile. "See? I am not quite so stupid as you would like me to be."

"You're not stupid at all," he said in disgust. "You really need to toss your ex-husband's words out the window. You know that, right? You're still hanging on to his attitude toward you."

"I tossed him out of my life already. Isn't that enough?"

Mack shook his head. "No, because he still governs you so much. For example, your thinking, your mind-set, and your lack of self-esteem."

She frowned at him. But his wording was a little too close for comfort. She turned the conversation around again. "Did Hannah have anything to do with Betty's murder?"

He shook his head. "You know I can't talk about an ongoing investigation."

"But can you tell me if Hannah lied about not knowing anything more about Betty's activities the last three months of her life? They were best friends, spending every night at each other's houses, and then suddenly Hannah doesn't know anything about what happened to Betty for three months?" Doreen scoffed. "That's not very likely."

"Friends fall out all the time," he snapped. "Betty got into trouble a lot."

"They both got into trouble a lot."

He nodded. "Okay, so they both got into trouble. That doesn't mean Hannah had anything to do with Betty's disappearance."

"I don't think she did. But I think she knows a hell of a lot more than she is saying. I think the family is protecting her. Or they're also protecting the person who Hannah is protecting." Even Doreen got confused at her wording. She raised both hands in frustration. "You know what I mean."

He looked at her. "No one in their right mind would have a clue what you just said."

She glared at him. "The only reason Hannah didn't tell the truth back then was because she was either protecting somebody or she was afraid of the person who was involved." She waited a minute, but Mack didn't say anything. "Right?"

"That makes sense, yes. But we can't go off on any other

assumptions. We need to focus on facts.”

“So the first thing you do is talk to Hannah. And, while you’re talking to her, you can tell her to lay off attacking me. And I want a damn apology.” She walked around the kitchen, not quite sure why it mattered so much to her. But the assault had been unexpected and unpleasant, to say the least. She had tried so hard to be good, no matter where she was, and to find somebody hated her that much was distressing. Especially someone who didn’t even know her.

“Look. I know she upset you. But I’m sure you can understand how you really upset her. The fact that you were dredging all this back up again …”

She spun on her heels. “Did you really just say that, Detective Mack Moreau of the RCMP Serious Crimes Division, about a cold case file on a murder? I didn’t dredge up anything. I stumbled across things. And I would think Betty’s family would like to know the truth. Hell, for that matter, I would think Hannah would like the truth about what happened to her best friend.

“So Hannah should go outside and smack the creek. Because it’s finally giving up its bounty. The secrets never stay buried forever. Eventually Mother Earth gives up the truth. We sometimes wait a long time, and, in this case, that’s thirty years,” she snapped. “But that doesn’t mean I am responsible because I happen to be the one who found the ivory box. *You* should know that.”

“I *do* know that. But I am trying to take care of all these threads without setting off all the alarms. If Hannah did have something to do with this, I didn’t want her to go to ground,” he said in exasperation.

“But you already said you couldn’t find her. So she’s already gone to ground. And that’s not my fault either.”

Mack paused, gave her a cautious look. "We need her accessible. And nobody is telling me where she is."

"I know somebody who could help us."

He held up a hand. "Whoa, there's no *us* here."

She snorted. "Of course there is. This is the only way you'll get this solved."

He stared at her suspiciously. "Who are you going to contact?"

She shook her head. "Oh, no you don't. I am not saying anything. You won't share with me, so I am not sharing with you." And then she realized she might have overstepped the mark ever-so-slightly with *Detective* Moreau.

His gaze narrowed, and he took a step toward her.

She was determined not to be bowed by his bulk and size and temper. "If I learn anything, I'll tell you. And that's more than you do for me," she said in a disgruntled tone.

He glared at her. "Remember that part about the *open police investigation*?"

"Remember that part about this being a cold case that nobody has been able to solve?"

"And why do you care so much?" he asked, stepping back slightly, tilting his head to examine her face.

"Because I hate to think of Betty, lying in pieces all these years, mostly forgotten by everyone." She shrugged. "You should feel personally affronted yourself. Somebody buried a lower leg and foot in your mother's garden, for heaven's sake."

He turned sideways and stared out the window. "Believe me. I am."

"I know Millicent had a gardener, caretaker, or handyman at the time ..."

"Not so much at that time. But over the years, yes."

"And, of course, you checked with the other neighbors?"
He glanced at her.

She gave him a cheerful, encouraging smile. "To know if the same gardener buried more body parts in other people's gardens."

"I am doing a cross-check right now. But I don't know how many other people he might have worked with."

"That's another question we need to get to the bottom of."

"He's dead."

She stared at him. "Well, darn," she said in outrage. "Are you sure?"

He nodded. "Yes. What I am not sure of is that this murder of Betty was a one-person job."

She thought about that. "It certainly could be a one-person job to cut up and bury a body part. Doesn't mean it was though. Although no one would want to cart the bigger pieces too far alone."

"That's what I was thinking."

"So you need to find the landscaper's family and friends."

"I am on it," he said in that tone that said, *Back off.*

She tapped her foot impatiently. "Okay, you track that down. I'll see if I can find any history on the landscaper." She waited a moment. "In order to do that, I need his name."

He just gave her a beautiful smile. "Not sure I can help you there."

She groaned. "You know I will find it. You could allow me to be useful and to get to the bottom of this that much faster by just telling me his name. And, of course, so I don't have to ask your mother."

Instantly his amusement fell away. "You will *not* ask my mother."

She glared at him. And then remembered the journal photos. "Fine. I won't. But then you have to help me. If you don't, you can't expect me to share my information with you."

He slammed down his coffee cup. "*Active investigation.*" He stormed out the front door. "Follow my orders or else …"

As soon as he was gone, she smiled. "It *wasn't* active, but it is now, and this time *we're* going to close it." And she sat down, transferred the photos from her phone to her laptop, and proceeded to go through Millicent's journal pages.

About the fortieth page in, she saw the landscaper's name. "Brian Lansdown."

She grinned and searched for Brian. The internet was a little sketchy on his data. That was all right; she had the next best thing. She picked up the phone and dialed a number. "Nan, you up for a visit?"

"Absolutely," Nan said. "I'll put on the teakettle." Nan hesitated but then added, "I do have dinner here. Someone brought me a tuna casserole. Would you like to share that with me?"

Doreen grinned. "Would I ever."

Nan laughed. "Good. I'll see you in a few minutes then." She hung up the phone.

Doreen took a few moments to write down questions she needed to ask Nan. Brian Lansdown was at the top of the list.

Chapter 24

WHEN SHE WALKED out of the house ten minutes later, Doreen took the back route to Nan's again. Not only did Doreen want to make sure the reporter wasn't hanging around the creek any longer but Doreen couldn't stop looking in the water to see if something new was to be found.

The animals walked with her, the route now memorized by all of them. It was such a joy to know that Nan was here for Doreen in more ways than she'd expected. She'd reconnected with her grandmother at a stage in Doreen's life where she'd lost her stability and foundation. And Nan had become so much more.

At the creek, Doreen stopped and studied the water flowing in the small circular eddy where they'd found the arm. She had checked the silt screen once, but it had nothing of value. The current had picked up and was flowing steadily down past the spot she'd found the box. It really saddened her to think other pieces had not been found. That poor girl. Then Doreen stopped to think about the foot they'd found and what that meant. The worst part was there were more body parts to find, even if just from Betty's body.

"Come on, Mugs. Come on, Goliath." She turned toward Thaddeus, stopped behind her. He didn't want to be carried today—he wanted to walk. He really liked this path. Then so did Mugs.

They kept walking down the creek bed, not seeing another person on either side of the creek. It was a good thing for her but a shame more people didn't enjoy the bounty here. She understood how easy it was to become accustomed to a beautiful view and to no longer find any joy in something because it became commonplace.

Whereas for her, she hoped she never got to that point. The creek itself had been a gold mine of unusual events in her life. Should they be written down? She wondered idly if she should write a book. There was something to be said about Millicent's journals. They were a lovely reminder of years gone by. Maybe Doreen should put all these thoughts and findings into her own journal of some kind, but she wasn't sure it would be of value to anybody but herself. Although it would be a great way to keep her memories clear, particularly if anything should happen and her memory started to fade.

Turning the corner on the first block, the four of them continued down the next couple blocks until they reached the far corner of Nan's place. Just as Doreen was about to cross the grass, the gardener straightened and glared at her.

She sighed. "If we cross here, we'll get in trouble," she said to Mugs.

Mugs barked and then barked again.

Nan stood and waved. Doreen smiled and waved back. "How are we supposed to get to you without walking on the grass?" she complained.

Nan finally understood what the problem was. She

turned to look at the gardener. "Why don't you put some stepping stones in so my family can join me?" she cried out.

The gardener shook his head. "They can walk around."

"But we can't," Doreen said. They'd had this argument many times. "The only way to get to Nan's patio without cutting across the grass is going through the building, and I am not allowed to take the animals into the building."

He gave her a big wide smile. "Exactly."

She glared at him and deliberately strode across the grass to Nan's patio. "He's determined that we can't come to visit you," she muttered when she hugged her grandmother.

"He's just grumpy. So many people here are cranky."

"Isn't that the truth?" She studied Nan's face. "And you are positively glowing."

"Oh, how lovely of you to say so." Nan reached up to clap her hands on her own cheeks. Adding to the bright pink color there.

Doreen studied her intently. "You have a definitely mischievous look to you. Just what are you up to, Nan?"

Nan gave her that innocent look which Doreen had come to recognize.

"Oh, no you don't. Tell me. What's up?"

Nan leaned forward. "Remember that horrible manager we had? The one we were taking bets on for when he would hand in his notice?"

"Oh, dear." Doreen sat back in her chair. "Grandma, you know you're not supposed to be betting."

"Well, I didn't set up this pool." Nan waved her hand as if to dismiss the issue. "Somebody else set it up. So it really doesn't count in this case."

"Okay, go ahead and explain this. What difference does it make?"

"Well, I won the pool," she said excitedly.

Doreen chuckled. "You're not supposed to be betting yourself or setting up any betting pools in the first place. Or do you think that, as long as somebody else sets it up, you can place a bet, and it makes it okay?"

Nan chucked with such glee that Doreen had to smile.

"And what will you do with the spoils of your pot?"

Nan grinned and held out her hand. "Give me your hand."

Doreen held out her hand and grasped Nan's. Stroking the paper-thin skin along the back of her grandmother's hand, she frowned. "Are you sure you're feeling okay, Nan? Your hands are really dry. Are you eating well?"

Nan's laughter rippled loud and free. "I am eating fine. You're not." She rolled Doreen's hand out so her palm was flat, pulled something from her pants pocket, smacked it into Doreen's palm, and then curled her granddaughter's fingers over it. "There. Now take that and spend it all."

Doreen stared at her, then looked at the money poking through the top of her clenched fist. "Oh, Nan." She didn't know what else to say.

Nan smiled. "I know how tough things have been for you. This is extra money. I don't need it."

"Maybe I don't need it either," she lied.

"You never could lie worth a darn, dear. And I know perfectly well you do need it." Nan smiled. "Don't be so proud as to turn down assistance when it's offered. And, if I can't spoil you, who else can I spoil? You're the only family I have."

Doreen felt tears in her eyes. She didn't want to count the money. She tucked it into her pocket carefully. "Thank you. But you know I don't come here to get money from you, right?"

Nan gave her the gentlest of smiles. "Even if you did, I'd be happy to help," she said. "You're my dearest granddaughter. And I love you. The fact that you visit me is a joy. Do you know how many people in this place never see their family?"

Doreen winced. "I am sure there are many. It's very sad. And I hate to say it, but, if I wasn't getting divorced, I don't know how much time I'd be able to spend with you either."

Nan smiled. "See? That's the thing. Maybe the divorce happened for this very reason, because I am delighted to have you in my life again." She clapped her hands. "Enough of this emotional conversation. There is a lovely tuna casserole in the kitchen. It's way too big for one person, so I'm delighted to share it with you. You sit here," she said. "I'll just pull it out of the oven."

Moments later Nan returned with a small casserole pan and set it in the middle of the tiny patio table. "It's so lovely outside. I'd like to eat here, if you're okay with that?"

"Always," Doreen said warmly. "This looks really good."

"It does, doesn't it? Sammy made it for me."

"Sammy?" Doreen hadn't heard that name before.

Nan served up a portion for each of them. As soon as she passed a plate to Doreen, a lovely cheese and tuna aroma filled the air. "Sammy. He was a dentist in town for years. He knows everybody."

"Even me?"

"Oh, my dear." Nan trilled with laughter. "Everybody knows who you are now. You're more famous than I am."

"Great," Doreen muttered. "That's not exactly what I wanted to be, you know?"

"That's all right. We all find our own path to happiness.

And, if finding dead bodies is yours, then I'm all for it."

Doreen stared at her for a long moment. "You did not just say that."

Nan nodded comfortably. "Hey, maybe you should have been a detective. Maybe you should join the police force and become a forensic something or other."

"I'd love to, but it's pretty late in my life. It's not that I'm old, but it takes a lot of years to get an education for a field like that." She shrugged, tried the first bite of the casserole, but it was so hot she couldn't eat it yet. "I mentioned something like that to Mack, and he shuddered."

"Of course he did." Nan chuckled. "If you want, just stay as the amateur detective. You can still make his life miserable, my dear."

They shared conspiratorial looks. Doreen blew gently on her first forkful and popped it into her mouth. Immediately warm, creamy, cheesy goodness filled her mouth. "Oh, this is delicious," she moaned.

Nan nodded. "Sammy is a great cook."

"He can come around and cook at my place anytime," Doreen said. "I am half starving."

Nan nodded. "I noticed. If you get any skinnier, you'll have to buy new clothes."

"Not happening. Can't afford that." She plowed through the tuna casserole until the first wave of her appetite was appeased. Then she settled back and ate a little slower. "Do you know a Brian Lansdown?"

Nan studied her. "Wow. I haven't heard that name in a long time."

"So you do know him?"

"*Knew* him, yes. He was the local handyman/landscaper/gardener."

"Did he ever do any work at your house?" The last thing Doreen wanted to think about was more bones in the back garden. It would be too much coincidence to have another person buried in Nan's garden.

"No, he and I never really got along."

"Why not?"

"I didn't like his manner," Nan said abruptly. "Honestly, he scared me."

Doreen slowly lowered her fork. "In what way?"

"He was a very rough-around-the-edges kind of a man. But there was a look in his eyes. One of those looks that said, cross him, and he'll take you out permanently."

She dared not tell Nan what she thought just now. Nan's questions would never stop if Doreen went down that path. So she asked another question instead. "Do you remember any more details about Betty Miles? I am also trying to get information on the Theroux family."

Nan looked up again. "Oh my. You are asking about the big families."

"Is Lansdown a founding family?"

Nan shook her head. "No, but he was always on the outs with them. And, of course, Betty Miles was part of that Lansdown family, on the black sheep poor side. Hannah Theroux is part of the poorer side of the Theroux family. But there's a big difference between Betty's kind of poor and Hannah's kind of poor."

"Do tell." Doreen was still stymied with the *of course* comment. Nan forgot that Doreen was new to town and hadn't lived with the history of the many long-running family dramas in town, but she didn't want to slow Nan's words. It could be hard to get her back on track again.

"After Betty disappeared, supposedly at the same time as

some of the Theroux family jewelry was stolen, the Theroux family was in an uproar. For so long everyone had thought Betty was just a runaway, and she'd pop back up like a bad penny again. But then her arm showed up, and again supposedly some Theroux jewelry was with her arm. Betty was from the poorest side of town, part of the Lansdown family. Not even the poorer part of the Therouxs lived on the poorest side of town. The rich Therouxs didn't want their name mucked about with this whole investigation, not even to get their stolen jewels back."

"Ah." Doreen understood now. There always seemed to be a black sheep in a family somewhere. Unfortunately for Betty, she seemed to naturally fall into the black sheep side of the Lansdown family, along with her scary uncle? "What about Hannah?"

"When Betty started going down a dark path, the Therouxs tried to convince Hannah to stay away from her. And it seemed like it worked because they weren't together very much over those last few months before Betty disappeared. But I always suspected Hannah knew more than she let on."

"It makes sense that she was protecting somebody."

"Oh, I don't know that she was protecting anybody. But she always had that fearful look in her eye, as if she thought she'd be the next one to go missing," Nan said in a low tone.

The hairs rose on the back of Doreen's neck. "Was there any Theroux connection to Lansdown at the time?"

Nan popped the last bite of tuna casserole into her mouth, then sat back as she chewed. With a very ladylike gesture, she picked up her napkin and dabbed at the corners of her mouth. "I know Lansdown did a lot of work for the Therouxs at the time. But then they were a big founding family, and everybody wanted to work for them. They had full-time gardeners, but, whenever they needed an extra man to pitch in, they brought Brian in."

"How do you know this?"

Nan looked at her in surprise. "It's not like it wasn't common knowledge. Besides, Gladys is here with me."

Feeling like the world just never quit going around and around in the circle of never-ending names she didn't have faces to put to, Doreen asked, "*Gladys?*"

"Oh, my dear, Gladys *Theroux*. She married Norm at least fifty years ago. Maybe more than that."

"So was she Hannah's mother?"

"Hannah's aunt."

"I'm trying to get the family tree together in my head. Did you ever ask her about what happened back then?"

Nan shook her head. "Gladys is on the rich side of the Therouxs. When the two girls were really tight, Gladys said that Hannah would spend a lot of nights at Betty's place. But then there was a big tiff and they stopped hanging out completely. That was about three months before Betty went missing."

"Any idea what caused the best friends to just cut off all contact like that?"

"Well, as everyone who's ever been a teenager knows, your parents don't understand anything, and it's all about finding someone to love—or misplaced as the sex act—but just gaining that sense of belonging somewhere, no matter how misguided or mismatched."

"Yeah, like breaking up with your boyfriend from math class, finding out the fairy tale wasn't there. Then to have your best friend dating him the next day. I remember those high school years."

"Yet we may never know what came between Hannah

and Betty." Nan sighed. "Nobody in the Theroux family was allowed to talk about the event from then on. Even now that she's a widow, just the mention of anything back then regarding their poorer relations is enough to make Gladys clam up."

"Suspicious."

"Very," Nan confirmed. "But I doubt you'd get anything out of her."

"Why?"

"Because she's dependent on the founding family for her livelihood now. This place isn't terribly cheap."

Doreen looked around at the large seniors' home and realized just how much the aged were dependent on the younger ones if they didn't have their own finances or control of their own money. "What about Hannah? She seems to have disappeared at the moment. Mack was looking for her."

"Why?"

Doreen gave her grandmother a lopsided smile. "Because she's the one who hit me."

Nan stared at her in surprise, then clapped a hand over her mouth and giggled. When she got a hold of herself, she leaned forward and whispered, "Really?"

Doreen leaned closer. "And the reporter who's giving me no end of grief is also a Theroux apparently."

"That's Sibyl," Nan said. "She was always like that. Pushy, pushy, pushy."

"Well then, she's in the right career, isn't she?" Doreen paused. "Her face turned seriously white when I asked her if she was related to Hannah."

"Hannah's her aunt."

"Can you think of any reason why Hannah would have

protected whoever killed Betty?"

"Not really. I always thought it had to do with the jewels myself."

"It always does," Doreen said. "It's either power or money or sex."

Nan laughed. "In this case it could be all three."

Doreen stared at her grandmother in astonishment. "Explain please?"

"Hannah's father liked young girls. I always suspected he had a relationship with Betty."

"How does that relate to the jewels?" Doreen asked, quite shocked, taking in that information. "If that was the case, would Hannah have tried to protect her father? Or blame him?"

Nan added, "I think they were being blackmailed." Nan sat back with a look of satisfaction after dropping that bombshell.

"Who was blackmailed?" Doreen asked. Nan wasn't making any sense. Or she was privy to a whole lot of information not many people knew.

"Hannah's parents. Gladys mentioned something way back then, that they had to pay up or else."

"And when did that stop? Do you know?"

Nan shook her head, leaning forward, and whispered, "But I bet it was when Brian Lansdown died."

"Did you ever tell any of this to the police?"

Nan looked at Doreen in surprise. "Of course not. I don't have any proof. That's just people talking."

"And theory or gossip or not, it doesn't explain why Betty would be carrying jewels when she disappeared."

Nan chuckled. "Well, it does if you realize Betty's father was Lansdown's brother."

Chapter 25

D OREEN WAS GOBSMACKED. "How is that possible? Why isn't Betty's last name Lansdown?"

Nan shook her head. "I don't believe Betty's mother and father ever married, or, if they did, it was so belated that everyone had the name 'Betty Miles' so stuck in their head that they just continued to call her that. You know what? I remember there was some question as to paternity. I think she ended up not listing a father on the birth certificate. Her and Stephen broke up and made up then broke up again a dozen times, she might have figured he shouldn't be listed on the paperwork. He's in jail now." She paused and frowned. "Or he was. I don't know if he still is."

Doreen asked, "Do you have a piece of paper, so I can write some of this down?"

Nan got up and came back with a small notebook and a pen. "I really like this hobby of yours," she said in a conspirator's tone. "It's very exciting."

"I don't think Mack agrees with you," Doreen said with a sideways look. She tried to write down the information in as straightforward a manner as possible. "So Betty Miles's father owned a jewelry store and is the brother to Brian

Lansdown, who was the gardener/handyman with the attitude that scared you, correct?"

Nan nodded.

Doreen wrote down the rest of the family relations the best that she could. "It's an assumption that Hannah Theroux's father was having a relationship with Betty, even though Betty was only sixteen, correct?"

"That's what the rumors were back then," Nan said easily. "But you know what rumors are like. Only half are true."

"It would explain why Lansdown was blackmailing Hannah's father. What was his name?"

"Glenn. Glenn and Rosie. But Glenn died some years back."

Doreen wrote down those names. "So they were trying to keep that a secret. And were probably paying the blackmailer in jewels in order to keep his silence."

"That would make sense."

"Then Glenn and Rosie would file a claim for the loss of the jewelry, supposedly a result of a break-in," Doreen said, working her way through this. "They probably got insurance money for the jewelry, so nobody was out anything."

Nan stared at her in surprise. "Wow. I never considered that."

"So why did Betty have any of the jewelry? Why was she considered the one stealing the jewelry?"

"That's easy," Nan said. "She must have found out Lansdown was blackmailing Hannah's father."

"And so she was getting jewelry in exchange for what? Her silence? She was blackmailing the blackmailer? Or in payment to keep seeing Glenn? Or, for that matter, maybe Glenn gave Betty the jewelry as a gift."

"And Betty's father, the jewelry store owner, was probably taking a bunch of those jewels to fence them for Brian, his brother the landscaping blackmailer. Or selling them outright in his own store."

"Stephen went to jail for theft."

Nan sat back. "That's how that happened?" She pursed her lips together, staring off in the distance. "He was caught with some of the jewelry missing from Glenn Theroux's place. Betty's father didn't have any way to prove he didn't steal them. And he couldn't very well tell the cops that he was blackmailing Glenn and that the jewels were blackmail payments to Lansdown and his blackmail partner, Betty's father." Nan stared at her granddaughter. "So it all comes full circle. The two blackmailers were brothers. One went to jail. The other one got away scot-free, and Glenn Theroux got the insurance money."

"One Lansdown got caught. The other Lansdown got dead, although years later," Doreen reminded Nan quietly. "So, who do we know in all this who would have taken out Betty?"

They looked at each other in silence for a second. "Lansdown," they said together.

"If Betty wanted to stay with Glenn or even if Betty saw her own payday coming out of her father and her uncle's blackmailing scheme, they had to buy Betty's silence to stop her from going to the cops," Doreen said. "The two brothers had a good thing going."

Nan clapped her hands in excitement. "This is wonderful."

"This is supposition," Doreen said. "It won't stand up in court."

"What court?" Nan asked. "Lansdown is dead. Betty's dead. Her father, Stephen, is already in jail. And Glenn is dead."

"But somebody was most likely working with Lansdown. Are you assuming it was his brother?"

"Quite possibly. And then maybe his daughter Betty got in the way."

"You think Hannah knew?"

"It's possible," Nan said. "She was friends with Betty. Maybe Betty warned Hannah about the scam. And maybe Hannah knew of her father's involvement with Betty and the insurance payout. It seems like everyone got something out of the deal, except Betty."

"But we don't know who killed Betty," Doreen said. "And that's the important thing right here. I don't care about the insurance scam, the blackmail, the jewels. Somebody killed Betty, and that's what I want to find out, to put them behind bars."

"You have to admit, my dear," Nan said, "there is a good chance he's dead or already behind bars."

Doreen didn't want to say anything, but one person was a little too riled over this whole thing to not have known or to not have played a larger part than had first been suspected. Doreen quietly put the notebook into her pocket. "I'll do a little more digging. If I find out the truth, I'll let you know."

Nan leaned forward. "Are you sure you don't want to talk to somebody here, like maybe Gladys? Questions might get answered."

Doreen shook her head. "No, because I don't want to upset anybody else or to alert anybody else. If I'm wrong, that would cause more hurt or problems for everyone."

Nan patted Doreen's hand. "You're a good girl."

Doreen wasn't so sure about that. She had a pretty darn good idea who had killed Betty. But it would upset a whole lot of people all over again. And that wouldn't do Doreen's reputation or her presence in the town any good at all.

She looked at the rest of the tuna casserole. Still quite a bit remained. "Are you going to eat that tomorrow?" she asked Nan.

Nan chuckled and stood. "Nope. You are. I'll wrap it up and send it home with you. The only thing is, I need the dish back."

Doreen chuckled. "No problem. I can do that." She stood as Nan returned with the wrapped tuna casserole. "Nan, don't tell anyone about our conversation, okay? Let's keep this a secret until I get to the bottom of this."

Nan leaned over and kissed Doreen on the cheek. "Absolutely. My lips are sealed."

But Doreen knew Nan had already told half the world. Probably while wrapping up the tuna casserole.

Chapter 26

DOREEN STARED SUSPICIOUSLY at her grandmother. "Nan, please tell me that you didn't tell anyone since I've been here."

To Doreen's horror, Nan's cheeks blushed red. Nan pulled out her phone. "I might have texted someone. But she won't tell anyone." ·

"Holy crap." Doreen stared at her grandmother in shock. "Gladys? You told Gladys, didn't you?"

Nan bit her lip. "It's just a little bit of fun."

Doreen stared at her in shock. "Murder is fun?"

"No, of course not, silly. But we had a betting pool on it," she confessed.

This information was a game-changer. Doreen stared at Nan, nonplused. "Wow." She leaned forward. "Then find out from her where Hannah is now, so I can talk to her."

A harsh voice behind them spoke out. "Leave that poor woman alone. Hasn't she suffered enough?"

Doreen happened to catch Nan's big beaming smile on her face at the male voice. So Nan obviously knew the intruder. Doreen slowly turned to stare at the gardener who was forever telling her off for walking across the grass. "What do you know about it?" she challenged.

He stuck his jaw out at her. "I know enough to leave well enough alone."

"So no justice for Betty?"

"She doesn't deserve any," he snapped. "That girl was bad news. Nobody mourned her loss either."

Inside Doreen felt something slide downward. That was a terrible sentiment. "How sad. She was just a teenager. She never had a chance to grow up and to understand the error of her ways."

Nan leaned forward and patted the gardener's grimy gloved hands. "It's all right, Dennis. I'm sure Hannah wouldn't mind answering a few questions."

Dennis snorted. "If she didn't mind, she would have gone to the police, now wouldn't she?"

"You mean, she was never asked to speak to the police?" Doreen asked in horror, turning from Nan to Dennis and back to Nan. "How is that possible?"

"She would have been of course," Nan said, "but she wouldn't likely have offered much."

"Hannah's delicate," Dennis said.

His explanation was simple, and yet, unbelievable. Doreen stared at him, remembering the woman who strode directly to her front door and smacked her hard across the face.

"I've met the woman. I don't see *delicate* the same way you do obviously," she said drily.

He gave her a disgruntled look. "Why don't you leave town? You're nothing but a busybody, getting into everybody's business. You should be leaving well enough alone."

"Dennis," Nan spoke up with determination in her voice, "this is my beloved granddaughter you are speaking to.

And I don't want her to move away from me. And this town's got plenty of busybodies, so don't be trying to oust one if you aren't going to evict all the others. Plus Doreen is solving a murder. Do you want a murderer to go free?" Nan stood, hands on hips, staring down Dennis.

He didn't have harsh words for her. Not after that.

"If the case doesn't involve Hannah, what difference does it make?" Doreen asked in a cool tone, hating that she'd already wondered about moving away. "It's not my fault that I find stuff to close cold cases."

He glared at her. "Of course it's your fault. You could have just walked away. You didn't have to go to the library and start digging for shit and talking to the detective. The police department has enough to deal with, without dealing with nuts like you."

"Dennis, mind your mouth," Nan snapped. "You know your attitude is upsetting many of the residents here. We pay a lot of money to live here. So I'm sure we can find a more pleasant gardener, like my granddaughter, to work here instead."

Doreen frowned at Dennis, happy to hear her grandmother standing up for her. "So, in other words, Hannah gets to run away and hide, instead of answering a few questions that would clear this all up?"

"That girl is innocent," Dennis stated.

"If she's so innocent, she won't mind answering a few questions."

Caught, again, he glared at her. And then he shrugged and walked away. "I can't tell you anything."

Frustrated, Doreen turned back to Nan. "Ask Gladys where I can find Hannah, please."

Nan nodded, picked up her phone. Instead of texting,

like she had earlier to keep it from Doreen's sight, Nan called. When the woman on the other end answered, she asked, "Where's Hannah right now?"

Doreen couldn't hear the full conversation, just Nan's side of it.

"Oh, she was gone for a few days, but now she's back, is she?" Nan listened for a bit. "She's at the house over on Oliver Street." Nan frowned. "That place is a bit of a mess."

The other woman was obviously speaking as Nan nodded her head as she looked at Doreen.

"No problem. I know Doreen just wanted to ask a question or two. ... No, no, no. I'm sure she won't upset her. We understand Hannah is delicate."

As soon as she got off the phone, Doreen glared at her. "*Delicate* my ass. She packed a wallop when she smacked me."

"She's easily upset."

"I wonder why?" Doreen said snidely as she shook her head. Carrying the tuna casserole in a bag, she called the animals to her side. "Nan, I will talk to you tomorrow." And she headed off.

The minute she was out of sight, she changed directions, trying to remember where Oliver Street was. Nothing at this end of town was very far away, and she was sure it was only a couple blocks over. She thought she saw it when she'd returned from the grocery store, and considering she and Hannah had shopped at the same store, it made sense Hannah might live nearby too. Plus she had walked to and from Doreen's house just to slap her.

Doreen went a couple more blocks, still searching for the street name, but found nothing. Frustrated, Doreen headed home to get her car instead. She drove blocks further and didn't find Oliver Street. Stopping at a gas station, she got directions.

"You must be new to the Mission," the guy at the pumps said, then staring into her car windows at the movement of the three animals inside. He just raised his eyebrows and turned back toward her.

With her nod, the man continued.

"You're in the nice part of the Mission. Oliver Street is in the really bad and rundown part of Mission several miles thataway." After a pause, he said, "I'll write down the directions for you. But I suggest you take a big strong man with you if you're going there in the dark. Hell, even if you go there in the daylight, you need a bodyguard."

Doreen nodded and said, "Thanks," grabbing the sheet of paper and driving off.

She only got turned around a couple times, not being familiar with this part of town. But, sure enough, as she crossed to the next block, she saw a side street that said it all. *Oliver Street*. She stopped and frowned. "Well, I certainly didn't see this area on the way home from the grocery store. This must not be where Hannah lives either."

As she parked the car and walked alongside the street, her trio of animals followed her on yet another adventure. Doreen found an odd back alley that disappeared in the distance. She didn't know how far it went, but it backed up to a good dozen-plus houses—all of which should probably be condemned.

"How the heck am I supposed to know which house it is?" she asked Mugs.

But Mugs was too busy sniffing along the street curb to give a darn as to what house he was supposed to be at.

And then Doreen saw Hannah's car. Doreen brightened.

"I guess it wasn't that hard after all." She stopped and studied the houses. They all appeared to be abandoned. Surely no one lived in these homes anymore. The reason Oliver Street was familiar to Doreen was because it was the same street that Betty Miles's family had lived on decades ago. Doreen had found it in her research. Not exactly a wealthy part of town. But it made sense that Betty's family had lived here and probably her uncle had lived nearby too. This wasn't where Hannah lived. She lived closer to Doreen.

Thaddeus cooed on her shoulder—maybe as a warning. Goliath on the other hand stopped suddenly, his butt down and a hind leg shot up in the air as he cleaned a spot.

Doreen walked up the driveway, found the garage door missing and an open door in the rear of the garage hanging by one hinge, which led to the backyard. No use going to the front door of an empty house, so Doreen headed to the backyard. And there she stopped. Hannah had a shovel in her hand at the far back corner. As Doreen stared at what was growing in the corner, her stomach knotted.

"Why begonias?" she whispered to Mugs who stood at her feet, his hackles roused. "They're such a lovely flower. Why does everybody abuse the begonias? They have enough trouble surviving winter without being mistreated at the same time."

She pulled out her phone. Mack would tear a strip of flesh from her if he knew what she was doing. She stepped back into the garage, hoping Hannah wouldn't hear her. When he answered, he sounded distracted, and she could hear other voices in the background.

"Sorry. I didn't mean to disturb you," Doreen said hurriedly. "I just figured that, if I didn't tell you, you'd get all pissy at me."

"Doreen," he said slowly with a warning. "What's up?"

"Well, I'm pretty darn sure I know who killed Betty Miles," she said in a harsh whisper. "But I'm not sure I'll be able to prove it." She heard his sucked-in breath and winced. "I know you told me not to interfere, and I didn't. Honest, but I was talking to Nan, and she knew some stuff, and Gladys knew some stuff, and before I knew it, I had it all figured out."

"This isn't some country-club game where you sit around the table and come up with your version of the truth. The way this works is we find facts and evidence to back up any theories."

"Or how about a confession?" She ended the call and set up her phone to record, put it in her pocket, and walked through the backyard to where Hannah was. "Any particular reason why you want to move the rest of the body parts now?"

The woman froze, spun on a heel, and stared at her. "What are you doing on this property?"

"I figured I'd return the favor. I mean, after you came to my house and attacked me, it seemed like a good idea that I should find you, maybe slap you back," Doreen said in a conversational tone. "Just kidding. I wasn't about to attack you." She motioned at the shovel in Hannah's hand. "Why did you plant body parts in begonias of all things? Why not tulips? Why not roses? And are they all pieces of Betty?"

Hannah stared at Doreen in disgust. "And *you* are telling people how you're a gardener and can take on all kinds of gardening jobs. You know what kind of root system roses have? You know azaleas and how touchy they can be? You can't put something like that at their roots." Hannah nodded at the ground before her. "In fact, the begonias haven't done very well either."

"And why, if you were going to bury the body parts, didn't you bury them all in the same place?"

Hannah looked at her. "What are you even talking about?" As if she'd suddenly realized this conversation was going the wrong way. "I didn't bury anything."

Doreen beamed. "I know. Technically that's quite correct. Technically you didn't bury anyone. You got Brian Lansdown to do it."

Hannah's jaw slowly dropped. "Are you nuts?"

She shook her head. "Oh, no, absolutely *not* nuts. But he's the gardener who had access to all these deep beds, so poor Betty could be buried in them."

"I didn't have anything to do with Betty's murder."

"That part is a lie," Doreen said, still in a conversational tone. "And of course, Brian found out about it. That's why he was blackmailing your father. The question is, how? And not only did he find out about it but he helped you dispose of her after the fact. And that's a very interesting little tidbit. Because Betty was his niece. And his own brother ended up in jail. So why didn't Brian go to the police and let them know what you'd done?"

Hannah snorted. "I don't know who you think you are, but you're not making any sense."

Doreen walked across the neglected lawn, her hands in her pockets. "See? Everybody says you're delicate. Everybody says you're easily upset. That worked for you for a long time, didn't it? I mean, it was just too awful what happened to you. You were so overwrought by the disappearance of your best friend that nobody could really question you about it. And, as time went on, the questions just fell away. But that whole persona of being so delicate meant *everybody* stayed away."

Something dark entered Hannah's gaze.

Doreen nodded. She'd seen it clearly for what it was.

Hate.

"You hated Betty, didn't you? Absolutely hated her. The thing is, I don't know why. Because she was sleeping with your dad? Were you jealous? Was Daddy also sleeping with you? Or were you upset for your mother's sake?" At that, she could see a shift in expressions cross Hannah's face. "Good. I'd really hate to think he was sexually abusing you too."

"What do you mean, *abusing* her? She loved being with him," Hannah said in a scathing voice. "He always bought her jewels and fancy little boxes. As long as she lay down with him, she could have anything she wanted."

"You were totally okay with her getting the gifts because you had enough of your own. Even though your family was deemed the poorer part of the Theroux family, you still had way more than Betty's family. Did Betty's mother know Glenn was sleeping with Betty? Did *your* mother know Glenn was sleeping with Betty? But *you* knew Betty was sleeping with your father. Except Betty wanted one thing you didn't want her to have. Betty wanted your father all to herself. She wanted to marry him. To get rid of your mother and you, and that you couldn't allow."

"We might have been the poorer side of the Theroux family," Hannah said, "but no way were we as low and as slimy as the Lansdowns. Betty's mother never saw anything happening around her. She couldn't be bothered. Drank herself into a grave a few years ago. Betty's brother took off a long time ago. Who knows where the hell he is now? The whole family is a mess."

"And so you couldn't possibly let your best friend marry

your father because that would attach those nasty slimy Lansdown bottom-feeders to the founding Theroux family. What would happen to the poorer side of the Theroux family, those existing members who had no intention of staying on the poor side of the family? I mean, look at you. After everything that happened, the wealthiest Theroux family tucked you away protectively, gave you a lovely house in the better part of town to live in, and looked after you. You remained the *delicate* one who they always had to keep an eye out for. And that suited you just fine." Doreen stopped and looked at Hannah. "That must have been difficult. Because, as much as you might have hated what Betty was doing, a part of you also loved her." Doreen thought about all the years since, thought about the fact that Hannah never had a family, never got married. And Doreen gave her a sad smile. "I'm so sorry."

Hannah glared at her, but now fear shone in her eyes.

"Back then it was even less acceptable, wasn't it?"

"I don't know what you are talking about." She took several steps back, the fear shining brightly in her eyes.

"You and Betty were lovers. She understood who you were. You could be *you* with her. But, at the same time, she was sleeping with your father. And that was a double betrayal. No way would you let your lover become your stepmother."

Chapter 27

H ANNAH'S FACE WORKED into an ugly red mottled grimace.

Doreen wanted to both hug her and hit her for what she'd done. "You never meant to hurt Betty. Or rather, you did at the moment, but you never meant to kill her," Doreen said thoughtfully. "What did you do? Hit her over the head? Knock her out? Suffocate her?" She studied Hannah's face, looking for an answer, but Hannah seemed beyond speech. "So, how is it Betty's uncle knew?"

Again Doreen looked for a reaction, but none came. Hannah appeared to be too involved in her own grief.

"Brian must have seen you."

At that, Hannah gave a slow nod. "He did. He saw us before, when we were curled up in bed together. And he knew. Then he heard the fight we had," she said slowly, sadly. "He came to see what was going on. But he was a little too late to save her."

Doreen wondered if that wasn't on purpose. It sounded like Brian was more interested in watching the two of them, seeing what he could get out of it. To confirm her thoughts, she asked, "Did he step forward and offer to help?"

Hannah nodded. "At the time I was desperate to hide what I'd done. And yet, inside I was breaking apart because I loved her. I really loved her. But I knew she was on a one-way track that just wouldn't stop."

"So it really had nothing to do with the jewels, did it?"

Hannah shook her head slowly. "No. Not then. She just disappeared, and nobody thought anything of it. But then Lansdown ran into a spot of trouble. He owed some money to some very bad and dangerous people, and he needed to pay up. He came to me. His way of finding a new source of cash. But I didn't have anything. So he went to my father. Brian told my father about Betty and me, about him having an illicit affair with Betty, a minor. And then Brian told my father that I'd killed Betty. My dad cheerfully cooperated at that point.

"He set it up to look like a robbery. Betty's father was hired to break in and to steal the jewels. I don't think Lansdown knew about that. But, when his brother got caught, Brian never stepped up and confessed either," she said bitterly. "I still don't understand why Stephen never told on Brian. But Brian was all about saving his own ass. He didn't give a damn about anybody else's."

Doreen could've told Hannah that men like Brian were the same all over, regardless of any perceived social position. "He couldn't let the money supply dry up," Doreen said softly. "Did Lansdown continue to blackmail your family until his own death?"

Hannah nodded slowly. "He did, but we didn't have any more money for him, not from our side of the family, not to get the sums he was always after. And the Theroux family might support their poorer relations, but they didn't pay blackmailers. So Lansdown tried to go behind my father's back by blackmailing my mother, but she kicked Lansdown out of the house and said she didn't believe any of it. After that, I honestly to this day don't know if Lansdown died a natural death or if my father finally had had enough of his blackmailer. Then Father died a couple years after Lansdown. It wouldn't surprise me if Mother killed him at that point."

"Was it Lansdown's idea to dismember Betty?"

Hannah nodded. "He was doing quite a few gardening jobs at the time. We put her in a chest freezer here at his house and then cut her up into pieces, so he could get them into the gardens without anybody knowing. The problem was, the creek went really high the following spring, and one of the garden beds washed out. A lot of properties along the creek washed out. We were lucky just one arm showed up. I stayed quiet. So did he. And the case went cold." Hannah turned on Doreen, her voice turning vicious. "Until you arrived and dredged it all back up again."

"We found a second arm," Doreen said quietly. "And a right foot and lower leg."

Hannah's mouth dropped open, and a small scream escaped. "Are you serious?"

Doreen nodded. "Mother Earth always gives up her secrets. She might take a little time, or she might take a long time, but eventually the truth rises to the surface." Doreen motioned at the garden behind her. "Which part do you have here?"

Hannah looked at the back garden and whispered, "Her trunk."

"What were you going to do with it?" Doreen waved at the empty backyard. "No one has lived here in forever. Why would you come here now?"

"Those rumors about you digging into things you shouldn't be and how you've been into the begonias."

"Why begonias?" Doreen couldn't help asking again. "Did Betty hate them?"

As a pained expression whispered across the other woman's face, Doreen understood.

"No, Betty loved them, didn't she?" At Hannah's slow nod, Doreen felt her heart wrench. As if words were beyond her, Hannah nodded slowly, the color in her face nonexistent, and Doreen understood further.

"I'm sorry. That's a heavy burden for you to carry all these years. I'm surprised about the ivory box too and the ring."

"I gave her the ring, but she threw it back at me when we fought that night. And the box was from my father," Hannah said softly. "I thought it fitting that she be buried with them. After she'd slept with him to get it, she'd sleep forever with the spoils of her actions."

Doreen hated to hear this, whether it was important or not. Then Hannah grew quiet and stared at Doreen for a moment, a cunning and calculating look entering her eyes.

Doreen shook her head. "Oh, no you don't. The game is up, and you can't kill me and bury me in the garden too."

"Why not? You have been asking questions all around town. Who knows who might have killed you? I know at least half a dozen people who would like to." Hannah glanced around slowly, as if looking for witnesses.

Down the street Doreen could hear a vehicle. She wondered if Mack had gotten the message. Not that she'd made it very clear. If he was any kind of a detective, he would have contacted Nan. Doreen backed up several paces to the garage.

The problem with this scenario was, if Doreen got caught in the backyard, and somebody from Hannah's family came here before Mack did, there was a good chance Doreen would end up cornered. And potentially in the garden in the begonias, along with poor Betty.

Doreen turned to see who had arrived and caught movement out of the corner of her eye. She spun. As the shovel came down hard on her shoulder, she defensively raised her arm, but the blow still knocked her down.

Mugs barked like crazy and went on the attack. He tugged on Hannah's pant cuffs. And Goliath ... Wow!

Doreen lay on the grass, partially stunned, and watched as Goliath clawed his way up Hannah's legs.

Hannah screamed, "Get them off me. Get them off me."

But her screams attracted Thaddeus. He flew on top of her head but couldn't quite get into position, so dug his claws into the nest of hair she had on top. She screamed even more. Thaddeus imitated her screaming. Mugs barked louder. Goliath howled.

And Mack walked into the backyard, his gun drawn and roared, "What the hell is going on?"

Doreen glanced up at him. "Hannah killed Betty."

And Hannah fell to her knees, crying. "I did. I killed Betty. Dear God, help me. I loved her too much to let her go."

Chapter 28

AT HOME, DOREEN couldn't stop shaking. Her whole body was racked with tremors. She knew she'd been extremely foolish, now that it was over. What was she thinking, confronting a killer like that—by herself? She was tucked up on the living room couch with a blanket around her shoulders. Nan—back in her former house for the first time since Doreen had moved in—sat beside Doreen, gently patting her hand.

Mack, finally freed from the craziness of forensic proceedings at Lansdown's former house, delivered Doreen a cup of hot coffee. He set it down on the coffee table before her. "Are you sure you shouldn't go to the hospital? That's a nasty blow you took on your shoulder."

Doreen shook her head. "No, I'll be fine. The last thing I want is more people staring at me and asking questions."

The truth about Betty had been postponed over these thirty years. Some of the questions still were not answered, but at least Mack now had the truth, once he'd heard the recording Doreen had on her phone. The entire town would be nothing but a gossip mill, rife with the latest news. She reached for the coffee on the table.

Mack said, "Just wait a bit. It's still hot."

She nodded. Goliath was currently curled up on her lap, but she scooped him up higher against her chest, so she could cuddle him closer. She had to do everything one-armed—the other one was in a fiery agony.

Nan looked at her granddaughter worriedly. "Are you sure you didn't hurt yourself? What if you broke your arm?"

Doreen shook her head. "I don't think so. It'll be one heck of an ugly-looking yet colorful bruise for a while." At least she hoped that was true. Maybe she *should* go to the hospital, but it wasn't her way. "If and when I try to move it, and it doesn't move, then I'll reconsider the Emergency Room. But right now I really don't want to go anywhere." Goliath's big engine purred in her ear, and she buried her face in his fur. "Thank you, Nan, for leaving me Goliath and Thaddeus."

Nan patted her leg. "You're very welcome. I think Goliath and Thaddeus are very happy with you too."

Mugs jumped up on the couch between her and Nan, finding enough room against Doreen's feet for him to tuck up in a circle. Nan rubbed him around the ears. "Of course I'm delighted too. And you're making me a lot of money." She beamed.

Mack, on the other hand, stood taller, his arms crossed on his chest, and glared at Nan, then at Doreen. "What will it take to keep you out of trouble? Both of you?"

Nan tried to look innocent. Doreen looked up at him and smiled. Then Thaddeus jumped up and landed on Mack's shoulder, trying to imitate the look on Mack's face.

Doreen smiled. "Maybe keep me out of the begonias?"

Thaddeus popped up and said, "Bones in the begonias. Bones in the begonias."

For the first time in a long time, Doreen laughed heartily, even though her shoulder radiated with more throbbing pain. "Listen to Thaddeus," she said to Mack. "He understands."

Mack shook his head and went to get himself a cup of coffee.

She exchanged a look with Nan, and the two of them smiled.

Nan leaned forward and said quietly, "You're doing good, bone lady. You're doing *real* good."

At the word *bone*, Thaddeus repeated ad nauseam, "Good bone lady. Good bone lady. Good bone lady."

There was nothing else to do but laugh. Still, Doreen would be happy to not hear that nickname directed at her again.

At least not for a few days ...

Epilogue

In the Mission, Kelowna, BC
Wednesday, One Day Later....

DOREEN SAT CURLED on the couch. All she had wanted was three days. Three days of peace and quiet. Was that in the cards? She doubted it. As much as she desperately wanted to be out of the lime light and rejoice in the peace and quiet of living in her Nan's house, she had a bad feeling in her gut.

Her brood was sedate—even Goliath, asleep on the other end of the couch with Mugs—all her furry or feathered babies obviously understanding how Doreen really needed that from them at this time. Thaddeus rubbed his beak along her cheek, then closed his eyes, happy to just sit on her shoulder.

Unfortunately she found no peace or quiet outside her home, not yet today—but it was early morning—and not for the last two days for sure. The reporters were still at her door, even at this hour. The newspaper journalists were still writing articles about how Doreen had helped solve the decades-old cold case of Betty Miles's death, and Nan and her cronies were still enjoying being the center of attention by giving numerous interviews, supposedly on Doreen's behalf. Doreen had told Nan how that was totally fine, just happy that Nan had found something, other than her illegal betting activities, to bring excitement to her life.

Indeed, Nan glowed with it.

But, as for Doreen, she wanted to be left alone. At that thought, her phone chimed. She glanced at her cell and groaned. But she hit the Talk button anyway. "You better have a good reason for bothering me, Mack." She slid farther down on the couch until her head rested on the armrest. Thaddeus shifted his position but refused to give up his spot on her shoulder.

"I figured for sure that, by now, you'd be all pepped up, raring to go," he said.

She could detect the worry in his voice and had to smile. "I am, and yet, I'm not. Have you any idea how deep the lineup of reporters is outside my front door? I know this is a small town, but it seems like the news hit the wires all the way across the country."

"You're a celebrity," he said, laughing. His voice softened. "But, no, that's not an easy position to be in."

"I didn't murder anybody," she exclaimed, sitting up straight to peek through the curtains. "Why are they haunting me?"

Thaddeus squawked, shot her a disgusted look when she had disturbed his nap on her shoulder, hopped up to the back of the couch, where he wandered over a few steps and then proceeded to close his eyes again.

"It's like everybody thinks I'm the one who's done something wrong," she said reaching out to pet Mugs, then stroke her fingers across Goliath's back.

"Remember the last time?" he asked. "This too will blow

over."

"Sure, but every time I find a new body," she said in exasperation, "they look at me as if I had something to do with it."

"Not that you had something to do with the *making* of the dead bodies," he corrected, his light humor sliding through his voice, "but that your arrival precipitated all this. Or maybe you have some sort of psychic ability. You don't, do you?" His voice held a curious note to it.

She chuckled at his tone. "I think, by now, both you and I would know if I did."

"Well, you need something to cheer you up."

"What have you got for me?" She stood, walking over to peer through the round window on the front door. Instantly camera flashes went off. She stepped back and walked toward the kitchen. "Have you got a nice puzzle for me to work on?"

"You mean, like another case?"

"It would get me out of the dumps." Her tone turned crafty. "You know how I like a good puzzle."

"You could pick up some jigsaw puzzles," he exclaimed. "That's a much safer hobby."

"Murderous puzzles are much more fun." She chuckled, knowing he'd hate her answer.

"And much more dangerous," he snapped. "You could have been killed last time."

She shrugged. "You live and you die. At least I'd be doing something I wanted to do."

"Solving cold cases?"

She grinned, hearing the hesitation in his voice. "You have another cold case you're looking into, don't you?"

Silence.

For the first time since she had awakened before dawn

today, her boredom and sense of a dark cloud hanging over her almost lifted. "It's not my fault this town is a den of iniquity," she stated. "Just think of all the nastiness hidden here for so long." She could feel that same sense of excitement surging through her when delving into Mack's cold cases. "Are you going to tell me the details?"

"No," he said, no hesitation in his voice this time.

"And why not?" She waited. If he wanted to play a waiting game, that was no problem. She could play that game too.

Finally he said, "It's not really a priority."

"Maybe not to you," she said. "Cold cases *are* a priority to the families."

"I didn't say a death was involved."

"That would be even better," she said. "Then I wouldn't trip over any more bodies, at least not right away."

"I'd be totally okay if you wouldn't trip over any more *anytime*," he said.

"Suits me," she said. "I'm okay to not find dead bodies ever again."

"Besides, it's not a cold case I wanted to talk to you about. I'll think about that first."

"Damn." She let out a heavy sigh. "So what is it then?"

"I was talking to the city council. They want to redo the big sign with the garden as you enter the city limits. You know the Welcome to Kelowna sign surrounded by flower beds?"

"Yeah, mostly begonias I think," she said. "At least one of the rings around the sign are begonias."

"*Ugh*," he said. "I'd be happy not to see any more of those anytime soon."

She nodded. "They're nice to look after, and they don't

grow too crazy outside, so they don't need a ton of maintenance. They're easy for large gardens and make great borders
or plots." At the word *plot* she winced.

He chuckled. "I can see that having you around will be a
constant reminder of dead things and everything associated
with them."

"Maybe. And what about the city council? What were
you talking to them about?" Her mind zinged to her ever-
dwindling pile of money, and she was deeply concerned
about it. "Hope it's important. And, if it involves money for
me, the answer is yes."

He chuckled. "You don't even know what it could en-
tail."

"Doesn't matter," she said. "I'm about out of the money
I found in Nan's pockets before donating and trying to resell
some of her unwanted clothes. Which means I'll be diving
into that little bit of savings I have."

"And the gardening you did at my mom's place? That'll
be a regular thing, if you're okay with that."

"I am absolutely okay with that," she said. "What you
pay me will put food on my table."

"Speaking of food," he said. "Did you turn on the new
stove?"

She pivoted and walked out of the kitchen. "What
stove?"

He sighed. "The stove you paid one hundred dollars to
replace. A lot of people went to a lot of trouble to make sure
you had something safe to cook on."

"There's the trick," she said, "the word *cook*."

"I'll tell you what. How about this Monday I bring over
the fixings for something simple for breakfast or lunch, and
I'll show you how to cook it."

"Simple would be, like, eggs," she said, "and I highly doubt you want eggs for lunch, do you?"

"Not an issue for me. I love eggs anytime," he said. "Don't you know how to cook eggs?"

She pulled the cell from her ear so she could glare at the blank screen.

"Okay, okay, okay," he said. "Stop glaring at me."

She gasped. "How did you know I was glaring at you?"

"I could hear it in the heavy silence of the phone's speaker," he said drily. "And eggs are easy. How about we do omelets? They are a little more substantial than plain eggs."

Her mind filled with the soft fluffy omelets her chef used to make for her. "With spinach and caviar and gruyere?"

Mack replied with that heavy silence again.

"Oh. Okay, so what do your omelets normally contain?" she asked.

"Well, spinach is one possible ingredient," he said, "but anything I have on hand. Like bacon, ham, leftover meat. You can put veggies in it if you want." His tone said he really didn't see the point. "Meat and eggs are a perfect combo. ... Plus cheese."

"Well, ham and cheese omelets are good too," she said. "Can we add mushrooms?"

"Sure," he said. "We can sauté a few mushrooms. So are you up for a cooking lesson?"

"Yes," she said slowly. But she needed to ask him something, and it was kind of embarrassing.

"Speak up," he said in that long-drawn-out sighing way of his.

As if he knew she was making a big deal out of nothing but needed to get it out first. "Am I paying you for it?" she asked in a rush.

He laughed. "No, you're not paying me for a cooking lesson. Not with money, not with gardening work, not with bartering or any other method."

She beamed. "In that case, I'm looking forward to cooking lesson number one coming up. Omelets it is."

"I'll bring the ingredients. You'll write down everything I do, okay?"

"Okay."

"And, on Tuesday, you'll repeat the menu, on your own," he said. "You'll take a picture and send the final results to me, so I can see how you did."

She chuckled. "Probably better if you come back and watch me make it the second time, and then you can taste the results."

"Done," he said.

She frowned suspiciously, wondering if he hadn't planned on that in the first place. "So you need to bring ingredients for two meals," she said swiftly.

He howled with laughter. "You know what? You might not know how to cook, but you sure know how to negotiate a deal." And, on that note, he hung up.

She grinned to herself, until she realized he hadn't told her all about the city's Welcome garden—or about the cold case. She called him back, but he didn't answer. Then she sent him a text. **What about the city?**

He sent her a map and a handout with his return text. **They're looking for suggestions about what to put in these two beds.**

She walked to her laptop, turned it on, and transferred the image and the PDF on her phone to her computer. There was the sign, Welcome to Kelowna. She could see the mature plantings around it. And the indicated beds were on each side of the sign. **Suggestions for what?**

Types of flowers, why those flowers, money, as in a guesstimate for the cost.

I haven't a clue on the money, she typed. **And, even if I do tell them what I would do, what's that got to do with anything?**

They're looking for bids. The winning bid gets to do the job and to make the money.

She perked up when she heard that. Then she opened the PDF and read the one-page document. **Okay, but it says to submit this by midnight tomorrow night.**

Yeah, he replied. **That's why I called you earlier this morning. So get at it.**

Getting at it was complicated. Doreen was in the third local greenhouse, checking out the prices of perennials, Mugs walking patiently at her side. She had all kinds of ideas from lipstick plants to carnations. She thought carnations would be gorgeous. But, to get the color she wanted at a wholesale price, that would be the trick.

So far nobody she had talked to was interested in giving her a bulk-buy deal. She knew somewhere in the Okanagan region she could set up something like that, but she hadn't done very well tracking that down. She wondered if she could put in a bid for doing the work and have the city pay for the cost of the flowers on their own. Surely the city gardeners had access to plants she couldn't even comprehend *and* at bulk pricing.

It made sense to her, but she didn't know if that was the proper procedure or, if not, if the city would go for it. Still, she could try. But, at the moment, she was running out of ideas of where and what she could put together. She loved the idea of roses, but they took work. Carnations, not the superlong stemmed ones though, she could do in layers.

Longer in the center and then shorter as they went out to the edge. That might look pretty cool.

With ideas buzzing in her head, she wandered through the greenhouse, writing down notes. When somebody called out her name, she turned without thinking, and a camera flash went off in her face. She growled. "Stop doing that."

"You're a celebrity in town." The man chuckled as he turned and walked away.

She sighed and slipped out the side entrance back to her vehicle, Mugs at her side. There she sat in her car for a long moment.

Somehow she hadn't associated getting out of the house as also being her first step into the public eye after the latest news had broken on Betty Miles. Doreen had been so focused on escaping the house that she had forgotten what she'd be escaping into. But her exit had worked out better than she had thought. She'd forced the media crowd to part to let her drive away, and she wouldn't return until she was darn good and ready.

As she sat in her car, she watched an old couple arguing nearby, standing at another parked vehicle. They looked so comfortable, as if the calm complaints had been told many times over. When they finally got into a vehicle and drove away, she wanted to laugh and to cry.

A loud engine had her turning to watch as a young woman drove up in a fancy scarlet Mini Cooper. Although what was *mini* about the new model, she didn't get. It looked bigger than her Honda. She watched as the woman got out, perfectly coiffed top to bottom. Doreen recognized all the work that went into that look; yet she had absolutely no interest in looking like that again.

She studied her currently close-cropped fingernails. They

were clean, but her hands showed the ravages of gardening—no weekly manicures or special fingernail soaks to keep her hands perfect anymore. Just healthy outdoor work in Mother Nature's glory. But still, Doreen needed to pick up some good hand cream. As she glanced back at the gardening shop, she wondered if they'd have a working hand cream—like, for professional gardeners. She was well-past using fancy hand lotions for her skin now. But the gardeners at her former home had small green pots of stuff they used daily. A drugstore might be a better option for that—and cheaper.

Then she thought about making yet another stop and decided she'd check here anyway. She hopped back out of the car, held Mugs' leash, and beelined to the far corner containing the walls of shelves for everything associated with gardening. Sure enough, the hand creams were on a triangle-shaped display.

As she studied the different choices, she could hear somebody speaking in the background.

A man said, "After what you've done, you'll now do as I tell you to." His tone was ugly.

Doreen stiffened. Mugs shifted at her heel, tugging at his leash to sniff the flowers an aisle away. She looked around cautiously to her left but didn't see anyone. She peered to her right, around the stand of hand cream, and saw two people around another corner. The man was large—six feet, maybe six two—glaring down at the stunning blonde Doreen had seen getting out of her car earlier. But, instead of being daunted, the blonde had shoved her face into his, and, in a hard voice, she said, "Well, with me or without me backing your decision, you'll end up planted in the daisies. *Not* me." The blonde turned in a huff and strode away.

Doreen tried to get out of her way, but the blonde deliberately knocked Doreen sideways. The air rushed out of Doreen's chest with an *oomph*. Mugs barked loudly, edging closer to the blonde.

The blonde turned, looked at Doreen, and said roughly, "Mind your own damn business. And keep that chubby pooch away from me."

"I didn't say a word," Doreen replied. Then, unable to help herself, she snapped, "And he's not chubby."

Just then the man came around the corner, towered over Doreen, and sniggered. "No, he's fat. And you won't say a word, will you?"

She glared up at him. "You can go murder and plant all the people you want. Just keep me out of it. And stop insulting my dog."

He laughed. "Wow. You've got a hell of an imagination, don't you?"

But she could see the worry in his eyes. He walked away but not before she grabbed her phone and took a picture of his profile as he turned a corner. It was probably a shitty photo, but maybe somebody could figure out who he was, if need be.

With her cream in her hand, she headed to the long line at the front counter. She watched the blonde ahead of her step out of the line, as if she couldn't be bothered to wait, and, in a hurried stride, headed for the front doors.

Doreen put down the hand cream on the counter, raced outside, and, with her phone, took a picture of the woman. As she walked to her car, Doreen snapped another picture of the Mini. She was getting damn good at using her cell phone at her hip to take images on the sly. She was pretty sure Mack wouldn't be happy with her doing this. Neither would the people she'd taken pictures of. But it seemed like everybody else snapped cameras in her face. So what the hell?

She wondered if it was safe for her to follow the woman. But that was an idiotic move. She had witnessed a minor tiff between two people who'd uttered empty threats. Nothing to do with Doreen. And hardly a life-threatening situation. She should just mind her own business …

Until she watched the big bully hop into a huge black truck and drive off aggressively behind the Mini.

Doreen chewed on her bottom lip indecisively, not liking the menacing growl of the truck's engine. Those humongous trucks always seemed to be driven by asshats.

At that term she grinned. Swearing wasn't something she was terribly comfortable with, but the words slipped out more and more. And unfortunately Thaddeus heard—and repeated—most of them. She wanted to utilize forms she could say comfortably that would give the same meaning without lowering her standards. The internet was full of alternate swear words, but she didn't want anything that just everybody used. Of course, *asshats* was a popular one. Still, she kind of liked it.

She hopped into her car and drove out, following the truck and the Mini Cooper. She didn't know why exactly. Was she that bored? It'd been three days since she'd solved the cold case of poor Betty Miles who'd been dismembered thirty years ago by her best friend, Hannah Theroux. Three days, that was it. What was she, some kind of a dead-body junkie?

Still, the argument between the two people had seemed like a viable threat, now that she thought about it some more in light of the demanding man now following the woman. Not that the woman had seemed threatened by the man's words. She'd given as good as she got.

While following those two, Doreen realized she was heading in the direction of the Welcome to Kelowna sign. She perked up at having a viable excuse to give Mack for going in this direction. She really did want to take a look at the two beds the city was considering updating. Doreen should have done that in the first place because, without knowing the size of each, she would have no idea how to budget for her time or for the number of plants needed.

It took another five minutes to reach that area. Both vehicles continued ahead of her. She frowned as they turned off and went around the corner and past the sign. She pulled into a small strip mall close by so she could park and walk to the sign the rest of the way up the road.

As she hopped out, she studied the direction the other vehicles had taken. It looked like a dead-end street. Maybe, when she was done here, she'd take a look there. In the meantime, she grabbed her notepad, and, with Mugs at her side, she strolled over to look at the big garden, about fifty feet across, with the Welcome to Kelowna sign in the middle.

She took several photos of the two smaller garden beds the city was looking for options on. The heart-shaped beds were pretty and could use something extremely unique. Her creative artistry piqued, she had almost too many choices to consider. As she wrote down more notes, she checked out the dryness of the soil, the type of mulch used, and saw how the city's gardeners had used a cutting tool to create a shallow trench at the garden's edge to keep the grass from encroaching. Which was smart because public-area maintenance requirements in a city this size were massive and expensive. Even though the city likely employed an army of gardeners, there was always too much to do and not enough man-hours to do it.

Mugs lay down in the grass, happy to be on a field trip. He rolled over and snuffled along the ground, enjoying himself. She chuckled. "I should have brought the others with us. They'd love it here."

Of course, the cat and the bird were much harder to control. She returned her attention to the gardens. Her mind buzzed with various plant options. She wondered if they could keep rubber plants here because they were huge statements that could be in the center of each of those heart-shaped beds. Not just one rubber plant but maybe four or five of them. She'd seen many big planters on the city's sidewalks and in the malls using the same idea. It would tie together the inner-city landscaping with the outer-city designs.

"Come on, Mugs. Let's go."

After letting Mugs into the car, she hopped back into her vehicle. Rather than going home, she proceeded where the two vehicles had gone. Just a quick trip to make sure everything was okay. She went around the corner to find the truck parked a few houses down on the left. With her phone, she took a picture of it, getting the license plate number. The truck appeared out of place compared to the run-down house it was parked at, which in her mind looked like a crack house. One of the typical druggie houses seen in a big city that others avoided. They were usually pretty easy to avoid because they were generally clustered with more houses of the same in a particular neighborhood. Yet the houses on either side here looked more upscale. This particular derelict house was hardly a place she expected the blonde to go.

Doreen was in the Rutland area of Kelowna, and Nan lived in the Mission area. Rutland was a poorer area, not low-class by any means, and the city was certainly doing a lot to revitalize the area. It had the lowest-priced real estate in town too. Great for enticing developers.

As she drove slowly past the truck, she could see the bright red Mini Cooper parked beside it. That looked really incongruous with the decrepit house. *Maybe those two were developers? Maybe they had bought the house and planned to level it and rebuild?* She shrugged, wondering what their deal was, but knowing it wasn't her business.

She drove ahead to a cul-de-sac at the end of the road. She pulled around in the circle and slowly drove past the house again. She had absolutely no excuse for doing what she did next—nothing that would pass muster with Mack. But she didn't even think twice about it.

She pulled up to a nearby house and parked. In a pretense of taking Mugs for a walk, she got out on the sidewalk and headed away from the house, crossed the road, and strolled on the sidewalk opposite the house in question. She was being nosy, and she knew it. But she and Mugs were just taking an innocent walk. Not like she was on private property with No Trespassing signs posted.

No harm done.

Spit. Spit.

She froze, wondering where to look, wondering if she could have mistaken that sound, but it came again. *Spit, spit.* Followed by a cry.

That all came from *the* house. "Mugs, let's go." She raced to her car, hopped in, and drove back to the garden store, where she called Mack from the safety of her car in the parking lot.

"What?"

"I think I heard gunshots," she said without preamble.

"What the hell? Where?"

She winced as she told him about the couple's argument and taking pictures of them and their vehicles and then following them.

"You did what?" he roared.

"Okay, okay. I know I shouldn't have followed them," she said, "but it doesn't change the fact I think I heard gunshots."

"It's also quite possible you heard something *other* than gunshots," he said. "Like a car backfiring."

"Yes, maybe," she said. "Maybe, maybe, maybe. But *maybe* not."

He groaned. "Fine. What's the address?"

"I don't know the house number," she said. "But it's on Hawthorne Street, the third house in from the corner—on the left side if you're coming from the Kelowna sign."

"Oh, that's what you were doing there."

"I had to see how big the beds were. How else could I give a decent bid?" She hoped he would believe that was her main reason for going there in the first place.

"I'll take a look," he said. "But you go home. Will you do that?"

"I will."

"Did you bring any of the animals with you?"

"Just Mugs." She reached over to pet the basset hound's head. Mugs let out a corresponding *woof* into the interior of her car.

"At least you've got him, although I don't know that he'll be much protection against an attack."

"As you well know," she snapped, "he's great protection—when needed."

"Maybe," he said. "But maybe not. I think you guys are

a comedy of errors."

"Okay, that's possible," she said defiantly, a trifle hurt. "But it works. We're all family." And on that note she hung up. She reached over and gave Mugs a big cuddle. "Let's go home. Back to the rest of the family."

Was there ever a better word? Nope. And she couldn't think of a better place she wanted to be right now.

This concludes Book 2 of Lovely Lethal Gardens: Bones in the Begonias.
Read about Corpse in the Carnations: Lovely Lethal Gardens, Book 3

Lovely Lethal Gardens: Corpse in the Carnations (Book #3)

A new cozy mystery series from USA Today best-selling author Dale Mayer. Follow gardener and amateur sleuth Doreen Montgomery—and her amusing and mostly lovable cat, dog, and parrot—as they catch murderers and solve crimes in lovely Kelowna, British Columbia.

Riches to rags. ... Chaos calms. ... Crime quiets. ... But does it really?

After getting involved in two murder cases in the short time she's lived in picturesque Kelowna, divorcee and gardener Doreen Montgomery has developed a reputation almost as notorious as her Nan's. The only way to stop people from speculating, is to live a life of unrelieved boredom until the media and the neighbors forget about her. And Doreen aims to do just that with a tour of Kelowna's famed Carnation Gardens. Plants, more plants, and nothing whatsoever that anyone could object to.

But when she sees a fight between a beautiful young woman and her boyfriend, she can't help but be concerned. Concerned enough that she follows the couple out of the parking lot and through town. And when gunshots interrupt the placid afternoon, it's too late to worry about how her nemesis, Corporal Mack Moreau, will feel about her getting involved in yet another of his cases.

With bodies turning up in the carnations, and a connection to a cold case of a missing child from long ago, Doreen has her hands full, not least with trying to keep her involvement in the investigations a secret from her Nan, Mack Moreau, and especially the media. But someone's keeping up with Doreen's doings… and that someone can't afford for her to find the answers to the questions she's asking.

Book 3 is available now!
To find out more visit Dale Mayer's website.
https://geni.us/DMCorpseUniversal

Get Your Free Book Now!

Have you met Charmin Marvin?

If you're ready for a new world to explore, and love ill-mannered cats, I have a series that might be your next binge read. It's called Broken Protocols, and it's a series that takes you through time-travel, mysteries, romance... and a talking cat named Charmin Marvin.

Go here and tell me where to send it!
https://dl.bookfunnel.com/s3ds5a0w8n

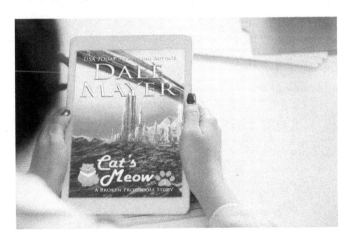

Author's Note

Thank you for reading Lovely Lethal Gardens, Books 1–2! If you enjoyed the book, please take a moment and leave a short review.

Dear reader,

I love to hear from readers, and you can contact me at my website: www.dalemayer.com or at my Facebook author page. To be informed of new releases and special offers, sign up for my newsletter or follow me on BookBub. And if you are interested in joining Dale Mayer's Reader Group, here is the Facebook sign up page.
http://geni.us/DaleMayerFBGroup

Cheers,
Dale Mayer

About the Author

Dale Mayer is a *USA Today* best-selling author, best known for her SEALs military romances, her Psychic Visions series, and her Lovely Lethal Garden cozy series. Her contemporary romances are raw and full of passion and emotion (Broken But ... Mending, Hathaway House series). Her thrillers will keep you guessing (Kate Morgan, By Death series), and her romantic comedies will keep you giggling (*It's a Dog's Life*, a stand-alone novella; and the Broken Protocols series, starring Charming Marvin, the cat).

Dale honors the stories that come to her—and some of them are crazy, break all the rules and cross multiple genres!

To go with her fiction, she also writes nonfiction in many different fields, with books available on résumé writing, companion gardening, and the US mortgage system. All her books are available in print and ebook format.

Connect with Dale Mayer Online

Dale's Website – www.dalemayer.com
Twitter – @DaleMayer
Facebook Page – geni.us/DaleMayerFBFanPage
Facebook Group – geni.us/DaleMayerFBGroup
BookBub – geni.us/DaleMayerBookbub
Instagram – geni.us/DaleMayerInstagram
Goodreads – geni.us/DaleMayerGoodreads
Newsletter – geni.us/DaleNews

Also by Dale Mayer

Published Adult Books:

Hathaway House
Aaron, Book 1
Brock, Book 2
Cole, Book 3
Denton, Book 4
Elliot, Book 5
Finn, Book 6
Gregory, Book 7
Heath, Book 8
Iain, Book 9
Jaden, Book 10
Keith, Book 11
Lance, Book 12
Melissa, Book 13

The K9 Files
Ethan, Book 1
Pierce, Book 2
Zane, Book 3
Blaze, Book 4
Lucas, Book 5
Parker, Book 6
Carter, Book 7
Weston, Book 8

Greyson, Book 9
Rowan, Book 10
Caleb, Book 11

Lovely Lethal Gardens
Arsenic in the Azaleas, Book 1
Bones in the Begonias, Book 2
Corpse in the Carnations, Book 3
Daggers in the Dahlias, Book 4
Evidence in the Echinacea, Book 5
Footprints in the Ferns, Book 6
Gun in the Gardenias, Book 7
Handcuffs in the Heather, Book 8
Ice Pick in the Ivy, Book 9
Jewels in the Juniper, Book 10
Killer in the Kiwis, Book 11
Lovely Lethal Gardens, Books 1–2
Lovely Lethal Gardens, Books 3–4
Lovely Lethal Gardens, Books 5–6

Psychic Vision Series
Tuesday's Child
Hide 'n Go Seek
Maddy's Floor
Garden of Sorrow
Knock Knock...
Rare Find
Eyes to the Soul
Now You See Her
Shattered
Into the Abyss
Seeds of Malice

Eye of the Falcon
Itsy-Bitsy Spider
Unmasked
Deep Beneath
From the Ashes
Stroke of Death
Ice Maiden
Psychic Visions Books 1–3
Psychic Visions Books 4–6
Psychic Visions Books 7–9

By Death Series
Touched by Death
Haunted by Death
Chilled by Death
By Death Books 1–3

Broken Protocols – Romantic Comedy Series
Cat's Meow
Cat's Pajamas
Cat's Cradle
Cat's Claus
Broken Protocols 1-4

Broken and... Mending
Skin
Scars
Scales (of Justice)
Broken but... Mending 1-3

Glory
Genesis
Tori

Celeste
Glory Trilogy

Biker Blues
Morgan: Biker Blues, Volume 1
Cash: Biker Blues, Volume 2

SEALs of Honor
Mason: SEALs of Honor, Book 1
Hawk: SEALs of Honor, Book 2
Dane: SEALs of Honor, Book 3
Swede: SEALs of Honor, Book 4
Shadow: SEALs of Honor, Book 5
Cooper: SEALs of Honor, Book 6
Markus: SEALs of Honor, Book 7
Evan: SEALs of Honor, Book 8
Mason's Wish: SEALs of Honor, Book 9
Chase: SEALs of Honor, Book 10
Brett: SEALs of Honor, Book 11
Devlin: SEALs of Honor, Book 12
Easton: SEALs of Honor, Book 13
Ryder: SEALs of Honor, Book 14
Macklin: SEALs of Honor, Book 15
Corey: SEALs of Honor, Book 16
Warrick: SEALs of Honor, Book 17
Tanner: SEALs of Honor, Book 18
Jackson: SEALs of Honor, Book 19
Kanen: SEALs of Honor, Book 20
Nelson: SEALs of Honor, Book 21
Taylor: SEALs of Honor, Book 22
Colton: SEALs of Honor, Book 23
Troy: SEALs of Honor, Book 24

Axel: SEALs of Honor, Book 25
SEALs of Honor, Books 1–3
SEALs of Honor, Books 4–6
SEALs of Honor, Books 7–10
SEALs of Honor, Books 11–13
SEALs of Honor, Books 14–16
SEALs of Honor, Books 17–19
SEALs of Honor, Books 20–22

Heroes for Hire

Levi's Legend: Heroes for Hire, Book 1
Stone's Surrender: Heroes for Hire, Book 2
Merk's Mistake: Heroes for Hire, Book 3
Rhodes's Reward: Heroes for Hire, Book 4
Flynn's Firecracker: Heroes for Hire, Book 5
Logan's Light: Heroes for Hire, Book 6
Harrison's Heart: Heroes for Hire, Book 7
Saul's Sweetheart: Heroes for Hire, Book 8
Dakota's Delight: Heroes for Hire, Book 9
Michael's Mercy (Part of Sleeper SEAL Series)
Tyson's Treasure: Heroes for Hire, Book 10
Jace's Jewel: Heroes for Hire, Book 11
Rory's Rose: Heroes for Hire, Book 12
Brandon's Bliss: Heroes for Hire, Book 13
Liam's Lily: Heroes for Hire, Book 14
North's Nikki: Heroes for Hire, Book 15
Anders's Angel: Heroes for Hire, Book 16
Reyes's Raina: Heroes for Hire, Book 17
Dezi's Diamond: Heroes for Hire, Book 18
Vince's Vixen: Heroes for Hire, Book 19
Ice's Icing: Heroes for Hire, Book 20
Johan's Joy: Heroes for Hire, Book 21

Gavin, Book 11
Shane, Book 12

Bullard's Battle Series
Ryland's Reach, Book 1
Cain's Cross, Book 2
Eton's Escape, Book 3
Garret's Gambit, Book 4
Kano's Keep, Book 5
Fallon's Flaw, Book 6
Quinn's Quest, Book 7
Bullard's Beauty, Book 8

Collections
Dare to Be You...
Dare to Love...
Dare to be Strong...
RomanceX3

Standalone Novellas
It's a Dog's Life
Riana's Revenge
Second Chances

Published Young Adult Books:

Family Blood Ties Series
Vampire in Denial
Vampire in Distress
Vampire in Design
Vampire in Deceit
Vampire in Defiance

Vampire in Conflict
Vampire in Chaos
Vampire in Crisis
Vampire in Control
Vampire in Charge
Family Blood Ties Set 1–3
Family Blood Ties Set 1–5
Family Blood Ties Set 4–6
Family Blood Ties Set 7–9
Sian's Solution, A Family Blood Ties Series Prequel
    Novelette

Design series
Dangerous Designs
Deadly Designs
Darkest Designs
Design Series Trilogy

Standalone
In Cassie's Corner
Gem Stone (a Gemma Stone Mystery)
Time Thieves

Published Non-Fiction Books:

Career Essentials
Career Essentials: The Résumé
Career Essentials: The Cover Letter
Career Essentials: The Interview
Career Essentials: 3 in 1

CPSIA information can be obtained
at www.ICGtesting.com
Printed in the USA
LVHW040953170423
744543LV00012B/432

9 781773 364018